"DO NOT DEN~~Y~~
LOVE, CARISS~~IMA~~!

Nando's arms tightened, hugging her against him.

Amy couldn't resist his kiss. The velvet caress of his firm mouth sent her blood pounding, as she had feared it would. In seconds he was inflaming her, filling her with heady excitement. He was stealing away her breath, her life, her very will....

A warning clanged within her: His lovemaking was so evocative, so expert. Was she being lured into a sensuous trap? Was he trying to make it impossible for her to deny him her share of the winery?

She pressed her hands against his chest. "Nando, please!"

"Ah, cara, do not say no to me." His words were skillfully persuasive, his plundering lips even more so. All thoughts of the winery were chased from her mind.

AND NOW...

SUPERROMANCES

Worldwide Library is proud to present a sensational new series of modern love stories— SUPERROMANCES

Written by masters of the genre, these longer, sensuous and dramatic novels are truly in keeping with today's changing life-styles. Full of intriguing conflicts, the heartaches and delights of true love, SUPERROMANCES are absorbing stories— satisfying and sophisticated reading that lovers of romance fiction have long been waiting for.

SUPERROMANCES
Contemporary love stories for the woman of today!

LOVE'S GLITTERING WEB

KATE BOWE

A SUPERROMANCE FROM
WORLDWIDE

TORONTO · LONDON · NEW YORK · SYDNEY

Published August 1982

First printing June 1982

ISBN 0-373-70028-8

CHAPTER ONE

AMY CONVERSE stood in the middle of her apartment living room, trembling with anger, her green eyes seething. *What a disastrous evening! What a dreadful man!*

The pounding on her door began again. "Let me in! You're a tease, you know that? A goddamned tease!" A man's voice was shouting. "You can't get away with this, you know, not after letting me think...." The words dwindled off into an indistinguishable murmur.

A number of angry kicks at the door followed, and the knob rattled furiously. Then came several moments of silence, and Amy let out a sigh of relief as she finally heard footsteps going back down the hall in the direction of the elevator.

Tossing her purse on the table, she crossed the room and went into the bathroom, flipping on the light. Reaching for a washcloth, she soaked it in cold water, then scrubbed hard at her face. Those wet warm kisses that he'd managed to force on her in the cab on the way home had been horrible, she recalled with a shudder.

Lowering the washcloth, she stared at her reflection and wiped again at a trace of smeared lipstick.

Her pale blond hair was in disarray, the result of trying to pull away from him. Amy stopped and looked down in sudden anger at the two-inch rip in the neckline of her pale green silk dress. That was where he'd tried to slip one of those nasty eager hot hands of his down inside. Her cheeks flamed hot in memory.

Never again, *never*, would she be so gullible as to allow a department head to foist an out-of-town relative on her.

This afternoon, just as she had been getting ready to go home, Mr. Richardson, the graphics head, had come out of his inner office, walking toward her with a beaming smile on his round pink-cheeked face.

"Ah, there you are, Miss Converse!" he said triumphantly. "I was hoping to catch you before you left for the day! My sister Grace's boy, Craig Layton, has just arrived in town for a visit with us. My wife called me a few minutes ago. I hope you're free tonight, and that you'll let our Craig bring you to a cocktail party Mrs. Richardson and I are having."

His balding head with its fringe of white hair nodded vigorously. "I know you'll like Craig. Fine young man! My wife and I think the world of that boy! He doesn't know anyone in New York, so maybe later you can introduce him to some of your young friends," he encouraged her, gazing at her expectantly.

The Richardsons had the reputation of giving elaborate parties, catered by some of the finest restaurants in New York. Other than taking her clothes to the launderette and writing a few letters, Amy had no plans for the evening. She hesitated only a second before saying, "Thank you, Mr. Richardson, I think I'd like that very much."

"Fine, fine. The party's from six to eight. Craig will be by to get you in a cab around six. I already have your address." Then he'd gone back into his office, a pleased expression on his face.

She wasn't a child after all, Amy chided herself. She was twenty-four, so she probably should have known better. But that was hindsight now.

The way Craig had acted in the cab coming home had disgusted her. He was drunk and aggressive and, in spite of her trying to push him away, his hot moist mouth had covered hers for several endless seconds while he fumbled futilely at her neckline.

Amy cringed at the memory of all that shouting outside her door. And calling her a tease! What a ghastly awful man! She wondered if the Martins, in the apartment next door, were at home. If so, then they'd certainly have heard him. And while she'd been struggling to extricate herself from Craig's feverish pawing long enough to escape into her apartment, she'd heard the elevator door at the end of the hall slide open. For the briefest flash of a second, out of the corner of her eye, she'd caught a glimpse of a man standing there.

If the Martins had been treated to an earful, he must have had an eyeful. She could only hope it wasn't anyone she knew, or who would recognize her as a resident of the apartment house.

Amy squeezed out the washcloth and spread it on

the towel rack just as the telephone rang. Going into the living room, she stood still for a moment, listening. She certainly wasn't going to answer it. That Craig person without a doubt had found a phone in the drugstore at the corner and would be trying to coax her back into an evening that had ended at eight-thirty. Or perhaps he wanted to do more name calling, his ego having been damaged.

Of course there was always the possibility he might wish to apologize, something she found a little hard to imagine considering his recent actions.

Amy stood her ground stubbornly. She'd endured all of Craig Layton she could take for one evening— or a lifetime!

The ringing stopped. But a few minutes later it began again, time after time, ringing insistently. Amy went over to gaze at the telephone, frowning, her lips compressing with irritation. This could conceivably go on the rest of the evening. She might just as well put an end to it now.

Reaching down, she picked up the phone. "Yes?" she said crisply.

"Miss Amy Converse?"

It was not Craig. Not a voice she recognized. And it had something unusual about it. An English accent, yes, but with a faintly foreign sound. Perhaps it was the lightly rolling r in the pronunciation of Converse.

"Yes, speaking," she said cautiously. Could it be that Craig had inveigled someone into calling her for him?

"By chance would you happen to be the Amy Converse whose mother was born Catherine Rinaldi, daughter of Gianpaolo Rinaldi? I do apologize for being so inquisitive, but it's really quite important.''

"Yes," Amy answered slowly, "yes, my mother's maiden name was Rinaldi." She hesitated, waiting for him to continue, wondering at the same time if this might not be some kind of advertising gambit.

"Ah!" There was satisfaction in the brief sound. Then he began again, "My name is Fernando Bonavia. Are you familiar with the name Bonavia?''

Amy felt the stirring of impatience. "No, I'm afraid not.''

"Well, no matter. That's not terribly important. I must apologize for calling this evening, Miss Converse. But I arrived in New York late today from Italy and unfortunately I will have to leave here for California early tomorrow morning. If it is at all possible, I'd like very much to talk with you this evening.''

Now came the first sign of hesitation in his voice. "I'm down at the corner near your apartment building—as I found it listed in the telephone book, anyway. I wonder if you'd allow me to come up and discuss something with you. A business matter. I assure you it is important—to both of us.''

Amy hedged at once, aware there were many ruses being used to obtain entrance to apartments.

"Really, Mr. Bonavia, I'm afraid that it would be quite—''

"I'm sorry, Miss Converse, perhaps I should have explained. I thought the name of Bonavia might be familiar to you. You see, if you are the Amy Converse I'm searching for, and it appears you are, then we are distant cousins."

Amy lifted a doubting eyebrow but didn't interrupt, since he seemed intent on continuing.

"Perhaps it will help if I explain the reason for my call. I'm searching for a cousin, named Amy Converse, who might have some information I need. I'm looking for a missing paper representing a share in a winery," the voice went on smoothly. "At least at one time it belonged to a Gianpaolo Rinaldi, presumably the one who is your grandfather."

He paused, then—just a little too casually, Amy thought—said, "This paper could possibly be of value to you. And to me."

She reflected swiftly. A share in a winery? Not that she was aware of. Her grandfather had been a man of limited income. Her mother hadn't mentioned anything about an interest in a winery, either. Amy gazed down at the polished tabletop, her eyes narrowing thoughtfully. What if this were actually on the level?

Despite a little stirring of excitement, she remained cautious. "Speaking of my grandfather, would you happen to know where he was born?" All right, she admitted to herself, it was a form of shibboleth, a testing. But one couldn't be too careful these days.

"Teolo." There was faint amusement in his reply. Obviously he knew why she was asking.

But she was reassured by his answer. "And you would like to come over right away?" Her eyes sought the clock ticking away on the bookshelf. Almost nine o'clock.

"Yes, it's very important that I see you at once. I need to get several things straightened out before I leave tomorrow, and there is very little time left. I'm certain we can resolve everything with a couple of questions and a few moments to talk them over." The firmness in his voice was reassuring.

"All right, Mr. Bonavia, my apartment is 486."

"Thank you, I'll be there shortly."

Amy set the phone down slowly, her eyes fixed on it unseeingly. The whole situation was very strange, she thought, but the man must be who he said he was—a cousin. Surely no one outside the family could have known about her grandfather's birth, which he'd always told her was a family joke. His birth had been registered as having taken place in Verona, Italy, but he'd actually been born in Teolo, a tiny hillside town. His mother had gone there to visit an old family servant who had returned to her own village and was ailing. Gianpaolo, not due to make his appearance for another full month, had discourteously decided not to wait. The family had stubbornly, and perhaps surreptitiously, registered his birth in Verona. "Born a lawbreaker," he'd always said with a slow grin.

Amy's thoughts returned to her family's share in the winery. If it existed, why had no one ever mentioned it to her? She frowned, trying to recall if she'd ever heard any discussion of it. She came up with nothing.

Amy's grandfather had died when she was fourteen. Her mother, if she had inherited his share of the business, had never spoken of it. Quite possibly no one had ever considered it important.

If there were any documents, they must be in one of the numerous boxes and trunks that had been stored upon her mother's death a year ago. Amy had been so involved ever since then in settling into her new job with Stewart and Newman Advertising that she had procrastinated in going back to Maryland to go through her mother's possessions.

She glanced around the room at the mahogany-edged Victorian sofa that sat against the wall. Not very comfortable, but it had a certain dignity and charm with its faded elegant needlepoint upholstery. That and the gleaming round drum table had been her mother's most cherished possessions, transported from army post to army post as they moved with Amy's father. Her mother had taken them on to Maryland after he had been killed in action during the Vietnam war.

Amy had never considered leaving these two belongings in the large dusty warehouse along with boxes and trunks after her mother died. Automatically she brought them to New York, to sit in solitary splendor amid the utilitarian pieces of her furnished apartment.

Crossing the room, she straightened the two small pillows on the sofa, gave another quick look around the place, then stopped to slide a green footstool over a faded place in the flowered carpet. Picking up her purse, she returned to the bathroom to repair her lipstick, reminded again of that impossible nephew of

Mr. Richardson's. She ran a comb through her shoulder-length blond hair and with her hand pressed the soft natural wave back into shape.

In the mirror she noticed again the rip in her dress, a dress bought less than a month ago and worn just twice. Sighing in exasperation, she walked back into her small bedroom, unzipping the dress as she went. She opened the closet to pull out a pair of soft gray slacks and a blue green shirt.

While she was changing, her mind went back to the voice on the phone. This cousin who'd called, was he old or young? She couldn't tell. Her mother had lost touch with her Italian relatives; her grandfather had been the only member of the family who had come to the States to live. When he had spoken of Italy, it was always with a reference to the beautiful weather and the fine food. Then he'd shaken his head and said a man couldn't make a living there.

When the doorbell sounded moments later, Amy hurried through the living room to open the door, feeling a faint surge of uncertain anticipation. The man standing there was definitely a surprise.

He was tall, tall and spare, with a casual European elegance about him. Except for his modern dress he could have stepped directly out of Bellini's sixteenth-century painting of an Italian gentleman. The same strong sensuous Renaissance face with its hawklike profile, its cool gray eyes, gazed at her. And, as in the Bellini portrait, there was evidence of classical arrogance in his bearing, a hint of temper lines etched about the firm mouth. Thirty-five? Thirty-nine? Amy could only guess.

"Miss Converse?" Abruptly the lineaments of his face softened slightly, even the arrogance receding, to be replaced by a courteous smile and an inquiring gaze. "I'm Fernando Bonavia."

"Yes, of course, how do you do? Please come in." Amy stood back, holding open the door. She motioned toward a chair. "Or the sofa, if you'd prefer."

As she closed the door, he walked toward the chair. But he remained standing until she joined him and took her place on the sofa, clasping her hands loosely in her lap. Then he sat down, leaned back slightly and crossed his long, elegantly clad legs.

"I'm sorry to intrude on you this way in the evening, Miss Conyerse, and to give you so little warning. But my time here is limited, and I do need to talk to you. I phoned shortly after I arrived. There was no answer, so I decided to take a cab over to slip a note under your door, or perhaps, with good fortune, to find you had returned. But I called one more time and, luckily, you were here."

He was very polite. He was a charmer, too, Amy realized; the type of man who could easily banish a woman's natural resistances. But while he was speaking, Amy found it hard to repress an uncertain feeling at something in the man's expression, that hint of sardonic appraisal in the gray eyes. What was it, she wondered, Latin machismo? Whatever it was, it made her vaguely uncomfortable.

"And you wished?" she asked, controlling a tinge of irritation.

He leaned forward. "I am looking for the missing deed to part of a winery, as I already mentioned. I have reason to believe it may have been in your grandfather's possession at some time. At least, that's the last record we have of it."

He hesitated, then said casually, "Are you familiar with the Monte Cielo Vino d'Oro of Italy?"

Amy shook her head slowly, reflecting that his question had sounded just a shade too casual. "Sorry, I'm afraid not, Mr. Bonavia."

The gray eyes flickered and for a brief instant held a glint of amusement. "This is a little ridiculous, you know. We are cousins, so we can't go on calling each other 'miss' or 'mister,' can we? I know your name is Amy. Mine is Fernando. But I'm called Nando by everyone, so I would be pleased if you would do so as well. That's known as a nickname in your language, isn't it?"

She nodded, then asked curiously, "You're Italian—from Italy, you said—so why do you speak English so fluently?" Winery or not, supposed cousins or not, she would feel a lot more comfortable when she knew more about this attractive self-assured man sitting across from her. She'd had her fill of experiences with strangers this evening.

He slanted a sardonic eyebrow. "After the war Italy was filled with American and British soldiers. They are not noted for their gift in speaking foreign languages, so as a child I learned theirs," he said dryly.

A child after the war; then she'd guessed his age fairly closely.

"Now," he said, "to get back to my mission here tonight. I'll try to be brief." Nando hesitated a fraction of a second, smiled, then went on. "Amy—may I call you that? Or do you prefer Cousin Amy?"

"Amy. Or whatever you wish." What she really wished, she thought, was that he'd get on with it and explain about her interest in the winery.

"Allow me to give you some background, Amy. Several generations ago one of our ancestors, a certain Guido Montagne, began making wine from his vineyard in northern Italy—only for his own use at first, then for his friends and neighbors. That was the beginning of the Monte Cielo Vino d'Oro Winery."

He lifted his shoulders in an expressive shrug. "It was quite loosely organized in a sort of partnership and has been run haphazardly, I'm afraid, even up through the time when it became the responsibility of the two later branches of the Montagne family, the Bonavias and the Rinaldis."

Amy felt a quickening of excitement inside.

Nando flashed a crisp disarming smile. "But it's a good winery, and I'm a vintner. I'd like to do something about reorganizing and modernizing the company."

He leaned back. "Somehow it no longer seems practical to call our cousins together during harvest time and ask them to tromp around barefoot in old wooden tubs. So we're going modern. And about time, I admit."

He seemed just a little too offhand, Amy thought, gazing at him carefully. "Does that mean becoming competitive?'' she asked. "Outside Italy, too? Even here in the United States?"

Nando nodded. "Yes, indeed. And because of that, our business must be brought into precise legal order, with all the original ownership certificates accounted for. They have been, except for Gianpaolo Rinaldi's, inherited from his mother and his mother's father before him.''

Amy gave him a quick look. "And that's the part you think is—was—my mother's?"

"Let's say I hope so. You yourself have no knowledge of it?"

She shook her head.

"Am I right in understanding that you have no brothers or sisters?'' he went on.

"I was an only child."

"No other family member, anyone who might have the document?" His voice grew more intent, still polite on the surface but pressing slightly. "That is, if you don't. I'm somewhat surprised you are unfamiliar with all this.''

Before she could answer he said swiftly, "You are quite, quite certain that you don't have the deed and perhaps have forgotten about it?"

The question was put blandly, but Amy was abruptly aware that her interest in the winery—if indeed it were hers—was vitally important to him. Why this gave her a feeling of satisfaction she couldn't say. Possibly it was that faint hint of arrogance visible once more on his face, combined with the cool male appraisal, that was irritating her consciousness.

Her eyes met his directly. "There is no other family; I do not have the deed myself, and, yes, I'm quite certain." Her words were crisp and clipped. "I'm not aware of any share in a wine company, though it is possible there might be something among my mother's effects, which are in storage. But I can't give you any real assurance. I simply don't know!"

"Is there any chance you could find out? Perhaps by the time I return next week?" He flashed her a breath-catching smile, but the pressure was still there.

"I suppose I could, yes," she said reluctantly. "But I can't possibly get away to search until this weekend. Everything is stored in Maryland."

"I'd appreciate it greatly if you could. As I said, I won't be back until Thursday or Friday of next week."

"And if I do find something?" The possibility erased some of the irritation that had been aroused within her.

"Then, my dear cousin, I'd be willing to make you a good offer for your share in the business," he said, his eyes on her. "If, however, you don't locate the deed, will you please see if you can find any record of when and where it was disposed of? I dislike being so insistent about all this, but it really is very important to me and to the firm."

"I'll certainly try, but as I said, I'm not very optimistic. If there ever was a certificate, I certainly never heard of it. And I'd think someone would have mentioned it at sometime."

"But you will search, won't you?" he underlined his words persuasively.

"I will." In fact, she realized, she was becoming anxious to do just that.

Pulling a card from his pocket, he handed it to her. "I'm on my way to the Davis branch of the University of California for a meeting of vintners. The number on this card will reach me, or word can be relayed to me. If you should locate anything I'd appreciate a call. If I don't hear from you, then I'll get in touch upon my return to check on further possibilities. Perhaps we can trace where the deed has gone."

He stood up gracefully. "I've imposed too much on your time, I'm afraid, my dear cousin. I must go now. Thank you for seeing me."

As she got to her feet, he clasped one of her hands in his, smiling down at her. "I'm pleased that our relationship is so. . . so many times removed."

The cool gray eyes were suddenly vividly alive as they met hers, and for a swift instant she was only too aware that he was looking at her as a man looks at a woman. It intrigued as well as disconcerted her.

But there was something else in his expression, something that tugged uncomfortably at the edges of her mind. For some reason that she couldn't isolate, she felt at a disadvantage. It was almost as if he knew something about her and that he was somehow judging her. But that was nonsense. How could he be when they had never met before?

"It's been nice meeting one of my Italian relatives," she answered. It seemed a safe reply.

"May I add that my new American relative is a

very pleasing surprise?'' he said as they reached the door. He still held her hand in his, and he lifted it to brush it lightly with his lips in continental fashion. To Amy's consternation his touch caused a curl of pleasure to flutter inside her.

"I shall be looking forward to seeing you next week, Amy. Good hunting! *Arrivederci*!''

Then, turning quickly on his heel, he walked down the hallway. Amy stood for a moment in the open doorway, watching his swinging stride. When the elevator swallowed him, she turned back into her apartment, closing the door.

It certainly had been an evening, Amy thought, locking the door and slipping on the safety catch. First the ridiculous fiasco with that impossible nephew of Mr. Richardson's. Then the appearance of this. . . this cousin.

She frowned to herself. Something about Nando sat a little uneasily in her mind. What was it? He was an attractive man, certainly, with a continental sophistication she wasn't used to. Was she bothered by the fact that he was so intensely masculine? Throughout his visit she had been very aware of the fact. The simple touch of his lips on her hand had given her a momentary thrill.

No, it wasn't that that was bothering her, she decided, not really. It was the fact that there seemed to be one man hidden inside the other. One man was delightful and warm, the other was remote, perhaps even calculating. Or was she simply imagining things?

Oh, men, she thought irritably. Thrusting herself

away from the door, she walked swiftly into her bedroom, unbuttoning her shirt as she went. After undressing she slipped into a robe and, reluctant to go to bed so early, returned to the living room, where she sank into an armchair. Reaching over, she switched on the television.

For some reason, however, she found herself unable to be completely absorbed in the BBC production that might otherwise have held her attention. She gazed reflectively at the figures moving about on the screen, their English accents constantly reminding her of her unexpected visitor.

Yes, indeed, she finally admitted to herself, there was more to her cousin Fernando Bonavia than appeared on the surface. A whole lot more.

NEXT MORNING AT WORK, Amy discovered she was not yet finished with the Craig Layton fiasco. She had left her desk to go upstairs and get some information on a layout she was working on. When she came back, Mr. Richardson was there, checking some copy. When he lifted his head and saw her, his thick eyebrows jutted into a deep V and his plump cheeks reddened.

"Good morning, Miss Converse." The words could have been chipped from ice.

"Good morning, Mr. Richardson," Amy said, all too conscious of his sour look and his air of disapproval.

He returned his attention to the copy. Then, when he had finished, he walked right past Amy's desk and into his private office without another word or look at her. His very walk, the way he shut the door, demonstrated censure.

Linda Daniel, who worked at the next desk, twisted around in her chair to stare at Amy. Her brown eyes were incredulous. "Well, that was quite a display, I must say. Why are you in deep freeze this morning?"

With heightened color, Amy turned slowly toward her friend. What kind of lies had Craig told, she wondered.

"I...I suppose because of something that happened last night. Mr. and Mrs. Richardson gave a cocktail party. Their nephew was in town so Mr. Richardson asked me—"

Linda swung around completely, clapping her hand to her forehead. "My God, Amy! Don't tell me! You were lured into a date with 'my sister Grace's boy,' that hundred-handed maniac?"

Amy nodded ruefully. "If you're talking about Craig Layton, I was. Much to my regret." She picked up the material she'd brought from upstairs, then set it back on her desk nervously. She was certainly in for something. Maybe her job?

"Well, I wish you'd said something!" Linda was shaking her head. "I could have at least warned you about him. My God, not one of us would get within twenty feet of him at high-noon Mass in Saint Patrick's Cathedral! He's a one hundred percent menace to any female. No one can stand him."

"I didn't know," Amy said feelingly, "but I do now!"

Linda nodded. "No doubt you were elected because you haven't been here long enough to have been exposed to one of Craig's visits.'' She gave Amy a sharp look. ''Just a word of warning. A date with Craig can have reverberations. A couple of years ago Polly Lind from upstairs in the copy department got cornered by him at the office Christmas party. He got her pinned against the wall and was pressing himself against her in the most disgusting way, right in front of everyone.

''Polly was struggling to get away when Jack Christian saw what was going on. He went striding over and yanked old Craig about six inches off the ground. Sent him sailing halfway across the room and onto a desk filled with glasses and bottles. It didn't hurt the little creep, sorry to say. But—'' Linda gave Amy a sharp significant look ''—I just want to point out that neither Polly nor Jack is employed by Stewart and Newman at the present time. So watch it!''

''Well, I will. But I'm a little afraid it's too late to do much about it. I'm certainly not anxious to lose my job, especially over something stupid like last night's episode!'' Amy smiled suddenly. ''However, I might voluntarily give up working for Stewart and Newman. And for Mr. Richardson! I just found out I may be the wealthy part owner of a foreign winery!''

Linda cocked her head, a speculative expression in her eyes. ''Are you sure you're not in shock, Amy, dear?'' She grinned. ''I wouldn't be surprised if you were, after an evening with Craig.''

''No, I'm serious, at least about having an interest in a winery.'' Amy told Linda about her visitor.

"And you think there's a chance you do own part of the business? And that it's worth something?" Linda asked.

Amy nodded. "Well, he seems to think that I must have a document somewhere. It was apparently traced to my grandfather. But to be truthful, no one in my family ever mentioned anything about a winery. I'm going to go through my mother's things this weekend and see what I come up with. I should have taken care of that project some time ago, but I simply haven't had time."

"This cousin of yours, what's he like?" Linda lifted an inquisitive eyebrow.

Amy hesitated a second before answering, then said thoughtfully, "Well, Italian, of course. Tall—over six feet—dark hair, tanned. Aristocratic-looking, I suppose you could say."

"Handsome?"

Amy started to shake her head, then didn't. "I was about to say no, that his features are too strong for that, but on second thought...." She smiled suddenly. "You know, he's rather the way I always pictured Heathcliff in *Wuthering Heights*. Dark, aloof, sensuous. When I first saw him I thought of some sixteenth-century cavalier, or maybe a Borgia."

Linda sighed, then reluctantly turned back to her desk. "Some combination! I wish I were the one who owned a missing share in the winery. If you don't want him let me know. He sounds like something I could use!"

Amy laughed. "All right. I'll give you first chance." Then she sobered, saying thoughtfully,

"But I have to find that deed, if it exists. I have a feeling that at present he may be a lot more interested in that than in anything else, even pursuing women."

They both turned to the day's work. In a few minutes Mr. Richardson came out of his office. As he passed Amy's desk on his way upstairs his haughty expression was as eloquent as his pompous stride.

Amy sighed. Right now missing deeds to a winery were the least of her problems.

CHAPTER TWO

AMY CAREFULLY UNFOLDED the yellowed parchment paper, her heart suddenly beating high and hard in her throat. At the top of the page, obviously hand-painted, a florid bunch of plump purple grapes nestled against green leaves and curling tendrils. The writing was hand-lettered in Italian. And there, in elaborate curlicues at the top of the page, was the name: Monte Cielo Vino d'Oro.

Her hands trembled as she glanced over the paper. Swallowing a couple of times, she took a deep breath. She'd found it!

Now that she had it, just how valuable was it, she wondered. Nando Bonavia had indicated that her part of the business would be bought out. Hadn't he said that it might be of value to her, and to him? She held the paper in her hands, momentarily daydreaming. There were so many things she could do with extra money. Take a cruise on her vacation next year. Oh, and move into another apartment, not one where the view consisted of a fire escape and where the furniture, except for her mother's sofa and table, had seen more than one tenant come and go.

Carefully refolding the parchment sheet, Amy regretted that she was unable to read the Italian words.

Perhaps she could persuade Nando to translate for her, she decided. Allowing her thoughts to drift back to her cousin, she realized that despite her slight feeling of unease about Nando, which still lingered for some undefinable reason, she was rather looking forward to seeing him again.

And not only for the transaction of the winery. There was something about him, something that made her other male friends pale in comparison. He was so thoroughly the Renaissance man, so strongly masculine. His cool manner seemed to be a thin shell, underneath which fires were smoldering.

Amy smiled abruptly at the thought. How poetic she was becoming!

Well back to work! With a sigh she eyed all the remaining boxes. She had unpacked five of them before finding the desired paper, and the contents were spread in small stacks around her. There was much she could get rid of, bits and tags that had for some reason been important to her mother. As for that—Amy gazed over at the table where she had placed the parchment sheet—it had been tucked in with some recipes and old postcards.

It was stuffy in the small corner cubicle of the storage building, but she realized that she might as well complete the entire task now that she was there.

Four hours later Amy had finished. Around her lay her past—her school report cards and a class picture of the fourth grade at Fort Campbell, Kentucky, where her father had been stationed for a time. There was a small handprint in plaster Amy had made for her mother in kindergarten. Her high-school diploma was there, as well as her bachelor of arts degree from the University of Maryland.

Amy picked up a color snapshot of herself and her mother, taken on campus the day of graduation. How like and yet unalike the two of them were in appearance, she thought. Both were small boned and slim. A board could have balanced on their heads, they were so even in height.

But her mother was a true Latin, with warm olive skin, dark glossy hair and eyes so brown they were almost black. Amy herself couldn't have been more opposite. Fair skin. Green eyes that sometimes shaded to hazel when she was tired or upset. Blond hair that she'd worn longer then. Now her hair was shoulder length, more practical for office life.

Somehow the photograph seemed to have been taken a long time ago, yet it had been only three years. It was probably the last picture of her mother. Amy felt her eyes sting as she slipped the picture into her purse.

Among the assorted mementos was a small case. She held it in her hand for a moment, then opened it. It contained her father's silver star medal, awarded posthumously. On his second tour of duty in Vietnam, he had been one of the last American soldiers to die there. Amy gazed at the medal, then gently closed the case and slipped it, too, into her purse.

Setting aside a few other items she wanted to keep, she began gathering up the debris around her, dumping most of it back into boxes. Her mother had apparently saved everything, a jackdaw habit that Amy suddenly appreciated. Though no one seemed to have had any interest in the parchment paper with its hand-painted purple grapes, it had not been tossed out.

ON THE PLANE going back to New York late that evening, Amy debated what to do next. How should she inform her cousin that she'd located the missing paper? He had said to phone. Should she do so first thing tomorrow morning, before she left for work? No, she thought, eight o'clock or even eight-thirty would be five or five-thirty on the coast. That was much too early for a call.

She bit at her lip as an idea occurred to her. It wouldn't hurt to call Bert Kester, a lawyer she'd been dating lately. He could most likely tell her whether she should consider herself an actual owner, and if she would be free to dispose of her share as she wished. She'd like to be certain of her legal rights. Then she could get in touch with Nando Bonavia.

At noon the next day, therefore, Amy reached for the phone. "Sorry if you're dashing off to lunch, Bert," she said when she reached the lawyer, "but I need to ask you something."

He listened as she explained, then assured her that she was within her rights to sell, if and when she wished. Her mother's will had left everything to her.

"You say it's all in Italian?" he went on.

"Yes, and handwritten. One of the layout artists speaks Italian, so I asked him to translate it when I came to work this morning. He said there wasn't much to it, but he read it for me. All it said was, "I, Guido Montagne, leave to my daughter, Giuliana

Montagne Rinaldi, her heirs and her heirs' heirs, one equal portion of Monte Cielo Vino d'Oro Winery.' "

"That's it? All of it?"

"That's what he told me."

"That doesn't give us much of an idea of what you own. A portion could be anything.... Say, Amy, wait a minute, something got past me there!" he said abruptly. "What did you say the name of the winery is?"

"Monte Cielo Vino d'Oro. It's in Italy somewhere."

"You know, that rings a bell of some kind. I think I've heard of it. Let me call you back. I'm going to have a word with Paul Clinton over at the investment company I deal with. He's a bit of a wine buff. Maybe he knows something about your winery or can give us some idea if your share is valuable."

"I'd really appreciate it, Bert," Amy said. "I don't expect it's going to turn out to be a bonanza or anything like that. My cousin spoke as if it were a small-scale family thing, with everyone tromping around on grapes in their bare feet. But they want to branch out now, make it a real business venture. I'd be glad to have any information your friend might have about it."

"My personal advice is not to run out and sell until we get a little background on the winery, Amy—find out what their plans are, if Paul can give us a report of some kind. As you say, it may be just a family business. But this Bonavia fellow came over here and looked you up, so maybe it's bigger than you think."

Bert's voice crackled over the phone. "Stay right

there, okay? I'll call you back after I talk to Paul."

As Amy set the receiver down she became aware of a flicker of excitement within her. This was turning out to be not only interesting but tantalizing, as well!

She propped her chin in the palm of her hand. She could certainly stand some good news, she thought. The atmosphere in the office was still frigid. She had the feeling that Mr. Richardson would dearly love to fire her if he could catch her making one small mistake.

She wondered again what Craig Layton had told her boss. No doubt he had bolstered his own image and torn hers apart.

The phone interrupted her thoughts, and Amy reached for it at once. On the other end Bert's voice was tight with excitement. "All right, Amy, let me lay it all out for you. You may just have a potential gold mine! Paul knew all about the company. It's a real comer.

"They're best known for a white wine. Not really white; more of a pale gold. Hence the name Vino d'Oro, or Golden Wine. The winery is located in northern Italy, near the famous Soave firm, which produces one of the top Italian wines. So the locale for making wine is right, Paul says, and from all reports the product is excellent. He couldn't find it listed on any of the stock exchanges—obviously because it's still owned by the family—so he can't give you any money figure on what your share in the business is worth."

Amy drew in a dazed breath while Bert continued. "And according to Paul, hardly anybody is drinking hard stuff anymore. Everyone's going for white wine. He told me the sale of white wine is going through the roof, up from twenty-four percent of total wine sales ten years ago to forty-nine percent a year or so ago. It's up again this year, too. And one little guess what country is leading the parade? Italy. How does that sound to you?''

Amy's hand tightened on the phone as Bert poured out more encouraging statistics. It sounded too dazzling to be true.

"And so, my dear lady, play it cool," he said firmly. "Bonavia may be your cousin, but though blood's supposed to be thicker than water, I've got a suspicion that wine could prove thicker than either. Paul suggests that you consider sitting on your share for a while and drawing dividends. But whether you hold or sell, I don't see how you stand to lose!''

Amy's eyes were fixed on the parchment sheet she had placed before her on the desk, and she was absently tracing the bunch of grapes with her fingernail. "Thanks, Bert. I'm not sure yet just what I'll do. I hadn't given much thought to holding on to it as an investment, but I might consider that as a possibility. I really haven't decided. But thank you, and please thank your friend Paul for me. I really do appreciate your help."

"It's been my pleasure. Now, if you do decide to sell, it might be a good idea to check back with both of us to be certain you're not getting rooked. Has he made any offer yet? I mean, a figure offer?"

"No. We weren't even certain I had the certificate."

"Well, whatever you do, think it over first. And by the way, now that I have you on the phone, how about a show and dinner with me this coming week?"

"I'd love to," Amy answered, "but let me get all this cleared up first. I'm not certain what day my cousin will be back."

"Okay, my dear. I'll call you toward the end of the week and check," he said. "But keep me posted. If there's anything I can do to help, give me a buzz."

"Thanks again, Bert. I'll remember."

For a few seconds Amy held the receiver in her hand, staring thoughtfully across the room. From Bert's report, her relative's winery didn't sound much like the modest company Nando had spoken of, one just a step away from barefoot grape stomping.

Slowly she put the phone down, letting her mind wander. What would happen if she decided to keep her share? As part owner she might have enough money to go to Italy. She had always wanted to see the home of her ancestors. Maybe she'd end up at the winery itself, just to have a look at it. And Nando Bonavia would be there. . . .

She felt an inexplicable flutter in her chest and frowned, instantly resentful. Pulling a brown paper bag out of her desk drawer, she began nibbling at a sandwich as she considered the latest surprising news. How much a part of the whole business would her own share represent?

Brushing the crumbs off her desk, she pulled a sheaf of papers toward her and began checking a layout. Linda returned from lunch, and within moments Mr. Richardson came in, as well, stalking past Amy's desk with frigid dignity. He never even glanced at her.

Linda lifted questioning eyebrows. "I may be wrong, but do I hear the sound of tumbrels getting ready to pull up at your desk?"

Amy glanced at Mr. Richardson's closed door, then shrugged. "I wouldn't be surprised. The silent treatment these past few days hasn't been exactly reassuring."

"Well, you said you'd found that winery deed. Maybe you should consider exiting into the wine business."

Amy hesitated a long moment, then said thoughtfully, "I might, I just might. After all, that share is mine by inheritance. It's probably been in my family for a long, long time. Maybe I ought to hold on to it and get involved in wine making."

Linda gave her an amused look. "Your modern-day Borgia wouldn't have anything to do with that decision, would he?" She laughed at the chagrined look on Amy's face. "Don't ever play poker, Amy. You don't have the face for it!"

"Well, I must say he has a lot more going for him than 'sister Grace's boy'!" Amy said tartly, turning back to her work.

As soon as she reached her apartment that evening she set down her bags, kicked off her shoes and padded over to the phone. Taking a card out of her purse, she dialed the number Nando Bonavia had

given her. He was not in, but, yes, word would be relayed to him to return her call.

Amy unpacked her groceries, then made herself an
omelet and a tossed salad. When everything was
ready she carried her plate into the living room and
sank down on the sofa. As she ate, her eyes roamed
about the room. If there was enough money coming
from her share in the winery, she reminded herself,
she'd certainly move out of this apartment. Tiny but
cute, it was all she'd been able to find when she came
to New York last year. Certainly she should be able
to afford a place where the faucets didn't drip!

Should she sell her part of the business, Amy wondered. Probably, unless there were very attractive
dividends. Actually, it was foolish for her even to
consider taking a trip to Italy. . . .

The phone jangled, and Amy picked it up gingerly.
Nando Bonavia was on the line, his crisp deep voice
barely concealing anticipation.

"My dear cousin Amy, I trust you have some good
news for me."

"I found the paper," she replied. "At least I think
it must be the paper you were inquiring about." She
spoke cautiously, not wanting to commit herself by
tone or by words.

"Marvelous. I'm returning to New York on Thursday night. Let's celebrate a successful conclusion to
your treasure hunt. If you aren't busy that night, why
don't I pick you up for dinner? There's no reason
why we can't conduct business over cocktails and
food. Can you make it?"

"Why, I—yes, of course," she answered, wondering if she was somehow obligating herself to the deal by accepting the invitation. After all, she hadn't come to any real decision yet.

"Excellent! Shall we say seven?"

"Seven will be fine."

When she had hung up the phone, she sat for several moments, absorbed in thought. Even if he quoted her a price for her share, she would be wise to delay before deciding whether to accept it or not. She really should check with Bert and his friend Paul before she signed anything.

It was obvious that Nando Bonavia fully expected to leave New York with her share of the winery in hand. Supposing she decided to keep her part as an investment, what would he do? She sensed that he wouldn't feel very pleased.

But from her own point of view, keeping her share might make the most sense. Her job at Stewart and Newman was hanging precariously by a thread, thanks to Craig Layton and Mr. Richardson.

If she did find herself out of work, maybe she really could learn something about the making of wine. Maybe she could even join the firm. The idea had certain appeal. Surely there was some aspect of it that a person as inexperienced as she could handle. And they must do advertising. She'd had plenty of experience in that.

The more she thought about the possibility, the more appealing it seemed. After all, why not? She was half Italian, even though she couldn't speak the language. As far as she knew, she had no relatives in the States. Why not meet the Italian branch of the family? They were her mother's people...and therefore hers. And she might like Italy.

She grimaced when she recalled Linda's knowing smile.

Nevertheless, on Thursday evening she dressed with particular care. Sliding open her closet door, she paused for a minute with narrowed eyes, examining her wardrobe. Finally she pulled a soft aqua wool jersey off the hanger. It was feathery light in weight and deceptively simple. But, she reflected as she smoothed it over her hips, it certainly wasn't unflattering. She might not have the exotic figure of some of the Italian movie stars, but she didn't look too bad at that!

She brushed her hair until it shone like a cloak of gold about her head. Then, reaching into a dresser drawer, she took out a gold chain necklace and clasped it on. She was ready.

Amy gave a sudden wry grin as she turned away from the mirror. She would dress with care for any date, she argued with herself. It wasn't as if Nando Bonavia was special. But she wasn't being exactly frank with herself, she knew. He *was* special. He was harshly handsome, an enigma in many ways, and a challenge.

He was prompt, as well. It was exactly seven when Amy opened the door to find him smiling down at her. Obviously he was pleased that she had located the missing paper.

"This evening we celebrate, eh, cousin mine?" He took her hand, and as he lifted it to his lips his eyes swept over her slowly, approvingly. "You're a lovely woman, my dear Amy!'' Then, touching her elbow, he said, ''Shall we go? Are you ready?''

A little breathlessly she smiled back at him. ''Quite ready.'' She would have started out the door but found herself detained by a surprisingly firm hand on her arm.

''The paper? You have it with you?'' He was doubtfully eyeing her small evening bag, which couldn't possibly have contained the parchment sheet.

She answered his look with a shake of her head. ''I thought we might discuss the subject over dinner and come to some conclusion. Then, of course—'' she gave a faint shrug ''—you could pick up the certificate tomorrow if you wish, or I could have it delivered to you.'' She wasn't going to allow herself to be stampeded into anything, she resolved. They could talk, he could make his offer. But she would consult with Bert and Paul before taking any action.

For the briefest of seconds something dark and clouded moved across Nando Bonavia's face, to be replaced by the calculated lift of one dark eyebrow. ''As you wish,'' he replied blandly. ''Or perhaps we can come back and pick it up after dinner.''

Amy realized that despite his smooth air, he hadn't quite been able to hide the fact that he'd not got what he wanted, and that he was used to having his way. The firm lines etching the corners of his mouth were evidence of that, and right now they were plainly visible.

She was right, Amy reflected, about there being fires beneath that sophisticated surface. Maybe more Borgia than modern Bonavia.

A taxi was waiting as they stepped outside the apartment building, and Amy's thoughts were interrupted. Nando opened the cab door for her to enter, then gracefully lowered his own tall frame onto the seat beside her.

The taxi, probably in constant use as most New York cabs seemed to be, smelled of stale cigarette smoke. The driver tore off into traffic, and the springs of the aging vehicle bumped and banged as they sped over potholes almost as ancient.

"I must admit our magic carpet leaves a little to be desired," Nando observed casually as he reached over to take Amy's hand. "But you, my lovely, are a charming bit of serendipity. Just think, the Amy Converse I was seeking could have turned out to be a dried-up spinster hoarding her share in a cobwebby attic. How fortunate I am to find not only the missing deed but an entrancing cousin, as well."

He had completely regained his poise, Amy noticed. Suddenly his words triggered a half-forgotten memory, something her grandfather had once said to her mother. "Every Italian man learns very young to 'make the compliment.' To tell every pretty lady many nice things, flowery things, even ladies not so pretty. Not important you mean them or not, or she believes you or not, but it makes everything nice, everyone happy. And costs nothing!" He had given his warm chuckle.

Nando had learned the lesson well, apparently. Even though she told herself she was secretly amused by his outrageous compliments, she had to admit the man had charm, a great deal of it.

"You aren't married, Amy," he was saying. "At least that's what I learned from a report. We hired an investigative agency to help us discover the whereabouts of your grandfather's heirs, you see. And I noticed your name remains the same as that of your father's. Unless," he added dryly, "you're one of these modern liberated women who insist on retaining their own names and independence in marriage. Something, I must admit, we Italian men don't particularly relish."

"No, I'm not married," she told him.

Gently his strong fingers stroked her hand and wrist. "Then American men are blind. You would not last two minutes in Italy!" In the flickering lights of passing cars and street lamps he gazed down at her. "Especially with that golden hair. It is not from our side of the family, that hair. Your father, perhaps?"

"Yes, he was blond. My mother had hair as dark as yours. She had lovely eyes, too—velvety and soft, the color of dark chocolate."

The cab screeched to a bumping halt at a traffic signal, paused as if to gather strength, then leaped ahead the second the lights changed.

"I suppose I'm a little tardy in bringing this up," Nando said, "but I've made reservations tonight at Windows on the World. I hope you approve. Perhaps I should have asked you first."

Amy whirled toward him, green eyes sparkling. "Oh, how nice!" she exclaimed. "That's absolutely marvelous. I've never been, and I've heard so much about it. Tonight is such a beautiful evening that the view of the city should be spectacular."

Wait until she told Linda, Amy thought. How had
Nando been able to secure reservations on such short
notice? She'd heard there was always a wait. She
sighed happily. She'd read so much about the restaurant, the extraordinary view, the food, the place itself, but she'd never dreamed she'd have a chance to
go there for dinner.

When the cab pulled up at the World Trade Center, Nando paid the driver. Then he took Amy's arm
and strolled with her through the lobby. The elevator
whisked them swiftly and silently to the one hundred
and seventh floor.

Amy caught her breath as they stepped out into a
glittering passageway. The walls and the entire ceiling
were covered in brilliant mirroring, with bold mosa-
ics of New York interspersing the glass panels.

For a second or two she didn't move, trying to ab-
sorb it all so she could tell Linda about it in the morning. They began walking toward the dining room, but
Amy had to stop from time to time to gaze at the immense golden seashells placed along the hallway,
their interiors filled with light.

She turned to her companion. "It's like stepping
into some kind of fairyland," she breathed.

His hand tightened on her elbow and he bent toward her to say, "You deserve it, my dear Amy.
Your discovery has made my trip worthwhile. Not to
mention the opportunity I've had of meeting you."

They reached the dining area and were led down a
few steps to a table placed right next to the window.
Floor-to-ceiling glass looked out over the lights of the
city spread out below. For a moment neither of them

spoke, their eyes on the brilliant panorama. Amy noticed lights of automobiles, visible as shining specks, moving along the strings of necklaces that were bridges.

She turned to say something to Nando, but a waiter had appeared at his side and the two of them were involved in a quiet interchange. She took advantage of his preoccupation, therefore, to study him secretly—something she'd had little opportunity to do before, at least unobserved. Curiously she examined that strong arrogant profile, the jutting dark brows, the firm lips. What came as a startling and not exactly welcome surprise was the realization she felt very much attracted to this man. Very much.

The thought left her a little unnerved. She stirred uncomfortably in her chair, turning her eyes hurriedly again to the view.

She wasn't successful in distracting her thoughts, however. They strayed back to the man seated across from her. Those strong expressive hands holding the menu; that proud hawklike profile.... She would have to stop herself from becoming a victim of such reactions, she warned herself. Knowing what made her feel this way about him, she could certainly do something about halting it. She wasn't even sure how much she actually *liked* Nando Bonavia. It was a disturbing combination of feelings.

The waiter left and Nando turned back to her. She was aware of a flickering change of expression in his gray eyes, a hint of intimacy. It wasn't blatant, Amy realized. But it was the gaze of a man who has had his success with women, probably many women, and was not inclined to pass up an opportunity.

"Because tonight is special I've taken the liberty of ordering for you," he said. "Let's see if I have read you correctly."

"I'm certain you have," she said easily. "It would be hard to miss. I like everything except gritty spinach and lumpy mashed potatoes." Looking around at the elegant decor of the dining room she added, "I don't think we'll be served either one here."

She watched as quiet efficient waiters moved among the tables, placing and removing food, unobtrusive against the background of crystal goblets and crisp white linen. It was, she thought contentedly, the most exclusive place she had ever eaten in. Linda was going to be absolutely green with envy.

The waiter appeared with a slim green bottle of wine. Opening it with a flourish, he presented the cork to Nando for approval. Her cousin looked at it, lifted it to his nose, then gestured to the waiter, who poured a scant half inch into a wineglass. Smiling at Amy over the rim, Nando tasted the wine and nodded. The waiter filled both glasses and withdrew.

Nando gazed at her across the table, then said softly, "A beautiful woman, a beautiful evening, a beautiful city. One couldn't ask for more." He touched his glass to hers.

Amy gazed thoughtfully at the pale golden liquid in her glass, then lifted her eyes quickly to his.

"Vino d'Oro?" she guessed.

Nando nodded. "Vino d'Oro it is. It's quite new to your country because for many years it was too light, too delicate to travel satisfactorily. But we have been studying and improving, and now we understand better."

Amy lifted it to her lips. The wine was fresh and light, with a subtle delicious fragrance. No wonder Paul had termed it a "comer"! A stir of excitement fluttered within her. This was her wine! Not entirely, though. It was his, too.

"Tell me something about my relatives, Nando, about the Bonavias. The Rinaldis, too, if there are any. It seems so strange to have cousins and not know anything about them," she said, sipping her wine appreciatively.

"There are not so many of us left," he answered. "Of the Bonavias, there is my mother, of course, and my sister, Anna Maria. Then there is a cousin, Franco Rinaldi, who is from Milano but who has come to live with us and to work with the winery. He's probably more closely related to you than I am. We all live at Villa Cielo, near the vineyards and the winery itself. We all own a share in it. There are some distant cousins whom we don't see very often. Their parents used to have an interest in the business but it has been turned over to us. So you see, your share is all we need to complete the company inventory, and we do need it at once," he said pointedly.

She sidestepped the implication. "And the winery? What's it like? I don't think I've ever visited one."

"On the small side as wineries go, I suppose, though we're going through some building activity now in preparation for expansion. Both the winery and the vineyards are out in the country, not many miles from Soave, the current most popular white wine of our country. We hope to give them some competition."

He leaned across the table and put his hand on hers for an instant. "Tonight, however, I give thanks to all the saints that I have been so lucky as to find you, dear cousin." His glance conveyed a lot more than his words. If a look could actually flatter, then his did, Amy realized.

"How did you locate me so quickly, if you arrived the same day you phoned me last week? Was that the work of the investigative agency?" she asked, adroitly changing the trend of the conversation. It wasn't that she minded his compliments, given with such an eloquent glance from those gray eyes, but with her share of the business still to be discussed, she didn't want the tone to become too personal. Just in case she decided not to sell.

"As I told you, the agency had been searching for some time. Only by sheer accident did they stumble on an old address of your grandfather's. Then, step by step, we were lucky enough to trace him to his last residence. Your mother was even more difficult to find because she moved so many times with your father, to many army posts."

He lifted his glass, took a sip, then said, "As for you, just before leaving Italy I got word that the agency had come up with a possibility, a Miss Amy Converse living in New York. There was a chance of a mistake, however, for the last address they had for you was in Maryland."

She nodded. "Yes, I lived there until a year ago. After my mother died I decided to come to New York to work. It sounded exciting, and somehow challenging."

He looked amused. "And has it been?"

Amy considered that. "In some ways, yes. The city is both those things. But I'm at work by nine and home by six, which is what I was doing in Baltimore. I worked in advertising there, too, so it isn't a lot different."

"I had a moment of doubt before I phoned, wondering if you were the right Amy Converse, the one I was searching for. If it hadn't worked out, then I was going on to California."

He was smiling easily now, and Amy was certain that it was with satisfaction.

"But fate was on my side," he said. "I found you, you found the deed to your share in the winery. So tonight we celebrate all those things."

Amy felt herself tense slightly. The time had come to be frank with him. Not that she was yet certain of what she planned to do; nevertheless, it had to be said.

"Nando, I've been thinking. What if—" she paused before going on unevenly "—what if I didn't want to sell? If I wanted to keep my share of the business?"

The warmth of the atmosphere dropped a dozen degrees. His eyes hardened abruptly and a muscle jumped in his cheek.

Amy twirled her glass between her fingers, her glance fixed on the small bouquet of flowers that graced the starched tablecloth.

"Keep your share?" There was stark incredulity in his tone.

"I really haven't come to any decision yet," she

said hastily. "I'm only discussing possibilities. I've even been considering taking a trip to Italy." Now she did lift her eyes, meeting his. She became aware that his lips were compressed, his fine nostrils pinched and white.

Amy attempted to keep her voice light as she added, "At least I've been thinking of it. I've never been there, you see. I think I'd enjoy visiting my ancestor's winery, and perhaps even learning a little about the wine industry."

He shook his head. "No, Amy," he said flatly. "That is quite impossible. If you have never been to Italy, then come as a tourist. No, come as our American relative, as our guest."

There was irritation, even anger in his face—an emotion he was barely keeping under control. Clearly he had not expected her response and did not welcome it. The gray eyes suddenly looked dark.

His voice tightened, as did his fingers on the stem of his glass. "You fail to understand the situation." He gave an impatient gesture with his head. "Women in a Latin country do not belong in industry. Oh, sometimes we must give token acceptance, but I assure you it is only token."

He regarded her for a second in silence, then added bluntly, "I am one of the worst what you call chauvinists, I admit. I prefer that women do not participate in men's business affairs."

His arrogant tone annoyed her. "I didn't say I planned to intrude," she said stubbornly. "After all, if your own mother and sister have shares—"

"Ah, but there is a great difference," he interrupted. "My mother and sister are Italian. You are not. Only by birth, perhaps, and that just partially. You may be half Italian, but you do not understand our ways. My mother and my sister do."

Amy failed to see what the difference was, but she had no chance to say so. He went on in a different tone, one that indicated the subject had been closed. "So, my dear cousin, let us complete our transaction. Sometime in the future—the near future, I hope—we will be delighted to extend an invitation to you to visit us for as long as you can stay."

He reached across the table to cover her hand with his. "My mother will be more than happy to welcome our American cousin. You can inspect our winery to your heart's content, for we often show visitors through it. And I'd love to introduce you to the beauty of northern Italy."

How deftly he was brushing off her proposal, Amy realized. And how little he knew her. If there was one sure way of making her resist, it was this bland assumption that women were inferior to men.

"You can be certain we shall be more than fair with you regarding the price," he was saying suavely. "A winery is no place for a pretty young woman, especially one who knows nothing of the industry."

"But I might like to learn, Nando," she said firmly.

"One might like to give a concert before having piano lessons, but—" his tone was dry "—but, my dear, it takes years to become a vintner. I myself grew up in the business. I've even stomped grapes with my bare feet."

Amy had a little trouble picturing this well-tailored handsome man in bare crimson feet. He had withdrawn his hand and was leaning back in his chair, relaxed and certain. "I assure you, no matter how romantic it sounds, the wine-making industry is no place for a novice, or for a woman. It's a hard, demanding, ferociously competitive business."

With unruffled self-command he added, "So let's forget this charming impractical idea of yours and have our dinner. Then we'll take a cab back to your place and finish the transfer."

What a typical chauvinistic male, Amy reflected stormily. She felt a lot more like holding on to her certificate than when they had set out.

To her relief, the first course arrived, effectively interrupting their conversation. As she anticipated, the meal had been chosen with care. Asparagus bisque was set before her, a soup of such velvety pale green in its snowy porcelain dish that she almost hated to disturb the dusting of deep jade parsley floating on top.

Then came Dover sole, delicately sauced, with a hearts-of-palm salad. And, finally, exquisite fresh strawberries in a glacé tart.

During dinner they chatted casually, as if in unspoken agreement not to mention the controversial share of the winery. Yet Amy was well aware that the man across the table was busy strengthening his position, camouflaging his strategies with charm.

And charm he certainly had. Effortlessly he regaled her with stories about the mores and morals of his countrymen, with insights into the European political arena. He was obviously intelligent, and

Amy found herself highly entertained by his sharp wit. She found herself relaxing into a pleasantly euphoric mood, pushing the whole problem into a corner of her mind.

The waiter brought them small cups of espresso, and while Amy was sipping at the strong aromatic drink she gazed out at the dazzling panorama. A ship, its lights aglow, crawled slowly along the dark river, then under the twinkling bridge.

With a sigh of contentment she turned back to Nando. As she did so she surprised a thoughtful look on his starkly handsome face. His eyes were fixed on his coffee cup and she sensed immediately that he was planning something. The realization made her uneasy and reawakened the undercurrents of their original conversation. For a while she had felt as if she were being courted by this fascinating sophisticated man. The experience had been a heady one. Had it been totally calculated?

For the briefest of seconds when he lifted his head she saw again the flash of cynical appraisal that she'd been conscious of that first evening. But as he met her eyes the expression vanished at once, to be replaced by a lazy seductive smile.

He was not planning to be denied, she realized. One way or another he was intent on obtaining her part in the winery.

When the bill had been taken care of, Nando graciously helped her to her feet. "This isn't the only dining area," he said. "While we're here we should tour the entire floor, to see the view from every side."

"I'd love to!" Amy agreed breathlessly. She hated

to leave this fascinating restaurant, knowing she might never have a chance to visit it again. She was glad to delay departure for another reason, as well. All too soon she would have to face this man with her decision.

They strolled slowly, stopping once to gaze in silence at the stark beauty of the Statue of Liberty brilliantly outlined against the night sky. As they reached the elevators, Amy took a last lingering look at the gold carpeting and the glinting mirrors. Then they were carried swiftly downward.

When they reached the taxi area, Nando said casually, "I would normally suggest a nightclub or a good piano bar I know, but I think we'll both feel better once we take care of transferring that deed."

There it was again, Amy realized. He was deliberately pushing her into a corner. He had treated her to a splendid dinner; now he was going to present her with the bill.

She didn't want to argue right there on the sidewalk. It would be better to handle the subject in the privacy of her apartment. So she made no comment as she slid into the cab except to say just as casually, "All right, let's go to my place." But she was crossing her fingers mentally.

As the taxi darted out into traffic, Nando slid his arm across the back of the seat. She felt the soft material of his sleeve tickle her shoulder.

"I wish I could stay in New York longer," he was saying in a low voice. His warm breath touched her hair, her neck, sending a tremor of pleasure through her. Amy couldn't make herself pull away.

Slipping his hand under her chin, he tilted her face

up toward him. For a moment, in the sheltering dimness of the back seat, they gazed at each other. Then his lips came down on hers.

Amy didn't resist his kiss. She didn't want to. The sensuous movement of his firm mouth on hers, the feel of his arms holding her against his muscular chest excited her almost beyond bounds. She was finding him far more compelling than any man she'd met in remembered time.

For spinning moments she returned the kiss, her heart pounding crazily against her ribs. His lips moved over her eyelids, the curve of her cheek. His warm breath was stirring her emotions. Then his mouth came back to hers again and his kiss, at first gentle, gradually became more passionate, until it was seeking, demanding, inflaming. He was stealing away her breath, her very will.... A small warning bell rang deep in her mind, chilling the ardor of her response. His lovemaking was so expert, so superbly evocative. Was she being lured into a trap? Was he trying to make it even more difficult for her to refuse to sell him her share? She, like a fool, had fallen for him. This whole scene must have been what was behind that contemplative look earlier!

Lifting her hands, she pressed them against his chest, at the same time trying to pull away from the seductive insistence of his lips. "Nando, please," she managed to gasp.

She couldn't see his eyes, but there was skillful persuasiveness in his voice. "Ah, *cara*, do not say no to me. We aren't strangers, nor are we so close in blood that we can't show affection."

His mouth continued to plunder hers and his arms drew her even closer against him.

"I promise you, as soon as I can possibly arrange it I shall fly back to New York. Then we shall see what can happen between us," he whispered. His lips were tantalizing her ear; then they moved toward her mouth again.

Twisting her head, Amy blurted out the one thing that might halt him in his far too successful assault on her senses. "Perhaps it won't be that long before we meet again. I really do think I'll come to Italy shortly."

He was abruptly still. When he did speak, his voice was even and relaxed. She hadn't affected him at all emotionally, Amy realized with dismay. His self-control had obviously been unimpaired by the passion of those kisses.

Not very flattering, she thought bitterly, conscious of her own ragged breath and unsteady heart.

"My dear Amy, of course you must come visit us," he was saying. "Surely your employer will allow you enough time off to tour your native country. And as I told you, Villa Cielo will always be ready to welcome you. I thought I made that... er...rather clear." This last was said almost teasingly.

Amy gazed straight ahead, her eyes fixed on the driver's head silhouetted against the passing lights. Her lips tightened. How smoothly Nando was glossing over any serious reasons for her visit. He *was* playing a game with her, laying an emotional booby trap to secure her part of the business. And she was furious with herself for having yielded so willingly during those few seductive moments.

The taxi pulled up in front of her apartment. Amy realized with something close to panic that she still hadn't made up her mind positively about her share in the winery. Nando Bonavia was going to pressure her into turning it over to him tonight, no doubt of that. Time was running out.

The cab door was being held open and Nando was helping her out. His hand at her elbow, he guided her through the front door, into the elevator and down the hallway to her apartment door.

There he looked down at her, a half smile on his lips. "All right, cousin, dear, may I be invited in to talk?"

Amy nodded, handing him the key so he could unlock the door. She would have opened it herself, but somehow Nando was so obviously the dominant male that she didn't want to rattle any cages until she could be certain of her decision.

Inside, she turned to him. "Would you like a coffee? Brandy?"

"Coffee sounds right; I never tire of coffee. Need any help?"

She shook her head, wanting desperately to be alone for a moment, away from the persuasiveness of his presence. She needed time to think. It simply wasn't like her to be so indecisive, she reflected irritably.

"I'll be back in a minute or two," she said quickly. "Make yourself at home."

He sank down on the sofa and leaned back, cross-

ing his long legs. He looked comfortable and somehow alert—not, Amy thought, the look of a man
about to become romantic. It was more that of a businessman contemplating the conclusion of a financial
deal, and exceedingly pleased about it.

As she stood in the kitchen measuring coffee, she
realized he had reason to feel gratified. He must be
thinking that what he wanted was now at last only
moments away from his possession. He was probably
concluding, too, that any resistance she might give
could be overcome one way or another—based on
her instinctive response to him in the cab. *Oh, damn,*
she thought angrily. It was a business deal. Why
hadn't she kept everything businesslike until the final
decision was made?

Amy hesitated, the can of coffee still clutched in
her hands. This attractive cousin of hers was absolutely correct about a couple of things. She didn't
know one single thing about the winery business. Sec-
ondly, she might very well feel out of place in a foreign country, especially a traditional country like
Italy where many people still looked askance at wom-
en in the competitive world of business.

She put the lid on the coffee can and set it back on
the shelf. She'd be a fool if she didn't take the money
and let him have her certificate.

Amy almost convinced herself. By the time she
handed Nando Bonavia a cup of coffee she was inwardly prodding herself, *go on, tell him you'll sell
out to him.*

For a few minutes they chatted idly, skirting the
issue. When he had finished his coffee, he placed the

empty cup on the table and smiled at her. "It's a shame to change the tenor of a lovely evening, but I really would like to complete our business transaction."

Despite her impulse to say yes, that she'd go get the paper in question right now and let him have it, something held her back, almost against her will. The words wouldn't come. "Nando," she began unevenly, "could I just think it over for a little longer? Say, until tomorrow morning? If I do decide to transfer my part of the business to you, I can have the certificate delivered to you before you leave. I promise."

"If? If? *Cara*, surely not *if*! I thought we had already discussed that." The smile he gave her now was frankly intimate. He reached over to take her hand, to kiss the palm and wrist. His gaze burned swiftly into hers. "Do not say 'if.' Let us quickly finish what must be done, then we can... enjoy the rest of the evening together."

Did he expect her to fall at his feet? Did he think she was that kind of woman? Firmly she withdrew her hand from his. "Nando," she began, her voice gaining strength, "when I promise, I keep my word. I'll decide and let you know by tomorrow. By noon you will have your answer."

"I'm quite sorry, my dear," he countered swiftly. "Shall we first dispose of your comment about tomorrow? It will run me too late. I shall be exceedingly busy all day and evening with vintners and dealers from New York state."

If her voice had become firm, his grew more so, and a trifle crisp. "So now will you please bring me

the deed? You will not be cheated, I assure you. Our
company is not large, but it's financially sound. I will
give you a receipt, then our accountants will forward
to you a certified check in U.S. dollars—full payment
for your fifth of the winery. As one of the family,
you will receive exactly the same amount as my sister
would, should she decide to cash in her share. The
amount will be based on market value the day the
share is received. I therefore can't give you an exact
quotation as of now, but it will be satisfactory, I'm
sure.''

Amy was dazed at the approximate sum he quoted
her. But when she spoke, it was in a voice just a little
too thin, too tense. "Thank you, Nando, I know you
will be fair; it isn't that, really. All this is just so new
to me—finding myself part owner of a winery that
has been in my family so long without my being
aware of it.''

She met his eyes candidly. "There's something
else, too. I'm twenty-four years old; for three of
those years I've worked in the glamorous advertising
business. And you know what? I hate it. I'm bored
with it. Right now I'm in a state of transition with my
present job.'' Well, that was one way of putting it,
she reflected. Then she added positively, "I'd really
like to try something else!''

"Then you should. But not—'' he flashed her a
smile that did not reflect in those remote glacial eyes
"—not in the wine business. Especially not in my
winery. As I have told you, I'm a devoted chauvinist.
Besides, you are holding up the parade, to use one of
your colorful American expressions.''

He was successfully stifling every objection she could raise. And every time he exerted more force, she found herself becoming even more stubborn. There simply was no use going on this way. She owned part of the business and had every right to take time to consider how she wanted to handle it. She said decisively, ''All I can promise right now is to carefully consider your offer, Nando. I'll call you first thing tomorrow. It's quite possible I'll turn over my share. But I think you can understand that I want to be completely certain first, so that I won't later regret my decision.''

There was such a long pause before he spoke that she finally glanced at him. How difficult it was to know what he was thinking! But behind that strong enigmatic facade something was stirring. He was deciding, she thought, whether at this stage to offer the carrot or the stick.

The carrot.

He took her hand again, bringing it to his lips and, as he had before, turning it over to kiss the palm and the inside of her wrist. And this time, too, she was unable to still the swift surge of blood through her veins. Oh, he had appeal all right, she thought bitterly.

He stood up, pulling her to her feet. Amy was certain he resented the delay her reluctance caused, but he concealed the fact.

''Very well, my dear, but consider what I said. It's positively no life for a woman. And as fond as I am of you already, I do not want you dabbling in the Vino d'Oro winery. Not in any way. You would not like having to work with me. In time bitterness could arise between us."

He looked down at her for a long moment, drawing her close to him. One hand lifted to touch her hair, his fingers subtly caressing the nape of her neck, turning her face up toward his. Then he kissed her. His mouth, arrogantly commanding hers, sent a spiral of emotion rushing through her.

Slowly, lingeringly, he drew his lips away, saying softly, "There must never be any bitterness between us, Amy. Never."

He stepped back. "Tomorrow, then, without fail, you will call me?"

She nodded. "Tomorrow," she said unevenly.

Lifting his hand in a gesture of farewell, he went out the door, closing it behind him.

Amy stood where she was in the middle of the room, still shaken by the fervor of his kiss. But she was shaken by anger, too—anger at herself. When she knew so clearly how carefully orchestrated that kiss had been, how in the world could she allow it to affect her?

And it had been planned, as an object lesson. If she kept her share and tried, as he put it, to dabble in the wine business, there'd be bitterness arising between them. And surely she didn't want that, did she? It would mean no more sweet kisses, no more fire-filled embraces. As if Fernando Bonavia knew he was God's gift to women and that she should be willing to give up everything for a taste of his charm! Who did he think she was?

Amy went striding across the living room toward

her bedroom. Her chin was firm, and green sparks leaped in her determined eyes. When it came to making her decision, it was going to be her own. She wouldn't be dangling like a puppet on strings pulled by that cleverly conniving man.

That night she lay awake for hours, the dulled sound of traffic floating up from the street below. Back and forth through her mind ran the two sides of the argument.

Nando had left no doubt about his wanting her share of the business, about his determination to have it. And she? Amy's eyes sought the clock on the dressing table. It was growing very late, and she still hadn't made up her mind.

CHAPTER THREE

AT NOON THE NEXT DAY Amy sat at her office desk with her hand on the telephone. She had just talked to Bert, then to his friend Paul.

"One fifth owner of the company?" Paul had whistled in surprise. No, he couldn't be certain exactly what it would amount to because there was no stock exchange listing for it, either in the States or abroad. The company was young from the international angle, but its reputation and prospects were good. He was able to give her a rough estimate, to say her share would be in the six-figure range at least. The news matched Nando Bonavia's own estimate of the night before.

Dialing again, she talked once more with Bert. He, too, had been impressed, and now asked if she'd come to a final decision to sell. Amy hesitated. The truth was, Nando Bonavia had fired a hot feeling of resistance within her—in spite of those emotional tempting kisses, or maybe because of them. Did she want to prove to him and to herself that her decision, either way, was not going to be influenced by him, she wondered. She answered slowly that, yes, the money sounded good to her, but she was still considering the possibility of keeping her share and maybe getting involved in some way with the family wine business.

Bert was startled. "Now hold on, Amy! Better give that one a little more thought! You'd be plunging into something that, if you'll forgive my saying so, you don't know one damned thing about!" His voice was definitely discouraging.

"Especially if the winery is in a foreign country. And...Italy? That's a whole different ball game over there. I honestly don't think a woman, especially an American woman, would be a big hit trying to integrate into a native wine business."

Amy could picture Bert shaking his head, his long lower lip protruding in concern. She didn't agree or disagree but thanked him, saying she'd let him know the eventual outcome. She hung up once again.

Looking across the room, she could see Mr. Richardson through the open door. He was sitting at his desk, probably preparing to leave for lunch. He bit at the end of a cigar, lighted it, then rose and started out of his office, crossing within a foot of Amy. Heading toward the outer door, he gave her a frigid nod as he passed.

She watched him go, then narrowed her eyes speculatively. So far Mr. Richardson hadn't found any grounds he could use for firing her. But it was only a matter of time. Anything of minor importance, her fault or not, and she would be out the door! It seemed as though the man wasn't going to relax until his precious nephew was vindicated.

And then?

For a full five minutes Amy sat in the empty office,

staring down at her polished desk. Her eyes were focused on a neat stack of copy material, but in reality they saw nothing. Then her hand stretched out slowly and picked up the telephone. She dialed the hotel where Nando Bonavia was staying.

His voice sounded stunned. "You are going to... to *what*?" he asked unbelievingly. "But you can't, Amy. I thought we had that all settled. I think I explained everything, why it won't work at all. You know how I feel about it."

She chose her words carefully. "I'm merely planning to come visit Italy," she said. "And I'd like to see the winery—not necessarily work there. I wouldn't be so presumptuous. But I will be between jobs. I'm giving my notice here."

"But, Amy, *cara*," he began softly, persuasively, "It really isn't—"

Amy was shaking her head even though he couldn't see her. "Please, Nando, don't misunderstand. I simply want to come over and take a look at the winery. I honestly don't know what my future plans will be, but you need feel no responsibility. I'd much rather you wouldn't. This is something that I need to do for my own satisfaction."

"If—if—" he began cautiously. "If you do come and we show you the winery—let you see what a complicated business it is—then will you turn over your share?"

Without waiting for her to answer, he went on swiftly. "I know you will; you simply aren't aware of the problems. So why not do this: let's conclude the transfer now, while I'm still here. It's so much simpler. Then your visit will be without problems. No great decision will be hanging over you, spoiling your trip. You'll enjoy yourself more.''

Amy had picked up a pencil while he talked and was rolling it about in one hand. Why couldn't she allow him to have his way, she wondered. She quite honestly didn't know. It wasn't because she wanted to continue seeing him; a little quickly she assured herself that that actually wasn't why. Maybe it was because she welcomed the idea of a challenge, a new way of life, a new interest. Like wine making. Somehow the process—so earthy, so natural—had an odd sort of pull for her. She would love to be involved in an industry so basic to life after her three dry years in graphics. If it didn't work out, if she didn't fit in or her relatives really didn't want her around, she could always take the money.

"I...I can't." Despite the hesitancy in her tone, both of them somehow knew that her decision was final, that there was no use arguing further.

There was a long silence from him, followed by, "You won't reconsider?"

"No, not yet. Maybe, if all these so-called problems are as complicated as you claim they are, I'll turn my share of the business over to you and then come back home. But I am very much interested in the business. I'd like to know something about the wine-making process, especially of a family winery. It might be a passing whim, Nando, but I would like to find out for myself.'' '

Again a pause, then he said grandly, "All right, my dear stubborn cousin, I surrender! Come to Italy, *cara*!''

That tone in his voice, the returned warmth, startled her. She hadn't expected it. And it was just a little too quick, a little too facile for comfort. What did he have in mind?

"When may we expect you, Amy?"

There really wasn't any need now to wait until she was fired, she thought, with a tingle of real pleasure and satisfaction.

"Oh, I guess I'll have to give two weeks' notice, then there'll be things to do about my passport and airline reservations. I suppose I might be arriving over there in about a month's time."

"A month? Nonsense. Come back with me tomorrow."

There was that velvet tone back, sensuous and inviting. The predatory male assuming she couldn't wait to be near him again.

"Oh, but that's impossible, Nando. I couldn't."

"Then, promise me, no more than a month. I'm eager to show you Italy. Venice by moonlight. And Verona—you'll like Verona, the city our family came from. There's so much to see, my dear cousin."

How transparent he was, and how badly he must want her share of the business, to be able to accommodate himself so quickly to the change in signals! Oh, he was planning on obtaining it, no matter how much she resisted. When he realized that argument couldn't extract it and that romantic persuasion had so far been ineffectual, he was going to increase the pressure.

"I'll write when I have a firm date," she said calmly.

As Amy put the receiver down, she found it hard

not to smile. What an easily read scenario would now unfold! She would arrive in Italy, welcomed as a guest rather than as a part owner of the winery. Then the campaign would begin in earnest.

She knew what would probably happen. The whole thing was going to be done as skillfully as any commercial venture. Nando, at his most charming, his most seductive, would try to lull her into a romantic mood. Instead of boardroom politics he would resort to candlelight and wine to buy out a bothersome partner. He might even attempt to make love to her.... She couldn't help a sudden shiver at the thought, and it served to return her to reality.

One thing was for sure, she thought, her eyes narrowing: she was going to have to be exceedingly wary. Already he must feel certain of eventual success where she was concerned. Part of that was her own fault. She had definitely responded to his kisses, more than she felt comfortable about.

She sat up abruptly in her chair. Well, he wasn't going to have his way! She was going to survey the situation fairly, judging it with as level a head as she could manage. Then she would decide whether to sell or not—on her own, not because he was pressuring her with kisses!

For another moment or two Amy sat staring blankly at the small calendar on her desk, biting absently at her underlip. Nando Bonavia attracted her more than was comfortable, it was true, but something else about him still bothered her. Sometimes she caught a glimpse of a certain... cool disdain. Was there actually a shadow of contempt? She shook her head slowly. No, not quite. But there was something about his treatment of her that she didn't understand or, for that matter, like. It was always so elusive, instantly smothered as he took her hand in his or spoke in soft seductive tones. Intuitively she sensed that he was a fine intelligent man. During their conversations she had been impressed by his wide-ranging ideas, amused by his wit, touched by his passionate concern for the have-nots of the world. And although he obviously knew very well how to arouse a woman, he spoke only with affection about his own mother and sister. Surely he had respect for women, in their proper place, of course. But did he have the same respect for her? Amy couldn't be certain which aspects of Nando were true facets of his personality and which were not.

Getting up from her desk, she started for the door and a hurried lunch at a sandwich shop. A feeling of anticipation was beginning to build within her. When she had played tennis in college, she'd never feared or avoided competition with a better, harder player. And sometimes she had won those uneven matches. But win or lose, it was the challenge itself she had enjoyed. Now she had a feeling that she was going to be stepping onto another type of court with just such a competitor.

Long before lunch hour was over Amy was back at her desk. Today of all days she didn't want to be late in case Mr. Richardson returned early and was looking at the clock when she arrived. She didn't want to give him the pleasure of firing her now.

Frowning, she rubbed her fingertips over her forehead, trying to decide how she wanted to word her resignation. Then she began to type. When she'd finished, she folded the paper, put it in an envelope and wrote Mr. Richardson's name on it. Rising, she went into his office and propped it on his desk. It would be facing him when he sat down.

Linda came rushing in right at one o'clock. She yanked the cover off her typewriter before slipping into her chair.

"Has our live-in ogre returned yet?" she asked, with a quick glance toward the office.

"No, he hasn't. I have a little surprise waiting for him. Maybe a disappointment." Amy smiled reflectively, a little pleased with the thought.

Linda stared at her curiously. "Just what have you been up to? You look like the proverbial cat that swallowed the canary." Abruptly her eyebrows shot upward. "Amy! You don't mean—you didn't—you aren't—"

Amy nodded calmly. "I do. I did. I am."

"When? Are you really going to go through with this nutty wine thing, then? Did you actually resign?" Linda was gazing at her, eyes only half-believing.

Amy crossed her arms, leaning back in her chair and smiling. "I wrote my resignation just a moment ago. I suppose I'm obliged to give the customary two weeks' notice. Anyhow, it's on his desk now. I'm afraid I've cheated him. I think he was really looking forward to firing me."

Her expression became pensive. "I'm going to Italy, that much I've decided. I don't know how deeply

I'll get involved in what you call my 'nutty wine thing,' but I have a yearning to see the winery itself, something I partly own. My own grandfather came from there, Linda! I feel I owe it to myself to have a look at it before...." Her voice trailed off uncertainly.

"Before you give up your share in the business? Or will you?" Linda asked, wholly interested now.

"I don't know. I really don't. My cousin wants to buy me out, and I'm sure he means to do just that. So I may simply go ahead and let him have my share. But not before I have a look at my winery!"

Linda's eyes narrowed with amusement. "I suppose that Renaissance cousin of yours has nothing to do with your deciding to go to Italy. He sounds mighty appealing to me."

"He's attractive in rather a lordly way, no doubt about it, but he won't get my share in the business because of that. It'll be because I'm convinced that dabbling in a foreign winery is not for me."

Linda's voice took on a serious tone. "Maybe it's none of my business, but you'll be out of a job. A trip to Europe isn't a prize that comes in a Cracker Jack box."

Amy nodded. "I know. Maybe I'm doing something a little crazy, but my mother left an insurance policy. Not a big one, not by any standard, but I've never touched a penny of it. I was saving it for something I really needed or wanted." She added simply, "This trip is it!"

She took a quick deep breath and laughed. "Well, Linda, it's done! I'm practically on my way to Italy!

Come over and have dinner with me tonight; we'll celebrate. I'll treat you to a bottle of Vino d'Oro, my wine. It really is marvelous." Her green eyes sparkled.

"My God, already she's a tycoon!" Linda observed dryly. Then she nodded. "But, great, I'll be there! Any chance of our Borgia showing up?"

"No, he didn't suggest getting together. He had said he had a lot of business things lined up for today and this evening."

"Too bad, I was looking forward to—"

Mr. Richardson entered, striding pompously across the office. He looked neither right nor left as he went into his own room.

"Darn it! He shut the door! I'd love to see his face when he reads your note!" Linda whispered as both of them turned to the afternoon's work.

AMY'S PROJECTED TRIP TO ITALY was the prime topic of conversation when she had dinner with Bert two nights later.

"I'm not at all certain I think you're doing the right thing," he said. His serious brown eyes met hers across the red-and-white checked tablecloth at the small steak and chop house they often patronized. "You don't know the language; you know nothing about wine, really; and you know even less about your relatives over there. You may not like them, they might not like you. . . . Though I don't see how they could help it," he amended quickly.

She looked at him fondly. Bert, with his neat brown hair, his square honest face and his three-piece

suit, was the type of man her mother would have
wanted her to marry. They had been dating for six
months already, long enough for Amy to know that
she liked him but would never love him. His good-
night kisses were gentle and sweet. In no way did they
send her heart plummeting and her pulse racing.

"You may be perfectly right, Bert," she replied
earnestly. "But it's something I need to find out for
myself. I'll never be satisfied if I don't."

He gave her a lopsided grin. "You know, Amy,
there are worse things than marrying a lawyer. If
hopping around on grapes with your cousins turns
out to be boring, you know where to find me."

What was wrong with her? Bert was fun, successful and certainly agreeable. For a moment Amy
almost wished that she did want to marry him.

"Well, I may be back sooner than you think, at
that," she said a little reluctantly. "I've been doing a
lot of reading on wine making and it isn't as simple
and primitive as I had thought. Besides, I have a feeling that my cousin Nando is intent on edging me
out."

Bert picked up his cocktail glass and grinned at her
over the rim of it. "Well, I think he's got his work
cut out for him. I get the feeling somehow that the
first time you two square off toe to toe out there
among the wine vats, he's going to find you can hold
your own."

Amy lifted her own glass, gazing at the glint of the
pale golden wine she had ordered. It was Vino d'Oro.
She smiled suddenly. "You may be right. My mother
used to say, 'Amy, you're usually very agreeable, but

when you feel put-upon you can be as stubborn as a Missouri mule....'"

"Not a bad trait, especially when you're going to be dealing with some pretty macho men over there. But speaking personally, I always find you agreeable." Bert looked at her affectionately. "Promise me that you'll hurry back, Amy. Make it as soon as you can. I'm putting in an order for two season tickets to the football games this year. Let's not waste them."

He repeated his plea almost in the same words when he saw her off on the plane one evening a month later. "I've got those football tickets. Don't make me invite anyone else to sit with me. I admit I'm besieged by beautiful show girls, but I'd rather have you," he groaned, making a dismal face.

She laughed. "And you want me to feel sorry for you! But who knows, I may be returning crestfallen before the season's over. Maybe before the Super Bowl, anyhow."

Her plane was called and Bert said goodbye, giving her a final hug and a kiss. "Take care, little one," he called after her.

She waved at him, then entered the boarding lounge. Not for the first time did she regret feeling nothing more than friendship for him. Those stupid glands or hormones or whatever they were; they lay so quietly around Bert and started pulsing so excitedly around Nando Bonavia....

As the plane lifted into the sky, on the way to Italy, Amy unloosened her seat belt, leaned back and dreamily half closed her eyes. Maybe it was wise, maybe it wasn't. Whichever, she was heading for her winery.

In her purse was a letter from Nando, saying how very anxious he was, how anxious they all were, to welcome her. There was a letter from his mother, too, written with a firm angular hand on stiff white paper, a politely phrased invitation to stay at Villa Cielo on her visit to Italy.

Visit. That was the key word. It wasn't underlined in Nando's letter nor in his mother's. But it might as well have been.

In the past four and a half weeks Amy had haunted bookstores and libraries, searching out information on wines, especially Italian wines. And, specifically, Vino d'Oro. There wasn't much that was of help. The general discussion of wines was just that—too general. The technical books were too complicated. She'd found only a few sparse references to Vino d'Oro, probably because the modernization of that winery and its foreign export had been so recent.

Amy had a worrisome feeling that Nando was right, that she was quite beyond her depth. She was still excited at the prospect of touring a winery that was, for a brief period anyway, partly hers.

It was too late to do anything about the language problem. She had first thought of taking a crash course at Berlitz, but she quickly gave up the idea. There was simply too much else that had to be done—storing her furniture, giving notice to her superintendent, having her phone disconnected. She did buy a small English/Italian dictionary and set out to learn a few words. She looked up the one Nando had used, *cara*. As she had surmised, it meant "dear." She learned how to say yes and, with Nando in mind, how to say no. Several other common words she committed to memory, but the sentence structuring and the grammar were still Greek to her.

When the huge jet landed and finally rolled to a stop at the Leonardo da Vinci Airport outside of Rome, Amy began gathering up her belongings, pausing for an instant to peer out the window. All she could see was the side of the large passenger terminal, but excitement foamed up inside her like warm champagne. She was in Italy!

Inside the airport building she was immediately surrounded by a clamor of voices. Even though it was early morning, all around her were dramatic farewells and exuberant welcomes, carried on in a clatter of foreign tongues. People were gesturing and embracing, laughing heartily and calling to one another. Bouquets of flowers and gaily tied packages were being pressed into the arms of travelers, and here and there white handkerchiefs were dabbing at eyes of people who hadn't seen each other for a long time.

Amy stood still, caught and held by the crowds swirling about her, her eyes shining with sheer exhilaration. She was enchanted at the very thought of being here, with those voices crackling about her. It didn't matter that she couldn't understand them.

She was anxious to wander around, to continue absorbing the sight, the foreign smells, the whole lively atmosphere. But her connecting flight for Villafranca was nearly ready to take off. She had barely had time to get through customs, much less take this brief look around her. She glanced down at her watch, then remembered she was no longer on New York time and turned to the large airport clock. With one more lingering look at the heartwarming dramatics going on around her, she started for her gate number.

She was still keyed up with excitement when she left the plane at Villafranca, but for a different reason. Immediately her eyes began scanning the milling crowd absorbing the disembarking passengers. She failed to see Nando, though he'd cabled he'd meet her flight.

Suddenly a tall arresting figure was striding through the crush of people toward her. Amy felt a sudden shock of recognition. Not recognition of who he was—Nando Bonavia would stand out in any crowd. This was more a stirring consciousness of him.

She felt instantly perturbed. This was no way for her to face the challenge that lay ahead. She threw up her defenses, determined that if he kissed her now she would be cool and unemotional.

He didn't kiss her. Instead he smiled down at her, lifted her hand lightly to his lips and said, "Amy, my love, it's been too long. I've learned a lot of things since I left you in New York—mainly that there has been something missing in my life!" It was said not seriously or dramatically but with a touch of dry amusement that prevented the words from sounding theatrical.

She was relieved, Amy told herself, that she hadn't had to arm her emotions. Of course he wouldn't kiss

her here among a crowd of people. He was too cir-
cumspect for that! She couldn't help feeling slightly
disappointed.

Nando claimed her luggage for her, then helped her
into a small sleek sports car. He slid into the other
side, gave her a quick smile, then skillfully nosed the
vehicle into a dense line of traffic, all of which was
moving at tremendous speed. Amy tensed her muscles
and caught her breath tremulously. The drivers, one
and all, appeared bent on self-destruction. She had
thought that exposure to New York traffic would have
hardened her to any other, but she was unable to resist
a sudden shrinking within herself as a car came bolting
out of a side road and whipped into a nearly nonexis-
tent space just ahead of them.

Nando glanced over at Amy. "You'll get used to
it, and shortly you'll be able to ride and drive without
clenching your fists the way you are doing now. We
Italians are still thwarted chariot drivers."

To Amy's relief, traffic congested and slowed as
they approached the outskirts of Verona, allowing
her to relax against the seat and uncurl her fingers.

By rights she should have been exhausted, but she
wasn't. Eagerly she fixed her eyes on the silhouettes
of church spires and the crenellated towers of castles
thrusting high inside walls that completely surrounded the city.

Even the sunlight of early fall seemed different
here. It bathed the high ocher walls and gray stone
buildings in a soft mellow glow, giving her the impression she was seeing not a modern city but an ancient oil painting.

Nando's hands turned the wheel sharply, sending the car through a narrow arched opening in the city wall, into a crowded, crooked street. Instantly Amy's ears were filled with the angry buzz of Vespas skirting dangerously in and out of traffic, reckless and unheeding; the dissonant pealing of church bells, as one, then another, rang out. There was an unending clatter of voices, shouting, laughing, singing. And again, as at the Rome airport, like a fragrant cloud, the scent of roasting coffee.

Amy turned enchanted eyes from one side of the narrow street to the other, trying to take in everything at once.

"Nando," she said simply, "it's everything I expected and more, much more."

He took a hand from the wheel to lay it briefly over hers. "We're prejudiced, we Bonavias. To us there is only one city in the world: Verona. The jewel of Italy, the most beautiful. It's also, as you no doubt already know, the home of Romeo and Juliet, a city of lovers. I hope to prove that to you, Amy." His fingers tightened on hers. "And you must not tell me no this time, as you once did."

Then he withdrew his hand to give his attention to his driving, dodging careless bicycle riders who darted now and then too close to the car.

Amy lowered her lashes in amusement. It was beginning already, then, the firing of the first salvo, laying the groundwork for what he was planning. Sliding a speculative glance toward Nando's strong face, she wondered if he had any idea of what was going on in her mind. He more than likely presumed she was overwhelmed with anticipation at the thought. Well, he had a surprise coming!

She turned her full attention to the city unfolding around her, iron grilles and balconies studding the fronts of buildings, crowded streets that had been built for horse and coach centuries ago and now allowed only constricted passage for cars.

Nando edged his way in and out, often barely missing pedestrians who stepped out of shops and houses directly into the street. At times they would wander almost casually in front of the car, trusting the driver— or, Amy thought, a guardian angel—for safe passage.

He crossed up and over a narrow arched bridge, nodding down toward the flat silver ribbon of a river that curved lazily through the city. "That's the Adige," he said as he headed toward the city walls once again.

"The rest of Verona we shall leave for another time. I simply wanted to tempt you with a small glimpse for now, but my mother will be waiting tea and she's anxious to meet you." Nando practically hurtled the car through an opening in the wall and out onto the highway leading toward Monte Cielo and the winery.

"I must say I'm relieved to learn your mother and I can communicate, Nando. She wrote me in English, so I gather she must speak and understand it," Amy said. "I feel embarrassed that I know so little Italian, but if my mother knew the language, she never spoke it at home. Even my grandfather spoke English, with only an occasional word of Italian thrown in when he got excited."

"I suppose our whole family speaks English of a sort, anyhow, so you won't have a problem," Nando reassured her. "We had English tutors, quite an accomplishment in those bad days after the war. But—" he gave Amy a wry smile "—my mother wasn't happy about our learning street English, including the usual colorful vulgarities, so she hired us tutors. How she managed I'm not certain, but she can be quite strong willed, as you may find."

It was surprising, Amy reflected, that he hadn't mentioned her share in the winery yet or asked if she had the certificate with her. Probably he assumed she had, for there was an air of supreme confidence about him. It was unspoken but present. He fully expected her to turn over her part of the business to him

Within fifteen or twenty minutes the scenery began to change, thickly clustering houses giving way to fields where trellised grapevines ascended the hillsides in formal rows. Nando slowed his car, then turned from the highway onto a winding road that led up between the vineyards to an ancient ochercolored castle perched far above on the brow of the hill.

"I can't believe I'm actually seeing real castles," Amy exclaimed, gazing up at the building. "Is it very old? It looks it."

"It is. And, my lovely one, this is also our winery. My father had been doing rather well, you see, and wanted to expand. He bought the land adjoining his own vineyards—and the sprawling old castle that happened to be on it."

She turned her head sharply to stare at him half in disbelief, then without a word gazed back up at the imposing edifice.

It was stone, a massive square of pale stone, rearing stark and forbidding several stories high against the twilight sky. Cupolas and turrets jutted from walls rimmed with crenellation. Amy could see windows, some of them mere slits, set deeply in the thick walls. Many of them were barred with intricate iron grillwork. At each of the two corners facing the valley below rose massive watchtowers.

As they drove nearer she could see a lowered drawbridge spanning a moat.

"It's utterly fantastic, Nando. It's unreal! Something out of a book of knights and chivalry. It's hard for me to realize that this majestic structure is actually our winery!" She hadn't meant to say it, not in that way exactly. Had she used an unfortunate adjective? She certainly didn't want to start problems at the very beginning of her stay.

Either Nando hadn't noticed or he had decided to ignore the "our," for he replied, "I'm afraid the drawbridge and moat are primarily window dressing. There's a large courtyard on the far side where deliveries take place. But visitors to the winery seem to enjoy the drama of a moat and drawbridge, so we leave them as they are."

As the road skirted the front of the castle, passing the drawbridge, Amy caught a glimpse of a graveled courtyard, wide stone steps and a heavily studded door.

Toward the rear of the building a high stone wall

billowed out in a huge half circle, enclosing the entire back section. Through the iron gates, which were swung open into a courtyard, Amy could see modern trucks lined up, one behind the other. They looked strangely incongruous next to an ancient castle. She could also hear the grinding sound of machinery coming from within, and the soft warm air carried a heady tart smell of wine making.

"How old is the castle, do you know?" she asked, twisting her head so she could gaze back up at the imposing watchtowers.

"The exact date? No. But I understand it was built sometime during the fourteenth century. Probably about the middle."

"It's incredible," Amy said wonderingly. "In the States we consider something to be very old if it dates back two hundred years." She glanced back again. "And it looks so untouched by the ages. I suppose it looks the same now as it did back then."

Nando shook his head. "I'm afraid not. Well, yes, the exterior, perhaps. But during the last year of World War II, planes going overhead—possibly one of yours—dropped a bomb right down into the center of the castle. Anyhow, we rebuilt that section, which now houses the winery. The rest, yes, is intact and unchanged."

No matter whose bombers had caused the damage, Amy reflected bitterly, she resented the act that might have caused destruction of this entire ancient building. She doubly resented it because the castle now seemed something personal to her.

They had turned up a road leading to a large

sprawling villa behind an iron-gated stone wall, a wall edged with sharp spikes. Nando sounded the horn, and an elderly man with a shock of unruly white hair pulled open the gate so the car could enter the courtyard.

Ahead of Amy lay a long two-story building, wrapped around a central courtyard in the shape of a U. It, too, looked timeless, she decided, a little worn by the passage of years but with immense charm and dignity.

The house, pale sandstone, had a double row of windows across the front, with four balconies jutting from the second floor. Sprawling ivy clung to the walls, softening the formal aspect of the building.

Nando stopped the car and turned to her, an enigmatic look in his flashing eyes. "My father had this old house renovated, too. Welcome to Villa Cielo, my home. And while you visit us, consider it your home, also."

There was that word again, Amy noticed. *Visit.* With the most delicate emphasis.

But she said only, "Thank you, Nando."

They got out of the car, Nando opening her door and taking her elbow politely to help her out. He was nothing if not solicitous, she thought as she gathered up her purse and smiled at him.

Together they went up the central walk, edged on either side by a stretch of smooth lawn. Here and there huge stone urns overflowing with brilliant flowers brought color to the otherwise formal layout. Up three steps was a large flagstone terrace fronting the entire breadth of the house. In the center of the terrace stood a gay red-and-white striped umbrella spreading over a table and chairs, looking almost hoydenish, Amy thought, where everything else seemed to be so very dignified and ancient.

Nando pushed open the heavily carved wooden door of the villa to allow Amy to enter a large reception hall. Dark oil paintings in massive gold frames stared down from the walls, a rich Oriental carpet of dark red spread across the gleaming marble floor. Amy stopped to gaze up at a magnificent tapestry covering nearly six square feet of wall space. It was a hunting scene, filled with horses in brilliant crimson trappings and hounds tugging at gold leashes. In the forefront a dashing young man wearing a plumed hat bright with green and gold feathers sat astride a coal-black horse, which was rearing up as if eager for the chase.

Ahead of her rose an imposing marble staircase, which separated into two balustraded wings. It was, Amy thought fleetingly, like stepping into an exhibit in some art museum.

"Come, Amy, my mother is eager to meet you. Do you realize you are the first American relative to come to Villa Cielo?" Nando asked. Without waiting for a reply he led her toward an open door, which was flanked by ponderous chairs of dark carved wood, standing at attention against paneled walls.

The next room Amy found nearly as somber as the entrance hall. It was longer than it was wide, and here, too, dark paneling prevailed. A delicate pastoral mural painted directly on a side wall did little to help lighten the stiff-looking chairs or the heavy green velvet draperies at the window. In the green-veined marble fireplace logs were laid but not burning in the warmth of late day.

Nando's mother was seated in a straight chair by the fireplace. As they walked toward her, Amy began to have the uncomfortable feeling that perhaps she should curtsy, as one does when approaching royalty. She wasn't immediately certain why she felt that way; perhaps it was the almost regal appearance of the woman.

Still, they were really rather alike, Nando and his mother. Amy was aware of the same strong face, the same aloof gray eyes and almost harsh profile. But while Nando was tall, the woman in the black dress, sitting so erectly in the high-backed chair, was small and slight, the bones of her face showing sharply through her pale skin. Not pretty, no—probably she never had been, Amy thought. But there was a certain stark majesty in the austere face, the white hair swept uncompromisingly back from her forehead. Her black dress was buttoned high and rigidly to her neck, incredibly old-fashioned and yet somehow unalterably right for this woman whose face was as unrevealing as a marble statue. Unrevealing except, of course, for the frosty appraisal in the gray eyes.

If Nando seemed to have stepped from a Renaissance painting, Amy reflected, his mother, too, might have gazed down from some dark canvas.

The woman did not utter a word until Nando and Amy were very near her chair, then she gave Amy an enigmatic smile. "My dear Amy, welcome to Italy, to Villa Cielo." The voice was cool and courteous. She held out a thin pale hand to Amy, who was surprised at the firmness of her grasp.

"You are very kind to have me," Amy murmured.

"Nonsense!" the woman said crisply. "It is not every day one has a long-lost relative arrive from America for a visit." With a slight directing nod of her head she indicated a chair.

Amy took the designated seat and found herself, too, sitting a little rigidly, almost by example. She moistened her lips nervously, trying to think of something to say. How should she address Nando's mother, she wondered. Surely not "cousin," though that was what she was; it hardly seemed suitable for some reason.

The older woman was quick to supply an answer to the unasked question, giving Amy the uncomfortable feeling that she had looked into her mind.

"I'm elderly enough that for you to call me Cousin Lucia is quite ridiculous. Why not call me Aunt Lucia? It seems far more appropriate under the circumstances. Besides, that is how your cousin Franco addresses me."

Something in the woman's intonation stirred a sudden inexplicable warning in Amy's consciousness. "Of course, I should like that, Aunt Lucia," she hurried to reply.

There *was* something—something intangible in the air. Amy had the feeling that she was being caught between two strong forces, Nando and his mother. Each was exerting invisible pressure; she was certain she wasn't imagining it. She had heard that animals can sense danger, that it lifts the ruffs on the back of their necks. The image was a little melodramatic, she hastened to assure herself. Surely this situation didn't contain anything as potent as danger. All the same she felt uneasy.

"We are planning to have tea shortly," Signora Bonavia was saying. "Would you like to be shown to your room first so that you may freshen yourself after your trip?" The woman paused, those gray eyes hiding all expression, the mouth forming a polite smile.

"Yes, if you don't mind, Aunt Lucia. I'd like to slip into something other than travel clothes. It will take only a few minutes."

The pale, almost translucent hand lifted, rings glinting on the thin fingers. "Very well. Nando, show Amy to her room, please. We've readied the guest room in the east wing."

Amy and Nando left the room, mounting the marble stairs together. "My sister is in town, but she should return in time for dinner. Franco is at the winery but will be home for tea, so you will be exposed to the whole family today," he said lightly, guiding her down a long hallway where heavily framed oil paintings decorated the walls on either side. He paused beside a pale cream-colored door decorated with gold curlicues, and opened it.

It was an airy room, and bright. With a balcony, she noted in delight. Through open shutters, soft white curtains fluttered lazily in a breeze from outdoors.

Before Amy could thank Nando and repeat that she would rejoin them in a few minutes for tea, he had slipped his arms about her. Pulling her close, he gazed down at her with those fathomless eyes. He did not kiss her—not yet, but let his lips trail tantalizingly around her ears, his warm breath stirring an unwilling response in her.

Amy tried to resist, tried to pull away. She wanted to seem a lot more casual and unmoved than she really was.

But he held her firmly, and as his lips moved nearer to hers, the hands that had been locked about her waist slid down the small of her back. He compelled her even closer, until their bodies were touching and she was conscious of every outline of his strong masculinity.

For a second more she struggled, reminding herself frantically that this was exactly what he had been planning—to assault her resistance with his powerful sexual appeal. But a sudden rush of traitorous response pulsed through her. As his lips hovered, so close to hers that she could feel the soft warmth of his breath, her mind lost to her emotions and her body, reluctantly then achingly, melded against him. Mindlessly she lifted her lips to meet his.

The sound of Nando's voice came like a splash of cold water. He had raised his head to bark a crisp sentence in Italian to someone standing behind her. Amy twisted her head quickly to see a manservant in the open doorway, her suitcases clutched in his hands. She caught her breath in dismay, her cheeks burning hotly in instant embarrassment.

The servant displayed only polite disinterest, however, as he nodded and replied to Nando. Giving a slight bow, and murmuring something in Italian to Amy, he entered the room, clumped across the carpet and set the luggage on the floor. He said something else to Nando, then pulled himself to erect attention until his employer lifted a casual hand in what was apparently dismissal. The man gave Amy the same slight bow, backed away a few steps, then turned and vanished out the doorway, closing the door softly behind him.

Nando once again reached out to Amy as if to continue exactly where he'd left off. Before she could protest, his lips covered hers and his hand slipped to the buttons of her blouse.

There was something so coolly premeditated, so almost crass in his approach that her mind began flashing red warning signals and her freshly aroused emotions went scuttling back to a place of safety. Did he think she was his for the taking, ready to leap into his arms whenever he snapped his fingers?

She pulled away, her voice forcibly casual if a little breathless as she gripped tightly at her gaping blouse. "Run along, Nando. I must change and we shouldn't keep your mother waiting."

He paused a second or two before leaving. "But I shall see you again shortly, won't I?" It wasn't a question. He gave her a slow sensuous smile, one in which amusement as well as that other illegible expression flickered.

She swallowed as she watched him go, then tried fiercely to regulate her thoughts and her emotions. *Damn the man, anyway,* she thought bitterly as she walked across the room toward her suitcases. She didn't understand him at all. How could he be so conniving and ruthless to squeeze a competitor to the wall with such a deliberate amorous assault. Wasn't he touched at all by what he was doing, by their passionate moments together? Amy herself was moved more than she had ever been by any man.

She was a fool!

Only now was her heart starting to slow down from its sharp knocking, only now was that sweet new aching ebbing away. She was going to have to do better than this, a whole lot better!

Quickly she stripped off the skirt and blouse she'd been traveling in. Opening a suitcase, she pulled out a simple silk jersey dress in a coffee-with-cream shade that was flattering to her blond hair. Slipping it over her head, she gazed at her reflection in the mirror. In exasperation she ran a chagrined hand across her breasts, as if she could somehow wipe away the tell-tale show of nipples evident through the soft material. She scowled at her reflection. Nando was a lot better in arousing emotion than she was in controlling it.

Opening her purse, she touched her lips with a faint coral lipstick, drew a comb through her hair, then went to rejoin the others.

As she reentered the room, a young man was standing near Aunt Lucia, carrying on a lively conversation. Apparently it was mostly one-sided, for the woman's face was stoic and her smile not particularly animated.

Nando, sitting in a dark green velvet chair, rose at once when Amy entered. "You were true to your word, my dear cousin. You took only a few minutes."

The young man, hearing Nando, whipped around and came toward her, his hand outstretched. "Cousin Amy, *benvenuto*! Welcome!"

"Your cousin, Franco Rinaldi," Nando said dryly.

The newcomer was not quite as tall as Nando. He was younger by several years, with dark chestnut hair that had auburn highlights in it. With his narrow face and his curious eyes he looked very much like a successful young stockbroker, Amy thought. Not at all like his cousin.

Franco took her hand in his. "Ah, my lovely cousin, how glad I am to meet you! We have just been speaking of you. How is it you say—your ears must have been burning." His accent was slightly more pronounced than Nando's or Signora Bonavia's.

There was a look of approval—of something more than approval—in his hazel eyes and in the gentle pressure on her hand.

Amy suppressed the flicker of amusement she felt. Obviously both the Rinaldi and the Bonavia men had one thing in common: they enjoyed the pursuit of women.

"Rinaldi!" she exclaimed, smiling at him. "The only other person I've ever known by that name was my grandfather."

"Ah, yes, and so you and I are more closely related than you and Nando are," Franco drawled. There was something in his tone that made Amy sharpen her glance at him. His face was bland enough, but for the briefest of seconds there was a flash of what could be malice in his hazel eyes as he tossed a quick look at Nando.

Amy wondered what it meant, but before she could attempt to analyze it, Nando was at her side. "What may we offer you, Amy? Would you like tea? Sherry? Vermouth? The vermouth is one called Punt è Mes, which we favor in this part of the country. It's slightly bitter in taste but very good. Or would you like to sample some Vino d'Oro Chiaro, our newest wine?"

She was conscious of Aunt Lucia sitting in her chair, a delicate teacup already balanced in her hand. The woman's eyes only partially betrayed the fact that they were shrewdly appraising her.

"But how could I choose anything other than our own wine? Wouldn't that almost rank as betrayal?" Amy asked lightly, slipping into the chair Aunt Lucia indicated. She forced herself to lean back and appear relaxed, despite her inner uncertainty. Then Nando was standing before her, handing her a thin crystal wineglass which contained a pale golden liquid.

Stifling a feeling of self-consciousness, Amy deliberately lifted the fragile goblet, turning it around slowly. Tilting it, she allowed the contents to trickle down the inside of the glass. These were the "legs" of wine she had read about. Slowly she raised the glass closer to breathe the delicate bouquet before tasting. She let the first few drops linger on her tongue before she swallowed—correct procedure according to the books she had read. Though she didn't glance at the other three people in the room, she was acutely conscious that they were watching her.

"Why, Nando," Franco's voice lifted in mock surprise, "what have you been hiding about our delectable cousin? I thought she knew little about the subject of wine. You've been keeping her to yourself!" He turned amused eyes on Amy. "My dear cousin, you'll have to confess. Are you a closet enologist?"

Amy lifted innocent eyes. They weren't going to trap her on that one. Some of those hours spent in the library were already paying off. "I make no claim to any expertise on wines. Not yet." *Let them mull over that for a while,* she thought swiftly. "Let's just say I'm an interested neophyte."

Aunt Lucia was watching her steadily, she realized, her gray eyes hooded. Amy had the uncomfortable feeling that she was becoming involved in a chess game of some sort, one she didn't yet know any of the rules to. And Franco was one more player to confuse the layout of the board.

The older woman lifted her teacup, meeting Amy's glance. As she returned the cup to the table beside her, she touched a fine linen napkin to her lips before saying, "You are a very lovely young woman, my dear, even as Nando reported. No doubt you are affianced to some fine young man in America?"

Amy shook her head. "No, I'm afraid not, Aunt Lucia. There are so many places I wish to see first, so many things I want to do before I settle down to marriage."

"Ah, indeed, but is that wise? If you'll allow me to give you some advice, do not make the mistake that some attractive young women do—that of letting things wait until tomorrow, then still another tomorrow. You may find that the right person has passed by unnoticed, and it is too late," Aunt Lucia said with a dry smile.

"I must say, I can't imagine our cousin ever being afflicted with such a problem," Nando observed lazily. He crossed the room, carafe in hand, to tip more wine into Amy's glass, though she held up her hand in a halfhearted protest.

She found herself relieved when he moved away again. Why was it, she wondered, that Nando affected her as he did? He seemed to have some kind of emotional magnetic field around him, one that entangled her helplessly even when he wasn't touching her. Franco was far better looking in a classical sense, but she didn't react at all the same way toward him. Oh, certainly he had his share of charm, but not that incredible "something" that constantly sparked from Nando to herself, however hard she tried to steel herself against it.

Did that same spark jump back from her to him, Amy wondered. Dismally she decided not. His amorous approach, with its studied passion, its experienced techniques, seemed too deliberate to be emotional on his part.

But what if it were a two-way thing? What if he felt it, too? What then? For one brief second her imagination leaped wildly out of control and she pictured him making love to her. That hard lean body pressed against hers, skin against skin. Demanding, possessing, his hands gripping her, his lips....

Amy glanced up suddenly and her face flamed.

Nando was gazing at her, eyes slightly narrowed, a trace of a smile on his lips.

For one ghastly moment she wondered if he could read her mind and if what he found amused him. He and his mother both seemed to possess the unnerving quality of being able to pry into her thoughts.... Amy brushed the idea from her mind. What ridiculous nonsense! She was being betrayed by her conscience, that was all!

She was relieved to find that the others were talking among themselves, even if it was about her. They were discussing what she should see in Italy.

Nando was saying, "Venice, of course! That is definitely a must." Turning to Amy, he nodded his head. "And you are going to see Venice as it should be seen. Both in daytime and by night. You shall be the tourist, I, your guide. During the day we'll take a ride down the Grand Canal by vaporetta, just for local color. That's Venice's version of a city bus. Then Saint Mark's Square, naturally. And because you are an American, a lunch at Harry's Bar. Perhaps an afternoon at the Lido, despite the season. But at night we shall take a gondola ride under the stars, with a gondolier singing."

Amy was aware of what he probably had in mind. She was to be taken to the attractions usually shown to tourists, her guest status emphasized. No doubt she'd be treated royally, kept busy, entertained. Then, after that, she would be expected to realize that that was it—hand over her share of the winery and *arrivederci*. With Nando's persuasive kisses helping her past the hard parts.

Aunt Lucia's aristocratic head was nodding in agreement. "Certainly you must see Venice, before it is too late. Sad to say, it is slowly being swallowed by the sea and by time. There are other places you must visit, as well. Verona, without a doubt. Perhaps we should plan a family dinner there one evening." The slender hand lifted in a vague gesture that almost had the air of a royal edict.

"It all sounds most interesting," Amy replied, sipping slowly at the golden wine. It was not going to be easy, she realized, to avoid being branded as a tourist-guest. But if she allowed herself to start out that way, it might become increasingly difficult to break the pattern—which was, no doubt, exactly what Nando was counting on.

"Now, Nando, let's be fair, you're not to monopolize all our cousin's time," Franco put in, reaching for the wine carafe and refilling his glass. He turned to Amy. "I would like to take you to Lake Garda for dinner some evening soon, possibly even tomorrow. I know a restaurant that overlooks the most beautiful body of water in the world." He slanted a quick look at Nando and smiled. "After all," he said, turning back to Amy, "our cousin here saw you in New York, so he's one up on me. It's my turn now."

Amy intercepted a flash of irritation in Aunt Lucia's eyes, a sudden tightening of her lips. The woman said tartly, "I might suggest that the two of you, before you fight over Amy's time, ask her what she herself would like to do. Why not allow her to decide?" Fixing an inquiring gaze on Amy, she said,

"Now, what would you prefer to see first, my dear?" Before Amy could respond to her question, she added, "We do hope you won't be in too much of a hurry to return to your home in America. There is so much to see in our country. When must you be back to your job?"

The question wasn't simply a hostess's desire to know how long the guest intends to stay. It was motivated by something more—a whole lot more. Amy decided it deserved an honest answer. If she had plans to approach this winery endeavor at all, it had to be done openly, frankly. She opened her mouth to speak, then waited as a servant slipped into the room, silent as a shadow, and began turning on soft lights. Their glow brightened the room, diminishing the heaviness of the carved dark furniture.

When the servant left, Amy carefully set her wine down on an ornate round table, then began candidly, "Aunt Lucia, I don't know if Nando has told you, but I have come to Italy not just on a visit, not just as a guest of your family, gracious as you have been to accept me. Quite honestly, I've come here to make a decision."

The older woman was watching her steadily, eyes slightly narrowed. No one else in the room moved. Aunt Lucia's slender, almost translucent fingers, heavy with their glinting ruby rings, were motionless on the arms of her chair.

Amy felt a slight constriction of her breathing as she said, "I...I am not certain yet whether I should retain the fifth of the winery that was my grandfather's and my mother's, or if I should sell it to

Nando, as he wishes. That was basically why I came, though I also wanted to see Italy and to meet my relatives."

There wasn't the slightest change in Aunt Lucia's expression. Her face stayed as cool and unrevealing as a marble statue's.

For a long second there was a tense silence, then Amy went on uncomfortably. "Under the circumstances I think perhaps it is better if I don't remain as a guest, knowing how much Nando would like to buy me out. It seems to me that my presence here at the villa would make for a certain amount of awkwardness for all of us."

"Oh, nonsense, nonsense!" Aunt Lucia said imperiously. "Of course you will remain. Not as a guest, but as part of the family And of course you must feel completely free to make up your own mind on the matter of the winery."

She paused, then went on. "If you do actually decide to keep your share—I hope you will pardon my curiosity—just what do you plan to do with it? Keep it as an investment?"

Unconsciously Amy raised her hand to smooth back her blond hair. It was almost as if she needed time to decide how to phrase her reply. She chose the straight answer, saying levelly, "It had occurred to me that I might become actively involved in the winery itself. Of course it may not work out, and I'm open to that eventuality. But I do have experience in advertising, and I know Vino d'Oro is just starting to sell in North America. You'll need someone who knows the American public.... The possibility appeals to me very much, though I realize I would have a great deal to learn.''

Aunt Lucia gave an unbelieving shake of the head. "Oh, no, my dear! Absolutely unthinkable! A winery is hardly the place for a young woman. It is impossible that you should consider it. My daughter owns part of the business, too, but she would never dream of becoming involved in the affairs of the winery, the vineyards or anything connected with the firm. You have no idea of the problems you would face. It's a man's work, Amy.''

"I did try to explain all that to Amy in New York, to convince her," Nando said smoothly, "but I'm happy to say I failed. Otherwise we might not have had the pleasure of her visit. However, I agree that once she is aware of how backbreaking the work can be—or, for that matter, realizes how dependent we are on the whims of nature for each season's harvest—I think she will discover she prefers sight-seeing and will be glad to leave the grapes to us. It's far from a glamorous occupation.''

Franco added nothing to their argument. He sat back in his chair, twisting his wineglass almost languidly in his hand, a slightly amused look in his hazel eyes.

Aunt Lucia had lifted her cup from the table and, before raising it to her lips, said, "Nando, you must be fair to Amy. She certainly deserves the opportunity to see and judge for herself—without our trying to dissuade her. Don't I recall we have at least one winery tour scheduled for this week? Why can't Amy be included, if she would like to be?''

Nando was quick to nod his approval. "Of course! A good idea!"

He turned to smile at Amy. "We have one of the tours set for tomorrow, if that won't be too soon for you. There's a blue ribbon representation coming—buyers, vintners, enologists, even some journalists, from several countries. Would you care to join them?"

This certainly was no spur-of-the-moment idea, Amy reflected. They had no doubt already planned to have her trail along in the wake of a group of experts, all speaking grape-growing and wine-making jargon, a completely foreign language to her. She was to be drowned in statistics and details, and thereby discouraged.

They couldn't have chosen a more effective method of bringing out every ounce of stubbornness in her nature. It was going to take a lot more than they had thought up so far to dissuade her, she vowed.

She lifted her glass. "I'd love to be included," she said calmly, taking a small sip of her wine. When she glanced up she spread an innocent smile among the three of them.

Franco was facing her directly. To her surprise and unseen by the others, he flashed her a surreptitious approving wink.

CHAPTER FOUR

AMY PARTED THE WHITE CURTAINS at her window and stepped out onto her balcony. For a moment she stood there, feeling the soft breeze sweep away the last remnants of the day's warmth.

A gauzy moon hung in the sky, enveloping the Gothic outlines of the winery down the hill. In the pale light the castle, with its jagged-tooth turrets and towers rearing skyward in a dark silhouette, appeared eerie and unreal, almost as if it had been lifted from an old etching.

But there was a glimmer showing through some of those deep-set windows. People apparently were still at work. Now and then flickering headlights and the faint rumble of trucks came up the winding road to pull into the castle courtyard.

After leaving the family when tea had ended, Amy had returned to her room to unpack, shower and rest for a while. Stretching out wearily on the white coverlet of her wide bed, she had for a few moments allowed her mind to tangle itself in the day's events. Jet lag had taken over, however, and she had slept.

Now she was awaiting the moment when she was expected to descend to dinner. Dining at nine-thirty struck her as peculiarly late, but her internal time clock was so mixed up by her flight that it really made little difference to her when she ate.

Gazing down at the castle, Amy thought that if it seemed unreal, then much of the rest of this venture did, too. She had left New York with a spirit of adventure, of challenge. A lot of that enthusiasm had ebbed away. Suddenly everything had taken on a far more serious aspect.

She leaned against the marble railing. Through the thin material of her dress she could feel that it still held some of the day's warmth.

It was entirely clear, Amy reflected, what Nando and his mother planned to do. Together they were going to apply enough steady pressure to squeeze her out. She frowned. It had taken a good deal of thought and no little time and money to progress this far. She didn't intend on this, the very first day, to let the two of them have their way. She was here, she was going to stay. And, in spite of Nando and his mother, she was going to stay long enough to learn something about wineries and grape-growing. If they didn't seriously object, she was going to go ahead with every phase of her plans as best she could. If at the end of the novice stage she changed her mind and decided she'd had enough, or if there wasn't a place for her after all, then fine, that was the way it should be.

There was one thing certain: she would not be pushed out for merely chauvinistic reasons. Not before she had her chance.

The soft wind caught at her hair, blowing it lightly across her cheeks. Lifting her hand to brush it back

into place, she paused, hand still raised. What about
Franco? What was that sly secretive wink supposed
to mean? Amy slowly lowered her hand, eyes narrowing in thought. Was it meant as encouragement,
urging her to stick to her plans?

Possibly. But if that were so, then why? *Why?* She
shook her head. It didn't make sense. Franco owned
a share in the business; he was part of the Vino d'Oro
firm. It would seem more logical that he would be in
favor of her promptly turning over her share for the
good of the company. . . unless he wanted to buy her
out himself. There again that didn't seem logical.
From the way Nando had spoken in New York, Amy
had the definite impression that everyone had an
equal share in the winery. He did, so did Anna Maria
and Aunt Lucia. That, of course, gave the Bonavias
three-fifths, the majority, which was no doubt why
Nando was running the company.

She and Franco held the other two-fifths. Maybe
Franco wanted her share to add to his to increase his
power and interests. That was the only reason she
could think of. She wondered a little nervously if
Franco was going to start pressuring her, too. That
would really complicate things!

What a nest of intrigue she'd tumbled into—all
very modern Machiavellian. The thought momentarily amused her. But her smile faded when she recalled
the look on Aunt Lucia's face when Franco had mentioned that trip for two to Lake Garda. Learning
about wine making might not turn out to be her only
hurdle, Amy realized.

The bright lights of a car came flashing up the

road, halted momentarily at the gate, then swung into the courtyard. After a sharp squeal of brakes a car door opened and slammed shut. Then there was the hurried sound of heels clicking on the stone terrace below.

Amy glanced over the railing, but already the newcomer was out of her range of vision. Probably Nando's sister, she decided, wondering if the girl could possibly contribute one more enigma or complication to the present dilemma.

She went back into her room, stopping to look again at the charming feminine decor. Fragile pale green Florentine tables scrolled in gold stood against the wall, and the green carpeting on the marble floor was woven with a border of pale pastel garden flowers. The sturdy bed had a carved wooden headpiece, and when she had awakened from her nap a little earlier she had made out figures in the carving—an animal that looked like a unicorn; trees, bending and twining; small woodland creatures peering out from underneath. The dressing table had a long pier mirror with a patterned beveled edge.

It was a delightful room and, as in the rest of the house, the furnishings looked very old and probably valuable. Amy ran a tentative finger along the gold patterning of one of the Florentine tables. How her mother would have loved owning one! Had she ever wanted to visit Italy? If so, she had never mentioned it.

Glancing down at her wristwatch, Amy hurried to the dressing table to repair the tangles the wind had made of her hair. A few quick strokes of lipstick, then she was ready to go below to join the others.

As she reached the foot of the stairs she could hear voices coming from the sitting room where tea had been served. There was a lively spatter of Italian, then a lilt of clear feminine laughter, followed by the murmur of Nando's deep voice.

Franco and Aunt Lucia had not yet appeared, Amy realized as she entered. But Nando was standing near a round carved table, where a carafe of wine rested. He held a glass in his hand. A young woman, her back to Amy, was gazing up at him. She was saying something in Italian, and her slim fingers were touching his cheek affectionately.

Nando's head jerked up. "Oh, Amy, come in," he said quickly.

The young woman turned. Amy could see there wasn't the slightest resemblance to Nando or to his mother, not at all. She was slim, yet her closely fitting frock did little to hide a figure that curved voluptuously, the low-cut neckline revealing a glimpse of high firm breasts. She was stunning, Amy thought, with that shining blue black hair falling gracefully to her shoulders. Astonishing black-fringed pansy-colored eyes met Amy's curiously over a wineglass that she held in her hand.

"You must be Anna Maria, Nando's sister," Amy said with a smile.

The violet eyes looked amused. "Must I? Oh, dear, I'm afraid I'm not. Sorry. I'm Elisa. Elisa Antolini. I'm—" she turned to flash a smile over her shoulder at Nando "—a family friend."

The girl's voice and manner conveyed that she was

perhaps considerably more than a family friend. To her consternation, Amy found she had sudden ambivalent feelings about that. She greeted the young woman pleasantly, however, aware that those extraordinary eyes were scanning her with open curiosity she made no effort to hide.

"Elisa is from what you might call the enemy camp," Nando drawled. "Her father has a nearby winery, so she's no doubt here to spy tonight."

Elisa wrinkled her delicate patrician nose at him. "And upon whose invitation, may I ask?"

She gave her attention again to Amy. "So you are the cousin from America whom Nando has been telling me about." The slender arched eyebrows lifted a trifle, a note of disbelief stealing into her voice. "Tell me, is it really true what he has been saying, that you want to help run the winery here at Monte Cielo?"

Amy shook her head. "Not run it, or even help run it, exactly," she said steadily. "Certainly not with the lack of information and experience I have now. But I would like to learn something about it. That's one of the reasons I came. Perhaps later on I might become involved in it in some fashion." There was nothing to be gained by hiding the possibility, she felt, especially since it apparently was being discussed by others.

Elisa gave a mock shudder and took a small sip of her wine before saying, "Oh, you can't possibly be serious! Sour smells and scrubbing out vats—absolutely ghastly! And everyone runs around testing and fussing all the time." She shrugged her slender shoulders, drawing attention to her bosom. "They are forever complaining. If it isn't about the weather, then it's the latest attack of yellow blight on the cork trees. All so incredibly boring and dull! You couldn't pay me to step inside our winery!''

Nando handed Amy a glass of Vino d'Oro, saying over his shoulder to Elisa, ''Good thing, too, Elisa!''

The lovely eyes flickered. ''You could be right, Nando, darling. My father, poor man, wanted a son to carry on the family business, but he got me instead. I suppose that's one reason why he—''

Her words were interrupted by the appearance of Aunt Lucia, Franco and a young woman. This time there could be no doubt about the newcomer's identity. Familiar gray eyes smiled at Amy, not with the cool arrogant expression apparent in Nando's or his mother's, but in open friendliness. She had dark hair, too, and the same strong aristocratic features, somehow gentled in this slender face. She was not beautiful, but she radiated warmth and charm.

''Oh, Cousin Amy, welcome, welcome!'' she said, rushing forward to take Amy's hand. ''Nando has told us all about you. And you are very attractive, just as he said. More than you can say for us Bonavias!'' She made a rueful face as she laughed.

''You might as well be warned that I'm planning on coming to visit you next spring, invited or not!'' she went on without a pause. Her gray eyes sparkled with mischief. ''Filippo and I are coming there on our honeymoon. We want to see the...the—'' her forehead puckered ''—oh, yes, the Big Apple. Isn't that what you call New York?''

Was this another planned move, Amy wondered fleetingly. One more gentle push out of the wine business, a hint that of course they expected her to return to New York? It was difficult to know in this case, for the young woman's smile was so open, her eyes so artless.

"Hush, Anna Maria, don't rattle on so!" Aunt Lucia snapped, adding a brisk phrase in Italian that brought a faint flush to Anna Maria's cheeks.

Then the older woman turned to Elisa. "*Buona sera*, Signorina Antolini. I'm sorry I wasn't down to receive you."

Her voice was polite enough. It was also definitely frosty. Amy had the uncanny sensation that she was watching a group of characters on a stage, a thought immediately followed by the realization she, too, was part of the drama, or comedy—whatever it was.

Aunt Lucia was moving toward her chair by the marble fireplace, hesitating for a second to say, "Why not be seated, all of you? It distresses me to see people standing about as if they were in a train station." Here again it was more a command than a suggestion.

Nando was standing by Elisa, glass in hand. Even in casual repose he gave off intense virility, Amy reflected uncomfortably. Was Elisa aware of it, too? The young woman turned her face toward his, murmuring something in Italian, then she sank into a nearby chair. Nando nodded, his gray eyes gleaming.

Franco and Anna Maria took chairs near Amy's so she turned to talk to them. Her mind was a bit distracted as she chatted casually, however, for she was conscious of a growing discomfort deep inside her. For a hideous moment she wondered if she was going to be ill.

When she realized what her ailment stemmed from she immediately felt worse. It was because she sensed that Elisa and Nando might be, and probably were, lovers. There was a suggestion of intimacy in the young woman's smile when she talked to him, in the way her fingers had trailed lingeringly across his cheek as Amy had entered the room.

Jealousy? It couldn't be! Impossible! She wasn't in love with Nando, not at all, she told herself firmly. Certainly he attracted her more than she found comfortable, but that was the extent of it. And he apparently felt little if anything for her. Once he secured her share she'd be out of his life completely. Firmly Amy focused her attention onto what Franco and Anna Maria were saying, and tried to ignore the rest of her mind, which was pacing about like a caged tiger.

Aunt Lucia sat in her chair like an empress surveying her subjects, answering briefly but not impolitely whenever addressed. Nando was serving glasses of wine, and Aunt Lucia held hers in her thin hand, taking only token sips. Her listening eyes seemed to miss nothing that was going on about her.

The part of Amy that was joining in the conversation found she liked Anna Maria. She actually felt more at ease with the girl than with anyone else in the room. Her laugh was bright and quick; her open honesty and guilelessness contrasted with the somewhat sophisticated impression the others gave off. Anna Maria was teasing Franco, who reached over to put his arm around her affectionately.

"Cousin Amy," he said, "can you believe that this

very irresponsible child is going to be married before long, and that a few words murmured over her by a priest are going to somehow change her into a staid matron? Impossible!''

Anna Maria turned a haughty look toward him, saying tartly, "My dear cousin, I'd appreciate some show of gratitude if you don't mind. I'm about to save your friend Filippo from the same dissolute life you lead.''

Reaching into her pocket, she pulled out a silver case and casually put a cigarette to her lips. Franco quickly lighted it for her.

"Anna Maria! I will not have it! If you must smoke you will do it elsewhere, not under this roof!'' Aunt Lucia's voice crackled icily from across the room.

"Sorry, mother, I forgot,'' Anna Maria replied, snubbing out the cigarette in a crystal ashtray. She seemed completely unruffled by the sharpness of her mother's tone, and she flashed a gamine grin at Amy. "At least I'm not being sent to my room without my supper,'' she said in a whisper.

Amy gave her a quick look. At least someone in the family had a sense of humor!

But there was no time for further reflection. A servant had appeared and was standing silently in the doorway.

Aunt Lucia rose. "Shall we go in to dinner?'' she said, as she swept across the room. She led the others down a long marble hall and through an arched doorway to a darkly formal dining room.

Wooden paneling covered the walls from floor to

ceiling. Candelabra placed down the center of the table threw a soft glow on the silver tableware. A large tapestry dominated the far wall, featuring a court scene with elegantly clad lords and ladies. Amy wanted to examine the details more closely but realized that that would have to come later.

She felt no surprise when Aunt Lucia went unswervingly to the head of the table. There a servant pulled back a dark, heavily carved chair to allow the elderly woman to be seated. Amy found herself directed to Aunt Lucia's right, next to Franco, with Anna Maria just beyond him. Across the table Nando took a chair beside Elisa.

Two servants began moving silently behind their chairs, placing gold-rimmed dishes in front of the diners. Amy gazed down at her own plate, which held a thin quarter moon of chilled melon wrapped in an almost translucent slice of Parma ham. The contrast between the pale green melon and the delicate rose of the ham was as delicious to the eye as it would be to the palate, Amy reflected.

When the empty plates had been whisked away, a soup course was served, a clear broth in which rounded curlicues of pasta floated.

Any glanced up, smiling. "This I recognize. Tortellini, isn't it? My mother used to cook tortellini in soup, and sometimes she covered it with cheese."

"Of course you know the reason for its particular shape, then?" Franco had turned to her.

"Franco!" The stern voice came from the head of the table.

"But, Aunt Lucia, I merely asked her if she was

familiar with the origin of the famous pasta. Are you, Amy?" he went on smoothly.

Any felt caught between the two but had to give some answer. "No, I don't think so," she said truthfully.

"Now, Aunt Lucia, it's really very innocent," Franco said, a laugh in his voice. "It may not even be true, but our cousin should be told the basic facts of life—regarding Italian pasta."

Amy expected another chill comment from Aunt Lucia, but there was none, so Franco, grinning irrepressibly, said, "One story has it that a cook was making pasta when he looked over at the navel of his unclad mistress. Presto! From then on, he rolled and twisted all the pasta he made into the shape of the lady's navel! Of course, the story has many variations. I've heard that the inspiration was none other than the delightful navel of the Venus de Milo. Still another version has it—"

"Quite enough, Franco," Aunt Lucia's dry voice carried authority, and Franco subsided with a grin.

Amy was relieved when the conversation turned to a more neutral subject. The soup with its offending tortellini was consumed and delicate mignonettes of veal replaced it.

At this point their glasses were filled with a pale yellow wine, clear and glistening. Amy noticed that Nando was eyeing the liquid sharply. Lifting his thin goblet, he held it so that the glow of the candle shone through it as he turned it in his hand. He sniffed at it briefly, then, with a sardonic lift of dark eyebrows, tasted a few drops.

Lowering his glass, he looked accusingly at Elisa. "So we have a serpent in our bosom tonight! This is your wine, no doubt!"

Long thick lashes lowered over the improbable pansy eyes. "My dear Nando, but of course! It was the last our vintner, Nino, developed before his death. At the gate I bribed Giuseppe to slip it into the kitchen tonight."

Amy tasted the wine and found it had a soft velvety texture on the tongue, a pleasant and almost woodsy flavor. Elisa was right, it was very good.

Nando took another taste, then, looking at Elisa, said dryly, "I presume your father, in accord with your firm's new aggressive advertising tactics, will be calling this, *Est! Est! Est! Est!*"

The girl gave a light tinkling laugh. "What better name? How better deserved!" she challenged.

There was some interplay here that Amy didn't understand, but Nando, twisting his glass in hand, came to her rescue by saying, "That's an inside joke, really. Are you familiar with the wine we are talking about?"

Amy glanced uncertainly down at her own glass. "No, except that it's apparently from Elisa's father's winery. And very good, too."

He shook his head. "No, I'm speaking of the famous Italian wine, *Est! Est! Est!*"

"I'm afraid I'm not familiar with it," Amy admitted, feeling she was revealing all too soon her lack of knowledge, to the probable satisfaction of some of those present.

Nando took another sip of the wine, then said,

"As the story goes, there was a German bishop, one Johann Fugger or Johannes De Fuger, back in the year 1110, traveling from Augsburg to Rome to visit the Pope. Our Johann loved his food and drink, so he always sent a scout on ahead to locate the best places to dine along the route they'd be taking. When the man located a good inn, with fine wine and all the other proper requirements, he was to chalk *Est!* on the door, meaning 'it is.' In other words, in this place the wine is good."

Nando sipped again at his wine and nodded approvingly at Elisa before continuing. "Well, Martin, the scout, arrived in Montefiascone. There he tasted a wine that sent him into such a complete frenzy of enthusiasm that he chalked *Est! Est! Est!* on the door."

Amy couldn't help giggling. This was Nando at his most entertaining. "And did the bishop agree with his scout's taste?" she asked.

Nando's gray eyes were amused. "Did he? He was mad about it! He never did reach Rome but stayed right there for the rest of his life. When he died the faithful Martin carved on his gravestone the Latin equivalent of It is! It is! It is! And through too much 'it is,' my master, Johannes De Fuger, dead is! Ever since then the wine from Montefiascone has been called *Est! Est! Est!* Capital letters, exclamation points and all, they're never omitted. And that's the joke, of course. I fully expect Elisa's father to pirate the name and add that one more superlative."

Elisa wrinkled her nose at him.

Anna Maria was nodding. "There's a statue of the

bishop in Montefiascone, and every year on the date of his death the vintners pour some *Est! Est! Est!* over his grave.''

Nando again lifted the wine to his lips, pausing as if to savour the bouquet. ''It's not bad, really, Elisa. Give your father my congratulations. But if this is meant for what I think it is, I'm afraid that my answer is still no. I'm simply not interested in forming a partnership with your father.''

Amy saw Elisa give him an amused smile, as if she were not at all convinced. Then the young woman leaned forward to say something to Nando, speaking softly. In bending she let her low-cut gown gape open, exposing those creamy rounded breasts if he cared to look.

Quite obviously he did. Amy saw his eyes lower and a twisted half smile curve his firm lips. Whether anyone else noticed, Amy wasn't certain, for the servants were placing crystal bowls of fruit in front of them.

There was little doubt that Elisa Antolini was using Nando's own tactics, she realized—the sensuous allurement, the deliberate tempting. It was apparent, from the trend of the conversation tonight, that her father wanted to be part of the Vino d'Oro winery or else have the two join together in some kind of partnership. Was Elisa the bait, sent to weaken Nando's resistance? Amy reluctantly wished she could feel pleased at the idea of Nando being subjected to the same kind of amorous treatment he'd used on her.

She held her wineglass in her hand, gazing at the golden liquid thoughtfully. Hadn't Elisa said, or at least implied, that she was here tonight on Nando's invitation? If so, then why—

Franco interrupted her thoughts by saying softly, "I'm looking forward to our dinner together at Lake Garda. I hope we can make it tomorrow evening. We have much to talk about, we two. Much in common, cousin mine."

Amy looked at him questioningly. He was implying far more than his actual words conveyed. Again he gave her that sly wink.

She hesitated a second or two. *Why not go,* she argued.

"Thank you, Franco, I'd very much like to. But it does depend, doesn't it, on whether anything else has already been planned? May I let you know tomorrow after I find out? I have no idea how long the tour will last, either."

It wasn't that she felt especially enthusiastic about going off with him alone. There was certainly nothing wrong with doing so, however. He was, after all, her cousin; it wasn't as if he were some stranger that had dropped by. And, to be honest, she was curious. If he indeed was encouraging her to keep her part of the business and not surrender it to Nando, then she wanted to know why.

"All right, let's see how tomorrow goes," he was saying. "The tour should be starting midmorning, followed by lunch for the visitors. Perhaps there'll be more viewing and business in the afternoon. Do you plan on sticking it out for the entire tour?"

Amy nodded. "I want to know everything I can. I'm here to learn."

A small porcelain cup of espresso was set before her, temporarily interrupting their conversation.

Franco turned to answer a question put to him by Aunt Lucia, and Amy was left for a moment with her thoughts. And they were confused ones. Granted, Nando had been affectionate—no, more than affectionate; he'd been amorous—in her room upstairs not so very long ago. Likely it was only step one in what he planned as the assault ending in her surrender and his victory.

That being so, why had he introduced Elisa into the picture at just this time? Unless... unless it was one more strategy of his Machiavellian mind. She could hear his seductive voice whispering, "Well, my dear Amy, you are not the only woman I can give my attention to. If you don't want to be squeezed out in the amorous sweepstakes, then be nice to me, give me the share! Otherwise...." In other words, he was deftly introducing the spur of jealousy.

Amy regarded the strong haughty profile turned toward Elisa. The fact that she guessed his intentions didn't prevent them from having some of the effect he must have desired. She sipped slowly at the strong bitter coffee, forcing her mind away from any further thoughts about Nando. Or Nando and Elisa. She succeeded only partially.

Amy answered Anna Maria's question about what it had been like to move from place to place in an army family. Yes, it had been interesting, she agreed, and yes, it was often hard to leave old friends. As the conversation became general she was rather pleased that she was able to field questions from both Nando and Elisa in a casual relaxed manner, the troubling knot remaining well beneath the surface. She was careful, too, to direct a polite comment or question now and then to the slender matriarch sitting so stiffly at the head of the table.

Though she laughed and chatted, she couldn't have recalled from one moment to the next what she said. It was as if she were two people, one brightly social, the other beginning to wander inside her brain, haunted by nagging thoughts she didn't want to recognize or accept.

At last Aunt Lucia stood up, signifying that dinner was over. Again she led the way, her proud carriage never once turning to see if the others were following, but presuming they would observe her example obediently.

As Amy was leaving the room she was aware of a faint scent of expensive perfume at her shoulder, a soft voice saying, "Don't even consider it, my dear. I have my own plans for him. You would not only be interfering, you would be wasting your time."

Amy didn't turn around. In a similarly low tone she murmured, "I have no plans for anyone." It was true. Wasn't her mission here to decide about the winery?

"Just as well. I suggest you keep it that way," Elisa replied in an amused whisper. Under the amusement there was certainty.

The group filed into the sitting room once again. Amy was beginning, despite her nap, to find the day extremely long. She was weary but tried not to yawn. It was with sheer relief that she heard Elisa say she really must be going.

The young woman went about the room to say good-night, bending her head respectfully toward Aunt Lucia and murmuring a few phrases in Italian.

When Amy in turn said good-night, she received a knowing secret smile from Elisa. Then the young woman walked over to Nando, who was standing by the door. He took her arm, then turned to say he was going to see Elisa to her car and would be right back.

His return was not immediate. Franco grinned. "Elisa doesn't give up easily, does she?"

Apparently Aunt Lucia read the meaning behind his words. "If she and her father think they can talk Nando into combining our two firms, she is mistaken."

Now Franco laughed. "I don't think *talk* is exactly what our Elisa has in mind."

For that he received a chilling glance from his aunt's disdainful eyes.

Anna Maria leaned toward Amy to say, "Elisa would dearly love to get her hooks into our Nando, but so far no success."

"Hooks! What a vulgarity! If you wish to speak English, you will not use such coarse words," Aunt Lucia amended.

"Sorry, mother," Anna Maria said calmly, then turned back to Amy, lowering her voice slightly. "It's just that Elisa's so terribly blatant about being after Nando, when she should realize by now it won't do her any good. Surely she knows that he's woman-proof, other than a little playing around. After the *affaire* with Ivanna Zaccone, he swore he'd never again trust a woman."

The girl slid a quick look toward her mother, then went on uninterrupted. "He was engaged to Ivanna when he was twenty-six; head over heels about her, of course. The wedding plans had all been made when she ran off with Pietro Rivella to South America, without a word to Nando. One day she was here, the next she was gone. He wasn't left waiting at the church, but he might as well have been. The banns had been announced.

"Anyhow, his pride was badly mangled and so he has sworn off marriage. He says he's already wed for life to Monte Cielo Vino d'Oro and no one else. Now, mother, there's no use frowning at me like that. Everyone knows about it, so Amy might as well, too. After all, she's family."

Anna Maria paused, her brow suddenly wrinkling. "He did invite her here tonight. I wonder why. It just encourages her." Then she shrugged. "Anyhow, Amy, you've just had a look at our family skeletons."

"And a close enough look, I must say," Aunt Lucia added tartly.

Amy was a little surprised that Signora Bonavia had let Anna Maria talk so freely about Nando's views of women. Perhaps she wanted the information about Nando's disinterest in getting married to be passed along as a veiled warning should Amy have any romantic notions about him. Well, she needn't have bothered.

Amy took advantage of a slight pause to get to her feet. "I wonder if I may be excused. The trip has been a long and tiring one, so if you don't mind...."

"My dear Amy, of course you're tired. We should have realized." Aunt Lucia's patrician head nodded. Her words were considerate, but her tone held little real warmth.

Saying good-night to the others, Amy went out and started up the stairs, her mind going back over Anna Maria's revelation about Nando. She could well believe that a man with such pride would be humiliated by a rejection—more, perhaps, than most men. But she had little time to think more about it before Nando had come in the front door and was loping up the stairs to join her. "Retiring already?" he asked.

She nodded. "Mmm hmm. The long day plus jet lag."

"I'll see you to your room."

"Please don't bother, really," she protested.

"Oh, but I want to," he said, smiling down at her, his eyes bold and disconcerting.

When they arrived at her door Amy reached for the knob, turning to say good-night to him. His hand closed over hers, however, and he drew her to him. Before she could protest or pull away his arms were tight around her and his face was a hairbreadth away. The tip of his tongue trailed distractingly along her lower lip.

"Let me come in, *cara*," he murmured against her mouth.

Mingling with his clean masculine scent was a delicate floating touch of the perfume Elisa had been wearing. He had no doubt held her in his arms, too.

Damn him! Amy angrily tried to wrest herself

from his hold, managing to twist her head so that his lips were no longer on hers. She was determined not to let him ever again arouse her emotions.

"Don't!" she snapped.

For a second he didn't speak, then he lifted her chin and gazed down at her. "You're angry," he said, a hint of surprise in his voice. "Dear Amy, surely it's not because of the presence of Elisa tonight. She's a family friend, nothing more."

It was said so soothingly, with just the right inflection. So she had been right! That had been his deliberate purpose, Amy thought swiftly. He had drawn Elisa into the scene to act as a spur. The stick again! And now here he was, proffering the carrot. His lips sought hers as if in confirmation.

She jerked her head away, saying dryly, "Nando, I'm exhausted. If you don't mind, I'd like to go to bed."

He paused, then said, "As you will. But you will not deny me forever, *cara*."

Lifting her hand, he brushed a swift kiss over it, gave a token bow and was gone, striding back down the hall.

Amy went into her room, closing the door behind her. That... that Don Juan! That arrogant overconfident Casanova! Making love to one woman, then another. The infuriating part was the hidden insolence of it. He could turn on his charm like a light switch.

She bit angrily at her lower lip, then stopped abruptly as the memory of his kiss surfaced disturbingly. And that was exactly the trouble. Her mind could be clear and determined, her words abundantly firm, but Nando didn't pay any attention. He must be aware of how quickly he could make her respond, even as she was fighting against it. He might even recognize the response was against her will—which must please him even more. No wonder he seemed certain he would eventually have his way with her....

Would he? Amy caught sight of her face in the mirror of her dressing table. Her cheeks were flushed and her eyes seemed enormous. She stood for a moment, staring at her reflection. *Would he?*

She felt something spring to life deep within her. Never before had she responded so eagerly, so excitedly at the mere touch of a man's lips, the caress of a hand.

Would she be able to tell him no? Yes, she would—now.

But could she keep telling him no—about her share of the winery? About herself? Her green eyes gazed back at her uncertainly from the mirror.

CHAPTER FIVE

AMY OPENED HER EYES to see a path of sunshine pouring through the open windows, spreading over her bed. The dregs of jet lag still held her half asleep, half awake. She blinked and yawned, gazing up drowsily at the high ceiling as her thoughts began to stir.

For a few lazy moments she lay there, allowing the events of the previous day to flow through her mind. It was like one of those Chinese box puzzles, she reflected. Everytime you opened one box, there was another inside.

Was Elisa Antolini Nando's mistress? Amy's eyes flickered. Was that why the young woman had warned her off?

She pushed herself up against the pillows. She had been here less than twenty-four hours and in that short time every problem she had had compounded.

She had come to see the winery, to find out if she wanted to be involved with it. That seemed simple enough. But it wasn't simple at all. Having Nando to cope with was enough of a challenge. Add to that his severe strong-willed mother, Franco and his curious little secret, and finally Elisa Antolini—it was more than she cared to contemplate this early in the day.

Swinging her feet to the floor, she wiggled her toes,

feeling around for her bedroom slippers. Just then there was a soft knock at the door, so she grabbed quickly for her dressing gown, which lay across a chair. For a moment she stood absolutely silent, her heart pulsing sharply against her ribs. Not Nando! If he thought she was going to let him in. . . . She gazed down at her thin transparent nightgown and the robe that hid little more.

"Signorina?" came a timid call.

She padded over to the door, opening it slightly to reveal a young maid holding a tray. *"Caffè, signorina?"* Dark eyes indicated a coffeepot and a small napkin-covered silver basket.

Amy felt a quick sweep of relief that she didn't have to face Nando. Opening the door further, she murmured, "Oh, yes, thank you... ah... *grazie.*" She stumbled self-consciously over the Italian word.

"Prego, prego!" The young woman bobbed her head several times in acknowledgement and crossed the room, placing the tray on a bedside table. With another bow, a quick shy smile and *"Permesso, signorina?"* she withdrew, closing the door softly behind her.

Perching on the edge of the bed, Amy reached over to lift the small white pot and pour out half a cup of coffee. It smelled wonderful. Filling the rest of the cup with hot milk, she swallowed a small mouthful before uncovering the silver basket, which held two hot crusty rolls. Then she paused, looking toward the large sunny windows. Last night out on the balcony she had noticed a wicker chair and a small round wooden table. How nice it would be to have her breakfast outside in the sunshine, overlooking the castle. Picking up her tray, Amy went over and edged her way through the opening.

Putting the tray on the table, she gazed down at the ancient brooding stone building with its medieval towers. It was difficult for her to realize that it was partly hers—at least for the time being.

She stood for a minute or two, strangely moved. How could she bear to give it up, this whole new experience, and return to some dreary desk job in what would likely be a replica of the Stewart and Newman advertising firm? Back to the noise and rush of a big city; back to living in an apartment. There ought to be some place for her here at the winery, some type of work she could handle, if she could only convince Nando she wasn't intending to interfere in any way.

Amy could see several cars parked in the winery courtyard and a number of people strolling about. She quickly glanced down at her watch, then relaxed. The tour wasn't starting for another two hours.

Pulling the chair close to the little table, she sat down, and for a moment did nothing but let the sun warm her. It was a marvelous day, all blue sky and golden light. The faintest of breezes was blowing, carrying a light fruity scent toward her.

Amy lifted her coffee cup contentedly, by sheer force of will thinking only positive thoughts. This was Italy; she was finally here. Though she had seen very little of the country so far, it appeared to be as fascinating as she had hoped. Suddenly she was flooded with a strange, sweetly sentimental feeling for this land. It was in her blood, if not until now in her experience.

She picked up one of the rolls, broke it in two and buttered it. As she bit into it the delicious crisp crumbs flaked off, dropping onto her dressing gown.

"Well, John, that should take care of everything, I believe. Now shall we have some coffee before the tour begins?" Aunt Lucia's voice, speaking English, to Amy's surprise, floated upward. There was the scrape of chairs on the terrace below. After a sharp clap of hands, Aunt Lucia snapped a crisp sentence in Italian, probably to a servant.

Then a man's voice said, "It's been a great year, a really magnificent one." It was a deep American voice with a flat Midwestern twang.

"You've done very well for us, John Delby. We made no mistake in selecting you for our American representative," Aunt Lucia replied.

"Well, Signora Bonavia, I couldn't have promoted Vino d'Oro so successfully without its appeal and quality, and that's the truth. It's a fine, fine wine! Before I left the States we received a report that the most popular order in American bars, restaurants— yes, even in private homes these days—is, 'I'll have a glass of white wine.' Cocktails are on the wane every- where. Mind you, before long we're going to see that instead of simply ordering a glass of white wine, folks will say, 'I'll have a glass of Vino d'Oro.' And this year's Chiaro might just do it." A contented chuckle.

Amy wondered if perhaps she should slip back into her room. Eavesdropping wasn't her usual practice.

But this conversation was about wine—her wine as well as the Bonavias'. She had a feeling she'd better learn what she could in whatever way possible. There didn't seem to be many people here willing to inform her.

Aunt Lucia, a majestic pride evident in her voice, was saying, "It should be a good wine. There are few better vintners, few better enologists in all Italy, perhaps in all Europe, than my son."

"True, Signora Bonavia. It's too bad the world can't know that the company has one of the shrewdest business heads in the country, too." It was a flat statement.

"My father and my late husband were my teachers. I only do as they taught me. But I much prefer to keep my role in the business completely out of the public eye. It suits me that it not be known any more than absolutely necessary. More so than ever, now."

Amy sat stunned, her mouth half-open. Aunt Lucia head of the company? That haughty woman who wanted nothing to do with the vineyards, the winery or the business? Who had so bluntly stated that women should leave such things to men?

Carefully she lowered her cup to the table, unconsciously brushing crumbs from her robe. Well, this was certainly a whole new ball game! Amy felt her cheeks grow hot with indignation. What an absolute naive fool she'd been to have been taken in so thoroughly by Aunt Lucia's regal austere manner, her cool assertions. *Leave the business to the men!* What absolute nonsense. And all the time, the woman was. . . . Amy exhaled a sharp angry breath. She disliked being lied to.

She leaned back in her chair, her eyes absently contemplating the sky. Very well, if Lucia Bonavia could run such a vigorous successful winery, however anonymously, there surely must be some place in it for another woman, even a beginner! It was going to be a lot more difficult for Nando and his mother to block her request now. Their argument had just been shot full of holes.

A rattle of cups from below interrupted her thoughts, then the man said, "I've brought along a new group of American buyers today, plus the fella who does the wine column for one of our most prestigious magazines. I think they're all going to be impressed. Nando met some of them at the conference in California."

There was a pause, then he went on. "I presume he bought out the share he was telling me about, the one he was so anxious to pick up in New York? I haven't had a chance to ask him."

Aunt Lucia's voice was thin and sharp. "No, he didn't get it. But he will shortly, I believe. There's been a slight problem, and that is something I'd like to discuss with you."

A pause, then, "There will be a young lady on the tour today, an American very much interested in wine making." A split second's silence was followed by a deliberate, "If you can do anything or say anything that will discourage her, I'd appreciate it greatly."

"Oh, she's the one?" the man answered thoughtfully. "She won't agree to turn over her share in the business to Nando?"

"Not yet. But she must! Without question she must. There is absolutely no place for her here in our company. I have no time to bother with her." Her voice was adamant.

Amy was sitting straight in her chair now, her eyes gazing blankly ahead at the expanse of blue sky. Her breath was coming a little unevenly.

The man was speaking once again. "I'll do what I can, Signora Bonavia. This is too bad, really. Certainly nothing must be allowed to disturb our progress. And if you consider that she might be a hindrance of some kind, might interfere in any way, then I'll certainly—"

Aunt Lucia sliced across his words. "She would be in our way, if only by reason of her inability and ignorance. No, John, she must not remain here. She absolutely must turn over her interest in the winery, and we want it now."

A pause, then, "And it is most important that she not be aware of my position as head of the firm. Of course it isn't widely known or publicized, and everyone here has been warned, but I thought it wise to pass along the word."

Amy's eyes narrowed. Whether it was poor manners to eavesdrop or not, she was glad she had stayed. Better to know just what was being planned to oust her.

There was a sound of footsteps on the terrace below. "Hello, John, sorry I couldn't meet your plane, but I've been putting the last touches on the tour arrangements." Nando's arrival was accompanied by another scrape of chairs, another clatter of cups.

"Hello, Nando. Your mother and I have been talking about our great sales record in the States. No doubt you've already heard the reports about what they're calling the Italian phenomena. We're going to be big time soon." The man again gave a contented chuckle.

"Yes, I've heard. That's great," Nando said almost absently. Then his voice became more positive. "John, there's a little something I'd like you to do for me. When you're on the tour today, you'll meet a young American girl, the cousin I told you about."

"Your mother and I were just discussing her."

Amy's lips tightened. Eavesdroppers seldom heard anything pleasant about themselves, she knew, but wild horses couldn't have dragged her away now. They were planning something, the three of them. Three against one.... So the more she knew about their plans, the better she'd be able to cope. Give up, get out, she conceivably might. But certainly not because of what these three might be plotting.

"Can you imagine how one of your top U.S. wineries would feel," Nando said with an ironic drawl "if suddenly a young girl in her twenties appeared—a foreigner at that—owning one fifth, *one fifth* of the company? Someone without a clue of what the business is about, who wanted to take part, to actually be involved in the production? We don't want her, John; we don't want her in our winery!"

"I don't blame you, Nando," the other man's voice replied.

"I want that twenty percent to ensure complete majority control. We've got to get it away from her!" Nando's tone was so determined that Amy couldn't help a sudden shiver of apprehension.

"What I'd like to have you do, John," Nando went on, "is to let her see the seamy side of the wine industry. Drop casual words about how hard, how grim the work can be. Concentrate, too, on the way women are out of their element in a winery, how she wouldn't find it the kind of work she'd like. As she goes through the plant, pour on the technical talk. You know the sort of thing." Nando's tone was more casual now, but it implied a firm directive all the same.

"You think it'll work?" came the other man's voice again.

"I hope so. It'll be a lot easier if it does. Lord knows I've been trying everything else to the best of my ability. In New York I started off with a straight offer to buy her out. But she began pussyfooting around, talking about how she wanted to come over here and see what the wine industry was all about. You know damned well it wouldn't work, and I know it, too, but she's a stubborn wench. So—" there was a pause, and Amy, sitting a dozen feet above, drew a sudden tight breath "—so I resorted to a more personal approach. You know what I mean."

No one said anything for at least half a minute, and Amy could almost picture the two men exchanging understanding glances. She wanted to get up, run into her room and close the shutters behind her. She wanted to hide!

Wanted to, yes, but she wasn't about to do it. She was determined now to stay right where she was.

"So far, I must admit, I haven't been successful," Nando said at last. "I don't mind saying I'm not proud of my activity in that line, either. She's a nice enough young woman, but it seemed to me that a more romantic approach might be indicated, for several reasons. I happened to witness a scene between her and a young man just before I met her, and I felt she was...I thought she was *that* kind of girl."

Amy's hands clenched in her lap as embarrassment and then sheer fury rose up inside her. So he had seen that encounter with Craig Layton! Then he had drawn his own chauvinistic conclusions—the wrong ones—and had decided she must have led Craig on! Revelation struck her. No wonder he'd come on like Casanova. No doubt Nando had used his own interpretation of the episode as a justification for his actions toward her—besides deciding a little casual hanky-panky must be what she liked from her dates.

Nando's voice was continuing, "As I say, I'm not proud of my methods, but I must have her share. And I will have it! I'll go to any lengths to get it, whatever it takes! Frankly, I'd be relieved if you could succeed in discouraging her about the wine industry. I don't like having to play the whore. Sorry, mother, but that's just about what I'm doing."

Amy closed her eyes in painful humiliation, cringing inside herself. Enough, she told herself. She'd heard enough! Rising unsteadily from her chair, she turned and went quietly into her room, leaving her breakfast unfinished. The muscles around her mouth felt tight, her shoulders rigid.

Going into the bathroom, she turned on the shower taps as wide as they would go—as if the sound would somehow drown the echo of Nando's words out of her mind.

She showered energetically, muttering into the soapsuds as she tried to get control of the feelings that swung wildly back and forth between fury and hurt.

When she had finished she dried herself roughly with the large white bath towel provided. What she found so galling, she realized, was the degrading approach he had seen fit to use on her, that cool deliberate lovemaking. It was insulting. And then...then to comment on it to others! That was completely unforgivable.

The mirror reflected back the hot sparks in her green eyes. She glared at her image. Why was she so fired up about learning something she already knew? Right from the beginning she'd suspected his amorous approach was just what it had turned out to be. So why this sudden furious reaction? Was it his misinterpretation of Craig's kick-at-the-door dramatics? She hated knowing he had witnessed that sordid little scene.

And Aunt Lucia! Amy shook her head. That had been a stunning surprise, an absolute shock. Yet perhaps there had been a hint when Nando innocently said that his mother was strong willed....

Very well, Amy decided, she was fully warned now. Some remnant of common sense tried to remind her that the wisest move might be to give up all this, go back to New York and to Bert. But a solid streak of tenacity firmed her chin and her will.

She had every right to her share of the business, as the others had to theirs. She had every right, too, to do with it as she pleased. They were holding on to their share, yet they expected her to relinquish hers simply because they wanted it. It wasn't fair.

Amy let her mind return again to Nando. How very ruthless he was. Knowing all she did about him, why couldn't she hate him? One by one she listed his faults. He was a deceiving Don Juan, using emotions and sensitivities like negotiable currency. He didn't care for her, yet he persisted in trying to arouse her sexually. As he had declared only moments ago, he was not unwilling to use extortionary means to get them.

Amy bit thoughtfully at her underlip. They were more evenly matched now. What she had at first only suspected, she now knew. So she was ready, and wouldn't be so easily fooled.

She turned toward the heavy wooden wardrobe that stood against the wall and carefully began selecting her clothing for the day. Under the circumstances she would present an image of the serious young businesswoman. Taking out a pair of tailored tan slacks, she laid them on the bed, then chose a severe silk blouse of woodsy brown. After dressing, she put on only a trace of makeup and brushed her hair until soft blond waves framed her face. Eyeing herself appraisingly, she finally dampened the brush and made her coiffure straighter, primmer. She gave one last look at the mirror, then left the room.

Nando was standing in the wide entrance hall, giving what appeared to be instructions to a group of men as Amy descended the stairs. He looked up suddenly, his eyes meeting hers. "Just a moment, Amy," he said graciously. "There's a little business I must take care of, then I'll be right with you." He turned back to the men, his deep voice rattling on in Italian.

She paused at the foot of the stairs, her hand on the newel, as one of the men spoke to Nando. The lift of his voice implied a question. Nando frowned, then nodded, and the men left.

"Last-minute preparations for today's tour," he explained as he came toward her. He lifted her hand to his lips, that disturbing hint of intimacy in his eyes. In spite of her firm decision, in spite of her new knowledge, she was still uncomfortably conscious once again of his masculine charisma and the effect it had on her. "You look very beautiful this morning," he was saying in a low voice.

She instantly withdrew her hand from his. "I suppose the tour will begin shortly?" She carefully ignored his flowery flattery. "Making the compliment" just like her grandfather had said, she reflected caustically.

Pushing a white shirt sleeve back from his tanned wrist, he glanced down at his watch. "We have about forty-five minutes before it begins."

He paused, lifting an eyebrow at her questioningly. "By the way, I think I recall your saying that you don't speak Italian. French, perhaps? No? German?" He gave her a quick sympathetic smile. "Nor Russian, either? Japanese?" he asked teasingly.

Amy shook her head, having a suspicion of what he was leading up to.

She wasn't wrong. All too casually he said, "Then perhaps it would be best if I ask John Delby, our American representative, to accompany you on the tour. He's really very knowledgeable. He can explain the whole process to you and answer any questions you may have. There'll be half a dozen other languages tossed back and forth in the groups, and you might not get a clear picture of what is definitely a complicated procedure."

Amy felt her nerves tighten automatically. If the real battle was to begin at once, she was prepared. She noticed that she felt no regret at all, no guilt about her recent eavesdropping. "Thank you, Nando, I'm certain he will be most helpful." Helpful, yes, but to Nando's cause!

"Sorry I can't be with you myself, but I'll be busy keeping the tour moving along and answering questions."

They were strolling toward the salon. As they entered the room, a ray of sunlight was streaming in through one of the long windows, stretching across the floor to Signora Bonavia's feet. The woman was seated in her usual chair. Even the sunlight didn't dare to trespass further, Amy thought wryly. A secret smile touched her lips. She was even prepared for the strong-willed dowager now.

"Good morning, Aunt Lucia," she said politely.

"Good morning, child. I fear I forgot to warn you, we cling to our Latin habits of the continental breakfast. You must be accustomed to other foods in the morning. You have only to make your particular wants known to Amalia, who is serving you."

How graciously it was said, and how subtly it stressed that she was a foreign guest with foreign habits. Amy realized she was being kept in her proper place.

"Thank you. It was very satisfying, however, and I certainly need nothing else. In New York I often had only toast and coffee—nothing as delicious as this morning's hot rolls. I shall very easily become accustomed to the Italian breakfast." There, the ball was tossed back into their court, Amy thought as she seated herself with a smile. She wondered what they were waiting for. There seemed to be an anticipation in the room.

There was little time to wonder, for almost at once a man arrived in the doorway. Amy recognized him even though she had never seen him before. His American voice was unmistakably the one that had floated up a short time ago from the terrace.

"Good morning, Nando, Signora Bonavia." He came striding across the floor, hand outstretched, as if this were the first meeting of the day.

He was short and stocky, with an ample waistline that indicated he probably enjoyed his food as well as the wines he was selling. His brown hair was combed carefully across a receding hairline, the pink skin shining through. The gaze he turned on Amy was disconcertingly shrewd.

"Amy, may I present John Delby, our U.S. representative?" Nando said. "John, this is Amy Converse, our cousin from America."

Amy made certain that, in acknowledging the introduction, her eyes revealed nothing.

Oh, she was from New York, he asked, then nodded. He, too, was half New Yorker, half Californian, for he spent part of the year in each end of the country. No, he wasn't born a New Yorker; he came from a small town in Illinois.

Their conversation was very congenial. Had Amy not been aware of what was going on under this easy social chitchat, she could easily have been entrapped.

"John, I wonder if you'd mind accompanying my cousin on this morning's tour?" Nando asked smoothly. "She'd like to see the winery, and I'd appreciate it if you'd explain the various processes to her as you go along."

The man's brown eyes beamed on Amy. "Delighted! It's really a very interesting tour." A pause, then, "Have you ever visited a winery before?"

In any other situation it would have been a polite conversation-making question. Here, however, Amy felt it was all too clearly an emphasis on her unprofessional status, probably planned to start her off at a disadvantage. She had to admit it was her first.

Delby took a chair and leaned back, obviously in no hurry to depart. It was Nando who kept track of the time, glancing now and then at his watch.

Amy made herself relax in her own chair as she secretly contemplated the others. Her eyes were drawn especially to Nando's strong face.

Proud and imperious, he was leaning idly against the marble mantel, his slim gray trousers molded snugly to lean muscled legs. Amy looked quickly away. Everything about him was so intensely masculine. Her eyes flickered. The male animal. The phrase fitted Nando. He was that, all right. Even knowing what she did about him, she had difficulty in not being affected by his presence.

"Good morning, all." Franco's voice entered the room almost before he did. "Hello, John. Glad to see you. When did you get in?"

John Delby shook Franco's outstretched hand. While the two men exchanged pleasantries, Amy's eyes shifted to Signora Bonavia. The woman's mouth, she noted, had visibly tightened. Why? And was she imagining the sudden faint frostiness in the air?

Then Franco was crossing the room toward her. "Good morning, my lovely cousin." He sat down beside her. "Ready for the grand tour?"

Amy nodded. "Yes, I'm looking forward to it."

He lowered his voice. "I've made reservations for dinner tonight, just in case you find yourself free. So far I haven't heard anything about conflicting plans." His eyes met hers. "And believe me, I'm looking forward to the evening." There was something conspiratorial in his voice, in his expression. He moved his leg slightly until it pressed gently against hers.

Amy's nerves contracted sharply. Not Franco, too! She had more than enough to contend with in Nando. Casually she changed her position so he was no longer touching her. But when she glanced up, she saw Nando watching them. His eyes held that same secret calculating expression that had bothered her in New York. The same cynical appraisal.

But now she knew the reason for it, she decided. He'd witnessed that awful scene with Craig Layton and he thought she was the type to encourage men. He must be making his own interpretation of Franco's behavior, probably thought she had invited it! *Well, let him think so.* Amy took a deep steadying breath. She wasn't going to try to explain anything to him—not now, not ever!

Nando glanced again at his watch, then looked up. "I think it's about time to go. The group will be gathering down at the castle."

Amy stood up gracefully. Turning to Aunt Lucia, she said politely, "Will you be joining us?"

The other woman lifted cynical eyebrows. "My dear, I wouldn't think of it! I'm quite certain you will understand why after you've been on the tour. Women should have the pleasure of sipping the wine, but not the labor of making it." She accompanied her words with a cool smile.

Amy found it hard to resist a certain admiration for this iron-willed woman. She was so calmly and firmly barricading her private domain against intrusion, taking whatever means she felt necessary. For that she deserved respect.

As Amy crossed the room, Nando came up to her. He took her elbow as if to guide her, but his hand tightened slightly and his thumb moved slowly in a mild caress. His eyes sought hers in an intimate glance.

This time an inner flare of anger spilled over and doused the eager leap of excitement she automatically felt at his touch. Amy was pleased with herself that she was able to stroll serenely across the large entranceway, through the front door and into the sunshine.

The contrast between the muted light of the villa and the brilliance of the Italian morning momentarily dazzled her eyes. She was unaware at first that Franco had joined her.

"Why don't I show you through the winery?" he offered. "I imagine you'll be busy with the rest of the group, Nando," he added smoothly.

"Delby's going to take her. It's all arranged. Thanks, anyhow," Nando said crisply.

Franco hesitated. "I see, I see," he said, a little oddly. "Very well, then, do you want me to guide any of the other groups?"

"They're pretty much accounted for. You might concentrate on the Japanese, however. One of their men speaks a little Italian. And they need extra treatment. The Japanese market is really opening up. See that they get all the details on the new Chiaro."

Amy saw Franco glance toward the American rep, who was walking some distance ahead of them. "What about Delby's group, the Americans. Won't he—"

"I'm going to take them. I know most of them already; met them in the States." That was brisk, too. Nando turned to Amy.

"Now, would you like to walk to the castle, Amy, or would you prefer to ride?"

"I'd like to walk. It isn't far," she replied brightly, her mind busy with that rigid little exchange between the two male cousins. Maybe Franco was right when he said that he and she had something in common. He, too, appeared to be more outside than inside the charmed circle of the Bonavia family.

Someone had recently cut the grass, and the fresh scent mingled with the tart sweet smell of crushed grapes as they passed the big iron gates and started down the road. The sky was an extravagant blue, and the sun poured over Amy's shoulders in a relaxing warmth. Despite her nagging problems with the Bonavias and the uncertainty of her future, she felt suddenly happy and excited as she gazed about her at the earthy beauty of the Italian countryside.

She could see row after row of terraced grapevines twining on their trellises. The vineyards stretched down the hill as far as her eyes could follow.

The very air seemed alive, the sounds of birds and insects strangely mingling with the noise of trucks and machinery.

Dominating the landscape, of course, was the massive ocher-colored castle, that incredible part of her heritage. She could barely wait to see the inside.

Cars were pulling into the courtyard as Amy and the three men walked through the big double gate. Nando waved as a man standing by an expensive-looking car beckoned to him. "Excuse me a moment. That's one of the Britishers," Nando said to Amy. "I'll be right back." Turning, he cut across the courtyard with his strong purposeful gait.

"Excited, Amy?" Franco asked, smiling down at

her. "Your cheeks are pink and your eyes are shining."

She nodded. "Oh, yes, I really am. It's the first time I've been in a winery, and this one, well—this is special."

He lowered his voice so John Delby wouldn't hear. "Now, don't let them overimpress you, *cara*. Maybe I should say, 'depress you.' Just remember, wine making isn't all that complicated."

She glanced up at him quickly, a question in her eyes. "I thought it was. Not only from the way Nando and Aunt Lucia spoke, but from some of the reading I've done."

He shrugged. "My dear girl, left to itself, a grape can make its own wine. The grape matures, the skin bursts and fermentation sets in. All we do here is what the grape does on its own, but we do it in a more sophisticated mechanical way and in greater volume. Remember that when you go through the winery today."

Nando was already walking back toward them. When he arrived he touched Amy on her arm. "We're starting now. John here will stay with you. John—" he beckoned to the man "—I'm turning her over to you. Give her a good tour."

"I certainly will! We'll follow you."

"All right. And Franco, the Japanese group should come right behind John and Amy. Give them the royal treatment; they seem to be eager to carry our line."

"Right, will do," Franco said airily. "See you later, Amy."

"All right, Franco," she said, then added impulsively, "and thanks." *For the encouragement,* she added mentally.

Apparently he understood, for he lifted his hand in a mock salute before heading toward the group of Orientals standing near the castle wall.

Nando was just joining his group, Amy noticed. His words ran through her mind again: "I'll go to any lengths to get her share, whatever it takes." Well, this little scheme wasn't going to work, she thought resolutely. As he confidently greeted the Americans, Amy quickly examined her emotional reaction to him now, after what she had overheard. She was pleased that the sight of that dark arrogant head meant nothing, nothing at all.

"Well, Miss Converse, shall we go?" John Delby was smiling down at her expansively. He nodded toward the castle entrance. As they started off together, he casually matched his steps to hers. "Nando tells me you might be interested in becoming more or less involved with the winery."

He was wasting no time obeying orders, she thought. "I'm here to see, to learn. There is a chance, yes, that I might like to do more than just hold on to my interest in the business." She might as well play the game as if she didn't know their plans.

He was shaking his head. "May I speak from an outsider's viewpoint, Miss Converse? I really can't see this as a business for women. Look around at the staff. And the buyers, too—all men. Of course, you must do as you wish. But I can't help wanting to give you a little fatherly advice."

"Thank you," she said blandly. He could interpret that as he chose.

The entire group had now gathered in the shaded area cast by the castle wall. Nando had told the truth about one thing, Amy realized. There were many languages being spoken, and many hands were waving excitedly as if trying to convey difficult meanings. They were a truly international group.

Nando led the way around one side of the building, where huge trucks were unloading large flat racks of grapes. Several workers were pouring the fruit onto a conveyor belt, which carried it along and dropped it into a long open steel vat, shaped, Amy thought, something like a huge bathtub.

As she neared the vat she peered into it. A long screwlike piece of equipment was crushing the grapes as it turned, sending out a wonderful fruity fragrance.

John Delby was droning on with technical jargon. The grapes had to be tested with a refractometer to determine the sugar content, he said. He emphasized the danger of too much sugar, too little acidity if the grapes remained on the vine too long. He used such involved descriptions, he almost succeeded in drowning her in details. Words like "botrytis cinerea" and "chemical conversion" peppered his sentences until Amy couldn't follow him anymore.

Suddenly she turned to him. "Would you mind if I asked you some questions as we go along?"

"Of course," he nodded expansively. "I'd be glad to explain anything."

"All right. Those grapes they're pouring into that

big vat—don't they wash them first?" This was not going to be a wasted exercise; she was determined to learn something in spite of him.

"No," he said reluctantly. "Not necessary or wise. Wash the grapes and you remove the natural yeast that's on the skin. And the water would serve to dilute the wine."

"What's that big vat called?" she persisted.

"A stemmer and crusher." His answer was crisp.

"So if they aren't washed, do they get, oh, I guess you could say purified, or sterilized?"

"They'll get doused with a little sulfur dioxide and they'll get filtered, too." He halted abruptly, as if he felt he was giving her too much useful information.

Clearing his throat, he went on briskly, "Wine making is a very difficult, very risky business, Miss Converse. There's always a hazard involved. The grapes must be crushed at once after harvesting. These were picked this very morning. If they don't reach the crusher within twelve hours they could deteriorate, and that's absolutely fatal. Just think what a terrible responsibility it would be, meeting such a deadline!" He shook his head almost gloomily.

Amy peered into the vat again. "Those grapes are all different colors! Pink, yellow, white...and some are greenish. Which ones do they use to make red wines?"

He gave her a reproving frown. "My dear young lady, I thought you realized we make nothing but white wines here. All of these grapes will be used."

"But what if you wanted to make red wine?" she persisted.

She could see he was reluctant, but he finally said slowly, "For red wines you need grapes with red flesh. These, whatever the skin color, have white flesh and white juice. Also, with red wines the skins are left in throughout fermentation, for alcohol draws out the color. For a rosé wine the skins are left in for twelve to twenty-four hours. But for white wines the skins aren't left in at all. Only the juice ferments. It's a very difficult, very exact process," he said pompously. Immediately afterward he launched into another spate of confusing technical terms.

Amy wasn't about to let herself be intimidated. She lifted her head to sniff the air. "I love that wonderful grapy scent. But there's something else I detect, too. A sort of yeasty smell."

Delby nodded shortly. She could see he was becoming not only impatient but more than a little irritated that he wasn't quite as much in control of the situation as he had planned to be. "Yes, yeast—natural yeast from the skins," he said tersely. "That's what turns the sugar in grapes into alcohol."

Just like a grape can do all by itself, she reflected silently, triumphantly. *Bless Franco!*

They followed the group to a large arched doorway. Amy caught the quick jerk of Nando's dark head as he turned to speak to someone. She couldn't control the sudden skip of her heart at that rugged profile, the arrogant swing of his shoulders.

Fool, she scolded herself angrily. She had thought

she was done with reacting to him. She should be, after all she now knew about him. Trying to trade his lovemaking for financial favors. Why, it was unspeakably crass. Amy deliberately pushed him out of her thoughts.

The group was filing into the castle itself. The walls, Amy could see, were at least three or four feet thick, and the low ceiling was hung with iron sconces fitted with light bulbs. Stark simplicity in this, the entrance room, although there was a large painting of the castle on one wall and a dark red Oriental carpet on the cool stone floor.

But they weren't lingering. Everyone was going in single file down a narrow stone hallway, to emerge into a large factory-size room where machinery filled the air with a clanking hum. Conversation would be difficult over the din. Delby's face smoothed and he looked relieved, as if he were glad to be free of her endless questions. Apparently he was going to allow the rows of industrial machinery and the tangle of pipes and hoses to present an object lesson of a complicated process.

Amy refused to be cowed. "Is there wine in those?" she asked, raising her voice and pointing toward towering steel tanks that had hoses leading into them. "Is that where the juice from the grapes is put?"

He nodded. "Yes, fermenting tanks," he called back.

She watched as workmen moved purposefully about the tanks, adjusting the hoses. Other staff members were pushing portable machinery, which increased the noise as they clattered over flooring made of latticed wood to enable spilled water or wine to drain through.

Delby touched her arm and pointed upward. Amy followed with her eyes. High in the air, around the tops of the tanks, ran narrow catwalks. A few men were making their way cautiously along them. Amy couldn't figure out what they were doing up there, or why John Delby had made such a point of indicating them to her. But the group was moving on and she didn't bother to ask.

In the next room rows of smaller casks lay side by side. "Wine is decanted from the larger containers in the other room. It comes here for further fermenting and aging," he said quickly, as if to circumvent questions.

It was quieter here, and Amy had a feeling he had been just waiting for an opportunity when he said, "You noticed those catwalks I pointed out to you, Miss Converse?"

Now it was coming, she thought swiftly. But she merely nodded and said, "Yes, I did."

"The men—" he emphasized the word "—who work here have to get around on those catwalks. Some of the tanks are open at the top and need attention from time to time. The catwalks can be slippery, you know. They're very dangerous. A fall from there, to the floor or into a tank...." He lifted his eyebrows and shrugged. "That, my dear, is why I'm recommending, for your own good and safety, that you think twice about becoming involved. Working around the tanks, lifting those heavy hoses, cleaning out the inside of the fermenting tanks—it's unpleasant work for a woman.''

"But I wouldn't necessarily work inside the winery. I was thinking of the public-relations department or advertising. Something like that," she retorted, letting a trace of stubbornness ring in her words. Why was she bothering, she wondered. She didn't need to defend her plans to a man who had been ordered to discourage her.

He turned an almost apologetic smile on her. "Oh, I suppose there are various minor positions like that open in some wineries. But frankly, not in this one. Nando—'' he shrugged in an offhand way "—well, Nando has strong feelings about it, I'm sorry to say. He feels this is man's work, which indeed it is. Even in the States women aren't hired by the firm, except as secretaries.''

Amy bit down on her lip. She had to, so that she wouldn't cry out, "And what about the 'minor' position of head of the firm? What about Signora Bonavia?''

But she kept quiet. If this was to be a war of sorts, it would be foolish to allow the enemy to know she had intercepted vital information.

As they approached the bottling area John Delby obediently switched back into his technical jargon. It seemed as if he was purposely picking the most difficult scientific terms he could, or that he took pleasure in describing the dire consequences that could arise should someone with little experience somehow make a mistake with the wine being processed.

It was in the bottling room that Nando left his group for a moment to come over to Amy. "I'd suggest you come along to the sampling room," he said in a low voice, "but since it's all men, and we may be talking business, you probably wouldn't feel comfortable. Perhaps John can take you back to the villa in time for lunch." It wasn't a suggestion, it wasn't even a question. Amy recognized shades of Nando's autocratic mother in the phrasing.

"Very well," she said calmly. This wasn't the time or the place to make a stand.

He turned to go, then looked back at her. "Did you enjoy the tour?"

She gave him a level glance with her green eyes. "I did, Nando. And please don't bother having Mr. Delby go back with me. I'm certain he will be needed here."

Turning, she said, "Thank you, Mr. Delby. It was very... enlightening."

He bowed his balding head. "A pleasure, my dear lady. I hope you will remember and consider the words of advice I gave you."

She smiled noncommittally and headed for the door, which Delby hurried over to open for her. "Are you certain you don't want me to walk back to the villa with you?"

Amy shook her head. "I'm going to stroll along and take my time looking around, since it's my first trip here."

"Goodbye, then. I'll probably see you again, but if not, I've enjoyed meeting you."

She knew exactly what he meant. He would still be

working for the company, but she wouldn't be here on his next trip.

She walked down the long stone hallway toward the reception room. The building was more winery than castle inside, she decided, but there was still an odd ancient feeling hovering over everything despite the gleaming stainless-steel tanks and the machinery.

As Amy stepped out of the cool interior into the warm sunshine, she halted, taking a deep steadying breath. All right, she told herself, she knew now. Knew for certain. Despite all John Delby's efforts to destroy her interest, she had become aware of a growing feeling as she went from room to room.

She wanted to stay. She wanted to learn the wine business, to become a vintner. It wasn't stubbornness. It wasn't because of Nando, or a desire to thwart him. She wanted this for herself, as a deeply important part of her life. In a way, Amy thought, she was like a sculptor who doesn't realize what he wants to do until he's confronted by a mound of clay. Then he knows.

She knew, too. Maybe there was something to the idea of genetic heredity. The winery was something more than a casual possibility of some new career. She couldn't explain it to herself, not exactly—but she wanted to stay, to become part of it. It was as simple as that.

And Bert? She was sorry about him, of course, but she wasn't going back to New York. He'd have to find someone else to sit beside him at the football games.

What if the Bonavias absolutely refused to allow

her to take any sort of job in the company, she wondered. The thought didn't daunt her. She'd still stay in Italy. She would just have to learn wine making somewhere else. She might even apply at Elisa's father's winery, she thought mischievously.

Anyhow, her decision had finally been made. And, more than likely, all hell was going to break loose when Nando found out!

CHAPTER SIX

As Amy neared the villa she could see the elderly gatekeeper peering through the iron rails. Reaching up, he unlocked the gate, swinging it wide for her to enter. Bowing several times, he murmured, *"Signorina, prego!"*

"Grazie," she answered, much more easily this time. She would have to learn Italian as quickly as she could!

Ahead of her, on the terrace, she could see Anna Maria and a young man sitting under the umbrella, glasses in front of them.

"Welcome cousin," Anna Maria called with a ravishing smile. "Come meet Filippo, my fiancé, and share some orange juice with us."

The young man got to his feet, then bowed over Amy's hand. *"Piacere,"* he said.

He was handsome, rather extraordinarily handsome, Amy noted. Not much taller than Anna Maria, but with the slim waist and broad shoulders of an athlete. His black hair curled close to his head and his eyes, a surprising blue in the smooth olive-skinned face, were fringed by thick dark lashes. He was saved from being almost too handsome by the firmness of his straight mouth.

"Filippo doesn't speak English, poor man." Anna Maria looked up at him in mock sympathy as he pulled out a chair for Amy to join them.

"I speak, I speak," he denied, smiling. "Some little."

"Damned little!" Anna Maria said. "And he understands even less. But isn't he perfectly lovely to look at? I'm glad he doesn't understand because I don't want him to know how completely mad I am about him."

Amy found herself suddenly envious of that happy glow in Anna Maria's eyes as she gazed fondly at Filippo. Maybe it would have been different, she reflected, if she had first met Nando in some other way, in circumstances that hadn't made them instant adversaries. But she hadn't, she reminded herself silently. She hadn't.

"Filippo isn't the only one who isn't fluent in a foreign language," Amy said to Anna Maria. "Tell me, what is meant by *prego*? The gateman said it just now, and so did the girl who brought me coffee this morning."

Anna Maria smiled. "It's confusing, I know. Basically it means please. He meant for you to 'pray enter,' or 'come in.' However, just to confuse you, if you thank someone for something, then the person will likely say *prego*, which in this case means the same as 'you're welcome.' But the former use is the one you'll be hearing most often."

Amy slid a quick look at Filippo. "And *piacere*?"

"It means please, too, in a way," she replied with a laugh. "It also means 'it's a pleasure,' or that sort

of thing. As Filippo just said. But if you ask someone
for something, then you say *per piacere*! Now, that
should confuse you!''

"Also to tell *Veronese tutti matti*," said Filippo
with a sly grin. "Anna Maria, Veronese!''

"Vicentini mangia gatti!" Anna Maria snapped
back at him tartly.

Then she turned to say, "This I'd better explain,
for if you are here for any length of time you are certain to hear it in part or in full. It's our poetic insult
to each other.

> *Veneziani gran signori*
> *Padovani gran dottori*
> *Vicentini mangia gatti*
> *Veronese tutti matti.*

"It means Venetians are great lords, while people
from Padova great doctors. Those from Vicenza—''
she slid another teasing look at Filippo ''—they eat
cats! Veronese, those from Verona, are all mad,
crazy. We Bonavias are considered Veronese, though
we live here now.'' She lifted an eyebrow at Amy. "I
might point out that Filippo is from Vicenza.''

He nodded cheerfully at both of them. Apparently
he was catching only bits of the conversation, but it
didn't seem to worry him.

Amy, however, found it a little awkward not to be
able to direct any comments to him or to understand
his occasional sentences. But Anna Maria chatted
along easily to both of them, not at all bothered by
the situation.

"Tell me, Amy," she said, "how did you like the tour? I would have found it dreadfully dull, I know. All those buyers can talk about is wine! However, it might have been fun to be the only woman having lunch with fifty or sixty men!"

So she had been excluded from the luncheon, too, Amy realized. But she might have expected that. After all, she wasn't a regular tour guest.

"Just as well I didn't join them," she said to Anna Maria. "I'm not very fluent in Japanese or Russian, either."

A maid came out of the house and approached the table. Politely bobbing her head, she murmured a few words in Italian to Amy.

Making a wild guess, Amy pointed toward the two juice glasses on the table. *"Per piacere,"* she said, trying not to grin self-consciously.

"Si, signorina, si," the woman said, bowing before she turned and went back into the villa.

"Congratulations!" Anna Maria said. "You'll be ready to teach Italian by the time you return to New York!"

Amy suddenly sobered. "Anna Maria, I'm not going back. My mind is made up; I want to learn the wine business."

The other girl's eyes were suddenly cautious. "Does Nando know? That you've really decided to stay?"

"I wasn't certain before, not definitely. I think he intended the tour to be an introduction. A chance to see how I felt after looking over the whole process."

And a chance for the troubleshooter, John Delby

by name, to talk her out of it, Amy reflected bitterly. Too bad for them it hadn't worked as they'd planned.

"I don't think Nando's exactly crazy about having women working for him," Anna Maria said cautiously.

Amy glanced up at her with a wry smile. "He hasn't made much of a secret of that."

The maid appeared and set a frosted glass of orange juice on the table.

"Grazie," Amy said.

She was childishly pleased when the woman said, *"Prego, signorina,"* before leaving.

It would be better not to return to the awkward topic of her future. "When are you and Filippo planning to be married?" she asked, smiling briefly at the young man to include him in the conversation.

"Spring. That's when the wedding is supposed to be. But Filippo is an impatient man. He keeps saying 'soon,' and 'now.' He is difficult to resist." Anna Maria reached over to lay her hand on his and immediately he entrapped it with his own. "However, we must now try to convince my mother we would like our wedding to be without delay."

Amy drank her orange juice quickly. She should leave the betrothed couple alone for a while, she felt, especially since theirs was by necessity a two-cornered conversation.

As she set her empty glass down, she stood up, saying, "I really must run along to my room. I have some letters to write." She turned a quick amused smile on Filippo, who had arisen when she did. *"Piacere!"* she said triumphantly.

He paused, then said, "Thank you. I please, too." He laughed, a sudden chuckle that lighted up his eyes. Amy suddenly understood why Anna Maria was so at-tracted to him.

"See you at lunch," the young woman called after Amy.

"Fine. What time will it be?"

"One o'clock. Filippo will be joining us."

Amy crossed the terrace and pushed at the front door, which opened easily. As she climbed the stairs to her room, she felt envy once again for Anna Maria. To be in love like that! And to be loved.... Her cousin could never really claim beauty, but her obvious happiness made her radiant, a quality far more mov-ing than ordinary beauty.

A soft breeze was billowing the white curtains at the open window as she entered her room. She crossed the floor and stood looking down at the castle. She was going to have to face Nando before long. How would he react? With anger?

Or would he resort to his old tactics, trying to sway her with the touch of his hands, his lips? Well, it wasn't going to succeed.

You've said that before, several times, she remind-ed herself guiltily. But this time she meant it.

When she went down to lunch, she found that Aunt Lucia, Anna Maria and Filippo were waiting for her in the salon. Together they moved into the dining room and seated themselves near one end of the long table. Then Aunt Lucia lifted her hand to indicate to the at-tending servant that lunch was to be served.

"Well, my dear, how did you find the winery?" she

began, turning those enigmatic eyes on Amy. "Rather a complicated affair, isn't it?"

"Yes, Aunt Lucia. Very...sophisticated," Amy replied dutifully.

The older woman nodded. "I thought you would find it so. It is certainly nothing I would care to have a daughter of mine exposed to. And, of course, that is why I have attempted to advise you, to discourage you, Amy." She lifted her spoon to begin eating the soup that had been placed before her. Apparently she was satisfied that John Delby had been successful in his mission.

"Even though it was complicated, I found the tour extremely interesting. There are so many factors that affect the process! What a challenge it must be to produce a good wine. I think I would like very much to learn how to do it." Amy lowered her eyes and began on her soup.

There was an electric silence, then Aunt Lucia drew in an impatient breath. When she spoke, however, her words were calm enough. "Before you decide finally, Amy, I suggest you talk it over more thoroughly with Nando."

"Yes, Aunt Lucia, I shall certainly do so."

Filippo looked up from his soup, no doubt aware of the tension in the air. Then he returned to his food, and it was only after finishing it that he spoke to Anna Maria.

The sentence in Italian was very brief and sounded like a question. Anna Maria frowned, then shrugged and nodded.

Filippo then addressed three or four sentences to

Aunt Lucia. There was a respectful tone in his voice.

It was met with a protesting gesture of Aunt Lucia's hand, a shake of her head, plus a stream of Italian. Anna Maria leaned forward, inserting a few words, a pleading tone in her voice. Amy looked from one to the other in fascination, trying to guess what was going on. Aunt Lucia gazed piercingly at the young man and woman for a long moment, then her expression gradually began to thaw and she gave a reluctant nod.

Filippo reached over quickly, took Anna Maria's hand and lifted it to his lips. Then he spoke rapidly to her mother.

At last Anna Maria turned to Amy, her eyes dazzled. "Forgive us, please, but Filippo wanted to ask permission for us to marry...this coming month. And my mother—" she twisted her head to look at the matriarch, who was lifting her hand to a servant "—my mother has agreed."

Aunt Lucia gave an ironic smile. "I fear I've little choice. Young people are so impetuous, so impatient. Well, perhaps it is best so. Time rushes past, and if one waits too long...suddenly it is too late." She didn't look at Amy; she didn't need to. The message was clear: Don't involve yourself in business. Return home, marry, settle down before it is too late.

Anna Maria was bubbling over with excitement, her voice light and lilting. "Oh, I have so many plans to make! Amy, you simply mustn't rush back to New York. You have to stay for the wedding! I'd like you to be my attendant." Her hand flew to her lips. "Oh, I'm sorry, I forgot. The winery. You *are* staying on..." she added a little doubtfully.

No one really expected her to stay, Amy realized. No one took her seriously—or those who did take her seriously were intent on changing her mind. But she couldn't stubbornly pursue the subject in view of the joyful news. They had a wedding to celebrate!

Chilled sole on a gold-rimmed plate was set before them, the fish artfully decorated with mayonnaise and a faint sprinkling of herbs. The food here was of gourmet quality, Amy thought. She almost regretted the necessity of moving out. But move out she should, if she held on to her share of the business and succeeded in her desire to work at the winery. She'd be *persona non grata* in no time!

After luncheon Aunt Lucia retired to her room, supposedly to rest. Naturally wanting to discuss plans for the pending wedding, Filippo and Anna Maria excused themselves and went into the library. Left alone, Amy strolled out to the terrace again, to sit under the umbrella. She had plans of her own to consider.

But the warmth of the sun, and the shreds of jet lag that still lingered, made her yawn and blink her eyes. Drowsily she leaned back in the chair, listening to the gentle twitter of birds and the hum of bees flying toward flowers along the terrace. A minute later she was asleep.

A touch of a hand on her shoulder brought her abruptly awake. She looked up to see Franco smiling down at her. "Sorry to disturb you, cousin mine, but I've a brilliant idea. I found out by devious means that nothing special is planned for tonight, so let's leave shortly for Lake Garda and spend the tag end of the afternoon sightseeing. Then we can have dinner on the lake.''

Amy sat up, brushing at her hair with her hand, then smothering the remnants of a yawn. The idea was tempting, partly because she wanted to postpone for as long as she could an encounter with Nando. And she did have some curiosity about Franco's veiled hints. Why not say yes?

"If you're sure no one will mind, and that nothing is scheduled for the evening...."

He held up his hand soberly. "I swear!"

"All right, then, it sounds very nice," she exclaimed. "I'll have to leave word with Anna Maria, since Aunt Lucia is resting."

"Good. Let's go!"

Amy suspected he wasn't overly anxious for Nando to arrive before they left. But then again, neither was she. As they entered the villa, Amy asked, "Is the tour all over?"

"It is. The luncheon, too. Now they all talk business, which I presume will center around the new Chiaro. Everyone seemed greatly impressed with it. Nando handles those questions, so I'm free to leave."

Amy wondered what Franco's role in the winery was, but she felt hesitant about asking him. Maybe they would talk about it later....

Anna Maria and Filippo approved of the trip to Lake Garda. "It's truly beautiful, Amy," Anna Maria said enthusiastically. "If you have time, take her to Sirmione, Franco. It may be touristy, but it's a wonderfully quaint town. And she should see the castle."

"It sounds delightful. Now, Franco, give me just a moment or two, I'll change clothes," Amy said hurriedly, starting for the door.

"You look fine, don't bother," he said a little impatiently.

"Five minutes; time me!" she laughed. Maybe she looked all right to him, but if they were going out to dinner she preferred to wear something more feminine.

She went flying up the stairs, and once inside her room she stripped off her clothes. Quickly she slipped into a simple silk sheath of pale green, topped it with a sweater of a faintly darker pastel shade, then strapped on a pair of sandals that would double for comfort and dress. A brush of her hair, a quick touch of lipstick and she was hurrying back down the stairs, to find Franco looking up at her from the landing.

"You look just like a spring nymph!" he exclaimed. "Let's go. I have the car outside."

Taking her arm, he led her out the front door and across the terrace to the driveway, where a blue sports car waited.

"My dearest possession," he said, patting the car. "Up to now!" He gave her a quick look and smiled. "I usually drive with the top down, but if it will bother your hair, I'll put it up."

"Not in the least," she said cheerfully. "I have wash-and-wear hair and I adore convertibles. You can see so much more as you go along."

He whirled the car down the driveway and pulled up at the gate, halting while the man ran out to open it. Then they drove on toward the castle. As they passed the entrance to the courtyard, Amy noticed that a few cars still remained. She caught a fleeting glimpse of several men standing in a group near the gate. How could she feel so certain that Nando was one of them? Did the sudden trip of her heart tell her?

Certainly not. That unexpected flutter was simply an unwelcome coincidence.

They followed the road around the castle, then drove down past the gray green vines braced on trellises. This time Amy noticed bunches of honey-yellow grapes hanging heavily among the leaves. There was a smell of hot, sunbaked earth as they raised a ruffle of dust along the side of the road.

They had no more than entered the highway when a car came racing up behind them. It passed at a sui cidal speed, finally whipping between two other cars that were some distance ahead. There was a concerted shrieking of brakes as the vehicles tried to avoid a collision.

Amy swallowed hard, grasping the door handle, while Franco shook his head. "I know!" he said. "We Italians have two ways of driving: full speed ahead, gas pedal flat on the floor, or jumping on the brakes. All of us. Italian kamikazes!"

"It's worse than New York," she managed weakly. Would she ever get used to this, she wondered. Franco drove fast, but so far at least he hadn't taken any idiotic chances. She couldn't really relax, but she did try to lean back against the sun-warmed seat, her hands knotting from time to time as other cars screeched past.

"I haven't asked you yet," Franco said, as if to distract her from the maelstrom of the highway. "Did you enjoy the tour? The wine tour?"

"Oh, yes! It was. . . well, I liked it."

"And our John explained it all to you?" he asked almost pointedly.

Just how much did Franco know about what had gone on? Had he, too, been in on the deception? She replied neutrally, "Yes, he explained everything quite thoroughly."

Some distance ahead, Amy could see turret and city walls rising against the sky. They looked faintly familiar.

"Verona?" she guessed.

"Right. Your home and my home, no matter where we were born."

"*Veronese tutti matti!*" she quoted, pleased that she remembered.

Franco gave a sharp laugh and reached over to squeeze her hand, his hazel eyes amused. "That we are, madmen all. Women, too. You're wonderful, Cousin Amy. I knew I wasn't mistaken in you!"

For a split second she thought he was going to say something else. He opened his mouth as if to speak, then didn't. It wasn't until they reached the walls of Verona and were starting to skirt the city that he said, "We go beyond Verona today, so we won't do the usual tourist crawl through the town. This way we'll have more time to spend in Sirmione. Anna Maria mentioned the castle. It's fantastic in its way. It was one of many built by our famous Veronese lord, Can Grande della Scalla, to protect Verona from marauders that came from other duchies and kingdoms. He especially feared those from Venice."

"How strange," she observed, "that two towns fought each other so fiercely. Verona and Venice aren't very far apart, are they?"

"Not far enough, certainly. But it really isn't strange that they should fight. You have to remember that Italy has only been unified since the early 1870s. Before that we were many individual duchies and kingdoms, each with its own ruler and its own ambitions, so raids and attacks weren't uncommon. We have a bloody history of internecine wars."

He laughed suddenly. "And to tell you the truth, Amy, we're still rather insular and provincial. Full of local dialects. For instance, I might hear someone speaking the Neapolitan dialect and not understand what he's saying."

"We have different accents in the States, but we can usually understand each other," Amy commented thoughtfully. "However, that didn't keep us from fighting each other in the Civil War."

"With us, too, there is the food question," he lamented. "We are almost as bad about our own provincial dishes. None of us believe other locales can compare with our own. Not long ago the family of a newly elected Pope actually brought food from home to him, saying, 'God only knows what the Romans feed him!'"

Interesting as the conversation was, Amy had the feeling that Franco was talking off the top of his head. That somewhere underneath something else was occupying his attention, perhaps something he was waiting for the proper time to reveal. She gave him a quick curious glance, but his cheerful face revealed nothing.

They drove through several small towns, along narrow hilly roads not much wider than the car. Several times Amy decided that if she held out her hand she could almost touch the walls. She was glad that Franco had chosen country roads instead of the main autostrada.

"I prefer these," he said. "And it will give you a taste of the real Italy."

Some of the streets were paved with cobblestones so old and worn that she wondered if, originally, chariots had rumbled along them. And the ever haunting scent of roasting coffee seemed to follow them from the moment they entered each village until they left. In the countryside they passed a small restaurant with tables set out under a shady arbor of grapes. By the building itself pasta was strung out on poles, drying in the sun.

Small piazzas dotted the towns. Usually there would be a spired church at one end, and in the center of the square a fountain, where sometimes a handful of women were gathered, their heads bent together in the age-old posture of gossip. There were schoolchildren, dark haired and rosy cheeked, in school uniforms, walking two-by-two along the narrow sidewalks. A few of them looked up and waved shyly as Amy and Franco whisked past in their car.

Then abruptly, like a curtain going up, Amy caught a glimpse of incredible blue. She watched in delight as it spread and became a vast expanse of sapphire water. Then she turned to Franco wonderingly. "What an absolutely unbelievable color. It looks like yards and yards of blue satin stretched as far as you can see, and there's not a ripple or a wave, it's so still!"

"That, my dear cousin, is Lake Garda. I told you it was the most beautiful body of water in the world. Don't believe, however, that it's always so smooth, or this color. When the wind comes racing across the mountains, the water actually hisses, and turns a dark purple."

He gestured with his hand. "Right ahead of us is Sirmione, a very old town—centuries old, in fact."

Amy dragged her eyes away from the lake. Ahead of them an immense castle suddenly sprang into view, dominating the landscape. And towers! She counted them: twelve massive towers edged with jagged crenellation, with one tower thrusting higher than the rest.

"Franco, look!" She touched his arm in excitement, not even conscious she had done so. "I've never seen anything like it! It's so big! That tallest tower...it sort of flares out at the top, as if someone had set an extra, larger story on top of it!"

He had quickly covered her hand with his, and it was only then that she realized she was still touching him. She tactfully tried to draw her hand away, but he held it tight as he explained, "That upper section has a very good reason for being there. It allowed the residents to pour boiling oil down on invaders trying to scale the walls."

Franco let her hand go in order to pull the car into

a parking place in the small city. "Let's have coffee, then wander around a little," he said, holding open the car door for her.

They stopped at a small coffee bar where tables were placed outside under gaily striped umbrellas. As they waited for their order, Amy looked about her. The small winding streets were filled with boutiques and an endless flow of tourists.

Franco gazed across the table at her. "Well, dear cousin, did today's tour discourage you about becoming a vintner or a wine mogul?" He added quickly, "How do you feel about it now? Going or staying?"

Was this what had been on his mind under his light conversation today? She somehow had a feeling that it was, for there was a certain tension in his voice.

"Staying, Franco."

"Does Nando know that? You haven't seen him since the tour, have you?"

She shook her head, waiting to speak until the waiter had set small cups of coffee in front of them and had left. Then she said, "No, I haven't told him yet. But I will tomorrow."

Franco made a wry face. "He's not going to like it, you know. He isn't keen on having women involved in the winery. In fact, he'd hate it. It's no secret, so I guess you already know that. And it's not just you, it's any woman."

"What about Aunt Lucia?" Amy could have bitten her tongue. The words had popped out without her volition. But it was too late to retract them, so she met his eyes directly.

"Well, well! So you know, do you? Yes, I can see you do. I wonder what little cat spilled the milk. But, no matter. You should know, you're part of the family. It's certainly far from common knowledge, though."

"I realize that. But she—they, I mean—don't know that I'm aware of the position she holds." Amy wasn't about to tell him how she'd heard.

He looked at her over the rim of his cup before setting it down. Then he drawled, "So are you going to keep your share in the business? I'm not idly curious. It's important that I know. Are you certain now?"

There seemed little reason not to tell him; everyone was going to know before long. Even Nando, and that was the thought that brought an uneasy feeling to the pit of Amy's stomach. Why couldn't she overcome that apprehension?

"Yes, Franco, I'm going to keep my part. But I know it's going to create a difficult situation. I'm a guest of the Bonavias, yet I'm thwarting their wishes. Perhaps under the circumstances I should move out, stay somewhere else."

He shook his head firmly. "They won't allow it. No matter what you do, or what you decide, they'll insist you stay. You are family. So am I. And, my dear cousin, you aren't the only one who is stubbornly holding on to a share in the winery!" He leaned back in his chair.

"Some time ago, shortly after I arrived here and they realized I wasn't surrendering my own share, I suggested taking up residence somewhere else. They wouldn't hear of it. And for more than one reason, I suspect. We Italians have our own version of the Oriental 'losing face.' We will go to almost any length to not *fare una brutte figura*—not make a bad impression. To allow either of us to stay somewhere else simply wouldn't look right. Besides, if we stay there in the house, they can keep an eye on us. Slight pressure can be brought to bear.''

A look of dry amusement crossed his face. ''However, I know wine merchandising, so I'm not as easy to get around as Nando hopes you may be. Especially since you've had no previous experience in the industry.''

''Franco, I really want to keep my part of the business. Maybe I'm being foolhardy, but I so much want to stay on here in Italy,'' Amy said sincerely, realizing how difficult it might be if Nando began deliberately closing doors to her. And that was something he might very well do.

Franco fished some lire from his pocket and tossed them onto the table. ''Amy, you and I need to have a serious talk without delay. But this is hardly the time or place for it. Let's take a quick look around town, then drive along the lake. Over dinner I'm going to level with you. Isn't that what you Americans say when you want to talk business?''

Amy gave him a sharp glance as she slowly got to her feet. ''Yes, Franco, that's the expression,'' she answered. No one could say her trip to Italy so far had been lacking surprise and intrigue, she thought to herself. She was curious; what did this cousin of hers have on his mind?

''A quick look at the castle?'' Franco was leading the way across the busy street.

"Love it!"

As they neared the imposing structure, Franco explained, "The castle has a moat to end all moats—Lake Garda itself wrapped around it. In fact, in some ways it's like a miniature Venice inside, with drawbridges needed everywhere as the lake flows in and out."

She and Franco entered the castle and climbed up into one of the towers. As Amy glanced around the somber interior, she could see that the walls were extremely thick and dotted with narrow slits he told her were firing ports. She tried to imagine the people who had lived here all those centuries ago. Had they sat here in this tower, crossbows ready, their eyes fixed on the nearby countryside waiting for an enemy to attack? It all seemed so warlike, she decided, then remembered that this castle actually was a fortress as well as a dwelling.

They crossed over lagoons, over drawbridges, and then, from the guard walk circling the north tower, stood gazing silently out over the lake. The water varied in color now from a lovely shimmering emerald to cerulean blue, then to a deep amethyst purple where it was shadowed by the mountains at the far side.

Amy turned to Franco. "You're right. It must be the loveliest body of water in the world," she said simply.

He reached for her hand, pressing it between his. "It is. And you, darling Amy, you, too, are lovely."

She withdrew her hand, softening the action with a smile. It was the second time she'd had to do that. Why, she wondered, did Franco's touch mean nothing, nothing at all? Yet had it been Nando.... She felt an immediate flicker of anger. Why did she continue to think such things? Nando was the deceiver. She had every reason to hate him.

If she had to be affected by the touch of a man, why hadn't she the sense to pick Franco? He was classically better looking than Nando; he was pleasant; he had been friendly right from the beginning.

So why wasn't he the one to startle her heart, to make her breath come unevenly? It was another case of Bert. Good company, but....

They continued to stroll through the cool stone rooms of the empty castle until they finally emerged again on the sunny streets of Sirmione. Amy stopped for a long moment in front of a window filled with exquisite glass objects—figurines as delicate as air, vases and glasses in glowing enchanting colors.

"From Murano, near Venice," Franco explained. "The whole tiny island is filled with people making this glass, which is sold all over the world. We Italians tend to specialize, you see. On another island near Murano people make lace. But—" he gently squeezed her arm, looking down at her "—I must say that all Italians make love!"

There was a familiar look in his eyes. The same intimate invitation that had flickered in Nando's eyes when he wanted something.

Amy felt her nerves tighten instinctively. So Franco was going to take a little firm handling, too! It would be easier than with Nando, however; she wouldn't have to be handling her own emotions at the same time.

She carefully ignored his words and his glance, paying exceedingly close attention to a glass clown balanced on one toe in the window. The moment passed and they strolled along the winding street. Amy was intrigued by all the people passing by. The sound of German and French accents mingled with the Italian. She could catch the inflections if not the words or meaning.

Franco nodded. Yes, there were many tourists here, but there always had been. "Romans flocked here before the birth of Christ," he said. "Warriors and poets, courtesans and nobles—they've all come here over the centuries. Sirmione is an eternal place, I suppose you could say, even though the castle is no longer used as a fortress."

They drove around the small peninsula, pausing at the old Roman ruins at one end, where tumbledown walls and arches reached down to the lake. Flowers and trees were everywhere, and stretching out in the distance was the incredible blue water.

Franco finally glanced at his watch. "Let's start up the lake. We have no great distance to drive, but we'll want to take our time. We should get to the restaurant while it's still light so we can look out over the water as we sip an *aperitivo* and order dinner."

They drove up the western shore, passing rows of lemon trees on the way. By the roadside, children held up bunches of lemons for sale.

Soon they were passing several beautiful hotels, their parks and gardens rich with palms, towering eucalyptus, laurel and magnolia. Intense shades of green contrasted with the extraordinary blue of the lake. Elegant flower-laden terraces, dotted with bright umbrellas and small tables, jutted out above the water. Amy could see tennis courts, shady flowered walks and people strolling leisurely about. The tourists hadn't all stayed in Sirmione!

"This is a completely different Italy from the area around Villa Cielo, isn't it, Franco? And not so far away, either. There it is mostly country, but this is as posh a resort area as I've ever seen."

"It's known as Gardone Riviera, and in its own way it rivals both the French and Italian rivieras." He turned a grin on her. "I told you we were insular. I like *our* Riviera best."

She nodded vigorously. "So do I. And I haven't even seen the others!"

He laughed, then reached over to pat her on the knee, letting his hand linger a few seconds longer than necessary before withdrawing it. "Good girl! Already you are turning into an Italian!"

Amy imperceptibly changed position so she was closer to her side of the car. She didn't want to make a scene about his touching her—maybe it was not an uncommon activity among Italian men. But she wasn't going to encourage or, for that matter, permit it. She would simply remove herself from ready availability.

The road changed, and they started passing through tunnels cut through the steep mountainside. Not just one or two tunnels, but one after another until Amy lost count. They weren't dark because they were punctuated regularly with portals opening toward the brilliant sparkle of the lake.

"It's like moving along a beautiful marble corridor of some kind," Amy said, catching her breath, "the way you can look out through those big arches at the water, as if you were seeing a series of framed paintings. It's. . .it's spectacular!"

They passed through villages nestled against the slope, where homes and greenhouses, surrounded by olive and lemon trees, could be seen through the deep flaring red of the oleanders that lined the roadside. The sun slowly began turning the peaks into frozen flames and sending paths of glowing amber across the deepening amethyst of the lake.

"We may be slightly early for dinner," Franco commented, "but as I said, I wanted you to have a chance to see the lake from the terrace by twilight. And if I'm not mistaken, we should be having a moon later."

The air was soft and still warm as they pulled off the road at the entrance of the restaurant. As they were led through the dining room and out onto the terrace, to a table by the railing, Amy understood why Franco had been anxious to get there. The deepening color of the satin water was so serene and beautiful that they sat at their table for a few moments without speaking. Amy found her chest tightening with a strange feeling of both happiness and sadness, a reaction she couldn't analyze.

"How about an Americano?" Franco asked her as the waiter approached.

"What's that?" she asked suspiciously.

"It's half Campari, half Italian vermouth, ice,

soda and a squeeze of lemon. Faintly bitter, but just right for a warm evening."

She nodded approvingly. "Another step in my Italian indoctrination. I'd love one."

When the glass was put before Amy, she lifted it in a toast. "Many, many thanks for the outing today, Franco," she said. "It has been lovely."

He turned his own drink in his hand, gazing at it rather than at her. "I also had a selfish motive in getting you off alone. I want to talk to you about it now." He lifted his eyes and looked at her levelly. "Amy, if you hold on to your share, you realize, don't you, that your chances of getting into the winery business through Nando are practically nil?"

"I . . . I suppose you're right." She had thought as much, but to have someone come out and actually say it caused her spirits to sink.

"All right. But maybe we can change that; in fact I think we can. What do you know about the division of ownership of the winery? I'm talking now about the original division."

"Not a lot. I know you have a share, and that Nando, Aunt Lucia and Anna Maria each own part of the business. And I do."

He nodded. "Right. Guido Montagne, a widower, had five children—two boys and three girls. As you no doubt know, his winery wasn't very big. But he wanted to be certain to leave equal shares of it to his children, just so there wouldn't be any arguing later as to who had been favored. The girls married. One became a Bonavia, two married Rinaldi brothers. The two sons, of course, retained the Montagne name. As the generations sifted down, your grandfather got a full Rinaldi legacy; so did mine."

"But Aunt Lucia, Nando and Anna Maria—they each have a share of the business, don't they?" Amy asked, puzzled.

"Oh, indeed they do, which is the reason for this talk with you. Nando's father was the one who really began building up the winery. He was an exceedingly shrewd businessman. He sought out the rest of the people who owned part of the business and bargained with them. He had his own share, of course, and he prevailed on the other families involved to sell him theirs. That gave him three-fifths. He went to my father, trying to buy ours, but papa refused to sell. Instead, he willed it to me. Yours they couldn't track down until Nando found you."

"I see! That accounts for why Aunt Lucia, Nando and Anna Maria each own a part of the business, then."

He nodded. "Right. And it gives them, united together, power as majority owners." Franco hesitated, looking at her appraisingly for a long second. "You do know, don't you, that under the present circumstances you'll never become an active partner in the business, even though you retain your share? Even though it's only right that you should? As long as they hold the voting power you don't have a chance."

She started to speak, but he held up his hand. "Wait, please. I want to finish what's on my mind first. I don't suppose you'd want to sell me your interest in the winery?" He eyed her hopefully. "No?

Well, I thought as much. Then how would you like to become a real member of the firm, an active partner, with the chance to learn and practice the wine business?''

She turned puzzled eyes on him. ''But how can I? You just made it clear they'll never agree to it. And I know you're right.''

Franco's eyes narrowed. This was no longer Franco, the easygoing amusing cousin. Suddenly he was as businesslike as Nando. ''It's true only as long as they retain majority control. But what if all that changes? You and I can join together as a voting bloc. It won't be easy, because Nando will keep putting on the pressure. He won't feel satisfied until your share has been turned over to him. But he needn't get it.''

''Franco, what good would it do? Even if we join together, it won't change the fact that they are still three-fifths against two-fifths.''

For a moment Amy thought that he hadn't heard her, for his face had a remote thoughtful look and he was silent. But then he met her eyes. ''Amy, I want to tell you something, something very important. I wouldn't have decided to tell you this so soon, but I have a feeling time is running out. However, I'd like your word that no matter what you decide you won't say anything, now or in the future, about what I'm going to tell you.''

''If it's that important, perhaps you hadn't better confide in me,'' she said a little uneasily.

''If you're sincere about wanting to keep your share in the winery and learn the business, then I promise you, that's exactly what you can do. There is nothing illegal about this, but I would like your word that you will not discuss it with anyone." His eyes narrowed, a muscle in his cheek twitched.

"Well," Amy said reluctantly, "if you're certain it's all right for me to know, and that you want to tell me, then I promise."

"Very well. If you and I join forces, each keeping our own share, we soon shall have the majority." There was quiet triumph in his voice. "After Filippo and Anna Maria marry, which is going to be shortly."

Amy looked at him uncertainly. "I know they're getting married, but how will that change our situation? Anna Maria will still have her share. She's certainly not going to offer it to us. Nando wouldn't let her, even if she wanted to."

He smiled a thin knowing smile. "Have you ever heard of *patria potestas*?"

She shook her head. "No. What does it mean?"

"It's an old Roman law. It assures a husband of full legal control of his children. In almost all cases, too, the husband controls the purse strings."

"I thought Italian women were liberated these days," Amy observed curiously, still not certain what his big secret might be.

"Oh, they are, theoretically. *Patria potestas* was repealed in 1975. But don't be misled; it's still widely practiced. Filippo is my close friend, so I know that he isn't the liberated type. Anna Maria is deeply in love with him, as you no doubt have noticed if you've seen them together for any length of time. When they marry, you can be certain *patria potestas* will be recognized in their household!''

''And...?'' Amy lifted her eyebrows questioningly.

''Then, my dear, her share will be under the control of Filippo. And he will join his share to yours and mine.'' Gold specks flickered in his hazel eyes.

''Then who will have the three-fifths?''

Amy sat back in her chair, relieved when the waiter approached them to take their order. It gave her time to think. When Franco asked what she would like, she gave him a perfunctory absent smile, saying, ''Why don't you order, please? You know what the specialities are.''

He nodded, then reeled off a string of Italian words to the waiter.

Thoughts were running in confusion through Amy's mind. The situation, she found, was rapidly becoming more complicated. Even if Nando's amorous approaches had been solely in pursuit of her share of the winery, she didn't quite like the idea of scheming against him. And yet, as Franco said, Nando would never accept her participation in the winery.

The waiter left and Franco turned back to her, a question in his eyes.

''I...I don't know, Franco. It's all so sudden. I don't know what to say. I suppose this sounds silly, but I feel as if I would be betraying Aunt Lucia... and Nando. I...'' she let her words drift off, not quite certain what she wanted to express.

''Do you think they feel any obligation or loyalty

to you? Turn over your share to them and you'll find
the door closing on your heels as soon as it can be
tactfully arranged. You do realize that, don't you?''

He was right. She was here on sufferance, and
barely that.

"I shouldn't think the decision would be much of a
problem," Franco said levelly. "It's a matter of our
getting in or being squeezed out."

Amy gazed out at the smooth surface of the lake.
It was dark now, barely touched by the promise of a
moon beginning to rise over the sharp-toothed mountains.

She was saved from an immediate answer by the
arrival of their waiter with their soup. It turned out
to be a golden aromatic broth with tiny bits of pasta
floating on its surface.

"Pasta in brodo," Franco said in an amused tone.
"You must start learning Italian now that you are going to remain with us. That one is easy. Pasta in
broth."

Was he that certain she would join him? Amy
lifted her spoon, not quite meeting his eyes.

"Amy, it's all so simple. I don't see your problem," he began again persuasively. "Nando came to
New York to find you and offer to buy you out. You
didn't sell—which, I must say, was shrewd on your
part." His eyes glinted. "You have come to Italy to
see for yourself what's going on. Correct?"

She nodded. Had it been only yesterday that she
had landed in Rome?

"Very well, then, I suggest you be prepared. Nando is going to put more and more pressure on you.

He wants that share, he wants it badly. Knowing him, I can imagine what method he will probably resort to. Nando has a way with women. He can be very persuasive.''

Amy continued eating her soup, eyes lowered.

''Amy, please understand that I'm not accusing Nando, not of anything. This is meant only as a warning.''

One that's a little late, she reflected. She lifted her head and looked at him steadily. ''He does not yet have my share, nor would I ever be persuaded in that way to turn it over to him.''

''Good. I may be wrong about his using that method, but he might resort to it if nothing else seems to work.'' He gave a short harsh laugh. ''It's the same thing Elisa Antolini is doing. She wants our winery to merge with her father's, and she wants Nando. And damned if I don't sometimes think she'll eventually swing it! You've seen her; she's beautiful and she's using the fact to fan Nando's flames. He's what you Americans call a tough customer. He swears he'll never marry, but he's flesh and blood. Hot blood at that, and a man can resist that temptation just so long.''

''But supposing Elisa is successful, what would that do to your plans?''

He shook his head. ''It would sink them. If he still controls the majority before she snares him, then the two wineries could merge just on his say-so, no matter how we feel about it. That's why Filippo is stepping up the pressure for an early marriage, and why we have to work fast, you and I, or our cause will go under. It's terribly important.''

"Franco, this is all so sudden, it's hard for me to come up with an answer. Let me at least think about it for a day or two. I'm going to have to let Nando know my decision to keep my share. Of course," she said a little doubtfully, "he *might* change his mind and let me become involved in some way with the firm."

He flashed a crooked smile at her, one eyebrow lifted. "You really think he might?"

"No," she said honestly, "no, I don't think so. But I feel he should be given the chance to accept me or refuse me as a contributing member of the firm, once he realizes my decision is final."

"I think we both know what his response will be." Franco's tone was dry.

"He really must let me stay," Amy said wistfully "Since I've come here I've realized that heredity, or whatever it is, runs strong in me. Vino d'Oro is more than just a wine to me, more than a new career. I can't explain it, but I know I really want to stay."

"Give this a little thought," Franco suggested realistically. "Why is it fair for the three of them to hold on to their share of the business yet demand that you and I give up ours? The pressure right now is on you, but I've felt it, too. No, we must act, and act now.

"If you join in with Filippo and me, you'll be a full third member of the new majority. Think of the future, Amy! Chiaro is going to be a real sensation. No more crumbs; we'll be handling the reins! Nando isn't a man to bend to the yoke, so he might under the circumstances even sell us his own share."

His eyes shone with excitement. "Sure, he's a fine

vintner, but there are other vintners available if he chooses to bow out. If Aunt Lucia wants to remain at the helm, fine. If not, we'll find someone else. We can't lose, Amy!"

The conversation lapsed as their soup plates were replaced by a pasta course. It was spaghetti, with a simple sauce that tasted of fresh tomatoes and herbs.

"Is food this good all over Italy?" Amy asked, wanting to change the subject.

"Of course not. Veronese cooking is best, of course! But everywhere it is good. We take eating seriously in Italy. Food, wine, love—these three are deserving of our time, our attention. Not necessarily in that order."

Amy was conscious that, as their pasta was replaced by trout, Franco's eyes were often on her—in a slightly disconcerting way. Finally he gave a trace of a smile and said, "There is another possibility, Amy. You are aware that in Europe, despite our swing to modern mores, marriages of convenience still take place to some extent. They say such a union often works out better than a blazing romance. When the passion burns out, as it does in time, two unhappy people are left without a common interest."

Amy darted a sudden swift look at him but didn't speak. There was more to come, she knew.

"Amy," he began again, his voice steady, "there would be a certain advantage to a marriage of convenience between us, you know. You and I."

She stared at him, started to say something, then closed her mouth without uttering a word. She wasn't sure any sound would have come out, she was so stunned.

"Yes," he went on, apparently not concerned with her silence, "it might do very well indeed. You and I can marry, join our shares and present a unified front to our dear cousin Nando." He reached over to capture her hand. "You are a lovely girl, Amy. I would be a good and loving husband to you."

Amy gave him a sudden shrewd look. "And, I presume, *patria potestas* would be observed in the marriage. Could that be what's on your mind?"

He gave a quick grin. "A very acute young woman. But no, my dear, not in our marriage. You are not an Anna Maria."

"And you're not serious, not really!"

"Yes, I am. I know this is sudden, but some marriages take place before the two principal parties have even seen each other. No, my dear, this is not meant for a romantic union, though that could well come later. It is sudden, yes, but time is important now. We both would have much to gain by the marriage. Nando would find it difficult to defeat us."

Amy sat back in her chair, gazing at him. "Of course I won't marry you! I've known you little more than twenty-four hours. And I certainly don't love you. Marriages of convenience may be all very well in a country where people are accustomed to them, but I'm not." She shook her head. "Thanks, but no thanks, Franco. I appreciate the offer, however."

A sudden thought entered her mind. "But, Franco, I don't quite understand. You say Filippo will eventually control Anna Maria's share. And you obviously had no idea that I would be appearing on the scene. So how had you expected to ever get a majority if I hadn't shown up. You would still have just two parts."

"Ah, we wouldn't have got control right away, perhaps, but eventually, yes. Our Nando appears adamant against marriage and so far has managed to escape it, which suits us very well. Surely Filippo and Anna Maria will have children. Aunt Lucia is not young. Someday she will be gone. And her share? Surely not to Nando, unless he marries and has children. So, who better to inherit Aunt Lucia's share than a child of Anna Maria? All in the future, yes, but meantime two shares against two. Then you arrive, and you have the golden share. You can tip the balance our way without our having to wait for Aunt Lucia's."

His eyebrow lifted. "My proposal will remain open should you wish to change your mind. Things may become more complicated than you expect. Nando doesn't accept refusal easily. Or maybe you know that already."

He nodded thoughtfully. "It could become a simple matter of choice, between you and Elisa. We all know that she's after him and the winery. But, just supposing he manages to escape her clutches, then decides he must have your share. If nothing else works—persuasion, veiled threats—marriage might be exactly what he offers you. I said he'll stop at nothing to get what he wants."

The thought of marriage to Nando brought a sudden jolt to Amy's heart, then a runaway beat. It was a reaction she couldn't control. *Remember that con-*

versation you overheard this morning, she cautioned herself harshly. Quickly she looked out over the water so Franco couldn't examine her traitorous eyes.

"And, my sweet cousin, *patria potestas* would most certainly prevail. Marriage with Nando might offer a ring, but not any power. I'm afraid he would consider it more a marriage of necessity."

"Well, I wouldn't say yes to him," she replied a little too vehemently. "I refuse to be anyone's pawn."

Their plates in turn were removed, and tiny strawberries, smaller than Amy's fingernail, appeared. They were different from any she had ever eaten at home. They had a strawberry taste, but one more delicate, more perfumed. And they were served in a Marsala wine.

"I'm running out of superlatives," Amy said, again trying to divert the serious conversation. "It has been a lovely dinner. Do you know what I'd be eating tonight in New York? More than likely salad or an omelet."

"I would promise you a lifetime of strawberries if you consider my proposal," Franco said lightly. "Better than that:

> Bonnie lass, pretty lass,
> Wilt thou be mine?
> Thou shalt not wash dishes
> Nor yet feed the swine.
> Thou shalt sit on a cushion
> And sew a fine seam,
> And thou shalt eat strawberries,
> Sugar and cream."

"Franco," Amy said with a startled laugh. "I can understand your knowing English, you all seem to speak it so well. But how in the world would you know a Mother Goose rhyme?"

"I went to school for a time in England. One is exposed to many facets of English life," he said. "Please do not overlook my qualities as a husband."

Amy still couldn't quite believe he was serious in his casual proposal, even for the reasons he had stated. Again she compared him to Bert. Why was it, she wondered, that the heart refuses stubbornly to go where the mind directs?

But for the moment Franco pressed her no longer. The moon had risen enough to send silver shards dancing across the water. The air, soft with the faintest of breezes, lightly feathered Amy's hair. There was a scent of lemon blossoms in the air.

It was a romantic night, a most romantic setting. Why, she thought rebelliously, was it Nando's face that forced itself into her mind? Why not Franco's? Though Franco had made her this astounding offer of marriage, at least he was honest about it. More so than that arrogant man who aroused emotions at a touch and who lied, lied, lied!

"As long as I'm in the confessional, my dear, I might as well tell you that I introduced Filippo to Anna Maria for a reason. Filippo is a very good friend of mine from Vicenza. He knows the winery business. They could have had a marriage of convenience, too. But...he fell in love with her, and she with him." He gave a wicked grin. "I think Anna Maria knows why I brought them together. She's gentle and sweet, but she's not unintelligent. And she's happy. You've only to see them together to realize that I actually did them a favor."

Then he added, "So you see, Amy, it can work very well, indeed. It could for us."

She sent him a light smile and shook her head.

The waiter appeared with their bill, and Amy and Franco left the restaurant. On the way to the car he gave her a quick probing look. "Problems, Amy? You're frowning."

"No, not really. Well, maybe so. I think I'm reluctant to face Nando tomorrow and tell him he won't get my share. He's not going to be very pleased."

Franco touched her elbow lightly as he opened the car door for her. *"Coraggio! Coraggio!"*

"Coraggio? That's courage, isn't it?" she asked as he slid behind the wheel. When he nodded, she said glumly, "I'll need it. I must say I'm not looking forward to the confrontation."

"Just remember, you can always say yes to me and solve that immediate problem. And once Filippo and Anna Maria are married, we will be in a situation of control."

The moon was almost overhead when they started back down the lake toward home. And it was quite late when they turned onto the twisting road leading up the hill past the castle to the villa.

Franco got out of the car to open the gate. "Giuseppe has gone to bed," he said in a soft voice. They drove almost soundlessly up the driveway, with only a faint scraping of tires as Franco braked to a stop.

Walking up to the house with Amy, he pushed open the front door.

The lights were still burning in the big reception hall, but no one appeared to be about as they made their way up the stairs. Franco saw her to her room, and just as she turned to thank him and say goodnight, he pulled her quickly into his arms, kissing her lightly. Then he drew back, saying, "Good night, sweet Amy. Don't forget what we talked about. It's never too late to change your mind and say yes."

But Amy's eyes weren't on Franco. They were directed over his shoulder down the hall.

Nando was standing not far from them, eyes narrowed, lips compressed. Apparently he'd witnessed that good-night kiss. Had he also heard Franco's last statement?

Amy took a sudden light breath. "Good night, Franco, and thank you for a lovely day and evening. Good night, Nando," she said calmly. Turning the knob, she went into her room without a backward glance.

CHAPTER SEVEN

AMY HAD COMPLIMENTED HERSELF on being so self-assured when she had airily said good-night to Franco and Nando, but morning found her not quite so confident.

Today she was going to have to talk to Nando. Then what? She let her mind go back over last night and that improbable proposal from Franco. He had spoken so lightly, it must have been more or less in jest. But was it? Amy considered that carefully.

There was the undeniable fact that John Delby had been immensely pleased with the success of Vino d'Oro. And everyone was predicting that the new Chiaro would be little less than a sensation. Both Nando and Franco, each in his own way, wanted control of the company, a most successful company whose sales were bound to spiral. It was her own share of the business now that could swing it either way.

Though Franco had at first offered her a full partnership with Filippo and himself, he must not feel secure around her, and Amy honestly couldn't blame her. And marriage, they both realized, would make her a lot less vulnerable to Nando's approach.

Amy slowly finished her morning coffee and rolls,

postponing as long as she could the inevitable encounter. When she felt she could no longer procrastinate, she turned to her wardrobe closet. Businesslike again today or feminine? She looked over her clothes thoughtfully, then drew out a white linen skirt and a simple blue blouse. They seemed to straddle the fence neatly.

Amy did her nails and carefully rearranged the toilet articles in her dressing-table drawer, guiltily realizing that she was still trying to delay going downstairs. Looking at herself in the mirror, she frowned. She'd never thought of herself as a coward, not before. But there were so many troubling facets about saying no to Nando!

Whirling about, she walked firmly out the door and down the hall. She almost expected to see him waiting at the foot of the stairs, but he wasn't there. She felt a sweep of cool relief but knew it was only postponing the meeting.

She peered in the sitting room as she went past. The draperies had been parted to allow in the morning light, but the room was empty. Aunt Lucia's straight chair looked strangely vacant. Amy realized that always before when she entered the room, Aunt Lucia had been sitting there.

Turning, Amy headed for the front door, deciding to go out into the sunshine and perhaps wander down the road toward the castle. Just as she reached for the handle to open the door, it was jerked from her grasp from the outside. Nando stood towering in front of her.

To her surprise, he was smiling as he held out his

hand. "Come out on the terrace and have a cup of coffee with me."

No wonder he was smiling, she thought uncomfortably. He expected John Delby's efforts had no doubt insured the delivery of her share in the winery.

"Of course, Nando. I'd like to talk to you this morning anyway. I'd been planning to." If he had any intimation of what she was going to say, there was no sign in those crystal-gray eyes.

As they sat at the table on the terrace, Nando clapped his hands and a maid appeared. When he spoke to her she nodded and vanished into the side door.

Almost by mutual understanding, the conversation skated carefully around the thin ice of the topic that loomed before them. Yes, indeed, Amy told him, she had enjoyed her trip to Lake Garda. It was beautiful, that extraordinary blue water, and the food at the restaurant was excellent. The words came out easily if a little thinly. Neither of them mentioned the good-night scene at her door the night before.

The coffee came, a white china pot on a silver trivet, and two small white cups. Then the maid bowed and disappeared.

It was coming now; Amy felt it, and knew it could no longer be delayed.

Nando sipped thoughtfully at his coffee, then set the cup down and smiled at her. "Did you enjoy the tour yesterday? Did John give you the information you wanted?"

How assured he was, leaning lazily back in his chair, Amy thought bitterly. He was presuming that

John Delby had swamped her with far too many complicated details.

"I did enjoy it. It was exceedingly interesting. Mr. Delby gave me a very informative description of each step of wine making."

He waited a second before continuing. "I think I was correct, was I not, that it's a very involved process, requiring a considerable amount of knowledge and experience?"

Amy lifted her cup to her lips and took a sip. "Yes, I can see that."

He leaned forward slightly, and she knew he was trying not to let his confidence show. "And I think now you can see why I say it is so impractical for you to consider having anything to do with wine making." He smiled. "So now, Amy, shall we talk about the matter we left unfinished back in New York?"

Obviously he was anxious. She escaped again to her cup of coffee, trying to think how best to answer him.

"Amy," he said, reaching over to take the cup from her hand and put it on the table, "We must talk. I'm not rushing you, you understand. But business affairs can no longer be delayed. When may I count on your delivering to me your share of the winery?"

Damn him! Amy felt a hot flare of anger flash through her. "Never!" she retorted. "I'm going to keep it!" Her tone was a lot more frigid than she'd intended.

The gray eyes narrowed, the mouth perceptibly hardening.

"Keep it? Now, really, don't tell me you are still possessed by that ridiculous idea of becoming a...a vintner." His smile was tight, edged with barely contained frustration.

"Nando, I came here to look over the scene and come to a decision. I now have decided: I am going to retain my share. I definitely do want to learn about wine making, and perhaps even have some part in the process. I don't expect to become a vintner tomorrow or the next day. I would like, however, to start at the bottom, the very beginning, and work my way up through the various procedures." She took a quick breath. "I hope you will allow me to do it," she finished simply, her eyes hopeful.

His silence lasted forever. It was almost as if she hadn't spoken, as if he hadn't heard. Amy, waiting, bit at her lip nervously. Why didn't he say something?

A bee landed on the table, buzzed for a moment, then took off. Amy shifted uncomfortably in her chair. Finally Nando broke the silence. "You are very, very sure this is what you want to do? You are not open to reason, or to an extremely good financial offer?" The expression on his chill unrevealing face didn't alter.

"This is what I want to do," she said steadily.

She could almost see the wheels turning in his mind. A strange fleeting expression passed across his eyes. *He's come to some decision,* she thought uneasily.

Then, surprisingly, he gave a slow reluctant smile. "Amy, my dear, you are a very headstrong woman.

But if this is what you want, what you are certain you want, then I suppose all I can do is agree. With a considerable qualm, yes, for you don't know what you are letting yourself in for. But...." He shrugged, then held out his hand. "All right, Amy Converse, welcome to the firm!"

For a second or two Amy wasn't able to realize she had been accepted. Uneasily she slid her hand into his, searching his face. Did he mean it?

He seemed to. Perhaps she had been misled by Nando's persistence, she thought. He might push, squeeze, try to buy her out. But when he was defeated and knew it, perhaps he could accept the fact graciously.

Perhaps. Amy wished she felt more confident about that.

Nando pulled a notebook from his pocket. "We might as well make plans," he said. "I'll see to the necessary arrangements. If you will appear at the winery...let me see...." He scrutinized a small pocket calendar. "All right, why not? Can you be ready to start tomorrow, Monday morning, at eight o'clock? That may be a little early for you, but it's the time everyone else starts. Signore Calabro will take you under his wing from there on." He lifted cool eyes. "Agreed?"

She nodded. "I appreciate this very much, Nando, knowing you really didn't want me to do it."

Nando flashed a rueful look at her. "I must admit that I still don't. I think you are being very foolish. But, let us say, I know when I'm defeated. And, from a very different angle, maybe I'm not quite as downcast as you would expect. Because this means you will be here with us for some time to come.''

Amy picked up her cup with a not too steady hand. Was his capitulation too abrupt? She couldn't quite erase a faint uneasy itching at the back of her mind.

Nando gave her a scrutinizing glance. "All right, Amy, stop worrying. I sense your distrust, and I can't say I blame you. I tried every way I could—that I'm not exactly proud of—to win your share. I failed and that's all over. Let's start anew. Friends?" He lifted his dark eyebrows.

Amy searched his face cautiously. "Well, okay," she said, then added almost hesitantly, "you really mean it, that I can start on Monday?" She wanted not only to reassure herself, but also to underline his promise to her.

"I'll tell Signore Calabro myself. I warn you, you won't find it the easiest work. But if you insist on learning by doing, perhaps it's best to begin under his direction. You will be starting out the way all our new people do, the way I learned myself."

His voice grew serious. "There will be no special treatment, no extra privileges, just because you're a member of the family. Still—" he looked uncertain "—perhaps as a young woman, you would prefer not—"

Amy shook her head. "I want to do it. Please don't think a woman can't learn on the job!"

"Very well, then that's decided. Tomorrow you become a working woman. Now, how about taking the rest of the day off? Let me show you a pleasant lake where we can swim and have a picnic lunch." He flashed her his heart-stopping smile. "It's your final day of vacation. Tomorrow you join the wage slaves. Which reminds me, you will be paid at the same rate as the other employees, but as a part owner you will also share in the profits."

Amy ventured a slow smile. It all sounded more believable now, after the first shock of his surrender. However, she was still not completely certain about Nando. She had seen too many variations of his character, the charmer, the amorous opportunist.... Was this at last the authentic Nando? A man not pleased with defeat but able to be relatively gracious about it? She wanted very much to believe it.

"I won't expect any special privileges at work, Nando. And, yes, I'd love to go swimming. Lake Garda?" she asked hopefully.

He shook his head. "No, as a matter of fact it's a private lake near one of our vineyards. I'll have Maria in the kitchen prepare us a lunch of sorts. Shall we leave in—" he glanced down at his wristwatch "—say, an hour? I want to run down to the winery first, but I'll be back shortly."

He stood up. "All right, junior member of the firm, let's make this a memorable day. Your last day of freedom!"

Amy shoved back her coffee cup and got to her feet, as well. "Nando, you're making it sound as if I'm going to be working in some kind of a sweatshop." She gave an unexpectedly happy laugh. Everything seemed to be working out at last.

He shook his head. "You may think so before you're through."

But she couldn't be discouraged by what must be his final oblique effort to sway her away from her decision.

While Nando was busy at the winery, Amy slipped up to her room, put her bathing suit, a towel and some suntan lotion in a beach bag and went down the stairs to wait for him.

Franco was just crossing the reception hall. As he saw her, he came over to the foot of the steps.

"You look cheerful this morning, Amy. I gather you haven't had your confrontation with Nando yet."

"Oh, Franco, but I have."

"And . . . ?" He regarded her sharply.

"He didn't mind!" Amy stopped and shook her head. "No, that's not exactly true. I'm certain he did mind, but when he realized how I felt about my share, he was rather nice about it. He agreed to let me learn the trade."

"Somehow that doesn't sound like Cousin Nando to me. Not at all." He scowled, thrusting his hands into the pockets of his gray jacket. "Was this in return for your handing over your share?"

"No. Once he realized that I was going to stay, that I was going to keep my part of the business, he didn't even mention it."

Franco took a short impatient breath. "I don't like it," he said sharply. "I don't like it for several reasons. Nando simply doesn't take defeat that easily; it isn't in his nature. And I must admit I don't like your going over to the enemy, so to speak. We need you on our side, Filippo and I."

There was that, but Amy now couldn't very well join them against Nando, not after he had given her the opportunity she had wanted so much.

She reached out her hand to touch him gently on the arm. "I think it will all work out, Franco. I'm not signing my share away. I'll still have it."

Franco gave her a flat look. "I wonder just how long you'll hold out."

"I—" she began, but the door opened and Nando came striding in.

"Ready?" he asked, eyeing the beach bag in her hand. "The lunch is in the car. Hello, Franco. It's my turn with our cousin. We're off to Lago di Verde. *Ciao!*" There was no invitation for Franco to join them.

"Coming?" Nando turned to Amy and reached for her bag. "Let's take advantage of a beautiful day."

She hesitated. "Shouldn't we tell Aunt Lucia?"

He shook his head. "I ran across Anna Maria and Filippo. They'll pass along the word. See you later, Franco."

As Nando drove past the winery, Amy was a little surprised to hear the rolling sound of the crusher working away on Sunday. She said as much to Nando.

"Grapes don't wait on the day. Twenty-four hours too long on the vine—" he shrugged "—spell disaster."

Amy gazed into the courtyard as they sped past. "What will be my first job tomorrow?"

"Whatever Signore Calabro has planned for the other beginners." His voice was a little terse.

Amy turned her head to look at him. She wished she could rid herself entirely of that small dark shadow of doubt that kept trying to crowd out her light mood.

They had driven only a half dozen miles on the highway when Nando turned the car onto a twisting country road. "We need more grapes than grow in the immediate area," he explained. "We could buy grapes from other growers, of course, but we prefer to keep tight control on quality and type. The new Chiaro comes from grapes grown here at Lago di Verde."

They approached a small village, and a dog ran out of one of the houses to bark at them. Several of the homes had lean-tos where chickens pecked and scratched.

Another turn in the road brought them to the center of town. Nando braked sharply, screeching to an abrupt stop, for a long string of people was crossing the street directly in front of the car. It was a religious procession.

Amy watched as a double row of darkly clad men marched solemnly past, carrying church banners on long poles. Small boys, stiff and self-conscious in what were so clearly their Sunday suits, were followed by twin rows of girls, dressed all in white like miniature brides.

"First Communion Day," Nando murmured.

Behind the children came a group of nuns in long black robes, some clutching prayer books and rosary beads. Bringing up the end of the line were uneven rows of women, veils and scarves draped modestly over heads and shoulders.

The entire procession moved silently and slowly past the car. While they waited, Nando's hand reached across to capture Amy's. She almost instinctively tried to withdraw hers, but he held it tightly, then lifted it to his lips.

His touch, she thought guiltily, was no less disturbing, no less pleasurable than before. Should she still rally her emotional defenses? The situation was more or less changed now. She was going to work in the winery, with Nando's permission if not his blessing. He had not mentioned her share; if he should, she could rearm herself then.

The procession passed the small tobacco store, the butcher shops, the bakery, circling the fountain in the piazza to trudge up the steps of the ancient church. Its tall tower, pockmarked with age, echoed with the steady bonging of bells.

"We have First Communion in the States, too," Amy said, "but I've never seen a procession like this through the town before."

"It's the custom for funerals, too. Family and friends walk behind the *carro funebre*, what you term a hearse. And if it's a prominent person who has died, half the town will follow the mourners through the streets."

Amy watched as the last straggler mounted the steps to the church and vanished inside. Nando released her hand, started the car and drove around the circle of the piazza, to exit out of town.

Before long Amy began to notice familiar rows of terraced vineyards. "Yours?" she asked, nodding toward the grapevines. She hesitated the least part of a second, then amended almost shyly, "I mean, ours?"

Those gray eyes turned toward her. "Yes," he said quietly, "yes, indeed. Ours."

Amy felt a ridiculous leap of her heart at the tone of his voice. *Don't,* warned a voice inside her. But she ignored it.

Up through the vineyards the road wound, until they pulled up beside a grassy bank, beyond which stretched a lovely lake.

Nando waved his hand. "Lago di Verde, an appropriate name for a green lake, no? And this, too, is ours, Amy." He smiled at her. Hoisting the basket out of the back of the car, he went over and set it down at the base of a poplar tree. "Why don't we have a swim first, then lunch?"

Amy glanced around and, seeing two small cabanas, nodded. "Let's! It sounds wonderful."

Taking her beach bag, she slipped inside one of the cabanas. As she undressed she gave her new bathing suit a faintly doubtful look. She'd bought it impulsively one day on a noon-hour shopping spree.

"It's too daring," she had said uncertainly at Linda's encouragement.

"Amy," Linda lectured firmly, "you are only young once. Ten years from now you might not get away with it. Now, with a figure like yours, you can. Go ahead!"

Spurred on by her friend she had recklessly bought the suit—the merest excuse of a green bra and a bottom that was not much more than two green triangles that tied at the sides. She wished now that she had reconsidered and bought something just a little more conservative. Well, she hadn't, so there was nothing to do but put it on. After all, some of her friends had suits equally revealing.

Amy stepped out into the sunshine, the grass soft and moist under her bare feet. Bending over, she slipped on a pair of thongs, and was just straightening up as Nando came out of his cabana. He stopped abruptly, his eyes narrowing appreciatively.

For a moment Amy couldn't take her eyes off him, either. His bronzed chest gleamed through the mat of crisp black hair; his stomach was hard and flat. He wasn't wearing boxer trunks, but instead a black jersey suit that was less abbreviated than jockey shorts and clung snugly to that muscular body. His masculinity was not at all obscured. Amy looked away quickly, industriously pulling on her bathing cap.

"My God, you're stunning!" he said thickly. Then silently he took her hand and together they walked across the expanse of grass to the edge of the water.

"All at once, or little by little?" he asked with a grin.

"Let's plunge in! I can't stand freezing by degrees," she laughed up at him, suddenly deliciously happy.

"You won't freeze here. The sun keeps the water pleasant at this time of year." He released her hand. "All right, let's go!"

They hit the water together in long shallow dives, emerging at almost the same second, their faces beaded with water. Then they swam side by side.

Amy found it exhilarating. Suddenly everything was all right—no, better than all right.

Eventually they turned around, almost by common consent, and started swimming back toward shore. Then, abruptly, Nando was no longer beside her. He had submerged, only to come up beneath her. Wrapping his arms around her, he half carried her in to shore, until she found she could stand on the bottom.

She was conscious of the wiry hair on his chest pressing against her skin as he pulled her close. She didn't protest as his mouth came down on hers, their lips wet from the lake water. Then, just as abruptly he lifted his head, holding her near him for a second or two longer before saying, "Maybe we had better have our lunch now... while we can keep our mind on it."

Amy was bemused. This was not the Nando she had known and distrusted. That Nando would have fiercely mastered her lips, demanding, deliberately arousing. Deceiving. But, Amy realized, that Nando had stirred only her emotions, her body. This one was stirring her heart.

The smile she turned up at him trembled ever so slightly.

"Let's eat," she said as he grasped her hand, leading her out of the water. "I'm starved!"

Nando spread out a blanket he took from the car, then brought over the basket. "Let's see what Maria has made for us."

It turned out to be a feast. Crisp rolls were filled with shavings of rosy Parma ham and slivers of cheese. There were even some tiny birds roasted to a golden hue.

Amy gazed at them hesitantly. "Those don't exactly look like regular poultry. More like hummingbirds, maybe, or doves."

"Try one," he invited.

She picked one up almost reluctantly and bit into it. It had a wonderful roasted taste, smoky with a hint of herbs. "It's delicious! But what is it?" she asked curiously.

"Larks," he said.

Again she glanced down at the small golden shapes. How could she possibly eat a lark and not feel like a cannibal? This time she picked up one of the small rolls.

Nando was pouring wine into a pair of delicate crystal goblets, and Amy exclaimed in surprise, "You astound me! On a picnic? We would have used paper cups at home."

He gave a wry smile. "Wine in paper cups? Savages!"

The warm sun, the food, the wine, followed by fruit and cheese, made Amy feel drowsy. She was not yet used to dining so heavily at noontime. The most she usually had while working was a sandwich, a cup of coffee and some fruit.

Almost languidly they gathered up the remains of the luncheon and put it back in the basket. "We shouldn't go in the water this soon after eating," Nando said. "Shall we stroll around the lake for a while?"

Amy nodded, feeling contented and lazy. As they walked along under the trees and out into the sunshine again, she marveled at how different the new

Nando was. Never once did he make one of his old blatant gestures toward her. Never once did he mention her share, or, for that matter, the winery.

He seemed perfectly at ease, too—charming and amusing, with no trace of the conniving adversary. Maybe they had passed the milestone....

Later, when they again ran hand in hand toward the lake, they found the water still deliciously warm. This time they swam out to a raft anchored some distance from shore and climbed aboard for several minutes before plunging back into the water. Nando was a powerful swimmer, Amy recognized. But he tailored his strokes to hers so that he wouldn't pull ahead.

Reaching shore, Amy wiped the water from her face and shoulders with the palm of her hand, then picked up a towel to rub at her hair. Finally she sank down on the blanket to let herself dry in the sun. Nando, his dark hair damp and curling and his broad bronze shoulders glistening, stretched out beside her.

A silence fell between them, a silence lasting so long that Amy turned her head toward Nando. His gray eyes, she discovered, were gazing at her with an expression that sent her nerve ends tingling in spite of herself.

Slowly he raised himself up on one elbow. "Friends, now, Amy? Starting over, yes?" Lifting a tanned hand, he traced the curve of her cheek with his finger. Amy was unable to stop the delicious tremor that raced through her body as she looked up at him.

"Okay, friends," she said, her voice not quite steady.

"*Cara, carissima*, you intoxicate me!" His voice was low and husky as he bent to press his lips gently against the pulse at the base of her throat. She knew he couldn't help but feel the wild betraying beat of her heart.

Slowly Nando lifted his head, his eyes meeting hers again for an instant before he let his lips trace intricate arousing patterns around her ears, along the curve of her cheek, her chin. He didn't touch her mouth but circled distractingly near it.

Gently he drew her closer to him until her body melded against his. She was intensely conscious of the stirring maleness, of his hardening muscles, the warmth of his bare skin.

"*Cara,* Amy, love," he whispered against her cheek, her hair. One hand slipped under her hip, pulling her even nearer. She caught her breath as she belatedly struggled to control the sweet hot flame that was spreading through her.

Amy's hands gave one futile push against his chest. Then her emotions began flooding her mind, her will. The nervous inner voice was smothered by the touch of his hands, by his pulsing male body.

Firmly he moved her hands aside and lowered his face until his lips covered hers. Then, as her mouth weakly submitted to his, his kiss became insistent, demanding. His exploring tongue excited her relentlessly, until she found herself responding to him with such throbbing eagerness that she lost all sense of time and place.

Amy was conscious only of the fact that she never wanted that disturbing searching mouth to leave hers. All her resistance was being drained in a whirl of emotions, leaving her completely vulnerable.

And however much she had tried to deny it to herself before, she knew now that she loved this man deeply and totally. Every doubt was swept away in this dizzying realization.

One of his hands moved down the slope of her neck to linger at her shoulder, before he pulled at the tie of her bikini halter and slipped it down to bare her breasts. His hand closed over one fleshy mound, then lingeringly moved to the other, catching each nipple gently between his fingers until it grew pointed and erect.

She tried to wrest her mouth from his to whisper raggedly, "No, Nando, no!" But he merely held her more firmly to him, his lips silencing her mouth. Inviting, then demanding, his strong virile body began to undulate slightly against her.

Then, a trail of hot fire, his lips slipped down her neck to the hollow between her breasts and lingered tantalizingly over her wildly pulsing heart. She felt his hand close around one breast, gently cupping it while his mouth sought and found the other one. His tongue trailed seductive patterns around the hardened nipple.

For one last time Amy tried to resist. Then she was lost, her treacherous body surrendering to a passion she could no longer control. Her hands went around him, sliding sensually down the smooth skin of his warm back, holding him close against her.

Once again he sought her lips, sweeping her along irrevocably as he murmured between kisses, "You are mine, *cara*, all of you. Don't deny me now, I must have you. Now, *now!*"

His body, pressing against hers, ignited fires that made her arch to meet and join the motion of his lean muscular hips. Her hands, pressing against the small of his back, tightened. She could no longer resist the surging invitation of his hard pulsing maleness. She was conscious of the fierce pounding of his heart.

Nando's hand slid down her body, exploring and caressing as it went. For a breathless moment it stopped to untie the strings that held the bottom of her bikini together, leaving her naked to the warm dappled sunlight.

Then his palm moved over her, gently intimate, and he once again withdrew his mouth from hers, his gray eyes smoldering. "Say that you want me, too, *cara*. Tell me you want me to take you. Now. Here."

She was lost, her whole body aching with sweet desire. "Yes, Nando, yes," she whispered brokenly, her eyes melting into his.

"Say it! Say, 'take me, Nando. Now. Please, I want you!' " he murmured, his lips again kissing her breasts, his tongue teasing the nipples with erotic torment.

Amy was past all thinking. All she knew was love for him, and desire. "Take me, Nando, now... please," she managed through uneven breaths. "I...I want you—"

Abruptly his exploring hand jerked away, and his intimate movements halted. He rolled to his side.

She opened bewildered eyes, only to meet his cold arrogant gaze. Nando got to his feet calmly and stood looking down at her with cynical amusement.

"There you are, my dear Amy! An object lesson for a tease. And how easy it was! You were there for the taking—if I wanted you. Your friend was foolish that night in New York. If he had approached you differently he could have had you, as I could have had you now. You see, a man can be a tease, too. How do you like being on the receiving end for a change?"

For a moment Amy was too stunned to think. His words whirled around in her mind, only gradually reaching her consciousness. She lay unmoving, her body throbbing, and she made no effort to cover herself. It was as if he had ground his heel on her heart.

She watched numbly as he gave her a twisted smile. "You had it coming!" Then, turning to stride away, he called back over his shoulder, "Get up and put your clothes on. I'm going to take you back to the villa as quickly as I can."

For a long, long moment she lay still. Then, out of her shock and bitterness, a realization emerged. For whatever reason he had done this, she knew one thing. When that long sinewy body had pressed itself so closely against hers, he had not been able entirely to control his own emotions, either.

CHAPTER EIGHT

AMY'S HANDS WERE SHAKING so badly she had a difficult time buttoning her blouse. Eyes blinded with tears, she stuffed her bikini into her beach bag, which she zipped closed.

She found it hard to breathe past the hard knot inside her chest. To think she had. . . had invited him to make love to her! Her hands tightened around her bag and she stared unseeingly at the closed door of the cabana. She felt crushed. Humiliated and sickened. But over all she felt a hot sweep of anger growing within her.

How dare he! She bit down on her lip, then suddenly she lifted her head, firming her chin. She had to go out that door, get into the car with him and endure the drive home. There was no other choice. There was no one else around, and even if there was she didn't know enough Italian to ask someone to take her there. She would have to face Nando sooner or later anyway. Might as well do it now.

Numbly she opened the door and walked across the grass toward the car. Nando was waiting there for her, his eyes fixed on the distant hills, those lean tanned fingers tapping impatiently on the wheel. He didn't move to open the door, but let her slip onto the seat without even turning his arrogant head.

Then he turned on the motor and stepped hard on the accelerator, almost spinning the wheels as the car raced out onto the road.

Amy knew her cheeks were flaming. She could feel their heat. She bit her lip to keep it steady, and her hands gripped in tight knots. She sat stiffly, as far over on her side of the car as she could get, and stared blindly out at the scenery.

Gradually her mind, edging past the shock, began unloosening to the point where she could begin to reason. Why had he done this to her? Why? Amy groped for an answer. Why would he try to pay her back for what he had presumed she had done to Craig? Somehow it didn't make sense. Franco had said that Elisa Antolini constantly tempted and teased Nando. Was that fact somehow in back of his insolent action?

And why had he pretended friendship, affection, then passion? Surely not just to balance the scales for her supposed treatment of Craig and, indirectly, Elisa's behavior. No, there had to be a deeper reason....

He had offered her the chance to work in the winery. But how could she do that now—go to work every day, stay on at the villa—knowing what he thought of her, seeing that contempt in his eyes? She could not. There was nothing left for her but to thank Aunt Lucia for her hospitality and go back to New York. Back to some nine-to-five desk job.

Something tugged at the edge of Amy's mind and she forced herself to concentrate. What was it that he hoped to reap out of the sordid little drama he'd just staged?

She slid a quick sideways look at that stern profile, as if she might find some answer there. All she managed was to bring on another sickening wave of humiliation. Over the aching lump in her throat she turned again to her thoughts. Now she would gladly sell her share, she decided. She never wanted to hear of Vino d'Oro again. . . .

Her share! Her eyes flew open wide. That was what he had wanted all along! Of course! His former romantic enticements hadn't induced her to turn it over to him. Would this latest fiasco work where seduction had failed?

A spark kindled in her green eyes and she lowered her lashes, almost as if she were afraid he might be able to read her mind. He had managed to lure her out from behind her defenses, her distrust, in order to insult and humiliate her. Under the circumstances she would naturally feel she couldn't possibly stay on. To do so would create an almost intolerable situation in the household.

Wasn't that what he was counting on? Underneath his righteous silence Nando must be feeling satisfied that he had finally won.

Nothing else really made sense. Her share in the winery did. "I'd do anything to get it, anything!" Wasn't that what he'd said?

And that generous unexpected offer to allow her to learn wine making—neatly intended to lower her defenses so she would be susceptible to today's sordid insult. That was exactly what it had accomplished.

Why hadn't she suspected his motives when he had been so gracious in defeat? Just a little too gracious, she conceded bitterly. She should have paid attention to Franco's warning.

Well, Nando's carefully orchestrated game plan wasn't going to work! Despite everything he devised, now or in the future, she wasn't going to fall for it.

The breeze caused by the speeding car cooled Amy's burning cheeks even though she nursed her anger and the memory of her painful humiliation all the way back to the villa. When they arrived, Amy picked up her beach bag and reached for the door handle.

As she stepped gracefully out of the car, she stated coolly, "Thanks for the...enlightening afternoon. I will report to the winery at eight o'clock tomorrow morning." She didn't wait to see his reaction but walked briskly up to the front door. To her relief no one was in the reception area, so she hurried up the stairs. She was in no mood to carry on a casual conversation at the moment—not with anyone.

Once in her room she furiously yanked off her clothes, grabbed a towel and headed for the shower, almost as if the water could help wash away the shameful incident at the lake.

But as she foamed soapsuds over her shoulders, her breasts, she was stricken with the memory of other hands, Nando's hands. Under the cool spray of the water, she felt her face once again flaming.

How could she have been such a fool! How could she have been such a willing, even eager participant? And thinking she loved him! Her hand, grasping the bar of soap, was suddenly still. Was it that mad rush of emotion that had prompted her to think that? Quickly she thrust away the unwelcome possibility.

Today's episode was past now, she reminded herself vehemently. It would bother her only if she allowed it to. Instead she would go ahead with her plan to learn about wine making. If she were somehow prevented from doing so here, if Nando Bonavia withdrew his offer, then she would go ahead with it elsewhere—even, if necessary, in the States.

There wasn't the slightest doubt in her mind that this was what she really wanted. One of her ancestors had chosen wine making as his profession. It was what she wanted to do, too. The fact that she was a woman shouldn't change anything. The hot sun on the grapes, their delicious scent when they were crushed, even the grinding of the machinery in the winery stirred something deep inside her.

After she toweled herself dry, Amy slipped into a robe and stretched out on the bed. For a long time she lay staring up at the white-and-gold ceiling above her. But eventually, drowsiness closed her eyes for a moment, then drew her into a troubled sleep.

The sun had begun to set, sending dull golden light filtering through the half-closed shutters when she awoke. Amy glanced at the clock on her dresser, realizing the tea hour was approaching.

Should she go down and encounter...what? Was Aunt Lucia aware of or involved in this latest unsuccessful debacle? Had she given her blessing to whatever Nando had in mind, no matter how despicable it was?

Tossing back the light sheet that had covered her, Amy swung her feet around to the floor. She certainly wasn't going to stay in her room, cringing like a frightened mouse!

Marching firmly over to the wardrobe, she took out a soft wisteria-shaded frock. If she was going to face her oppressors, she would do so with banners flying.

Fumbling in the bottom of the wardrobe, she pulled out a pair of violet linen pumps. She couldn't remember when she had last dressed with such care. This was not to impress Nando, his mother or anyone else. This was the way some queens would have gone to their beheading, dressed with exquisite care in defiance of their executioners.

The touch of lipstick she applied blended soft pink with an undertone of lilac. After putting on a hint of eye shadow, Amy brushed her hair until it fell like a soft curtain of gold. She caught a glimpse of her intent face in the mirror and reluctantly smiled. She was girding for battle like a knight going to the wars rather than like a gentle queen going to her execution. She was going to show Nando that she didn't give a damn, that it would take someone stronger, and wilier than him to defeat her.

She left her room and had reached the bottom of the stairs when she met Anna Maria. The girl halted, giving Amy a frankly admiring glance. "Now if I looked like you instead of like the Bonavias, I'd be so happy!" Then she shrugged, giving a wry grin. "However, Filippo says he loves me, so I'm happy anyway." In a sudden burst of confidence she added,

"I adore him, you know. I can't believe my luck, he's such a darling!"

Amy smiled in understanding. Anna Maria was fortunate to be so in love, and to be loved in return. "Yes, he's certainly handsome, Anna Maria, and very nice indeed."

The girl nodded contentedly. "He is. I'm so blissful I can hardly bear it." She gave a sudden sly look at Amy. "And how are things between you and Nando? I'll be truthful—I'd love to see a romance blossom between you two. I can't bear the thought of that conniving Elisa Antolini prowling around after him. You might be the very woman who could change his mind about marriage."

Amy was glad they were approaching the drawing room and that she didn't have time to answer her cousin.

Signora Bonavia was sitting in her usual chair, a fragile china teacup in her hand. She greeted Amy with a polite nod of the head and a few murmured words, then lifted the cup to her lips. Anna Maria began chatting about plans for her wedding, so Amy had a moment of respite.

Then Franco came sauntering in, his eyes raking the room until he spotted Amy. After greeting the two other women he came over to sit by her.

"And how was your day at the lake?" he asked cheerfully. "Beautiful place, isn't it?"

"Yes," she said tightly, trying to keep her voice casual, "it is indeed."

Her success was minimal, for he gave her a quick shrewd look. Lowering his voice, he said, "Is Nando still agreeable about your taking part in the operation of the winery? I must admit I'm still rather surprised that he capitulated so promptly.''

Amy, reluctant to make eye contact with this perceptive man, merely said, ''Well, yes. He hasn't said anything about changing his mind.'' That much was true.

There was a pause before Franco said slowly, ''Amy, what's the matter? You look as if you were chewing on glass. You're all edges—sharp edges. Did something happen?''

She shook her head. ''If you mean, has he gone back on his word, no.'' Almost desperately she searched for a way to change the subject. She was almost relieved when Nando came striding in, his offhand greeting to those in the room not quite hiding the grim set of his mouth, those deep temper lines.

''Oh, no!'' Franco said softly. ''Storm warnings out! I know this mood. It can't be in any way connected with yesterday's tour. That was a glorious triumph.'' He turned a mocking, accusing gaze on Amy. ''So it has to be you, little cousin. What have you done to our temperamental Nando?''

''Me?'' she prickled. ''Nothing!'' Her answer, she realized, was just a little too quick, a little too vehement.

Franco wasn't deceived. ''Well, well. I might suggest, dear Amy, that you reconsider my invitation of last night. Perhaps both invitations. You can see what dealing with Nando could mean, considering his mercurial temper.'' In his normal tone he added, ''Wine, cousin?'' He lifted the carafe from a nearby table.

Amy shook her head, then reconsidered. "Yes, please," she amended. Everything as usual. No change. She couldn't allow Nando to see that she was in any way intimidated by what had happened.

"Amy, you will promise that you'll be my attendant, won't you, when Filippo and I marry next month?" Anna Maria's eyes were shining.

"Perhaps Amy has other plans," Aunt Lucia said briskly. "One must not presume on relatives to be constantly at one's disposal."

"Oh, but this is so important. I want her at my wedding. So you will be my attendant, won't you, Amy? It's just a short month away. You're not going to change your mind and do something silly like leave before then?" the girl said pleadingly.

"No, indeed, I'm not leaving. As a matter of fact, I'm starting to work tomorrow at the winery," Amy stated calmly.

There was a sudden silence, a total absence of sound and movement. Amy fastened her eyes firmly on the glass of wine that Franco had brought her.

The silence was shattered by a sniff from Aunt Lucia. "Is this so, Nando?" she asked, her voice thin and frigid. For the first time, however, she sounded a bit uncertain. "Surely it's no work for a young woman."

"Yes. It's decided." Nando's voice was dry. He wasn't doing well in hiding his feelings, Amy thought with some satisfaction. The score was a little more even now. He hadn't expected her to stay, and he didn't like it.

Anna Maria gazed at Amy, openmouthed. "Really? What are you planning to do? Secretarial work? Promotion?"

"She is going to start as anyone starts, the way I learned," Nando stated, turning to pour himself some wine.

"She's a young woman, don't forget, not a man," Aunt Lucia began hesitantly. "Perhaps it would be better—"

Nando fixed an unwavering gaze on Amy. "You did say you wanted it that way, didn't you? To learn the way we all have, beginning with fundamentals?"

She nodded, green eyes meeting gray ones unflinchingly. "Yes, I did."

"You heard her decision," Nando stated to the room at large, turning away with a shrug.

Immediately Anna Maria spoke up. "That's not fair! She doesn't know how hard it is! It's not at all pleasant, Amy. It's hard work, really it is."

"It won't be anything she can't handle if she wants to badly enough," Nando replied curtly, sharply adding a sentence in Italian that Amy didn't understand.

Anna Maria tightened her lips into a straight line, but she only shook her head and shrugged.

Franco himself gave Amy a strange look but said nothing. The conversation turned to yesterday's tour.

"Yes," Nando was saying, "our visitors were all impressed with the winery and the wine, especially our Chiaro." He gave a brittle smile. "The Japanese suggested we trade some for *sake*." It was obviously intended as humor, but it sounded forced.

Somehow Amy managed to drag herself through the rest of the evening. There was no further mention about her work in the winery. It was clearly too touchy a subject, one that none of them seemed to want to open up again.

Amy was aware of the way Nando's eyes coldly avoided her. The few words he directed to her by necessity were distant and formal, his manner forbidding. It created an uncomfortable strain among the rest of them and Amy began having a very uneasy feeling about tomorrow.

When she finally felt she could excuse herself to retire for the night, Franco got to his feet, as well. He would have accompanied her to the door, obviously wanting to have a few private words with her, but Nando strode decisively across the room. Taking Amy's elbow with a cold proprietary grip, he said, "I'll be right back after I see our cousin to her room."

Amy cringed within herself, every nerve pulling tight. She didn't want him to go with her; she didn't want to be alone with him! Yet there was little she could do about it that wouldn't seem childish and impolite.

Not a single word was spoken between them as they went up the stairs and down the hall. When they reached her door Amy felt for the knob, saying, "Good night, Nando," in a carefully expressionless voice.

"Just a minute!" he ordered sharply. "I have something to say to you. I want to remind you again that you are not to expect any special treatment from

Signore Calabro. You certainly aren't going to get any! You are going to be given a chance, but it will be your only chance!''

Amy unwaveringly faced those dark scowling brows, the hard mouth, but she made no response as the cold angry voice swept on. "If you find the job isn't what you were so eager for, or that the work is more than you can handle, then I'll expect you to give up this ridiculous idea. You will surrender your share to the proper owners under the original offer and return to New York as soon as it can be arranged.''

Turning sharply, he strode off down the hall, his footsteps harsh on the marble floor.

Amy opened her door, closed it behind her, then sagged against it. The whole thing was turning out to be a Pandora's box. She wanted to work in the winery, and she was finally going to have the opportunity. But Nando, damn him, was not going to give up the fight. He'd be waiting, watching, hoping she'd fail. Even now he might be planning to make certain she would fail, Amy reflected warily.

She could, of course, go over to Franco's side to protect her share and her rights—join him, and eventually Filippo, in a concerted power play. But she didn't want that either, not now. She had something to prove to herself and, in a way, to the rest. There was but one way to do it.

She pushed herself away from the door and slowly prepared for bed, setting the alarm clock for an early hour. When the lights were off and she lay back on her pillow, all the turbulent events of the afternoon came creeping out again, taking over her thoughts. The shock, the humiliation rushed over her again, but so did the inflaming touch of Nando's hands, his mouth....

Amy stared up into the darkness, her eyes stinging. For there was one more emotion that had to be faced—her love for him.

How could she feel this way, after his cruel actions? She would just have to learn to hate him again! It shouldn't be hard. But how, she wondered, did one actually go about falling out of love? She tossed restlessly, knowing this was no time for thinking. She should be asleep, for tomorrow wasn't that far off and she would need all her energy.

But the memory of his lips, that hard eager body, followed her into her tumultuous dreams, and in her dreams she did not deny him.

AMY AWAKENED to the insistent ringing of the alarm clock and fumbled sleepily to shut it off. She lay for a moment, her dream still disturbingly fresh in her mind. Then she thrust herself upright, her cheeks burning at the memory. She moved one foot searchingly across the floor, feeling for her slippers, then padded to the bathroom to prepare for work.

Moments later she was gazing speculatively at her wardrobe, trying to decide what to wear. Both Aunt Lucia and Anna Maria had hinted that it wasn't going to be easy work, but the clothes Amy had brought on the trip seemed too much like vacation wear, which, of course, they were.

Finally she unfolded a pair of jeans, hesitated,

then slipped them on. Designer jeans at that, she thought, and they'd cost a lot more than she cared to remember. But she had nothing else that was even remotely worklike. She chose a plain white T-shirt and pulled on a pair of tennis shoes.

There was a light knock at the door, and her coffee and rolls arrived. The young maid who brought them bobbed her head, saying, *"Momento, signorina,"* and ducked back outside the door to return with a neatly tied white box. Handing it to Amy, she gave a shy self-conscious smile. "Iss launch!" she pronounced carefully, obviously having memorized the brief English phrase to explain what she had brought.

"Grazie," Amy thanked her. After the girl vanished, she eyed the box thoughtfully. Someone had ordered lunch for her; the early breakfast, too. Of course she wouldn't be expected to return to the villa for a leisurely meal at midday. No special privileges, Nando had warned.

She finished her coffee and rolls with one eye on the clock. Twenty minutes later she was slipping quietly down the stairs in the still-silent house, out the front door and across the terrace. To her relief she met no one except a gardener, digging on his hands and knees in a flower bed. As she passed he lifted his head and touched a finger to his worn felt hat in a polite salute.

As Amy went through the gate and started down the road toward the castle, a feeling of excited anticipation began bubbling up inside her. She had won; so far she had bested Nando in his dogged reluctance to let her learn. Hard work? Yes, it might well be, but if others had learned the rudiments of wine making, then so could she.

The gate to the castle courtyard was wide open, and trucks laden with grapes were pulling up to the far end where the conveyor and crusher were located. Amy stopped just inside the gate and looked around her. Just where was this Signore Calabro? She bit her lip, then, seeing a man leaning against a truck with a cigarette hanging out of the corner of his mouth, she hurried over to him. Only belatedly did she realize she couldn't question him in Italian.

"Calabro?" she began uncertainly. "Mr . . . Signore Calabro?"

The man, his soiled leather cap pushed back on dark oily hair, took the cigarette from his mouth and with it gestured toward the far corner of the castle. "Calabro? *Là!*" Another pointing gesture. *"Là!"*

"Grazie," Amy stammered, flushing when the truck driver gave a low wolf whistle as she walked away in the direction he had indicated.

As she reached the corner she saw four men standing with their backs to her. One man was gesturing as he talked, the others nodding.

"Uh . . . Signore Calabro?" Amy raised her voice slightly as she approached.

One man who had been gesturing looked up. He was short, squat, with a leonine head of white wiry hair. A Roman nose dominated the swarthy face, which held eyes as dark as coal.

He gave her a quick appraising glance, and an odd expression filtered across his face. But it was instantly gone again as he said, "Converse?" When she nodded he beckoned to her.

Signore Calabro, Amy could tell, was not looking particularly pleased. He sighed, then said, "Converse," pointing to her. Then he pointed to each of the men in turn—all of whom were young. Amy tried to memorize the foreign names. Petri was the tall thin one, with a shock of uncombed black hair. Martini was muscular, with a narrow sun-darkened face and a nose that must have been broken sometime in the past. Solari had carefully combed wavy hair, a bold manner and a petulant-looking mouth.

All three young men were dressed in sturdy clothing that showed signs of long hard wear. Martini had a ragged patch on the sleeve of a sagging brown sweater. All of them were wearing boots.

Each murmured something in Italian and Amy hurriedly summoned up *"Piacere!"* hoping it was the right response. She was uncomfortably conscious of their eyes sweeping boldly over her, lingering on her T-shirt, which clung to her firm young breasts. They grinned, nudging one another.

Calabro snapped something in Italian, the lift of his impatient voice indicating it had been a question. He stood looking at them, fists planted on his hips.

Solari took a step forward. "I es-speak the English. Some." Then he nodded understandingly as Calabro spoke to him. Turning to Amy, Solari said, "Is boss!" He directed a thumb toward the older man. "He say we all new, we begin today. All start. Now you follow."

The four young people trotted obediently after

Signore Calabro, who walked along the castle wall until he came to a door, which they entered. Amy found herself in the large room with the steel tanks.

Following the boss, they wound in and out among the towering structures, stepping over hoses, until they came to a storage room at the far end. There Calabro pulled out brushes, buckets and scoops, which he passed out to each of them. In momentary frustration he stopped to look at Amy then he handed her a bucket and the rest of the items. Taking her lunch, he set it on a shelf and pointed to it, apparently indicating that she could pick it up later.

When he jerked his head they again trooped after him. Halfway down one of the rows he stopped. "Petri!" He nodded toward a tank and said a few words in Italian. The young man walked uncertainly over to the tank and looked at a door in the lower part. It was a very small door.

After a moment he pulled it open, bent down and poked his head inside. Then he took his bucket, brush and scoop and tossed them into the tank. Raising his arms over his head, he managed to slither in behind them, his feet disappearing last.

Martini was assigned to a tank a little farther on. He, too, placed his equipment inside and then wormed his way in through the opening.

Amy was beginning to feel perspiration raising on her upper lip. She didn't particularly like dark closed-in places, but she had a feeling that was exactly what she was in for.

"Converse!" Calabro motioned toward her, indicating a towering tank at the end of the row. She moved toward it uncertainly as Calabro gave information to Solari, who stepped forward. "He say clean all inside. Then, with hose, clean. Also say you stick head out. Fumes, they bad. Go back. Work more, okay?"

Amy nodded, giving a nervous look over her shoulder. Then she walked toward the small door and opened it. It seemed barely large enough for her to squeeze in. But the others had managed and they were bigger, so she carefully set her bucket and other equipment inside, then, following the example of the other two, managed to edge herself in. It wasn't dark, not really; rather it was like twilight, with dustlike particles rising and floating in the air around her.

She started to get to her feet, but they abruptly slipped out from under her and she sat down hard. For a second or two she stayed there, then gingerly tried again, every motion sending the light feathery sediment swirling around her. Finally she was able to stand up and look around. The sediment, she discovered, wasn't all fine and powdery. In places where it had not yet dried it was as sticky as oatmeal or wet clay. Permeating everything was the heady smell of fermented wine and of yeast. The wine smell wasn't exactly unpleasant at first, but soon it began to be overpowering, sending her slipping and sliding to the small door to stick her head out and gulp fresh air.

As she did so she noticed that Signore Calabro was standing a half dozen steps away. Was he measuring her work, she wondered, seeing if she was doing it correctly? Or was he making certain she had brains enough to breathe fresh air from time to time so she wouldn't be overcome with the fumes?

Before long Amy's world had shrunk to the mess beneath her feet and a grim determination to keep going in spite of her aching arms, her tired back and wet feet. Over and over she would clean, scrape, scoop. Wash down the remainder with a hose that had been passed in to her, then rush to gulp some fresh air. She had no sense of the minutes going by; time seemed to be standing still.

"Converse!" Dimly she heard her name being called and she looked up, shoving back her lank hair to stare almost unseeingly at the tank door. Then Signore Calabro's white head appeared in the opening.

"*Mangiare!*" he called impatiently.

Amy stared as he made motions of his hand toward his mouth. "*Mangiare!*" he repeated.

Eat? Was it lunchtime? Or dinner? She glanced down at her watch but couldn't read it in the dim light of the tank.

She nodded numbly toward him and began to make her way cautiously toward the opening. He hesitated, glanced quickly over his shoulder, then again at her, and held up a hand to aid her in climbing out.

"Thank you...uh...*grazie*," she said wearily. Then she halted for a moment while she let her numb mind remember where she had left her lunch. The storage room, that's where Signore Calabro had put it. She headed in that direction, opened the door and picked up the white box. She was startled to hear her

name again. This time it was from Martini, one of
the other beginners, beckoning to her from between a
row of tanks.

As she neared him, he pointed to a door and she
followed him outside. Stupefied, she stopped to look
around her. It felt as if she had never seen the sunshine before.

Seated on the ground, leaning back against the
stone wall of the castle, were Solari and Petri. They
were chewing hungrily at slabs of bread heavily
coated with a sauce that smelled of tomatoes and
garlic. Petri patted the ground beside him and Amy
wearily sank down, her lunch untouched in her lap.
For a few moments all she wanted to do was take
long staggering breaths of the sweet fresh air.

"Hard, hey, okay?" Solari grinned at her and
shook his head.

"Yes. Hard," she said in a small flat voice.

"You eat, feel more better!" the young man ad-
vised.

Amy awkwardly undid the package. Her hands,
she noted, were stained, and two of her nails broken.
She looked down at two crisp rolls, one stuffed with
slices of ham, the other with creamy Bel Paese
cheese. The box also contained an orange, some
cookies and a small bottle of wine.

At first, too exhausted to eat, Amy found it hard
to lift the roll to her mouth. But she forced herself to
bite, to chew, to swallow. Bit by bit she ate more
quickly, feeling better with the stimulus of food and
the cool bite of the wine.

As she ate her eyes wandered over her wet soiled

jeans and her soaked shoes. Her T-shirt was stained green and clinging damply to her figure. She needn't have worried about what she wore for her job! The young men sitting near her were stained and wet, too, but they hadn't paid for designer jeans that had been worn but twice before. Jeans that looked permanently colored from the debris that clung to the bottom of the tank.

"For why you work?" Solari, chewing on his bread, spoke to her between mouthfuls. His eyes were curious.

"Because I want to be a vintner someday and I understand this is one way to learn," she replied.

A glazed look of incomprehension came over his face, and Amy realized that she had spoken much too quickly. His knowledge of English was limited, possibly learned in school or picked up here and there from tourists. But he knew a lot more English than she knew Italian!

When she shook her head helplessly he shrugged and applied himself to his food once more.

Amy peeled her orange and leaned wearily back against the warm stone wall, eating the fruit mechanically. She was so exhausted that she let her eyes close, not in sleep but in a smothering fatigue that leadened her bones..

"Hey, Converse!" The voice penetrated her numb cocoon.

She opened her eyes to see Solari standing over her. He jerked his thumb toward the castle door. "We go. Work now."

Amy nodded, gathered the remnants of her lunch

together and stuffed them back in the box. Suddenly
her hands were still. She couldn't go back in there
again! Every muscle, every bone in her body ached.
There was no need to subject herself to any more
punishment, she told herself. All she had to do was to
get to her feet and walk up the hill—with defeat on
her face and in her words.

She watched the door close behind the other three
novices. Then she rose slowly and trudged after
them. Placing her lunch box once again on the
storage-room shelf, she walked back down the row
and climbed once more into her tank.

By midafternoon she had finished cleaning it.
Signore Calabro inspected her work, nodded, then
turned to look at her sharply. He opened his mouth
to say something, but didn't. Giving a slight shrug he
pointed out another tank to her.

Amy took a long trembling breath, then wearily
crawled into her second tank of the day. It was as
dirty as the first one had been, with light feathery
sediment floating all around her.

Somehow the endless workday drew to a dazed
finish. Amy half crawled, half stumbled out of her
tank, and with her co-workers put away her equipment. The three young men were less talkative now,
their faces streaked and dirty, ribbed with fatigue.

Amy noticed other workers, clearly more experienced, sauntering away toward other storage rooms,
talking and joking as they went. She stared after
them, her mind only half registering everything she
saw.

The sun was beginning to lower behind the trees,

laying a lattice pattern on the roadway as Amy made her way out of the castle courtyard and turned toward the villa. She trudged slowly, wearily, her feet seeming to carry an unsteady burden.

The elderly servant opened the gate, giving her a swift glance of sympathy, but he said nothing. Amy felt she could just possibly make it up to her room and the heaven of a warm bath, then bed.

As she plodded across the terrace, head down, a voice intercepted her. "Well, I'm surprised! The return of the working woman! Hello, Miss Converse!" It was a woman's voice.

Amy looked up. Seated under the umbrella sipping iced drinks were Nando and Elisa. The girl, sheathed in sleeveless white linen that contrasted with her lovely bronzed shoulders, was immaculately crisp, cool, elegant. Her dark hair was caught up with a white ribbon.

Nando, his gray-trousered legs extended lazily under the table, was wearing a soft gray shirt with a blue ascot at the throat, a blue reflected lightly in his gray eyes. Those eyes were gazing at her with an expression she found impossible to analyze, tired as she was. In anyone else it might have been concern, but in Nando she couldn't be certain.

She was agonizingly aware of her own stained clothes, her hair plastered against her face, her cheeks no doubt as grimy as her hands. With effort she straightened her shoulders and said, "Hello, Miss Antolini. Nando."

"My dear, you actually did it, didn't you? I simply can't believe it!" trilled the elegant young woman, amusement in her violet eyes. "Wasn't it simply ghastly? And difficult?"

Amy nodded grimly. "It was. Now, if you'll excuse me, I must get cleaned up," she said, feeling she was using her last ounce of energy to make it past them with some show of dignity. As she headed toward the door she was aware that Nando had not uttered a single word but still sat there with that strange look on his face.

Anna Maria emerged from her room as Amy moved slowly up the stairs, and came hurrying up to her.

"Oh, Amy, Amy, you poor dear, you look absolutely exhausted! You should never have tried to do it! And a whole day! Nando shouldn't have let you try. It's. . . it's nothing short of criminal! And I certainly plan to tell him so! Here, please let me help you. Can't I do something for you?"

Amy shook her head. "All I want to do is to get to my room and have a shower!" She tried to smile, but it took too much effort, so she headed doggedly toward her door. "But thank you anyhow, Anna Maria," she said over her shoulder.

When Amy reached her room she wanted more than anything to fling herself heedlessly down on that snow-white bed, dirty clothes and all. But she forced herself to go straight into the bathroom and turn on the warm water.

She caught a glimpse of herself in the mirror and spun away quickly, grimacing. She looked worse than she'd thought. Her hair was like limp rope, her face streaked from the tank sediment.

She found she had to actually peel the clinging sticky clothes from her body. Leaving them in a heap on the floor, she stepped toward the hissing shower.

It felt heavenly. The warm water carried away some of her monstrous fatigue as it sluiced off the grime. Amy stood under the spray for long minutes, letting it cascade onto her uplifted face.

When she toweled herself later, she peered at the pale haggard face in the mirror. *This,* she thought wearily, *is how I'm going to look when I am old.* Pulling on her robe, she headed straight for her bed, hauled down the coverlet and slipped between the sheets. . . .

Amy had little more than begun to relax when there as a knock at the door. For a few seconds she didn't move but lay there with her eyes shut tight. *Whoever it is, go away,* she thought. But the knock came again.

Sighing with irritation, she swung her bare feet to the floor and padded over to the door.

Nando was standing there looking down at her, suave and elegant in his tailored clothes. He seemed taller somehow, she registered vaguely; tall and remote.

But he also looked exasperated. "Amy, I certainly didn't expect you to be so foolish as to try to stay the whole day! Just look at you, you're completely exhausted! I know you don't want to go on with it! It won't get any easier, and it could get even harder."

She didn't answer. It didn't matter, really, for he went on. "I think we both know this ridiculous experiment must come to an end. I was certain you would find the work too difficult. You were warned that it would be, not only by me, but by others, too."

Amy didn't reply to that, either. She only pulled her robe more tightly around her and leaned unsteadily against the door frame.

His voice lost its firm tone and gentled slightly. "All right, my dear, so that's that. You had to see for yourself what the work was like. I trust your common sense will tell you how absurd your idea was from the start. A winery is no place for you, but apparently you needed to find out for yourself. I gave you your chance, as I promised I would. Now I suggest that sometime tomorrow we settle our affairs."

Amy looked up at him. He had definitely approached her at the wrong time. Her nerves were raw; she was still smarting from the episode he'd subjected her to yesterday. And he'd chosen this moment to arrive at her door to give the final coup de grace. All at once a hot surge flared up inside her, replacing fatigue with anger. Drawing herself up rigidly, she gave him three seconds of hostile silence. "You can just go to hell, Fernando Bonavia!" she finally exploded. Stepping back, she shut the door with a bang. Two minutes later she was sound asleep.

The room was growing dark when the sound of voices in the hall awakened her. Struggling to sit up, Amy squinted at the clock on the bedside table. It was a little after nine. Soon it would be nine-thirty, dinnertime.

She lay down again. She didn't want any dinner: she didn't want to move!

For several minutes she remained there, letting

thoughts flow into her mind. All right, she admitted
to herself, she couldn't go through another day like
this one. She'd barely made it to quitting time.

Nando, for all his pretended concern, had purposely given her the hardest dirtiest task at the very
outset, believing, of course, that she could never last
through the first day. Well, she had! A momentary
glow of triumph warmed her, only to be followed by
the knowledge that, yes, she'd survived today, but
only by forcing herself beyond her strength, her en-
durance. She couldn't possibly do it again. So Nando
had won after all.

Amy sat up in bed. She would go home. Back to
New York, away from the clannish Bonavias. Write
this off as a bitter lesson and forget the whole
damned thing.

She would go in her own way, too—with dignity,
not letting them see how she felt. She was even going
to go down to dinner tonight, no doubt her last one
with them all. She might look tired, but she refused
to look beaten.

Choosing a soft blue dinner frock with an attractive scoop neck, she laid it on the bed and began to
get ready, even though every muscle protested. When
she had dressed, a glance in the mirror did little to
reassure her. Dark half-moons lay under her eyes.
Even her hair looked tired, she thought a little hyster-
ically.

Sitting before her dressing table, keeping a cautious eye on the clock, she began to apply makeup
with care. A touch of blush on her pale cheeks gave
them a little color; then blue eye shadow, mascara on

her eyelashes. She tried a bright lively lipstick, then wiped it off with tissue. The contrast was too garish; she settled for a soft pink.

Her arms were heavy as she lifted them to comb and smooth her blond hair, but finally she was finished. She stood up, eyeing herself appraisingly. Her fatigue was not gone, but at least it was less obvious.

She stood at the door, gathering every spare ounce of resolve. Then, taking a deep breath, she went out into the hall, heading for the stairs.

As Amy reached the bottom step, she halted, her hand still on the newel post. She could hear streams of Italian rattling back and forth furiously inside the salon. Aunt Lucia's dictatorial voice was more than a little sharp. Then Nando spoke, sounding stubborn, adamant. Again Aunt Lucia held forth. When Anna Maria said something plaintively, Nando snapped a reply. Amy could tell that the vigorous disagreement must involve the whole family.

She remained where she was for another moment or two, not wanting to walk into the room while all this was going on. But when it still didn't show any sign of abating, she moistened her lips nervously, straightened her shoulders and went in.

There was an abrupt cessation of sound, and four heads turned in her direction. Amy sensed that they really hadn't expected her to appear this evening.

"I hope I'm not late for dinner, or that I've kept you waiting," Amy said in a light thin voice. She moved toward the sofa and sat on the edge of it, feeling that if she relaxed one single muscle she would never make it through dinner.

"My dear child, I was planning to send your dinner up to your room this evening. You must be very tired," Aunt Lucia said, a strange new note in her voice that made Amy glance quickly at her. But the stern face revealed nothing.

"I'm tired, yes, but not too tired to come down to dinner," Amy replied.

Anna Maria was shaking her head, her cheeks flushed, her eyes sparking angrily. "I just told Nando exactly what I think of him! He simply had no right to send you to the winery on such a job. Absolutely criminal! That's man's work, it's hard, it's dirty and...oh, everything!"

Nando was lifting a wineglass to his lips. He took a slow deliberate drink, then said, "I think Amy was fully warned that it was no work for a woman. And when she returned this afternoon from the winery, I went to speak to her and suggest that she not go back. That it was clearly too much for her. Isn't that so, Amy?"

Amy, feeling a swift resurgence of that earlier anger, curled her fingers in her lap so that her nails bit into her palms. "Yes," she said coolly, "so you told me."

"And I was correct, was I not? It is too hard for you, or for any woman."

Green sparks leaped into her eyes. "I cleaned one tank completely today, and did most of another one," she replied steadily. "I didn't notice that any of the other three beginners did better. And they were all men." She finished the sentence a bit tartly, she realized, but he had it coming.

Amy was aware that Franco was in the room, too, sitting in his chair but not saying a word. He let his eyes move from one person to another, an odd contemplative look on his face.

"Amy, Nando has the habit of being a bit lordly," Aunt Lucia said. "He means well, I presume, and in this instance I admit he is correct. The work is far too hard. What truly surprises me is that he allowed you to start by working in the fermentation tanks, and I have just finished telling him so."

"Amy said she wanted to learn! I think most of us learned exactly that way, by starting in the less attractive jobs. You may recall, mother, that that is the way I began—cleaning out the tanks."

"But you are a man! It isn't the same thing at all!" his mother said, frowning.

"Exactly!" Nando smiled. Then, lifting the carafe, he said, "Cousin, may I offer you some wine?"

Amy blinked. Wine? She had been surrounded, inundated by it all day long. The fumes from the fermented wine dregs still lingered in her nostrils. But she nodded anyway. "Yes, thank you."

As he handed her the glass, his hand touched hers, sending an irresistible electric tingle to her heart.

Amy tried not to frown, but her automatic reaction disturbed her. His behavior of the day before was unforgivable. His calmly sending her to do the worst possible labor in the winery was in a way just as bad.

Then why couldn't she hate him? Why was it that he still had the power to affect her? The mind can order the body around, but not the heart. Why, she wondered irritably, can't the heart do as it's told? And how had she ever allowed Nando Bonavia to become in some unaccountable way nearly the very center of her life? Now she did frown.

"Well, Amy, I hope that scowl means you are looking with more favor on our conversation of the other night." Franco had suddenly appeared at her side on the sofa, his voice low.

She shook her head. "Tonight I don't know what I think about anything. My mind is as tired as the rest of me," she said, lifting her glass to her lips.

Franco gave her a shrewd look. "I'm not surprised. You shouldn't have been allowed to do it."

At that moment, Filippo appeared in the doorway, flashing a charming smile. His astounding good looks were highlighted tonight by an elegant dinner jacket. Anna Maria's face lighted up and she rushed over to him. He took her hand in his to lift it to his lips, but she boldly held up her face and he kissed it instead.

"Anna Maria, please save your demonstrations of affection for private moments," sniffed Aunt Lucia in her most grande dame manner. "I realize that television and motion pictures make such things quite common. But I watch neither, and therefore do not wish to witness them in my own salon.

"I'm afraid, Amy, that my daughter has seen far too many American films," she went on.

How incredibly old-fashioned the woman was, and yet her words and actions seemed so much in character, Amy reflected. Even her oblique derogatory comment about American movies could be expected, and therefore it lost any possible sting.

The appearance of Filippo had at least changed the tenor of the conversation. Because he couldn't enter into an English-speaking dialogue and because Amy herself couldn't understand Italian, the talk turned to lighter subjects with much translation.

Amy sat quietly, at times almost dreamily, trying to stay awake. She said a few words now and then, but basically she longed for bed. She ate dinner but she had little memory of it, and not much of the rest of the evening penetrated her shell of fatigue. She was conscious, however, that Nando's eyes were often on her, hooded, thoughtful. He was quick to move his glance away when she encountered it unexpectedly.

As soon as she could, Amy escaped to her room. She simply could not tell anyone that she wasn't going back to the winery, she told herself. She was too tired.

She started up the stairs, bone weary. To her surprise and dismay, Franco came loping up to join her. She sighed inwardly. She didn't want to talk anymore tonight, to anyone. But he wasn't to be thwarted.

"Amy, dear, please don't let him do this to you! I've been worried all evening. That work is far too hard! I never thought Nando would allow it, but I should have guessed," he said bitterly. "He has gone completely overboard on this. It can be dangerous, you know. Stay too long in the tank and you could be overcome. That's carbon dioxide in there; in time it might be fatal."

"I think," she said slowly, only now realizing it was quite possible, "that Nando has Signore Calabro watching me to see that nothing happens."

"How gracious of Nando," Franco snorted. "How extremely thoughtful! Amy, I should think that now you'd want to get back at him. After what he's done to you, wouldn't you find a certain pleasure in retaliation? Join Filippo and me."

Amy looked up at him, tears of exhaustion and strain not far away. "Please, Franco, not tonight. I can't think."

He took her hand. "Sorry, little one. Didn't mean to press you, but I'm so worried. Don't let Nando manipulate you this way. He's hard and he's ruthless. You won't change him, nor can you get him to change. He thinks he's got you where he wants you at last. But he doesn't have to win, Amy, not if you join us. Think about it." He squeezed her hand gently, bending to kiss her lightly on the cheek. "Good night, rest well."

Amy went into her room, undoing her dress as she went. She had made it through the day; she had somehow got through the evening. It was over, she thought wearily. It was all over.

Her head had barely touched the pillow before she fell into a deep sleep. She didn't dream of Nando or of anyone.

In the morning she was awakened by tapping on her door. She sat up, her eyes seeking the clock. It was early, as early as yesterday. But today she need not get up. She grasped her robe and went over to the door anyway, to open it to the young girl holding a tray.

Not knowing the Italian words to say "Later, please! Much later!" she motioned the girl to come in. Only tardily did she remember *"Prego!"*

The girl set the tray down, stood for a second or two in confusion, then said, *"Momento!"* She stepped back through the door to return with a box.

"Launch?" she asked, this time hesitantly, uncertain.

So even the help suspected she wasn't going back to work, Amy thought. But how do you explain in a language you don't know? She thought it simpler to take the box with a *"Grazie."*

But the girl was not finished. She again ducked out the door and came back with a neat pile of laundry in her hands. Amy recognized the blouse she had worn on her flight and, carefully folded on top, a pair of designer jeans, deeply wine stained but otherwise clean. A greenish T-shirt and her sneakers were there, as well. Someone had slipped into her room last night while she was at dinner and taken away the soiled clothes—probably one of the routine household duties.

When Amy took them, again saying, *"Grazie,"* the girl bobbed her head, smiled and left.

She set the clothes down on a chair, gazing at them. This was certainly going to make an amusing tale to tell Linda when she got back to New York. "These jeans," she would tell her, "have been around! You won't believe this, but one day I worked in the winery and. . . ."

She picked up the jeans and went over to the window, where she opened the shutters and gazed down at the castle.

So Nando had won!

He had known he would, one way or another. He had been so certain he could triumph over her . . . !

Something stirred deep within Amy. No, not entirely, she thought. He hadn't yet completely defeated her. She still had some fight left in her. She frowned, her lips straightening into a firm obstinate line, one her mother would have readily recognized.

Amy kicked off her bedroom slippers and stripped off her robe. Then she began dressing—first her underwear, then the jeans and T-shirt, and finally her dry stiff tennis shoes.

She ate her breakfast hurriedly, then with an eye on the clock, went out the door. She was going back to the castle. It wasn't yet eight o'clock.

CHAPTER NINE

FRIDAY found Amy still doggedly heading down the hill each morning, then trudging back to the villa every evening. She was weary, yes, but not quite as weary. She had learned by now how to pace herself better, how to work more efficiently and therefore finish the day less exhausted. Even Signore Calabro had noticed and no longer hung around to keep an eye on her.

There were still times when she had to grit her teeth not to give up, but she persisted. Nando certainly couldn't justify keeping her in this job forever, so she was determined to stick it out. And she was learning.

In a way it was all worth it, just to be able to give Nando a calm untroubled smile each evening over the dinner table, thinking how it must irritate him. She figured that he had it coming, especially after subjecting her to such humiliation at Lago di Verde. However, she thought, her face flushing at the memory, he hadn't emerged from that little charade as impassively as he had planned, either.

It was less than an hour before quitting time on Friday afternoon when Amy began to find the air in her tank becoming oppressive. It was time to gulp some fresh air, she realized. She had been working

with her back to the small door, and when she turned
around she was startled to see the door closed. That
struck her as strange, but she quickly slipped and
stumbled toward it and pushed hard against it. It
refused to budge. She tried again, small beads of
perspiration springing up on her upper lip. The door
ordinarily opened from the inside, she knew, but now
it wouldn't. Someone must have accidently latched it
from the outside, not realizing she was in there.

Amy's heart began to pound heavily. Panic made
her legs shake, her feet grow unsteady on the slippery
surface. Trying to breathe shallowly, she turned and
fumbled for her brush. She was unable to find it at
first, but she finally located it and, grasping it tightly,
began to pound hard against the steel shell of the
tank. The sound of her blows reverberated in her ears
until she felt surrounded by clanging.

Then, abruptly, the door was jerked open and a
workman peered inside, his face a combination of
alarm and bewilderment. Amy stumbled toward him,
gasping fresh air as he drew back to allow her to lean
out. He looked at the outside of the door and shook
his head, saying something to her in Italian. She
could only shake her head, murmuring, *"Grazie,"* as
soon as her breathing steadied.

He waited a few more minutes, then, apparently
satisfied that she was all right, gave her a puzzled
frown, shrugged his shoulders and walked off to his
own work.

Someone must have latched it, she thought. That
was the only answer. But why would they without
checking first? As she drew in long shaking breaths,

she went over everything again in her mind. That's what must have happened, unless...unless it had been done deliberately.

The thought came like a blow. Nando couldn't have! He wouldn't have! She couldn't be that wrong about him! Surely he would never have moved her feelings, her heart, if he was so...so criminal. Amy felt a sick lump at the pit of her stomach.

But he must have known there wasn't much chance of its being fatal. All she had to do was draw someone's attention; there were many workers around who would be alerted by pounding. And unless panic paralyzed her into inaction, she would naturally call for help. Was he using this as one more means of warning her off?

Amy stood unmoving, thoughts running distractedly through her mind like confused mice through a maze. She couldn't quite reconcile such an action to Nando.

Well, she argued, how about his actions out at the lake? Certainly they hadn't been all that admirable, either. She shook her head. If Nando hadn't shut the door, then it would have to be what she had thought at the beginning—a mistake. But surely any of the winery staff would have checked first! There she was, right back at the beginning and no nearer an answer.

Amy slowly turned back to her work, sluicing out the tank, pulling the plug in the bottom and watching the water swirl out. Her thoughts were troubled.

As she left the castle a bit later she wondered how Nando would react. Would he bluntly tell her that this was just a sample of what might happen if she

persisted? Or would he present an innocent face and
not say a word, letting her own imagination provide
her with unnerving answers? She sighed in frustration.

Amy was so deeply involved with her thoughts as
she made her way out the castle gate that she failed to
notice a low-slung car parked under a tree nearby.

"Amy! Amy Converse!"

Amy looked up, surprised to see Elisa Antolini sitting in the car, beckoning to her. "Can you spare a
few minutes? I'd like to talk to you," the girl said,
reaching over to open the far door.

Amy didn't feel much like conversation at the moment, but there was little chance of avoiding it. She
went slowly around the side of the car, but before
getting in she halted. "I'm afraid I'm not very clean.
These jeans might get the seat dirty," she said, looking uncertainly down at the pale cream leather of the
upholstery.

The young woman waved a casual hand. "Think
nothing of it! We have help who can clean it if necessary."

As usual she was exquisitely dressed, in a sleeveless
pale sapphire silk frock that molded itself to the seductive curves of her body. Amy was conscious of
her own damp bedraggled appearance as she got into
the car, and she wondered what had prompted Elisa
to wait out here for her.

The reason wasn't long in coming. The girl turned
those deep violet eyes on Amy and said, "I simply
had to talk to you. I hope you don't mind my calling
you Amy, because I want you to think of me as a

friend, one who has your best interest at heart. And, speaking of that, I understand you had a fright in the winery a short time ago. Something about a door closing in one of the steel fermentation tanks, wasn't it?"

The words, spoken so casually, startled Amy. How had the news spread so fast? And how could Elisa have heard?

"Well, yes, it was frightening for a moment. But someone came right away, so it wasn't really dangerous," Amy said. But as she spoke a cold ripple ran down her spine and she remembered that awful moment when she feared the door wasn't going to open.

"Ah, true, true," Elisa nodded, pink-tipped fingernails tapping idly on the steering wheel. "But it could have ended otherwise, couldn't it? I really do believe that if I were you I'd give some thought to it, perhaps consider it a warning of sorts." She smiled. "Quite frankly, I'd wonder if someone didn't want me to stay around. And," she went on airily, "you would be perfectly correct. Because I don't want you here. I don't want you in the winery, I don't want you in Italy, and I most certainly don't want you around Nando!"

Amy swallowed in surprise. *Elisa?* She turned to gaze at the Italian girl in bewilderment. "Do I understand you had something to do with the incident?"

Elisa nodded. "Yes, of course. Everything."

"But you...you...?" Amy's voice halted. It was too incredible! Elisa was admitting doing something that could be considered a criminal act. It certainly would have been if anything had happened. But she was confessing to it as carelessly as if it were nothing at all.

"Now, Amy, don't get excited. You wouldn't have remained in there long enough to be in trouble. We both realize that wouldn't have happened. Someone held the door shut for just a moment or two—that's all there was to it."

Amy stared unbelievingly at Elisa. How could a woman who looked like she did, wearing a form-fitting silk dress, walk unobserved through the building with workers everywhere.

"Why weren't you seen?" she asked.

"I? Oh, I didn't do it myself. Heavens, no! One of the workmen did it." She slanted a sly glance at Amy. "One of *our* people. You see, we have spies, if you want to call them that, planted in competing wineries. For a price they'll do almost anything." She laughed. "Why, we knew about the new Chiaro almost as soon as Nando did. He more than likely has someone in our winery, too. That's the business world. And one in which you don't belong, at least not here in Nando's winery."

"But why did you do it? Why have one of your workmen shut the door?" Amy asked, still a little stunned by the whole thing.

"Because you didn't seem to get the word that first night. I told you Nando was mine, that I didn't want you to create problems. But you stayed on, and even went to work in the winery. You're starting to get a permanent look about you. So I told one of our men to wait until no one was around, hold the door shut long enough to scare you, then vanish. I hoped it would shake you up enough to realize someone doesn't want you around.''

"But I own a share in the winery," Amy protested. "And I want to learn wine making. That's the only reason I'm working."

"No doubt. But I never dreamed Nando would give you the chance, knowing how he feels about women in a winery. And the gossip around the castle is that you're going to be given a step up next week."

Amy's eyes grew round, but she didn't interrupt.

"And that's what I don't like," Elisa continued, "for it means Nando has begun to take an interest in you. In addition, you're not only working with him by day, you're there at the villa in the evenings. Together."

"If you think that means I'm pursuing him, then you are quite wrong," Amy said quickly. "He's not the least bit interested in me."

"Wrong, am I?" Elisa's slender eyebrows arched. "Then, my dear, you don't know Nando. I know him a lot better than you do; I know what he's like. He's a hot-blooded Italian and quick to passion. Not hard to arouse. You are there where he sees you all the time. You are attractive. I know enough about propensity—and Nando—to realize that sooner or later, if he hasn't done so already, he will put his hands on you. And God knows what will happen then. I say God knows, but so do I. Nando will have you on your back before you can catch your breath."

Amy looked indignantly at Elisa. "And I'll have nothing to say about it? Do you think I have no mind

of my own? What if I don't find him appealing?"
Amy felt guilty the minute the words were out, knowing all too well the answer to each of her questions.
But more than anything in the world she wanted to
keep her feelings safe from this prying young woman. . . and Nando.

The girl laughed, a light silvery sound. "It doesn't
matter in the least. I want you gone from here, out of
the way, before you cause more problems."

Amy reached for the door handle. "I presume that
if I stay, I can expect more. . . problems from you?"

Again Elisa laughed. "No, that was a one-time
thing. It was only to let you know I'm serious about
wanting you to leave. Call it a practical joke with a
hidden meaning. Otherwise do you think I'd be telling you about it?"

She gave Amy a knowing look. "I've given Nando
almost everything he wants. . . *almost*. Kisses,
temptation—but not what he wants most of all. And
he knows that the only way he can have that is
through marriage. The night before you came here I
had him half out of his mind with desire, almost
ready to say the fatal words." She gave a petulant
frown. "Next time he will forget his vows of
bachelorhood—if you aren't around to distract
him."

Amy got out of the car. "If you have finished, I'd
really like to go. I'm rather tired."

Elisa nodded. "I've said what I wanted to say to
you and I hope you take the message to heart. Also,
if I were you, I wouldn't be tempted to tell Nando
about my own part in today's episode. I'll only deny

it. I'll say that you more than likely panicked when
the door closed unexpectedly and are trying to cover
it up by accusing someone. Frankly, I imagine everyone at the winery already thinks you became overex-
cited when you saw the closed door.''

Elisa was probably right, Amy reflected uncomfortably, recalling the puzzled look on the workman's face. He had opened the door without any
difficulty and so had failed to understand the reason
for her frantic pounding.

Elisa started her car, gunning the motor several
times. "Hands off Nando, remember, and keep his
hands off you!" she called as she whirled the car
around and went speeding down the hill, leaving a
curl of dust behind her.

How incredible Elisa was, Amy thought. Brazenly
arranging to give someone several terrifying moments, then not only freely admitting it but being so
completely casual about it, as well. As if the whole
thing were merely a lighthearted prank.

. As Amy walked slowly up toward the villa her
mind was on Elisa's words. Not about the incident at
the winery now, but on the things she had said about
Nando.

"Half out of his mind with desire." Amy had
no trouble picturing that. Those few brief encoun-
ters she herself had had with him made her realize
that for all his deliberate romancing there was
always a hint of hot fire below the surface. And at
Lago di Verde for a brief moment it had suddenly
flamed.

Amy found that thinking of Nando and Elisa to-

gether, in each other's arms, upset her. She tried not
to picture it.

Even harder to forget was the fact that at the lake,
unlike Elisa, she had not been going to deny Nando
anything. She had actually offered herself to him!

Amy kicked at a small stone, sending it bounding
ahead of her. It was just as well she wasn't in open
competition with Elisa for Nando's love. Not only
was the girl extraordinarily beautiful, she was fiercely
determined. And there was little doubt but that she
would get exactly what she was after.

The evening, as Amy was getting ready to go down
to dinner, she flinched at the thought of having Nando comment on today's incident. Certainly he would
have heard of it by now. More than likely it would
bring forth one more observation that the winery was
no place for a woman.

She needn't have worried, for he was not at dinner
that evening. Dressed in evening clothes he had
brushed past her on the stairs, murmuring a greeting
to her as he went by.

Sunday evening he was again missing. Aunt Lucia
gazed in disapproval at the empty chair. Arching thin
eyebrows, she turned to Anna Maria. "Signorina
Antolini?"

Anna Maria nodded. "Dinner again at Villa Antolini. I took the message this time. There are important guests tonight from out of town, people she
wants him to meet. What nonsense! How transparent
she is, chasing after him harder than ever." She
added a sentence in Italian that brought a frown to
her mother's face and a gesture of distaste.

The girl turned to Amy. "You know, I think your presence here has made Elisa nervous. She is afraid Nando will slip from her grasp."

Aunt Lucia lifted her proud head. "She does not have him in her grasp, not at all, and she will not."

"I'm not so certain," Franco remarked. "She's very beautiful and, I might add, a very determined young woman. In spite of Nando, he may find wedding bells beginning to ring, and not just for Anna Maria and Filippo." He gave Amy a swift glance as if to remind her of their conversation on just that subject.

Aunt Lucia drew herself up stiffly. "She shall not marry Nando. Not ever! Whether he wishes it or not! I shall not allow it." Her voice held such an odd note that Amy turned to look at her curiously, but no word followed and the dinner ended with nothing more said about the subject.

If Aunt Lucia seemed concerned, apparently Franco was even more so. After dinner he cornered Amy. "We must talk, Amy. Things are developing too fast."

"You mean. . .?"

"Yes. Elisa. You heard that conversation at the dinner table. The girl has the family worried. And it should worry you," Franco persisted.

"Me? I'm not involved. It has nothing to do with me," Amy said uncomfortably.

"Oh, but it has. You know very well that the marriage would be a two-pronged deal. I told you before, the wineries are sure to be part of the picture. Do you think our Elisa wants a beauteous, very distantly related cousin of Nando's to be present with him in the winery every day, especially as a part owner? If you think she'll permit that you are incredibly naive. Once they were married, I think you would find yourself with a one-way ticket to New York. She doesn't like competition.''

Amy knew better than he did on that particular subject. As she cast about for something to say, Franco pushed on with a further argument.

''If we, you and I and Filippo, don't solidify our situation, it will shortly be too late.''

Amy hesitated. ''I know that, Franco, and yet I don't feel I'm quite ready to take the step of joining you against Nando and Aunt Lucia.''

''You have another choice, Amy,'' Franco said quietly, taking her hand in his. ''My offer of marriage is still open. However you may feel about it, don't overlook the fact that Elisa can't very well insist that you leave, not if you are married to me.''

She gave him a faint smile. ''I know, Franco. But a marriage based on financial interests seems a little fragile to me.''

He nodded. ''Perhaps. Marriages have been founded on less, however. I admit the idea may seem preposterous to you, but it is not. We are compatible, I believe. Love could come later, you know.''

''I like you, Franco, I really do. You have become a friend in this short time, and you have been kind. But I can't marry you. I've known you little more than a week! I'm not in love with you, and you are not in love with me. Without love, to me at least, it would not be marriage.'' She gave him a gentle look.

"No, Franco," she repeated, "not even to save my chance to work in the winery. I'm sorry."

But Franco's warning did little to reassure her. He was correct in predicting that Elisa wouldn't want her around after marrying Nando. She didn't want her there now!

Thoughts of Elisa reminded Amy of the "step up" she had mentioned. Was it true, Amy wondered. No one else had said anything about it. She hoped that if it were a fact, that her new job wouldn't be any worse than cleaning tanks.

But Elisa was correct, Amy found, when she went to work on Monday morning. Signore Calabro appeared at the storage-closet door as Amy was gathering up her equipment.

"Converse, *andiamo!*" he said, beckoning her to follow. He shook his head at her brush and bucket. Quickly she put them back in the closet and hurried after him. She did have a new job, she thought eagerly.

He led her into a room filled with rows of wine casks and there he held up his hand, signaling her to wait. He stood by, arms folded, his eyes on the door.

Amy was startled to see Nando walk into the room. "Signore Calabro reports you have been doing well, and he recommends you be given further instruction in a different department," he said. "It was entirely his idea, you understand. I had nothing to do with it. He is in complete charge of indoctrination."

A muscle jumped in his cheek. He seemed unusually stiff and formal, his eyes not on her as he spoke.

She wondered why, but had long since given up trying to interpret Nando's actions.

"It is I who must explain because of the language
barrier," Nando went on. "You must understand that
these casks have to be topped from from time to time,
so there will be no air space left inside. This will be
your job now. Each winery handles this in its own
way. Signore Calabro will demonstrate how we do it."

With that, he swung around and left.

Amy watched carefully as Signore Calabro picked
up a wooden mallet and gave a sharp blow to the
wooden bung protruding from the cask, knocking it
off. Then he took a container filled with wine and
gave a hard suck on the end of the siphon hose attached. As the wine appeared, he stuck the hose into
the cask, letting the wine run into it. When the cask
was filled he removed the siphon, pounded the bung
back and turned to Amy.

"Ha capito?" he asked.

She nodded, guessing at his meaning. "I understand."

He handed her the mallet. Taking it in her hand,
she went over to the next cask and tapped at the
bung. It didn't budge. Realizing she was going to
have to put a little more force into the blow, she tried
again until it worked.

Taking the wine container, she sucked gingerly at
the siphon. Nothing happened. She tried once more,
pulling in her breath hard and steadily. The wine came
up the tube so quickly it surprised her, and she ended
up with wine all over the front of her shirt. Quickly she
stuck the end of the hose into the bunghole until the
cask was filled, then she replaced the bung.

Signore Calabro gave a quick unexpected grin. "Okay!" he said, patting her on the shoulder. Then the grin disappeared and he looked stern once more as he walked off.

Amy began moving down the row, knocking off bungs, inspecting the level of the wine within each cask and adding more as needed. It was much nicer work than cleaning tanks. The air was fresh, and she was exhilarated at learning something new. As hard as the cleaning had been, it was a hurdle she'd cleared. Now she was truly beginning to feel part of the wine-making process.

That evening when she walked back to the villa she was far less weary and her step was lighter. But in back of her mind still loomed Elisa's shadow and the ever increasing possibility that things might change.

Amy had just stepped out of the shower a short time later and was toweling her hair dry when there was a knock at her bedroom door. Grabbing a robe off the chair, she went over to open the door. An elderly female servant stood there, gaunt and faintly stooped in her neat black uniform.

"*Signorina*...." Then came a string of Italian words.

Amy shook her head apologetically. "I don't... ah...I don't...*no capito*," she tried, resurrecting Signore Calabro's words.

"*La mia signora, la signora Bonavia*...." The woman frowned, looking baffled. She gave a nervous shrug of thin shoulders.

Apparently Aunt Lucia must want something and had sent the maid to fetch her, Amy decided. It was still too early for dinner, so it must be something else.

Pointing to her robe, then back at her clothes she had laid out on the bed a little earlier, Amy held up her hand and said, *"Momento!"*

The elderly face brightened with relief as the woman nodded her gray head, then stepped back, closing the door softly.

Amy crossed the room, wondering what the summons was all about. Well, she told herself philosophically, she would know soon enough.

In moments she was slipping into a simple white sheath and buckling a slender gold belt about her waist. As she did so she thought of her first day at the winery, when she had wearily dragged herself up the road only to encounter the vision of Elisa, so crisp and elegant in her sleeveless white dress.

She scowled at herself in the mirror. Elisa's presence seemed to infiltrate everything.

Amy drew a quick comb through her still-damp hair and hurried to the door. Upon opening it she was surprised to see the servant still there waiting, her hands clasped patiently. The woman bowed her head, murmured, *"Prego,"* and started, not toward the stairs, as Amy had expected, but in the opposite direction.

Prego. Amy's mind almost automatically translated it. It was that omnibus term again, the one that could mean many things. Pray come in, please do, a reply to thank-you and, in this case, please come along. Here she was, she told herself, beginning to learn a few helpful words in Italian. But of what use would they be, how much chance would she have to learn many more, if Elisa triumphed?

Why am I taking such a negative attitude about things, Amy asked herself. Today there had been a promotion, or certainly what amounted to one. Signore Calabro seemed to be pleased with her progress. Yet Amy found she couldn't fend off a feeling of unease, or of impending... impending what? She couldn't analyze it. Nevertheless there was a strange hollow developing in the pit of her stomach. Animals, she had read, can sense the coming of an earthquake and begin to stir restlessly. If animals have that kind of premonition, Amy thought, then who was to say that people didn't?

She tried to shake off such thoughts, only partly succeeding by the time the maid stopped in front of a door and tapped lightly. Upon hearing Aunt Lucia's voice from within, she opened the door and stood back to allow Amy to enter.

It was a charming bed-sitting room, Amy's eyes registered as she went in. A soft rose and pale green Oriental carpet covered the floor, and rose velvet draperies at the windows were pulled back to allow the late rays of the sun to enter. Marble-topped tables were covered with gold-framed photographs and the mantel of the marble fireplace held a number of delicate porcelain figurines. It seemed a very feminine room for this austere woman.

Aunt Lucia was sitting in a tapestried chair, with a square of needlepoint on which she had been working resting on her lap. She motioned Amy toward a green velvet chair.

"Sit down, Amy, I'd like to have a talk with you."

As Amy slipped tensely into the designated seat,

Aunt Lucia said, "We shall have our talk in a minute, but first Maria is bringing us some tea."

Almost immediately a servant came into the room, carrying a tray, which she set upon a small table beside her mistress. As she left Amy gave a quick oblique look at Aunt Lucia.

It was like gazing at the face of a marble statue, cold, withdrawn, unrevealing. Yet, Amy thought, it was seldom any other way.

Aunt Lucia carefully placed her needlepoint in a basket on the floor beside her and began pouring tea. Handing a cup to Amy, she said, "I understand that you have now left your work in the fermenting tanks and have begun on the topping process?" She lifted thin eyebrows.

Amy took her cup, saying, "Yes, Aunt Lucia. And to be truthful, I like it better than cleaning tanks." She smiled ruefully. "That wasn't the most pleasant work I've ever done."

Aunt Lucia's eyes fixed on Amy with an intense unwavering gaze. "I assume you still insist on learning what you can about wine making, despite my warning and despite the knowledge that Nando certainly doesn't want you working there?"

Amy shifted uncomfortably in her chair. Was this why she had been summoned, to be given another lecture about women working in the winery? The whole subject was more than a little ludicrous when it was being talked about by a woman who was much more involved in it than anyone.

But Amy was not going to be intimidated. "Yes, Aunt Lucia, I do want to continue," she said. "I'm sorry if it doesn't meet with either your approval or Nando's, but I honestly do want to learn."

"Why?" The word came sharply.

"Why do I want to learn?" Amy considered how to phrase her answer. "I don't know why I am so drawn to it, Aunt Lucia," she said earnestly. "But there's something about it, about the sound of the crusher and the way it sends out that wonderful smell of grapes, the look of the new wine, the bite of yeast in the air— Well, I just can't describe it." She shrugged. "All I know is that when I came here I was curious about the industry. But now I'm certain that it means something. . . something important to me. Or—" she looked candidly at Aunt Lucia "—or I wouldn't have stuck it out, cleaning the tanks.

"Maybe I was trying to prove something to myself, too," she added honestly. "And perhaps to you and Nando."

"You are certain that no matter how hard the work, you will stubbornly insist on staying on?" The words were blunt.

Amy's eyes met the older woman's directly. She refused to be intimidated by what might be a veiled warning. "Yes, Aunt Lucia. No matter how hard the work," Amy said firmly.

Aunt Lucia nodded slowly. "I see, I see." Abruptly the whole atmosphere seemed to take on a less tense, less stern feeling.

The older woman lifted her teacup and took a slow deliberate swallow. Putting the cup down again she said, "Very well. All right, Amy, I must say I believe you. So after you have been exposed to several more of the processes in the winery, you will then go into the laboratory where testing is done. In time you will receive all the practical instruction possible, to help you to take your place with us."

Amy opened her mouth in astonishment. This was certainly not what she had expected! Not at all! "Why, I...this is very kind...of you, Aunt Lucia," she stammered.

"Kind? Nonsense. You had the determination, the tenacity to endure the hard task of tank cleaning—work I highly disapproved of, as I told Nando. But you did it without whimpering or complaining. I respect you, Amy; I admire your spirit. In the brief time you have been here you have become one of us." The gray eyes warmed with approval, and a faint smile curved the usually firm mouth.

What an abrupt change! Amy's mind had trouble accommodating itself to the woman's sudden and immense switch of attitude. "Why...thank you, Aunt Lucia," she managed.

Abruptly the gray eyes darkened and the skin seemed to draw tight on the older woman's face until her cheekbones stood out sharp and white.

"I am, however, displeased," she said harshly. "Very displeased."

Startled, Amy could only stare. She couldn't keep up with such abrupt reversals. Now what had she done?

But the woman gave her a quick understanding look. "Oh, not you, my child, not you. It is my son who displeases me." She paused for a long moment, so long that Amy wondered if something in the way of a response was expected.

Apparently not, for the woman continued, "You have met Elisa Antolini!"

Indeed I have, Amy thought vehemently. But, though Signora Bonavia's statement was in no way a question, Amy dutifully nodded, agreeing that she had.

"I presume you have noticed, also, that my son has not been much in evidence these past few days. We were commenting on it at dinner last evening, you no doubt recall."

"Well, yes, I do," Amy replied. Aunt Lucia actually looked distrait, she thought, which was very unlike a woman who always seemed in such rigid control of herself.

As abruptly as before, the subject changed again. Amy was kept busy trying to follow the older woman's shifting train of thought.

"I am certain, Amy, that you are already aware of the history of Vino d'Oro, how for generations it has always been under the ownership of the same family. The Bonavias...." She paused, then with a slight show of reluctance added, "And the Rinaldis, which you and Franco represent. But all stemming from the Montagnes, and all part of the same bloodline. This is most important. It is a matter of heritage, it must be guarded jealously, and it must always be kept in the family!"

Preferably the Bonavia family, Amy reflected, recalling how hard Nando had tried to pry her share of the business away from her.

"There is, however, an immediate danger," Aunt Lucia said. "Signore Paolo Antolini has a winery, but it is having problems. Their chief vintner died recently and his replacement can't seem to produce stable wines. They have lost business and respect. Nando offered to buy them out, but Signore Antolini refuses, wishing instead to go into business with us. He knows Nando can reestablish good wines, and he wants Nando very much.''

He is not the only Antolini who wants Nando. Elisa wants him, Amy thought, picturing the determined look on the girl's face when she had said, ''He's mine!''

The older woman unknowingly echoed Amy's thoughts. ''And so, I may say, does Elisa Antolini. She is brazen and aggressive in her pursuit, acting in a manner no young woman would have dared to in my day. And few, I trust, would do so now. She is blatantly using—'' the woman's lip curled ''—carnal temptation. Not, I hope, successfully as yet.''

Aunt Lucia paused before saying in a slow measured tone, ''She will not succeed; I forbid it. My son will never marry an Antolini, much less as shallow a young woman as Elisa Antolini is.''

''But,'' Amy began, feeling that some response was required of her, ''but if they fall in love—''

''Nonsense!'' The older woman almost spat out the word, her eyes blazing. ''Absolute nonsense! Nando fall in love with Elisa? Not a son of mine! He desires her perhaps. He is a man, after all, and she possesses obvious allurement. But marriage? No! And he must not be tricked into it!''

Wearily she turned wise eyes on Amy. ''I am not unaware that the sexual urge can exist strongly out of wedlock, but it is no foundation for a marriage.''

Her mouth hardened. "Such a marriage would be doomed to failure. Fires may burn hot, but they eventually cool, and only ashes remain."

Amy was beginning to feel embarrassed. All these confidences the woman would surely regret later. And, though Amy didn't like to say so, she wondered if Aunt Lucia might be fighting a losing battle. Elisa's beauty, her sensual appeal and her determination might well lure Nando away from his present opposition to marriage. In such a circumstance it was not likely that a mother's objection would be able to prevent a strong-minded son from doing as he wished.

"However, for all the Antolinis' plans to force themselves into our winery, they are doomed to failure!" Aunt Lucia said contemptuously.

A change came over her thin face—a look of satisfaction, of triumph. "It is very simple, my dear Amy," she said. "You shall marry Nando."

CHAPTER TEN

FOR A FEW SECONDS there was absolute silence in the room. Then Amy set her teacup down so abruptly that it rattled in the saucer.

"Aunt Lucia—" she began, but the other woman cut calmly across her words.

"Of course it's the only solution, Amy. I should have seen it from the first. I am sorry, my dear, that when you arrived here I was not as hospitable as I should have been. I admit that I did not especially welcome a distant cousin, particularly one from America, whom I felt was selfishly holding on to our missing share of the winery. But now I see it was fate that you should arrive at just this time." She nodded her head with the air of one who has not only come to a decision but is pleased with it.

Amy managed a firmer tone this time. "You must listen to me, Aunt Lucia. It's absolutely out of the question. Nando certainly does not want to marry me. And I am not going to marry him." This woman was incredible, Amy thought, arranging people's lives like this! Marriage to Nando? She closed her mind immediately to the thought.

Aunt Lucia held up a placating hand. Amy almost expected her to say, "Tut-tut, my dear!" But she didn't. She said, "You told me you were not affianced to anyone. I believe that if you give some thought to this, you will see advantages. You and Nando shall marry; upon my death he will inherit my share. You will have children—sons, I hope—and the family winery will be secure." She nodded several times.

The whole thing was so ridiculous, Amy thought. She had to dissuade the woman before Nando was brought into it. And she refused to allow herself to imagine his reaction! "But, Aunt Lucia, if neither Nando nor I wishes to get married, we certainly shouldn't. It would be misery for both of us!"

Aunt Lucia was already shaking her head. "My dear, you are not Italian. You are not European. We have our ways, and they are good ways. The marriage of convenience is not new to us. Even in this age it is sometimes practiced, particularly by those of us who appreciate the advantages. I speak from my own experience."

The woman was twisting one of the heavy rings on her fingers. "My father was a vintner. We had a very small winery, which was successful for its size. But he had a large family, too many daughters. He had a friend, a Signore Bonavia, who also had a winery, and a son. Our marriage was arranged between the two families. My husband and I did not know each other well at all, for whenever we met we were accompanied by a stern chaperon."

The cool gray eyes abruptly softened. "It was a good marriage. For thirty-three years we were happy. When he died, something died in me."

"It worked for you, Aunt Lucia," Amy said gently, "but you are right when you say I am not European, not Italian. I'm afraid we don't do things this way in America."

"Ah, perhaps, but you are not in America now, and Nando is not American. He is not unaware of the custom." The words were emphatic. The woman calmly picked up her needlepoint and began stitching on it.

Marriage to Nando? A nerve jumped in her throat. She barely dared consider it. A man who didn't love her? Who loved someone else? Never! Not even if he were willing. But how could he be? Had he agreed? Aunt Lucia was perfectly calm, as if it had all been discussed and decided.

"Aunt Lucia?"

The woman glanced up. "Yes?"

"Does Nando know about this idea of yours?"

Aunt Lucia nodded, taking her scissors and cutting a length of thread.

"And what does he think of it?" Amy asked, her voice not at all steady.

"Oh, he objects, or so I gather. At present, anyhow. But he'll come around. The winery is important to him, very important, as I presume you know." Aunt Lucia looked up from her needlepoint and nodded her head confidently.

"But if he doesn't want the marriage, and. . .and I don't, then how—"

Aunt Lucia's expression became impatient. "Love comes after marriage, if it is a good marriage. And this one would be good. You are both dedicated to the winery; you each own a share of it. You are very pretty and you are intelligent, young enough to have children. It is ideal. Nando has a temper, and he is stubborn, but he is no fool.''

Stubborn, Amy thought. *It's Aunt Lucia who's stubborn.*

"Besides, Amy, I know my son. I should; we are alike, both headstrong. He is angry and frustrated because you have bested him about your share." Aunt Lucia gave a dry amused smile. "But he is aware of you, that I know, quite aware. He will not be that difficult to persuade, I am certain."

"But, Aunt Lucia," Amy began again, wondering a little hopelessly how she could get through to this inflexible woman. Before she could say more there was a light tap at the door.

Aunt Lucia glanced up in satisfaction. "Nando," she said. "I have asked him to come so we could discuss this matter together."

If Amy could have sunk through the floor, she gladly would have done so. Nando had humiliated her thoroughly once, and she had a feeling he was about to do so again, in quite another way. To be told, however politely, that he wouldn't think of marrying her was not exactly something she was anticipating with any pleasure.

Amy quickly lowered her eyelids, reluctant to make eye contact with him. He greeted her briefly, then to his mother said something in Italian, his voice bristling.

Aunt Lucia said calmly, "Speak in English. After all, Amy is to be considered, you know."

Nando whirled around. "I suppose my mother has told you of her ludicrous idea of forcing a marriage between us?"

"She has." Amy felt temper beginning to stir inside her. Perhaps he wasn't interested in marriage, especially this one dreamed up by his mother, but he ought to realize that he wasn't the only one concerned.

He strode over to Amy, his eyes unreadable. "And what do you have to say about it?"

She replied suddenly, and more tartly than she planned, "I said no, of course. I said I would not marry you."

Nando turned back to his mother. "You see? It's exactly what I told you. You can't possibly force—"

"Nando, will you hold your tongue? Perhaps I haven't made myself clear. You know what will happen if you marry Elisa Antolini. Our winery won't be our winery any longer," Aunt Lucia said grimly.

"And who said I was going to marry her?" Nando's lips compressed and his dark eyes snapped.

"You might not have a choice in the matter. There are certain ways you could be forced into it. Women have used them for centuries. And you had better pray to your Maker that, if you have been intimate with her, she is not already expecting a child!" Aunt Lucia said frankly. "I certainly wouldn't put it beyond her to use that means of securing what she is after, knowing that a Bonavia does not turn away from his responsibilities."

"I am not a child, nor am I a fool. Though I feel it is not necessary for me to explain, Elisa would have no reason upon which to base such a claim. I am not her lover," Nando said hotly.

"Ah, perhaps not, not yet. But I can read the signs and the motives of that young woman. You may not be a fool, but you are a man and you could be susceptible if temptation is sufficient," his mother sniffed.

Nando's lips firmed in a hard line. "Nevertheless, you cannot force a marriage between Amy and me."

His mother jerked at a thread, then glanced up at her son. "Very well, then you leave me no alternative. I'm quite aware that Franco would like to have more power. His demeanor does not hide that from me. He would, I am certain, be eager to join me and Anna Maria in refusing to allow an Antolini into our winery. As majority owners we could prevent it. And should you not agree with our decision, we will, if necessary, replace you as vintner." The words were stony.

Amy listened to the two of them, stupefied. Nervously, she picked up her teacup and took a sip. The tea was cold.

"But you forget, Anna Maria will soon be out of your control. She will be married," Nando said.

"Not if I don't allow her to marry. She is more obedient than you, my son."

"You wouldn't do that! Not when she and Filippo—"

Aunt Lucia lifted cold gray eyes to meet angry gray eyes. "Wouldn't I? Then you don't understand your mother very well when it comes to family matters!"

"My God! What a mess!" Nando drew in his breath harshly. "If you have no consideration of my feelings, think of Amy. You can't force her into a marriage she so obviously doesn't want. You can't!"

It was like stone wall meeting stone wall in a steady pressure of will, Amy thought, watching them silently. Neither of them seemed willing to yield an inch.

"My son," the woman began in a more conciliatory tone, "consider this. Our winery is growing in prestige. Will you allow the Antolinis to insinuate themselves into Vino d'Oro with their flashy advertising, their often mediocre product? Never! You must not allow it. I will not permit it. Marriage to Elisa Antolini would cause nothing but conflict and chaos. Please discontinue seeing the young woman. I do not trust her motives, and I do not trust your resistance."

Then she leaned back stiffly in her chair, her high arched nose, the sharp angles of her cheek and jawbone harshly dominating her thin face. "Very well, I have said what I have to say. I expect both of you to do as I recommend. No, not recommend—" she gave a slight inclination of her head "—let us say instead that I insist!"

She lifted a dismissing hand. "You may go. I suggest you talk this over between you and make plans for the wedding. I shall expect you at dinner shortly. Both of you." She gave a sharp warning look at Nando.

Amy rose, her knees unsteady beneath her. She felt as if she had been blown about by a hurricane. As she started toward the door after a polite but admittedly cool nod of her head toward Aunt Lucia, she found Nando beside her.

Together they went out into the hall. Nando turned to glance back at the closed door of his mother's room. *"Dio mio!"* he breathed in exasperation. "Have you ever heard anything like that? Ordering us, *ordering* us to enter into a marriage of convenience. I'm afraid my mother has delusions of monarchy!"

Amy walked along silently. For the moment she was too stirred up to offer any comment.

Nando said unexpectedly, "You know, you mustn't underestimate her. My mother is a very determined woman, and she is intent on having her way about this. We might very well end up married at that."

"I very much doubt it!" Amy replied hotly. She felt nothing but embarrassed over the whole affair.

"She is stubborn and she is clever, so don't count her out," Nando said reluctantly. "I've heard stories about her—things that happened during the last days of the war. The Germans were retreating through this part of the country, commandeering and destroying as they went. In Verona they senselessly bombed all the ancient bridges over the Adige, then they came on through here.

"My father was away with the army, but my mother had all the local people—women, children, the elderly men who were left—gather up every single bottle of wine and hide it. There were bottles under hedges, in stables, even in people's beds. She was not going to allow the Nazis to have one swallow of Vino d'Oro."

They paused outside Amy's room and he continued, "My mother was not elderly then, but she dressed to appear so. She sat behind the big desk in the reception room of the castle with a shawl over her head, waiting for the Nazis, whom she hated bitterly. When a German colonel came into the castle demanding wine, she apparently told him in a shaking, whining voice that there was none, and that there had been none for a long time.

"He didn't believe her at first and threatened to blow up the castle. But—" Nando lifted a wry eyebrow "—luckily for him she convinced him, and he withdrew without bothering her or the castle itself. I say luckily, because I understand she was holding a revolver in her lap—a weapon she was perfectly capable and willing to use to save the family winery."

"Your mother may be stubborn, but so am I," Amy said. "I don't intend to be forced into a marriage with you!"

Nando looked down at her, his eyes suddenly chilled. "If you'd only had sense enough to listen to me in New York, to sell me your damned share of the business then and there, none of this would have happened."

So it was her own fault! Amy felt that right now she had taken all she could stand of the Bonavias, mother and son. A wave of indignation boiled up inside of her.

"I happen to own part of the winery, Nando," she snapped. "It is legally mine, and I am going to keep it! Also, I am not going to marry you. I can't imagine anything I would like less! Is that clear?" she flung out impulsively. Then she went into her room and shut the door emphatically.

It was not yet time for dinner, so Amy went out on her balcony and sank into a chair, staring moodily down at the dark silhouette of the castle.

Could Nando be right? Could his mother somehow force them into this marriage? But how could she? Still, Nando hadn't seemed completely certain that it was an impossibility. "Don't underestimate her," he had said. But. . . just supposing that it did happen? What then?

It was a little difficult to contemplate that eventuality with complete composure. In fact the very thought of it caused something within Amy to break loose from all bonds. There was no way she could evade the truth—that she deeply cared for this troublesome man. That she actually loved him. And it wasn't just a purely physical attraction. Not anymore. Now it was something she feared she would never get over.

Amy let herself open to her feelings for him, the love that was soft and warm and gently enfolding. . . and hopeless.

She gazed off into the distance. She was a fool, perhaps all kinds of a fool, to feel like this about someone who didn't care about her. But it changed nothing.

If Aunt Lucia had her way, what kind of a marriage would they possibly have? Would she remain a virgin bride, Amy wondered. No, surely not, not with a man like Nando. Though he had coldly, calculatingly staged that scene at Lago di Verde, planning to disturb and arouse her with his lips, his hands, his virile body.. had it been *all* artificial fire? That fierce inflamed insistence as he pressed against her might have been planned, but he hadn't been able to restrain it, either.

"A hot-blooded Italian, quick to passion," Elisa had said. Amy leaned back in the chair, a speculative look in her eyes. A celibate marriage? Somehow, considering how macho, how sensual Nando was, it seemed improbable.

Amy thrust herself out of the chair. She must not go on thinking this way! She certainly wouldn't want a marriage that he didn't want. It would be a travesty, ending in unhappiness for both of them.

She wished she didn't have to go down to dinner, but she felt there was not much choice. In the mood Aunt Lucia was in, she might send up for her.

At nine-thirty Amy went reluctantly down the steps and into the salon. They were all there. Franco was chatting with Anna Maria, about her wedding plans. Nando, his face dark, was gazing down at his glass of wine. And Aunt Lucia, Amy thought, looked supremely satisfied. Irritatingly satisfied!

The older woman glanced up, giving Amy a surprisingly warm smile. She held out her hand, lifting her paper-dry cheek to be kissed.

Amy was startled but complied. She turned to see a look of astonishment on the faces of both Anna Maria and Franco.

"Nando, the Chiaro, please," Aunt Lucia lifted the heavily ringed hand in a grand gesture. "Yes, for me, also. For all of us. Fill the glasses."

Amy saw Nando shoot his mother a sharp look, a nerve pulsing angrily in his temple. But he poured wine into fresh glasses, taking one to his mother first, and shaking his head warningly at her while he did so. Then he brought a glass to Amy, giving her a narrow appraising stare as if to probe her thoughts. Amy, biting her lip in concern over what might be coming, looked quickly away.

"What's the celebration about?" Franco asked, glancing around. Then, taking his glass, he turned to Amy. "For you? I heard you had been paroled today from the fermentation tanks! On to bigger and better things, I trust! Congratulations!"

Observing the sudden tensing of her mouth, the fingers trembling around the stem of her glass, he stopped smiling, but before he could say anything more Aunt Lucia was speaking.

"I suggest we all toast the *fidanzati*, the betrothed pair who will shortly marry."

Franco made a half gesture with his glass toward Anna Maria, saying, "But, Filippo...?" Then, conscious that something was not right, he turned and looked at Aunt Lucia, who was smiling and nodding regally.

"To Nando, my dear son, and to Amy, my cousin and future daughter-in-law."

There was a moment's silence so stunned that one could almost hear it.

Amy clung tightly to her glass, afraid of dropping it. How dared she! How dared Aunt Lucia push ruthlessly ahead like this!

Nando was shaking his head, saying something to

his mother in Italian, his voice biting. Amy didn't have to understand what he was saying, she could sense it.

Aunt Lucia remained completely unruffled. She ignored the Italian and replied in English, "But, my dear son, of course you will. Of course you must."

Anna Maria, who had been looking at her mother, then at Nando, her large eyes wide and puzzled, slowly turned to Amy. "Are you really going to marry Nando?" Then her usual bright nature broke through. "Oh, Amy, say you are! I've always wanted a sister! And you, more than anyone. It's absolutely marvelous. I didn't want...I was so afraid...not that really impossible Elisa!"

Whirling about to gaze at her mother, she said, "Why not a double wedding? Amy and Nando, with Filippo and me?" Her eyes sparkled. The older woman hesitated, then nodded approvingly.

But Anna Maria was the only one sparkling, Amy realized numbly. Aunt Lucia had now reverted to her imperious air, eyes like an eagle's, sharp and unyielding. Nando was half turned away, leaning against the mantel, staring down into his glass as if he were in another world.

Franco's voice was tense and wary as he said, "Is this true, Amy?"

Amy was shaking her head, but Aunt Lucia, missing nothing, said, "But of course it is. Amy, Franco, is either of you inclined to see the Antolinis affiliate with our winery? Ah, I can see you aren't. Well, this will prevent it."

Nando lifted his head and seemed about to speak,

but his mother gazed at him forbiddingly. "Enough. I do not care to discuss this further. It is not open to argument. Now, shall we finish our Chiaro and go in to dinner? I have asked Maria to prepare a betrothal feast for tonight."

I should be Alice in Wonderland instead of myself. Only Alice could have found herself in such a bizarre situation, Amy thought dazedly, lifting her glass, the wine for the first time tasteless in her mouth.

Almost on cue a servant appeared in the doorway. Aunt Lucia rose, setting her empty glass on a table beside her, then moved regally across the room. She smiled fondly on Amy as she passed.

"My God, Amy," breathed Franco, touching her elbow as if to guide her, "this is insane."

She nodded. "It certainly is. And it's not true. I don't intend to marry Nando."

He gave a sigh. "That's a relief to hear! But I warn you, I see trouble ahead."

Amy agreed. "So do I. But it just isn't going to happen."

As they filed into the dining room, Amy halted at the door, aghast. White roses entwined with silver cord were placed along the entire length of the table. White tapers flamed steadily in silver holders.

The woman was incredible! Aunt Lucia was completely deaf to protests, going firmly ahead with her plans. For a few giddy moments Amy wondered if, in spite of everyone and everything, Aunt Lucia was forcibly going to have her way.

The dinner was as splendid and impressive as any betrothal feast could be, but Amy had little appetite.

The lobster bisque, then the saltimbocca made of tender veal and delicate ham, were as tasteless as ashes in her mouth.

There was tension, too, around the table. Only Aunt Lucia seemed impervious to it. Conversation was politely kept balanced like a spiritless ball, but Nando confined himself to monosyllables—dour ones at that. Amy found herself twisting her napkin in her lap with taut fingers between courses, avoiding Nando's eyes.

It was over coffee, served in tiny white porcelain cups, that Aunt Lucia calmly forced her plans along.

"Amy, my dear, for this auspicious occasion I have a small gift for you. Nando, will you hand this to her, please?" Aunt Lucia gave him a small white box. He took it but hesitated, gazing down at it suspiciously.

Aunt Lucia's voice sharpened. "I said it is for Amy, Nando!"

Nando touched his lips with his napkin, pushed back his chair and stood up, walking around the table to Amy. He handed her the box with a warning look in his eyes.

Amy swallowed hard, her hand unsteady as she took it from him. She didn't want to open it, premonition making her uneasy. But other than causing an awkward scene, there was no way of refusing a present.

Nando went back to his chair and sat down as Amy lifted the lid of the small white box. Then her eyes abruptly widened. It was a ring, a lovely glittering ruby surrounded by small rubies in a charming old-fashioned setting. It was exquisite.

She looked up at Aunt Lucia. "Oh, but I can't, I truly can't accept anything like this. It's lovely, Aunt Lucia, but...I simply can't."

"It is yours. It was Nando's grandmother's ring, her betrothal ring. When I married Nando's father, his mother was still living, so he had one made for me exactly like it." She held up her left hand where the rubies flashed.

"Perhaps I should have entrusted it to Nando to give to you, to place it on your finger, but in his present rebellious mood I preferred this way."

Amy was appalled. How could this woman meddle in people's lives, manipulate them like this because of her own personal wishes?

She sat there looking down at the ring for another moment, then carefully closed the lid. This was neither the time nor the place to thrust the gift back at Aunt Lucia. But it must be done. Lifting her eyes, she met Nando's. He gave a slight shake of his head then a resigned shrug, as if he, too, knew this wasn't the moment to continue the battle.

But something had to be said. Aunt Lucia was waiting.

"Perhaps...perhaps we can talk about it later," Amy said lamely. It wasn't much of an answer, she realized, but she could think of no other words to avoid confrontation in front of the servants.

"No need, no need." Aunt Lucia brushed away all problems with a casual wave of her hand. "It is yours. And someday it will go to your eldest son for his bride. Or perhaps I should say mine will, for I shall certainly predecease you. But the two rings will bind generations together."

It was impossible to differ with the woman, Amy realized. She simply did not hear opposition.

It was a subdued group reentering the salon after dinner, that is, everyone but Aunt Lucia was subdued. She seemed completely unaware that the others spoke in strained tones. Even the normally talkative Anna Maria was quiet, her eyes looking from Nando to Amy worriedly. She, too, was uncomfortable with the pressure being so firmly applied, in defiance of the desires of the two people concerned.

Amy glanced up at one point to see the older woman gazing at her in a strange contemplative way. It was disconcerting.

Finally Aunt Lucia spoke, for the first time with some show of hesitancy. "My dear Amy, I feel that now is the proper time for you to be given certain information. You will soon be family. I have not spoken about it to you before; no need for a foreign cousin to know everything."

She paused, then added, "I have not been exactly candid with you. I . . . I do have some part in the running of the winery."

Amy was not in any mood to evade issues at the moment. Her emotions and her feelings had been too thoroughly shaken during the day. "Yes, Aunt Lucia. I know."

"You know?" The older woman turned accusingly toward Franco. "Then it must have been you who took it upon yourself to inform her! You had no right!" Her words were tinged with acid.

Amy couldn't allow that. "No, Aunt Lucia. Franco did not tell me."

The probing eyes swung back to her. "Then may I ask just how...who had the temerity...." There was sharp anger in her voice.

Amy felt the blood creeping into her face. "I...I overheard it." She might as well go on now, she decided grimly. "I was having breakfast out on my balcony the morning John Delby came. You were sitting on the terrace below."

Nando's voice sliced in like a knife. "And I—was I there at the time?"

Amy avoided looking at him. She had to swallow before answering, for her throat had gone suddenly dry. "Yes." That was all she could seem to get out.

A silence followed her reply, broken by Nando. *"Dio!"* His one word rang in the room like the stroke of a gong.

He got up out of his chair and stood looking down at Amy. "So you heard that, too," he said quietly, "my comments about you."

Amy glanced up to meet his fathomless gray eyes, then quickly looked away. "Yes, I did. I realized then why you had treated me so...strangely. A mistake of judgment on your part, by the way."

She was conscious that he stood there for a long minute before turning on his heel and walking to the other side of the room.

Then Aunt Lucia spoke up in her cool precise voice. "What is done is done. We Bonavias have not come out of this favorably, I must admit. But in spite of all you overheard, what you learned of our plans, Amy, you still took on that despicable work in the fermentation tanks. And you never said a word to us."

"It didn't matter, not really," Amy said frankly. "I wanted to work, for it was the only way I could learn."

"I suppose there's no use asking what this is all about?" Franco asked, his voice reflecting his doubt.

"There isn't," Aunt Lucia said dryly. "It is enough that Nando, Amy and I know. It doesn't apply to anyone else."

Resolutely she changed the conversation. "From now on, Amy, since you have passed one of the most arduous tests at the winery, perhaps you would like to come back to the villa for lunch instead of taking yours with you. Especially since your fellow workers will soon learn that you're to become a member of the family, the immediate family, I mean. You might find it more. . . more appropriate."

"I would prefer to continue on as I am," Amy said firmly. "I believe Signore Calabro has been instructed that I'm not to have special privileges or special treatment." She paused, then said uncertainly, "Unless my being moved from the tanks to the wine topping might be considered—"

"You were given that because you earned it, and for no other reason," Nando broke in tersely. "One of the young men who started with you has also been given another job."

Amy stood up with a tight-lipped smile. "Then I must be certain I do well—which means I must go to bed now. Morning comes around rather quickly, I find."

Franco also rose and would have accompanied her

had Aunt Lucia not said, "No need of that, Franco. She knows the way to her room by now."

Nando himself made no move, so after a brief good-night Amy started up the stairs, grateful to be left alone. Her body was weary, her emotions in a state of chaos.

Each time an anxious thought tried to push up into her mind, she roughly thrust it down. Not tonight! She felt incapable right now of making any sensible decisions.

She found the tiny white box in her pocket as she undressed. With a grimace she dropped it in a drawer. She would have to deal with that problem later, too.

She had not thought she would sleep, but she did, a sodden dreamless sleep that found her unrefreshed by morning.

If Nando was around the winery that day, she didn't see him, or Franco, either. However, when she was ready to leave late in the afternoon, Franco was waiting outside the gate for her just as Elisa had been the week before.

He moved quickly toward her as she stepped outside the courtyard. "I must talk to you without delay, Amy," he said, a sharp edge to his voice.

She knew what he wanted to talk about; it wasn't difficult to guess. "It's really quite a situation, isn't it?"

She nodded. "I feel as if I've fallen into a millstream and am being swept along no matter what I try to do. Aunt Lucia is difficult to reason with."

"Difficult?" Franco gave a short derisive laugh.

"No, not difficult. Impossible! Now that she has this marriage in mind, don't be surprised if she finds some way of managing it to a conclusion. If she can sit up there in the villa looking fragile and elderly, seldom putting a foot in the winery yet running the whole business with the skill of some international oil tycoon, she can certainly maneuver two seemingly reluctant people into a marriage."

They started walking slowly up the hill. It was a bright day, the sun only now beginning to dim slightly. Small veils of white clouds were sifting across the sky. Why, Amy thought, was everything here so beautiful and the people so difficult? Only Anna Maria and Filippo seemed free of complications—unless Aunt Lucia actually meant what she said about stopping their marriage in order to put pressure on Nando.

Franco gave Amy a quick sideways look. "It is not too late, you know. You still have time to join us. Aunt Lucia can do nothing if we stand together, you, Filippo and I. And I might point out, certainly not for the first time, that marriage between us would solve your present dilemma."

Amy turned her head and gave him a wry smile. "A marriage of convenience versus a marriage of convenience?"

Franco shrugged. "No, not quite the same. In this particular case the groom is willing. Nando may be a fine vintner and not a bad sort really, but he is ferociously stubborn and arrogant. He doesn't like the fact that you got around him to work in the winery. That's no secret. Can you imagine what marriage to a reluctant balky Nando would be like? It would certainly have some disadvantages.''

He was right, of course. But it wasn't going to happen. "I'm not married to him, nor do I plan to be, Franco. I still fail to see how Aunt Lucia can possibly force us into it. She could, of course, make life unpleasant for me—enough to make me move out of the villa. But I still own a share of the business, so there might be second thoughts about forcing me out of the winery itself.''

As they neared the gate of the villa Franco made one more effort. "Amy, I know you think you can resist. Perhaps you can, but only for a short time. I've seen Aunt Lucia putting on pressure before. She doesn't hold back!''

The old servant pulled open the gate, and Amy and Franco strolled up toward the terrace. Before going inside, Amy hesitated for a second to say, ''I simply cannot accept the idea of a marriage of convenience. Not to you, not to anyone else. Love is important to me. I...I don't want to be bartered for my share.''

Aunt Lucia was crossing the entrance hall as they came in. She turned toward them, and for a moment there was a grim look on the thin face. But her greeting was cordial enough. It was only as Amy headed for the stairs that she thought she detected a contemplative look in the woman's gray eyes.

If anything could make Amy more uneasy about Aunt Lucia, it was that calculating look, there for a second then gone. But she trudged on up the stairs with Franco, then left him to go to her own room.

When she was alone at last she sank down on the

edge of her bed and stared unseeingly at the carpet. It was one hell of a situation, she thought angrily. If she married Nando she would be tied to a man who resented not only her but the situation itself. And if she didn't marry him, more than likely Elisa Antolini would, ensuring Amy's own hasty return to New York.

She got to her feet restlessly and went over to the window. There it was, the precious winery. The source of all the trouble, for to the Bonavias the winery was everything.

It might even be more important than Anna Maria's happiness! Surely Aunt Lucia wouldn't ruin her own daughter's joy in order to force her will on Nando! Would she?

Amy turned away from the window. Going over to her dressing table she pulled open a drawer and took out the ruby engagement ring, looking at it with sober green eyes. This gift had not been given on impulse. Aunt Lucia must, at least in her own mind, be certain she was doing the best thing. Turning the ring about, watching the light sparkle in its many facets, Amy wondered what to expect next in the way of surprises from the strong-willed woman.

IT WAS NOT AUNT LUCIA but Nando who surprised her next. He sat down beside her on the sofa after dinner and said, "We've been invited to a wine festival in one of the hill towns this coming weekend, on Sunday. A representative from the family or the winery is always expected to be present." He paused, then added stiffly, "Would you like to go?"

Of course she would! Anything about the winery held interest for her. And this sounded rather like a matter of Vino d'Oro business than any personal invitation."

"Oh, yes, I've heard of wine festivals," Amy exclaimed. "Will our wine be available there?"

He nodded. "Perhaps not the new Chiaro. But we will send a number of our regular wines. It's really a matter of quantity rather than quality that is in demand, I'm afraid."

Anna Maria laughed suddenly, her eyes glinting. "Oh, just you wait, Amy! You'll come home exhausted. Maybe even a little *ubriaca*," she said mischievously. "There'll be so much wine about and so many people wanting you to drink with them that you may find you've suddenly had a drop or two too much."

There wasn't laughter in Franco's voice or face when he managed to get her alone a little later. Giving a quick look over his shoulder as if to be certain the rest of the family were occupied, he said urgently, "Have you told Aunt Lucia or anyone about our... our conversations?"

Amy shook her head. "Not if you mean about the ownership of the winery, or about you and Filippo," she replied softly. "Or about anything else."

He gave a nervous hunch of his shoulders. "Aunt Lucia sent for me before dinner and gave me a firm lecture about not trying to force my attentions on you. She said that if I had any idea your share of the business would be turned over to anyone but Nando, I was mistaken. It was a warning, and a pretty strong one, to leave you alone."

"Perhaps she's only trying to cover all possibilities," Amy offered. "Anyhow, she heard nothing from me!"

She felt slightly guilty. Should she tell him about Aunt Lucia's threat about postponing Anna Maria's wedding? And the fact that in that case Filippo might not have a share to offer? She decided not to. Apparently the word had not been given to Anna Maria yet, either—one more unnerving sign of Aunt Lucia's determination.

Franco sighed. "The internecine intrigues of the Borgias have nothing on us! Maybe you are right, though; maybe this was nothing but a precautionary move. But I was suspicious. She often makes me feel that she can pry into my mind at will and knows exactly what I'm thinking."

Amy nodded. "I often feel that, too. She can be very disconcerting at times." It was an understatement.

AMY CAME OUT OF HER BATHROOM Saturday evening clad in a pale green nightgown. Vigorously toweling her blond hair, she let her thoughts turn to the wine festival tomorrow.

She had mixed feelings about it. Of course she wanted to go; it was the first event connected with company business that she'd had a chance to attend.

But the situation between her and Nando was awkward and, if anything, becoming more so. Both of them felt uncomfortable under the pressure being applied by Aunt Lucia. They spoke to each other little more than was necessary, and that warily. Amy realized that they were going to be the only two representing the family at the festival, and she was not exactly looking forward to spending a whole day with him.

Twice this week and again this evening, Amy had made an effort to return the ruby ring to Aunt Lucia, only to meet with unshakable refusal. And tonight Aunt Lucia had replied placidly, "Oh, no, it is yours. And you must not worry. It will be a good marriage, in spite of Nando's sometimes stormy nature. You will temper him. And I wish to hear nothing more about returning the ring."

I will not keep it, Amy had thought rebelliously. If Aunt Lucia wouldn't take it, then Nando must. And at once. She didn't want the responsibility any longer.

But after dinner there had been no chance. Nando had quietly absented himself as they left the dining room, and Amy had heard the heavy front door close behind him.

Aunt Lucia had been far from perturbed. She merely nodded approvingly, saying, "Nando is going to take care of some unfinished business this evening."

As Amy finished drying her hair and returned the towel to its rack in the bathroom, she wondered if Elisa Antolini was the "unfinished business." If so, then perhaps Aunt Lucia wasn't quite as wise as she thought, sending Nando into the velvet trap baited by those pansy eyes, that sensuous appeal. . . .

As she started toward her bed, Amy heard a tap at her door. At this time of night? She stopped, frowning a moment, then went over, opened the door a few inches and looked out.

It was Nando, wearing a dark blue dressing gown. He looked down at her steadily. "What is this all about?" he asked quietly, holding out a small white box.

"It's the ring, the Bonavia ring," she whispered. "Your mother won't take it back, so I put it in your room."

"As I discovered a short time ago when I came in. Very well, we must have a talk—tonight. Partly about this." He gestured with the box.

Amy shook her head in bewilderment. "Tomorrow, Nando. Whatever you want to talk about, surely it can wait until then. It's late."

His voice was low pitched but undeniably firm. "I am going to talk to you right now, either in the privacy of your room or out here in the hall. But I think anyone going past might draw the wrong conclusions, my being here. . .dressed as we both are."

Amy hesitated. She didn't want to let him in, yet she had a hunch he was going to do exactly as he said. Feeling she was probably making a mistake, yet not certain what to do about it, she said, "Just a minute, let me get my robe." At least she wouldn't have to worry about any amorous advances from him, not anymore, she thought swiftly.

The second she left the door he had slipped inside, closing it behind her. "Don't worry about your modesty. I've seen you in less than this, remember," he said, amusement in his voice.

Amy grabbed her dressing gown and wrapped it

around her, her hands trembling on the tie. As she turned back, her eyes snapped angrily. "I suppose I might expect a comment like that from you. I thought you were out taking care of unfinished business tonight," she said tartly.

"Quite right," he conceded, "and now there are other details to be discussed."

He motioned her toward a chair, and he himself sat on the end of the chaise longue. "We never seem to have a chance to be alone. The family is always around or we are at work. But we must get some things straightened out—before our wedding."

Amy sat back suddenly in her chair. She looked at him, stunned. "Our wedding?" Her thoughts skidded to a standstill.

Nando nodded. "Yes. Mother has finally managed to convince me." He gave her a slow appraising look that seemed to penetrate the thin material of her robe and gown. Then his eyes met hers. "Franco, it seems, has begun to be much too . . . too attentive."

Amy found her tongue. "If you mean toward me, you're crazy. We drove to Lake Garda once. That's all!"

"I believe I saw him kissing you. Quite cousinly of him, I'm sure," he drawled. "But you see, my dear Amy, our Franco is nobody's fool. Flirting, yes, that's one thing. But a Franco bent on marriage is something else entirely. If he can talk you into marrying him he will have a double share in the business, and that becomes a little threatening. And if Anna Maria marries Filippo . . . then a pattern evolves."

Nando looked at her sharply. "Anna Maria is so

infatuated with Filippo she would be persuaded to do anything he says. Filippo—" Nando looked at her sharply "—Filippo is a close friend of Franco's. In fact, it was Franco who introduced him to Anna Maria. Does that give you any ideas? About what Franco might have in mind pursuing you?"

Franco's secret wasn't that much of a secret any longer, Amy realized, but Nando wasn't going to pry anything from her. "This so-called plot involves a lot of 'ifs.' I, for one, am certainly not going to marry Franco." She managed an offhand shrug.

The gray eyes narrowed. "So the possibility has been discussed between you! I should have guessed as much. You see, your eyes always shift and there's a becoming flush across your cheeks when you try to evade a direct question. But you are quite correct, my dear. You certainly aren't going to marry him! It would not only disrupt my own plans, it would cause immense problems for the winery."

"Everything for the winery, right? It's the only thing that matters to you," Amy said coldly. "I'm quite certain your interest in marrying me is solely for the good of the winery."

He lifted an amused eyebrow. "Indeed? You are quite certain of that? Then you are mistaken. However, it does happen to benefit both of us. You've been so enamored with Vino d'Oro; now you are in the position of adding to the success of it. With our part of the business joined to my mother's, we need not have any fears about what Anna Maria will do with hers. Nor care what plans Franco may have had."

"And you'd plan on taking over my own share, I suppose," Amy snapped. "*Patria potestas* and all that?"

"Naturally." He shot her a quick suspicious look. "And how, my dear, did you learn of *patria potestas*?"

Amy sidestepped the question. "I know that it is no longer the law in Italy. Women now have the right—"

Nando shrugged, interrupting her. "Don't be misled. In your own America, I believe, you once passed a law forbidding people to drink alcoholic beverages. Did they all stop? It is the same with our *patria potestas*."

"Nevertheless, Nando Bonavia, it is useless for you or your mother to keep talking about marriage," Amy retorted hotly. She was becoming more and more irritated with his cool assumptions. "I simply refuse to do what seems expected of me. In this case, marry a winery!" She caught her breath sharply. "When I decide to marry, it will be to a man of my own choice. To someone I love."

"We'll see about that, *carina*," he said with a wicked smile. "In the meantime, catch!"

Instinctively she lifted her hands to catch the small white box he tossed to her, but it dropped into her lap.

Amy looked up at him defiantly. "I am not going to wear it, I am not going to keep it. You might as well take it back."

"Oh, but you are. It will let Franco, and everyone else, know our plans." He rose and walked slowly toward her. As he reached down to take the box from her lap, his fingers brushed the thin material of her robe, sending an unwelcome ripple of emotion through her. Taking her hand in his, Nando pulled her to her feet.

Slowly, deliberately, he lifted the lid of the box, took out the ring and slipped the gleaming ruby onto her finger.

"So now, my dear Amy, we are truly betrothed. Engaged, I suppose you call it. This changes everything, does it not? Tonight I went to the Antolinis to take care of some unfinished business, that of announcing that you and I are to be married." He hesitated a second, then added, "Perhaps you should know that my mother was not correct. I have not been. . .intimate with Elisa. And whatever else there was between us, that, too, is done with.

"Now," he said softly, gazing down at her with fathomless eyes, "you and I also have some unfinished business. Something that was not completed the day at the lake. Something that I should like to change."

His arms encircled her, pulling her close to him. He bent his head, lips seeking hers.

Amy tried to pull away, turning her head quickly one way then the other to escape him. "Stop!" she said hoarsely. "I'm not marrying you, not to save your interest in that damned winery! I. . .Nando, don't. . .don't. . ." she ended raggedly.

"Ah, my dear, don't argue. . . ." He stopped talking as he swept her up into his arms and carried her to the bed. He laid her on it, then lowered himself beside her. "If you can only forgive what happened that day, then perhaps we can start over, *cara*."

Before she could reply, before she could do anything at all, his arms were around her and his mouth closed over hers.

For one endless moment Amy struggled to free her lips from his, trying frantically, too, to halt the treacherous sweet warmth that began flooding through her. Her mind clutched frantically at every reason she could think of to stop herself from responding. Once he had said, "I'd do anything...." Was this, too, part of the anything? Marriage, lovemaking?

While her mind was trying to throw up barriers, her emotions were beginning to respond to the mesmerizing invitation of his kiss.

All she could feel was her own weakness as his hands gently brushed back her hair, then slipped to her shoulders. Sliding down under her robe, his fingers reached for and captured the tip of one breast through the filmy nightgown.

"Nando, no, don't, please...Nando!" she gasped unevenly, trying not to want him.

His lips were at her ear, a tormenting sensation that made her blood beat in her veins.

She felt his hand slip down and jerk at the tie of his robe. With another quick motion, a twist of his body, the garment was dropped to the floor beside the bed. He turned toward her again, pulling her close, and she was vividly aware of the hot contour of his body pressing against her gown.

He raised himself slightly to open her robe. Amy tried to hold it shut with one last effort at restraint, but he slid it from her shoulders, letting it lie beneath her. Untying the ribbon straps at her shoulders, he slowly slid the loose gown down, his lips trailing fire as they followed its descent, pausing a moment to caress her breasts. Then they continued along the curve of her body, her thighs, bringing her exquisite pleasure.

Amy was beyond all halting now. She knew only a mindless aching desire and an overwhelming love for this man, blotting out everything else in the world.

His body pressed close to her, skin against skin, feeling as she had once imagined he would. His hand possessed one breast as his lips again took hers. Then both his hands moved down the curve of her back, imprisoning the faint swell of her hips and bringing her tightly against him, against his aroused body and the strength of his long supple thighs.

"*Cara*," he whispered hoarsely, his heart throbbing heavily against her, his breath hot and uneven, "this time we will not stop." She could feel him stir. "Look at me, *cara*. Don't hide your feelings from me. Look at me."

Amy lifted her eyelids to see burning desire in his gray eyes. "This time, *cara*? *Carissima*?" She closed her eyes, but he had seen her helpless answer.

One of his hands caressed her body slowly, intimately, making her gasp with exquisite arousal. His hot blood was firing hers, inflaming her with undeniable passion. He gave a soft groan as their bodies locked together, straining against each other, then, abruptly, finding what they sought.

For one brief second, Amy felt a swift thrusting exultation of pain, which vanished as Nando's own passion sent her spiraling higher and higher, almost beyond consciousness. At last she was swept into a swirling maelstrom of rapture that left her gasping and spent....

Nando's breath, which had rasped so hard and unevenly in her ear, had slowed. He lifted his head slightly and gazed down at her, his lips and eyes only inches from hers. There was a thin veil of perspiration on his forehead.

"Ah, Amy, *cara*," he muttered hoarsely, "if you think I plan to marry you solely for the sake of the winery, how can you explain what has just happened between us?" He kissed her gently on the eyelids, the barest touch of his lips. "It seems we may have a bit more going for us than a common interest in Vino d'Oro."

Amy felt drained of all emotion, all thought. From somewhere deep inside her she was vaguely conscious that she should be feeling something. Shame that she had succumbed to him so readily, or perhaps regret.

But she didn't. Her body's memory still retained the touch of his hands, his enraptured passion, that sweet tumultuous invasion.

Nando sat up, swinging his long legs to the floor, his sensual masculine body glistening in the lamplight. Wrapping his robe about him and knotting the tie, he stood gazing down at her.

"Well, my dear, have you decided to keep the ring now? To wear it?"

Amy nodded, not trusting her voice.

He gave an unexpected smile. "Very well, then, I

shall start plans for our marriage. It takes time here, there is much red tape. But it shall go forward.''

Nando turned toward the door, then looked back over his shoulder at her. "You are a very. . .exciting young woman, Amy Converse. It appears that our marriage of convenience might turn out to be a lot more than that.''

He stepped back to the bed and lifted her hand to his lips. "Good night, Amy, *cara*."

Finally she found her voice. "Good night, Nando."

He went out, closing the door softly behind him.

Amy lay unmoving, filled with a sweet exhaustion as she listened to Nando's footsteps going down the hall.

Lifting her left hand, she gazed at the sparkle of the ruby. How strange that she was soon to marry this man whom she had once hated and mistrusted. . .and now loved so deeply.

For several languid moments she gave herself over to the memory of their lovemaking, her eyes soft, her lips trembling. Her gown and robe were still lying crumpled beneath her where Nando had left them. She thought drowsily of putting on her gown, but did not. Her eyelids fluttered several times, then closed, and she drifted into a dreamless sleep.

CHAPTER ELEVEN

AMY AWAKENED to a bright world. Sunlight was flooding across the room, and the day already held the promise of warmth. She sat up abruptly, wondering if she had overslept and would be late for work. Then, realizing it was Sunday, she lay back on her pillow dreamily.

She felt the soft folds of her nightgown and robe beneath her, and memory flooded through her once again. "Nando," she whispered to herself, smiling gently. Nando, whose touch had lighted a wild passion within her, a passion she had never dreamed of experiencing.

Then a thought came slipping treacherously across her mind, bringing a frown to her face. She loved Nando—with her entire being she loved him—but did he love her? Not once during the whole time he made such consuming love to her had he said so.

The heat of his passion had been real, there was no denying that... hadn't Elisa said he was quick to passion, easy to arouse? Had the sole emotion he had felt last night been sexual desire?

Amy stared up at the ceiling. Granted, she was to become his wife. Would she also be his mistress, his only lover, or would he turn to other women? Having obediently gone through the ritual of a wedding for the good of the winery, would he consider that enough had been demanded of him and that he owed his wife nothing but his name?

She bit at her lip. Was she anything to him but the owner of one-fifth of Vino d'Oro? Would she ever be anything more?

Amy pushed her pillow back against the head of her bed and sat up, turning the Bonavia ring back and forth on her finger. Did she honestly want to marry him when such questions were prodding her mind?

Even after what had happened she had a choice, she reminded herself. She could say no, and choose a world without Nando in it....

Or she could accept this marriage, not absolutely certain if it would be a true marriage in every sense of the word. A few phrases spoken over them by a priest, a wedding ring, a new name—perhaps a quick feverish tussle in bed now and then when he felt inclined. Was this what she could expect in becoming his wife?

"I'd do anything...." She remembered his words and her hands twisted the sheet. Did "anything" include this marriage?

Amy shoved back the sheet and slipped out of bed, trying not to dredge up any more troubling thoughts to depress and disturb her. She picked up her nightclothes and for a moment stood holding them to her, remembering. For that instant Nando seemed once more with her, loving and reassuring.

She glanced at the clock, then went over to the

closet to hang up her gown and robe and decide what to wear to the wine festival. Slacks? A dress? She paused thoughtfully. It was a festival, a fiesta, wasn't it? Nodding, she drew out a dirndl skirt, the black background spattered with tiny bunches of yellow flowers, and a white cotton off-the-shoulder peasant blouse. Her white sandals would go perfectly with the outfit.

Amy suddenly grinned. *I shall look,* she thought, *just like a travel poster for Austria or Switzerland.*

Aunt Lucia nodded approvingly at her choice of clothes when Amy came downstairs a little later. "You look quite charming! Very pretty and very young," she said. Her manner was definitely thawing out. "One would never guess you were a determined career girl—a vintner at that. And I am pleased to note that at last you are wearing your ring. You will discover that I am quite correct, you know. Infatuation does not sustain a marriage; respect and a common interest will."

Amy gave a restrained smile. "You may be right, Aunt Lucia," she said tactfully, wondering if the only common interest she and Nando shared was Vino d'Oro.

Her mind flashed back again to last night. What she and Nando had shared for that brief impassioned span of time had been more than a common interest in a winery. Surely it had!

"Nando has gone down to the castle for a short time to be certain our wine is ready for the festival. He will be back shortly," Aunt Lucia said.

"I think I'll go out on the terrace and enjoy the sun

while I'm waiting for him to return," Amy replied, wanting to escape for a while.

It was an extraordinary day, the sky a glistening inverted bowl of blue with no hint of clouds. The air was warm and sweet, heavy with the scent of rosebushes. A small bird sat on top of the wall near the gate, lifting its head to chirp from time to time, then returning to its search for food.

Amy walked over to the rosebushes and strolled among them breathing in the fragrance of the flowers. Glancing up suddenly, she saw Franco striding toward her.

"You look as if you just stepped out of *The Sound of Music*," he said, smiling and taking her hand in his. Then his face sobered. "I've come to put in a good word for myself again this morning. With you and Nando away together for the day, he might just decide to take his mother's advice and...." His voice trailed off as he became conscious of the ring.

He lifted her hand to look at it, saying nothing for a few seconds. Then, raising his eyes to meet hers, he said, "So it *is* too late. I hope you know what you're doing, Amy."

"I...I hope so, too," she answered, not quite able to hide her own uncertainty.

"This is a surprise, and not exactly a welcome one." Franco fell into step beside her. "Last night I thought the field was still relatively open. How did he manage to convince you in so brief a time?"

How? I couldn't possibly tell you how, Amy reflected. "I...I...." She sought for an answer. "I just told him last night that I would." That really didn't qualify as a reason, she knew, but it was all she could come up with.

Franco halted and lifted her chin with his fingers, gazing down at her. "Are you in love with him?" he asked shrewdly, his eyes probing. "I suppose I have no right to ask, but are you?"

She nodded, unable to lie. If she didn't admit it her face would no doubt betray her anyway, according to Nando.

"I see," Franco said stoically. "And Nando...? I think in this case I do have the right to ask, because I, too, proposed to you. And to be truthful, I believe I'm already half in love with you. So I'm hoping that despite the ring there's still a chance for me. Is he in love with you?"

He still held her chin and she couldn't avoid looking up at him. "I don't know, Franco," she was forced to admit.

He frowned, then released her. They began walking along together once more. "If you are intent on going through with this, I hope he is in love with you. Otherwise...."

Amy nodded. "Yes, Franco, I know."

Again he lifted her hand and gazed at the ring. "This has a disturbingly final look. But the hesitation and uncertainty I sense in you give me some hope."

"But wasn't the reason you suggested marriage all because of my share of the winery?"

He nodded. "I must admit it was, yes. Originally, anyhow. But now I find myself growing more and more fond of you. But I suppose only you can decide whom to marry, which of us would bring you happiness. I suggest you give that a good deal of thought.''

Before she could reply the gate swung wide and Nando came in. Catching sight of Franco and Amy, he strode directly over to them.

He gave Amy a quick meaningful smile and leaned over to brush a light kiss on her cheek. Then he lifted her left hand. "You see, Franco, it's too late, old man," he said dryly. "It's hands off for you from now on."

Franco gave a nod of his head, shielding the expression in his eyes, and said, "Yes, I noticed the Bonavia ring. Yet until the banns are read, until the final important words are uttered over you—you'll forgive me for saying so—it does leave me some room." He said it lightly, but Amy could detect the sharp challenge beneath the surface.

Nando took Amy's arm. "Don't count on it, Franco. It's all settled."

"Pardon my curiosity, but whatever happened to Nando, the professional bachelor? The man who swore he'd never marry?" Franco asked provocatively.

"What happened? That should be obvious. Amy arrived," Nando replied coolly.

"Bringing with her her precious share of the business?"

Nando gave Franco a cynically amused smile. "Nice try, Franco, but that won't work, either. Amy's share of the winery was what the Americans call serendipity, or an unexpected bonus. And now we're off to the wine festival. *Ciao!*"

"Goodbye, Franco, wish me luck at the festival,"
Amy called over her shoulder. "I hope I don't become—what was it Anna Maria said about having
too much to drink—*ubriaca*, wasn't it? Or something
like that." She spoke quickly, trying to leave the
three-way encounter with a lighter, less rigid atmosphere.

She could feel Franco's eyes following them as she
and Nando headed for the car. But her main aware-
ness was of the tall, roughly handsome man who was
striding along beside her. With Franco present she
hadn't been so vividly conscious of the Nando who
had been her lover last night. Now it came back as
strong as ever, her heart crowding up into her throat,
beating irrationally. This was the first moment she
had been alone with him since then. She felt a warm
flush stealing up her cheeks as she looked at him out
of the corner of her eye.

If Nando was remembering the episode he didn't
show it. Nor did he mention it. He was busy starting
the motor and backing the car around, then headed
for the open gate.

"I imagine I've thrown a spanner into Franco's
works," he observed dryly. "He's disappointed at
having been edged out." His hands were lean and
brown on the steering wheel. "I think he had other
plans for your future."

Amy glanced away from the sight of those strong
supple fingers. Why, she wondered uncomfortably,
did every single thing about him remind her so vividly, so embarrassingly, of last night? It was hard to
connect this Nando—his austere profile, his hawklike

gray eyes—with last night's impassioned lover. Yet she couldn't get the memory of his sensuous possession out of her mind.

The brief kiss he had given her today, was it meant more as a warning to Franco to stay out of the race or as a token of affection for her? Why didn't he stop and take her in his arms, now that they were alone again? The way Nando was acting it was as if their lovemaking had never happened.

"Uh...tell me more about the wine festival," she asked finally, becoming a bit tense with the protracted silence that had fallen between them.

"A number of villages have them at this time of year, celebrating a good grape harvest and the new wines. This particular festival is popular for several reasons. Most of the local wineries will be represented. The wine flows freely; there's to be a parade, food, music."

He gave her an amused glance. "When I went out to California to that conference I heard someone use a saying that I think might apply to today. 'Hold on to your hat!' In other words, this could turn out to be a wild rollicking afternoon and evening."

Nando turned the car off the highway onto a side road that ran steeply up a hillside, winding its way through vineyards. Small farms were set into the slopes. The road was narrow, for a while following a tumbling stream that raced on down toward the flatlands below.

They came upon a truck loaded with dark wine kegs. Nando geared down until they came to a wider place in the road, then he slipped past the lumbering vehicle.

"Ours?" she asked.

He shook his head. "No. I don't recognize either the truck or the driver—which makes me think of something you should know. Our wines, not just ours per se but all Italian wines, are strictly controlled by law these days. From the very composition of the soil the grapes are planted in to the label that goes on the bottle."

He slammed on the brakes to avoid a chicken that was scrambling across the road, then went on. "The controls are very strict, and with reason. The wine industry had a scandal in the 1960s, you see. Some unscrupulous people hired some equally unscrupulous chemists to make up a tremendous quantity of wine, or supposed wine. Actually the brew was composed of alcohol, bone meal, ox blood and some other unattractive ingredients.

"It was sold everywhere. Almost half the unbottled wines in Italy turned out to be this artificial stuff, vended in jugs and kegs. Until the gang was caught."

Nando gave a sharp laugh. "You can't say the culprits didn't have imagination. They were also convicted of grinding up plastic umbrella handles to add to the bulk of grated cheese they sold."

Amy gave him a incredulous look but he nodded."It's true!"

Again Nando had to apply the brakes quickly, this time for a small ox-drawn cart filled with hay that pulled directly onto the road in front of them. The cart was decorated with ribbons and had heavy bunches of grapes dangling from the railing. Perched on the hay were three jaunty-looking young men, already in an obvious mood of revelry. They waved wine bottles at Amy, whistling at her and blowing kisses.

Amy laughed. "They seem to be getting an early start."

"And it's going to be a long day. I suspect they aren't going to be in shape for much fun tonight, at this rate," Nando said, holding the car to a crawl behind the slow-moving cart.

"Luckily it's only another kilometer or two," he observed. "We certainly can't pass on this stretch of road."

Amy saw a long stone wall on the rim of a hill ahead, stretching across the horizon. "Is that it? Is it a walled city?" she asked.

Nando nodded. "Walled and very old. It used to be a fortification centuries ago, but now age and decay—and wars—have turned the old castle into nothing but tumbled stones where the village children play."

The wheels of the ox cart rattled noisily across wooden planks before passing through the arched opening in the walls. Nando followed, crossing the wooden bridge that spanned what had long ago been a moat.

Inside the walls cars were parked everywhere, with motorbikes and bicycles laced in between them. Nando edged down a small street that hugged the outer wall, guiding his car past tobacco shops, a flower stall and a bakery. The tables of a small outdoor café were all empty and the proprietor, his hands tucked under his apron, stood in the doorway. The city wall was plastered with old torn posters, and someone had chalked slogans on the empty spots.

Nando turned up a cobblestone alley, so narrow that two cars couldn't possibly pass each other. Laundry hung like banners from poles jutting out overhead, and iron balconies lined the faded terra-cotta-colored buildings. Over all floated the tangy delicious smell of food cooking.

Nando drove the car into another alley, past a number of commercial buildings, and finally pulled into the courtyard of a long two-story winery. There was a large sign painted with bright purple grapes attached to the wall.

"They save a place for us each year," Nando said, turning off the motor. "Ready?"

Amy nodded, a feeling of excitement beginning to replace the uncertainty of early morning. Stepping out of the car, she followed Nando out of the courtyard and onto a street that headed down the hill.

They passed several factories, their doors locked and barred, before Nando turned at a corner. Across the street was an opening where a dozen cobblestone steps, worn and uneven, led to a piazza below.

He held her elbow to guide her down the stairs, until they emerged into a giant town square. It was surrounded on all sides by ancient buildings with grilled iron balconies. And on the opposite corner from where Amy stood rose the church, somber and gray, its twin towers lifting starkly against the shining blue of the sky.

Cars had obviously been barred from the piazza, and all along the sidewalks crowds jostled one another cheerfully, stopping at stalls that lined the streets.

In front of Amy stood a giant Bacchus, fully thirty feet tall. The animated leering creature was crowned with grapes, and he rolled his large eyes, his arms alternately lifting a bottle then a glass.

Voices, laughing and shouting, filled the air. From time to time music blared out above all the noise. Nando looked around, then said, "Let's be certain our booth is in operation and dispensing wine before we do anything else."

They edged through the crowd, Amy's eyes darting from stall to stall. The wine booths were hung with large bunches of purple and golden grapes, and glasses, filled to the brim, were being handed out. Food counters were piled high with stuffed rolls, pink ham and creamy cheese visible between the pieces of bread. Olives, salami and an endless display of sweets were being looked over by prospective customers. And everywhere was an air of excitement and celebration.

Amy was amused to see a group of young men, locked arm in arm, moving systematically from one wine booth to another. They would reach out for the well-filled glasses, drink down the dark red or pale golden liquid, give back the glasses, then go on to the next stall.

Nando shook his head. "They may make it around

the piazza, though I doubt it, and then... asleep on a park bench or propped up in an alley! No parade for them."

Amy noticed, however, that most of the people were conducting themselves decorously. Families with children, gnarled old men with faces like beige leather, stout matrons dressed in the inevitable black strolled along, pausing to eye the booths or chat with friends. Some of the children carried balloons, and there was an occasional cry from a young tot as a balloon escaped and went soaring over the crowds.

"Here we are," Nando said, stopping before a stall framed with green-and-gold grapes. Amy was surprised to see Solari, one of the workers who had started with her the first day, standing behind the counter. His dark hair was carefully combed and oiled, and his brown eyes flashed at the passing girls. When he saw Amy, his face lighted up in recognition.

"*Ciao*, Converse!" he called. Then, belatedly noticing Nando, he abruptly became obsequious. "Signore Bonavia," he said. He didn't tug at his forelock in an ancient token of respect, but he might as well have done so, Amy thought with amusement.

Nando acknowledged the greeting with a curt nod of his head, his eyes sweeping appraisingly over the stall as the young man turned to fill glasses for the eager tasters who pushed up to the counter. Nando murmured something in Italian to Solari, who nodded and replied. Then Amy found her fiancé steering her away from the Vino d'Oro booth.

"Shall we look around, maybe sample some of the

wares of other wineries?" he suggested, looking down at her.

"Love to!" she agreed, finding herself suddenly happy just to be there, just to have Nando's hand touching her arm.

They pushed onto the crowded sidewalk, to stop a half block further on at another stand. A buxom young woman was pouring a glowing red wine into glasses. "*Buon giorno*, Signore Bonavia," she called.

He answered her, then said something more in Italian, ending with Amy's name.

The girl gave a quick glance at the ring on Amy's hand, then said, "*Vi auguro felicità*, Signorina Converse."

"Signorina Testa wishes you happiness," Nando translated. "Her family owns the local winery where we parked."

"*Grazie*, Signorina Testa," Amy replied.

The young woman lifted an empty glass. "*Signorina?*"

Amy nodded. "*Prego.*" She was easily falling into the simple responses. *Grazie*, thank you. *Prego*, please. But she had such a lot more to learn, she thought, glancing up at Nando. Not only about the language.

The wine was full-bodied and fragrant, with a faint afterbite on the tongue. Nando tasted his, glanced down at the glass and nodded approvingly. The cheeks of the young woman behind the counter grew pink with pleasure. "*Grazie*, Signore Bonavia, *grazie.*"

After finishing the wine they strolled along in the

direction of the church. Amy gave a sudden startled jump.

"What's wrong?" Nando questioned quickly.

Amy turned around to glare at a group of young men walking several paces behind her and Nando. Their expressions were innocent, but their lips were tightened as if to hold in laughter.

She turned back to Nando, her face flushed. "Someone pinched me!" she said indignantly.

Nando laughed. "An old Italian custom, my love. When a woman has a derriere as delectable as yours it is bound to invite a complimentary pinch."

Amy was ruffled. "I'm not sure I appreciate the compliment," she said tartly.

They were approaching the fountain that stood in the middle of the piazza. A crowd encircled it, holding out cups and glasses. Amy stopped, blinked, then turned to Nando.

"It really is, isn't it?"

"Yes, it's wine. It's fixed so that the fountain will spray wine all day long, and what isn't caught by the people will fall into the basin to recirculate. Fun, if not terribly hygienic."

Some of the younger men, those without cups or other vessels to catch the wine, stuck their faces into the spray, licking their mouths and laughing.

A group of strolling musicians walked by, and the noise increased as some of the exuberant drinkers began grabbing hands and dancing around the fountain.

Nando nodded toward them. "We Italians, you understand, usually drink wine with considerable discretion. We are not used to immoderate drinking. But today is special, it is a day to celebrate a rewarding harvest and perhaps to let down our hair, as you Americans so aptly describe it, after a year of back-breaking labor.

"Before we sample any of the other wines around the piazza, shall we have something to eat?" he went on, looking down at her. "The parade shouldn't be starting for another hour or so."

"Food!" she ordered lightly. "I'm famished."

"We have a choice. We can settle for rolls and cheese from one of the stalls, but I'd suggest a small *trattoria* I know around here. We'd be more comfortable."

"What's a *trattoria*? A restaurant?" she guessed, putting the word away into her memory.

"Yes, but usually a simple one, not quite a *ristorante*, which tends to be a bit more formal. You're quite intent on learning everything, aren't you?"

Amy couldn't quite decide if there was a touch of cynicism in his words but decided to ignore it if there was. She simply nodded.

"The *trattoria*, then?" he asked.

Amy lifted her head, blinking a little at the glare of the overhead sun. "I imagine it will be cooler. It sounds fine to me."

The day had grown warm, and she found that her cotton blouse was damp against her back. Nando grasped her hand to draw her through the crowd, which seemed to be increasing as noon approached.

For one fleeting second Amy thought she caught sight of familiar dark shining hair and a face with pansy eyes moving through the throngs toward them, but suddenly a tall man obscured her view. If it had indeed been Elisa Antolini she didn't catch sight of her again. Yet she couldn't avoid a quick tightening of nerves, which the ring on her finger did nothing to halt.

Nando led her down a narrow winding alley until he came to a wooden door set in the wall of a building. He pushed open the door and they entered, going down two steps to a cool dusky room that had a long wooden table running down the center of it. Several people were sitting on long benches, eating and drinking. Some of them glanced up and nodded as Amy and Nando took their places at one end.

It was blessedly cool. Amy took a deep refreshing breath and brushed back the damp hair from her forehead.

An empty glass was set before her, and Amy looked up to see a plump, dark-haired, dark-skinned man. He had eyes like ebony and was wearing a bibbed green apron that had traces of tomato sauce down the front.

He grinned, a gold tooth glinting, and spoke so rapidly in Italian that not a single word was intelligible to Amy. When Nando replied, the man went to a table in the corner and returned to fill their glasses with a sparkling wine. Then he headed back into the kitchen.

"Spumante...a little like champagne," Nando said, lifting his glass to Amy. "I propose a toast! A banner year for Vino d'Oro and the new Chiaro! And success to our merger!"

And in that order, she reflected, lifting her glass.

"Yes, to both," she said quietly, tasting the wine. It was delicate, faintly sweet and aromatic, tingling the tip of her tongue.

Then, as a sudden pause fell, Amy said, "That man, the one who waited on us. I'm not really used to Italian yet, but he sounded...somehow different. Not that I could be certain, of course. Would that be another dialect, maybe?"

"You're right. It's the one that's commonly used around Verona. People in Rome might not understand it at all."

"So I understand. Franco was telling me about it," she observed absently, taking a drink of the effervescent wine.

Nando turned his glass in his hand, looking down at the bubbles rising to the top. "Did he also suggest you marry him and turn over your share of the winery into his care?" he asked bluntly, his gray eyes disconcertingly shrewd and cool as he lifted them to look at her.

"No," Amy said, deliberately answering only part of his question, "he said nothing to me about surrendering my share to him."

Nando shrugged. "He's a fool, then. Generous, but a fool."

"I think I hear *patria potestas* raising its ugly head again. Tell me, if we marry, what will you do if I don't care to surrender my share to you?" She said it lightly, but she was certain he would pick up the thread of her resistance.

He gave her a slow seductive smile, reaching across the table to imprison her hand. "Oh, but you will,

my dear. Believe me, you will. Like a good Italian
wife.''

Amy was relieved when the waiter appeared at that
moment and Nando surrendered her hand. All he
needed to do was touch her that way, look at her like
that, and she wasn't sure that she wouldn't do whatever he said. And she hated herself for her weakness.

A huge bowl of soup was placed before them with
a ladle and soup plates. The waiter plunged the ladle
into the cauldron and brought out large helpings of
vegetables and steaming aromatic broth, filling their
plates. Then he plunked down a glass container with
an aluminum lid.

As he left, Nando smiled at Amy. ''It may seem a
lot, and a bit warm for a day like this, but believe me,
before today's over you'll be glad for the inner stok-
ing! As you might guess, the soup is mincotrone. And
this—'' he pushed the glass dish toward her ''—is
grated Parmesan cheese.''

Amy peered suspiciously at the cheese. Then she
lifted amused eyes. ''Guaranteed to contain ground-
up plastic umbrella handles?''

He slanted a wry smile at her. ''Your memory
serves you well.'' Then he sobered. ''I hope there are
some things you will be generous enough to forget.''

From Nando this was a surprising concession. He
was different, she thought, now that he had given up
trying so hard to buy her out. A nasty little corner of
her mind reminded her that a moment ago he had
casually assumed he would easily obtain her share of
the business. Amy scowled inwardly, letting her
thumb rub absently over the band of her ring. A

troubling doubt came crawling back into her mind. Was marriage the price he was prepared to pay to gain her share of the winery? Impatiently she tried to thrust such thoughts away.

The sparkling wine had been removed after their toast, and with the soup arrived a robust red wine that Amy and Nando barely sipped.

"We may be expected to sample some of our competitors' products later," he warned.

They ate cannelonni, the stuffed pasta covered with a delicious mushroom sauce, and Amy held up her hand in protest when Nando suggested a bunch of grapes and a small piece of cheese.

"All I want to do is find a corner and take a nap," she said weakly. "The warm day, the wine and all this food—I'm in a state of complete lethargy!"

He took her hand and pulled her to her feet. "The day is just getting started. The parade will be going by before long. Let's go find a place to watch it."

When they reentered the piazza a band had started playing, and the church bells were chiming with a loud dissonant counterpoint. The throngs were now retreating to the sidewalks to allow the parade to progress around the piazza. Amy and Nando were caught in the crush as the crowds compressed. She found herself pressed against him as he stood behind her. His arms slipped around her waist, locking in front of her, pulling her close as a blare of trumpets heralded the beginning of the parade. Amy was honest enough with herself to admit she found it very pleasant to stand there leaning against him, feeling an irrepressible joy at his nearness.

Another loud blare of bugles, then came a church banner held high by a solemn young man. The white-and-gold pennant swirled in the air. A few steps behind him came a large plaster statue of the Virgin. The platform that bore the statue was carried by four older men, their dark suits looking uncomfortably warm and wrinkled in the heat of the sun. As the Virgin passed, many of the onlookers genuflected in reverence, then went right back to laughing and drinking their wine.

A group of children carrying bunches of balloons and dressed in what were obviously homemade costumes trailed along behind the Virgin, followed by a small noisy band.

Amy glanced around at the crowd. There was no sign of Elisa, at least that she could see. Perhaps she had been mistaken earlier.

Gaily decorated donkey carts carrying barrels of wine and small mountains of grapes came next. They were followed by paper-festooned floats bearing young men and women dressed in red and green, who tossed grapes at the onlookers.

Nando's arm tightened slightly, and he bent to rub his chin gently against her hair. How, Amy wondered, could such a simple gesture be so erotic? The movement sent little ripples of longing through her.

The crowd seemed to increase every few minutes until Amy felt she had been squeezed to half her size. She was warm, she was in the midst of a suffocating crush and she was completely happy. Everything, she thought, was going to be all right. Different than she had ever dreamed, maybe, but in the long run, all right.

The festival queen, a smiling pink-cheeked maiden with a crown of deep red grapes on her dark hair, came riding past. From her grape-covered throne she waved at the onlookers, bringing shrill whistles from the sidelines as young men eyed her well-developed charms. Four teenage girls seated precariously on the corners of the float pelted everyone with showers of grapes.

The procession moved toward the church, where the banner carrier and those bearing the Virgin marched up the steps and disappeared inside. The rest of the parade made a lumbering circle of the piazza.

After that the afternoon seemed to fly by. Amy and Nando strolled about, watching the people. At one point they stopped by a small wooden stage where a wrinkled old man dressed in black cloth knee britches and a faded green coat was playing a lively number on an accordion. There was a stir in the group watching him, and finally a plump middle-aged woman, urged on by her friends, mounted the platform, grinning with embarrassment. She hesitated a second, then, hiking her dark skirt up to her knees, began to dance, a whirling, swooping display that brought cheers of encouragement from the crowd gathering around.

"That's the *tarantella*," Nando murmured in Amy's ear. "Not many people know how to dance it anymore, especially the young."

The music changed and the woman was joined by

two other women her age, then three or four men. They all waved their arms as they danced, making up in enthusiasm what they lacked in style. The accordion player grinned, revealing a toothless mouth, and tapped his foot energetically while the dancers swung one another around, their laughter coming faster and faster as the tempo of the music increased.

Finally the accordion stopped with a windup flourish. The dancers sagged with exhaustion, their cheeks flushed, as the crowd cheered and begged for more.

Amy looked over her shoulder at Nando, her eyes shining. "It's all wonderful," she said. "I've never seen people having so much fun."

He nodded. "They deserve a day like this. Tomorrow these same people will be out working in the vineyards side by side, weeding, spreading fertilizer, watching over their vines as closely as they would their children."

Nando glanced down at his watch. "I think it might be a good idea to drop around to our stall again, to see if the wine supply is adequate or whether more barrels should be brought around."

As they started back around the square a small band began playing a rollicking tune. The music quickly inspired a group of young people to link hands and begin a serpentine dance in and out of the crowds. A few of them were weaving a trifle unevenly as they threaded their way in and out of the bystanders.

Nando turned to watch them. "Some of those fellows will have large heads by morning, but they'll have a whole year to get over it."

Amy noticed a calm tolerance of the goings-on by the more staid and sedate villagers. Older couples moved to one side to allow the serpentine line to slide past as it circled the piazza. Whenever a pretty young girl was spotted by the dancers, a passing hand would quickly reach out and detach her from her friends or even from her escort, and she would be swung away in the exuberant queue.

Nando and Amy were approaching the Vino d'Oro stall, which was still surrounded by patrons, when the serpentine line neared. At this point it was being led by a vigorous young man with dark hair curling close to his head. His white shirt sleeves were rolled up, baring his sun-darkened arms and hands, and he was holding on to a bright-eyed girl who was laughing and gasping for breath as they sped along.

Nando and Amy pulled back to allow the dancers to pass. The procession was quite long by now, and as its tail finally neared them Amy was suddenly grabbed by the hand. Before she could open her mouth to protest she was swept away and she had to move right along with the dancers to keep from stumbling.

She threw a quick distressed glance back at Nando, who simply waved at her with a grin. Momentarily she felt indignant, then the enthusiasm and the exuberant gaiety of the celebrants caught at her spirit and she found she was laughing, too, having to gasp now and then for breath.

In and out of the festival crowd, the serpentine wove its giddy way, collecting more and more participants. They wound once around the wine fountain, where a few of the dancers dropped out to refresh themselves by sticking their faces under the spraying wine. Their clothes quickly became splashed and stained; their places in the line were instantly filled by other eager volunteers.

Amy decided she'd wait until they had made a complete circle around the piazza and drop out of the line as they approached the Vino d'Oro stall. She was perspiring when the circuit was nearly completed, but she was still having great fun, gasping with laughter. Her laughter halted abruptly as she caught sight of Nando in the distance. He was still standing by the wine stall, but he was no longer alone. By his side, her hand on his arm, was Elisa Antolini. Nando's eyes were on the girl, and Amy saw him shake his head once, pause and then nod.

She had a hollow sinking sensation in her stomach as she saw Nando bend to say something, then take Elisa's arm to guide her through the crowds. They disappeared together between two of the stalls.

CHAPTER TWELVE

AMY STUMBLED and only the two firm hands grasping hers kept her from falling. She didn't even think of breaking away now, but let the serpentine carry her along, her eyelids stinging.

It was no doubt something quite innocent, she struggled to reassure herself. A chance meeting, perhaps; nothing to get upset about. After all, this fiesta was for wineries and wine makers. But Amy, reflecting on this possibility, found it hard to accept.

Oh, Elisa had warned her, clearly and firmly, that Nando was panting after her. But hadn't he said only last night that he'd never been intimate with her, that whatever the relationship had been between them, it was over, and all unfinished business was taken care of? Amy bit her lip. Apparently there was still more to it.

Her feet were still carrying her along, but the joy and laughter that had been there before had evaporated. She moved like an automaton, only vaguely noticing that new people had broken into the line and that now two different masculine hands grasped hers.

As the dancers neared the fountain once again, they began slowing down, their original enthusiasm overcome by heat and fatigue. The serpentine gradually disintegrated.

However, the hands holding on to Amy's didn't let go. Instead they grasped more tightly, separating her from the other dancers who were idly strolling about now, melting into the crowd.

Amy glanced up to see two young men grinning down at her, their sturdy roughcast faces flushed with wine. The two exchanged glances with each other and suddenly Amy found herself being swept up into one man's arms as if she weighed nothing at all. He dashed over to a two-wheeled cart decorated with grapes and ribbons, the back of which was piled with hay.

Amy was tossed onto the hay, and before she could scramble out or even protest, the two young men had raced around to the wooden shafts and were dashing off with her to the whistles and encouraging shouts of others standing by. As they ran they were pelted by a shower of grapes.

The cart bumped and clattered over the cobblestone road. Amy had to cling tightly to one of the side railings so that she wouldn't be jostled out.

"Stop! Please let me out!" Amy called nervously. Fun was fun—at least to the men it might be fun—but this was carrying it too far.

One of the men glanced back over his shoulder, his bold eyes flashing as he shook his head. Obviously he didn't understand English.

Amy slid toward the back of the cart, trying to decide if it would be safe to jump out. They were moving at a trot, and though that wasn't especially fast, it was enough to make her consider waiting until they either stopped or had to slow down for pedestrians crossing the street.

But they were veering away from the main piazza, turning down a deserted twisting alley that ran between iron-gated industrial buildings. There was no one else around. The strains of music and the noise of the crowd had dwindled behind them, and the only sound now was the rattle and clatter of the wheels of the cart.

Thoughts of Nando and Elisa no longer dominated Amy's mind, and the present situation actually began to frighten her. She had no idea where the fellows were taking her or what they had in mind. Terrifying possibilities began occurring to her. Her shouts for them to stop were met with nods and laughter, and they kept on going.

Finally they panted to a halt, letting go of the shafts, which dropped down to the ground. Amy was thrown on her back against the hay.

Before she could move, one of the young men had quickly climbed up on the cart, running a quick hand over the expanse of bare leg that had been exposed. He threw himself beside her, his feet braced against the railing and his arm pinning her down as he tried to force a warm kiss on her mouth.

Amy struggled frantically to free herself. He smelled of sweat and sour wine, and he was still panting slightly from the run. But his face, as he pulled back to look at her, was not mean or vicious, only young and not quite sober. He said something to her in Italian, grinned, then squeezed her breast through the thin material of her cotton blouse.

"Stop! Leave me alone! Let me go!" Amy cried frantically as she tried to push him away. The other man leaned over the railing, laughing at the struggles of his friend. "Ah!" he said, *"Una signorina Americana!"* Then he shook a warning finger at the one who was trying to subdue her.

The man in the cart drew back again to grin at her as if he were having a tremendously good time.

She sat up, free at last from his fumblings, and quickly pulled down her skirt and straightened her blouse. Then he jumped out of the cart, holding up a hand to help her out. She hesitated, not knowing whether to trust him, but finally allowed him to aid her in stepping over the railing.

It was a mistake, she found out, for as she slid to the ground the other man slipped behind her and gave her a quick pinch on the bottom. They both laughed, patted her on the shoulder and, picking up the shafts of the cart, trotted off, apparently looking for more victims.

For a full two minutes Amy couldn't move. She leaned against the warm brick wall of one of the buildings, her knees turned to jelly. She reached up a trembling hand to wipe the damp hair back from her forehead and took a long uneven breath. She realized the prank was only meant in an exuberant male spirit of fun and had been spurred on by the imbibing of a considerable amount of wine. But as she pushed away from the wall and began to walk along the deserted alley, she felt shaken and brittle.

Her scare was over, but now the memory of Nando

and Elisa walking off together came back to trouble her. The happiness she had felt earlier, the joy of simply being with Nando, the man she loved—had that been self-deception? Suddenly the thought of marriage to Nando became once again disturbing. Was she going to have to share him with Elisa in the future? Certainly Signorina Antolini was not the type who gave up easily.

For a while, a very little while, really, Amy had almost believed that Nando had given up Elisa. Had she been wrong in hoping that?

She frowned. Was she drawing conclusions that simply didn't exist? There very well could have been a reason Nando had to go off somewhere with Elisa, his hand on her arm. But she couldn't think of one.

As she came to the end of the alley she was at once plunged into the crowd again. There was laughter all around her, and some enthusiastic voice was singing opera arias, not even faintly in accord with the music that was blaring from the center of the piazza. Amy hesitated, trying to orient herself, then began to push her way back to the Vino d'Oro stall.

Nando wasn't there. Behind the counter, Solari was still pouring wine. "The *signore*, he...." Solari searched for the word. "He come back, soon come back. He say you to stay." Lifting a jug, he poured wine for an elderly man in a black coat who looked over at Amy with a shy smile. Lifting his glass to her, he took a drink, carefully wiping his mouth with his coat sleeve.

Amy returned the smile distractedly. Nando had said for her to stay. Of course she would stay. Where else would she go? Certainly not back to the villa, for how would she get there?

She stood in the warm sun of late afternoon, waiting for her prospective husband to return from a tryst with his former woman friend. Former, Amy wondered.

The minutes dragged. Her face was moist with perspiration and her clothes sticking to her. She realized that not much time had passed since her return, but it stretched out endlessly.

She felt a tap on her shoulder. Solari was leaning toward her. "The *signore!*" He nodded toward the far end of the piazza.

Nando was walking quickly toward them, evading pedestrians as he approached. When he reached Amy he smiled, taking her hand in his.

"Sorry I had to be away when you came back. Business," he said briskly. Then he added, "Well, how did you enjoy the serpentine? A little vigorous, isn't it?"

Business; so that was his explanation! Did he think it would satisfy her? "The serpentine? It was rather fun, but exhausting," Amy answered. She decided against mentioning the two men and the cart. Nando might think the incident funny, as they had, but for several moments her fear had been real and she didn't yet feel in the mood to joke about it.

"What would you like to do now?" he asked, tucking his hand under her elbow as if to guide her through the crowd. Exactly as he had touched Elisa. She jerked away sharply, instinctively, without even thinking.

Nando looked down at her, his gray eyes suddenly cool. "I'm sorry if you felt I'd abandoned you. You surely can't be upset because I had something to take care of. Business matters do not always come up at convenient times or places." The reprimand was not entirely hidden.

Amy's mouth tightened and she felt a coldness stealing over her. She would have had a lot more respect for him if he had simply said he had gone off for a while with Elisa. She wouldn't have been particularly happy, but it would have been better than the way she felt now, as if he had tried to deceive her. What kind of business could he and Elisa possibly have with each other?

All at once the heat was depressing, the crowds and the noise a bit overwhelming. Added to all that, her recent experience with the two young bloods had left her exhausted.

"If you don't mind, Nando, I'd like to go someplace quiet and just sit down for a little while."

Nando must have seen the fatigue in her face, for his voice lost its edge. "Are you tired, Amy? Wine festivals have a way of wearing one out, especially if you aren't used to them. I should think most of the excitement is about over, anyhow. I notice the crowd is thinning out. There'll be a few who won't leave as long as the wine flows, but unless you particularly want to stay, shall we go?"

Amy nodded. "I really would like to. Even though it has been...fun."

"We can have dinner at home. That is, unless you'd like to stop somewhere on the way."

She shook her head, forcing a smile. "What I'd really like is a nice cool shower and a glass of Maria's orange juice. I think I've had enough wine and sun for today."

Nando was right; many of the celebrants were leaving. Small children drooped sleepily in their strollers, older people walked along slowly, all heading out of the piazza. But the center of the square, particularly around the fountain, was still filled with a younger crowd. They looked energetic enough for several hours yet, Amy thought as she and Nando began making their way up the steps in the direction of the car.

As they drove down the curving hill road their conversation was minimal. Nando seemed to be preoccupied, his stern profile remote and inexpressive. Amy, leaning her head back against the seat, glanced at him out of the corner of her eye.

Who or what was he thinking about? Clearly there was something on his mind, something he didn't want to share with her.

Amy glanced down at the ruby ring on her finger. What a strange marriage this was going to be—if indeed, she thought uncomfortably, there should be any marriage at all. She had blown hot and cold on the subject all day. For a while it had seemed as if it would work out, but now she was far from certain. She loved him, but was that enough? Would it always be enough?

Perhaps it was the fatigue of the day, perhaps it was that feeling of uneasiness that she couldn't seem to shake. In any case she let her mind wander where it wanted. Once she had heard Nando say he didn't like playing the whore. Last night he had slipped this ring on her finger.... Had he forced himself to play the whore in order to convince her she should marry him? And, in marrying him, surrender her share of the business? Amy closed her eyes.

His passion had not been all pretense. It couldn't have been. She'd felt the wild beating of his heart on her own, the rough gasp of his breath, the final exultant shudder of consummation. That much had been real.

"You're very quiet." Nando interrupted her thoughts.

"Yes," she admitted. "I'm not used to wine festivals." It was feeble but the best response she could think of at this particular moment.

"Ah, but you shall grow used to them. We'll be expected to be present each year at one or more. Which reminds me, when shall we set the wedding date? Do you wish it to coincide with Anna Maria's, as she suggested? Or would you prefer a separate ceremony? I'd like you to decide as soon as possible because, as I've said, there are certain details that must be taken care of."

So he really must feel that getting her share was worth the emptiness of a marriage of convenience, Amy thought. Probably because he felt that such a marriage wouldn't deny him his extramarital pleasures.

"Nando," Amy began uncertainly, "I'm not at all sure that we...that we...."

He shot her a quick look. "I thought that had all

been decided." He reached over to take her hand. "Last night," he said softly.

"But—"

"But of course you will marry me," he said firmly. "It's all settled. The only remaining question is what day."

She had to say it. "Nando, if you're marrying me only for my share...." Her words dwindled off.

"If you are in doubt, you could always offer me your share now." He turned teasing amused eyes on her.

Amy hadn't quite expected that suggestion, but maybe she should have, she realized. "Sorry, I'm keeping my share," she replied firmly.

He didn't answer at once, having come up suddenly behind a motorbike. The tiny vehicle carried not only the driver but also his wife, sitting behind him clinging to his waist, and a small child, perched between his arms near the handlebars.

Nando waited until he could pass them without throwing up a wake of dust, which might momentarily blind the driver. When they finally regained the highway, he said, "Now, then, what day do you want to get married?"

"I...I really don't know," Amy answered. "I haven't thought about it."

"Then I shall take care of it," he said dryly. "You seem so determined and obstinate about some things, it's unlike you to vacillate so about this."

That stung her, especially after his own clandestine activities. "I've never had my fortune proposed to before," she snapped tartly.

Nando merely laughed, turning up the road that led to the castle and the villa.

When they arrived, Amy hastened up the stairs to her room. She was hot, she was fatigued, she was frustrated. The first two she could take care of; she wasn't so certain of the last.

But before she could strip off her clothes there was a knock at the door, and a young maidservant stood there.

"Telefono, signorina." She held her hand up to her ear to demonstrate her meaning. Then she beckoned Amy, *"Prego, signorina."*

There was a small round mahogany table at the end of the hall with a telephone on it, a chair beside it.

Amy sat down and picked up the phone, a puzzled frown on her face.

"My God, Amy, where the hell have you been?" Bert's voice came booming over the miles as clearly as if he were in the same room. "You promised me you'd let me know how things are going in the land of wine and olive oil, but what have I heard? Nothing! Not even a postcard. I've been getting worried!"

For a fleeting second Amy's throat choked up. It was so good to hear a familiar voice from home! She had to swallow hard before she could speak.

"I'm terribly sorry, Bert, but I've really been busy. I know that's no excuse; it's the truth, though. I'm working in the winery, learning to be a vintner."

"You're *what*? Do you mean you've become part of that Vino d'Oro setup now? And working in the winery? That's some surprise. Doing what?"

"Well, rather a lot of things, really. Learning right from the beginning." She wasn't going to enlarge on that, particularly about the tank-cleaning part. Bert would explode with indignation.

"How about the family, the Bonavias? Are they treating you all right?"

"Yes, I'm staying here with them at the villa."

"So I gathered. I've been trying to get you all day. Say, how about what's-his-name, the fellow who came to New York and wanted to buy your share of the business? Did you ever sell it to him?"

"No, Bert, I still have it."

"How does he feel about that? Still pressing you to sell? He was rather persistent about it while he was here, if I remember correctly."

"I still have it." There she was, repeating herself. She was rapidly running out of safe things to say. Perhaps she'd better tell him about her marriage to Nando, and yet....

"Look, Amy, honey, come on home," he was saying. "You don't belong over there with a bunch of foreigners, even if they are your relatives. Come on back! The weather is beautiful now; yesterday I saw our team knock the socks off the Dallas Cowboys. I was all by myself on the fifty-yard line. Your seat was beside me, empty. It's still waiting for you."

"Bert, I told you, get someone else to go to the games with you. And . . . find someone else, you really must," she urged.

"Now, how could I do that? I'd probably end up with somebody who'd ask what those men were doing, running up and down the side of the football field with sticks. Or who'd want a hot dog when it was fourth down and goal to go. Not on your life.'' He had evaded the second part of her statement.

"Besides," he said, "your little friend Linda called me Friday to see if I'd heard anything from you. She said that if I talked to you, to tell you she knows of a good job you can get if you return pretty quick, a better one than you had. And that you can stay with her until you find another apartment.'' He paused, then repeated, "Come home, Amy."

Amy sat there, the phone in her hand, her eyes brimming with tears. Homesick was something she'd never felt before. Maybe Bert was right. Maybe New York was where she belonged.

Maybe she'd even get over Nando if she went back.

She gazed down at the ring on her finger, a little blurred before her eyes. It wasn't fair not to tell Bert. Even if she hadn't fully made up her mind yet, it wasn't fair.

"Bert," she began unsteadily, "I may not be coming back. I may stay here. I...I think I may be getting married."

There was complete silence on the other end. For a second Amy wondered if they'd been disconnected. Then he burst out incredulously, *"Married*? To whom, for God's sake? You just got there a short time ago!''

"My cousin Nando. Fernando Bonavia."

"Say, wait a minute. That's the same one, isn't it? The one who—"

"Yes, Bert, that one."

"I'm kind of bowled over. Here I was, all set to

talk you into coming back home, and you hand that kind of news to me, Amy. But I want to tell you something; you don't sound very certain to me. You say you *may* be staying, you *may* be getting married. That's not like the Amy I know. Are you absolutely sure he's the right one for you?"

"I...yes, I think so, Bert." There she was, doing it again, sounding indecisive! "It's just that it isn't completely settled yet. But I thought I should tell you now."

"Yes, well, I'm glad you did. I guess I am. But you should be a lot more certain than you sound to me. You're not only going to be marrying a strange man, remember, you're going to be taking on a whole different way of life in a different country. Things aren't exactly the same there as here, you know."

"I realize that, Bert, but I already love Italy. It...it means something to me, maybe because I'm partly Italian. I know, too, that the winery offers me the work I want to do more than anything." She realized belatedly that she hadn't mentioned Nando.

"All right, Amy," he said resignedly, "I'm not going to fight you on it. But I want you to know this: if you change your mind, I'll meet any plane, at any time. And if you should need it, I'll send you a ticket home."

"Thank you, Bert. I...I'm sorry if you were really expecting me to come back. It's just the way things have worked out."

"I'm sorry, too. But remember, let me know. Whatever you decide, let me know."

"I will, Bert, I promise." She wondered what the message would be.

He hesitated, then said slowly, "I guess that about covers it then. I wish it had turned out differently. I suppose I hoped that once you got that wine idea out of your system you'd be content to come back and consider being a lawyer's wife. But if you feel this man is for you, then you've got every good wish from me for your happiness."

When Amy put the phone down she gazed at it unseeingly, blinking back tears. Why couldn't she love a man like Bert? Someone who was good, warm, considerate. Which would be better, she wondered— to marry a man she loved but who possibly didn't love her, or to marry Bert and be grateful that he loved her, no matter how she felt about him?

"Something wrong?"

Amy's head jerked up to see Nando standing beside her, his hands thrust deep in the pockets of his gray jacket, his eyes searching hers.

"No, nothing wrong. It was just a call from a friend. Back in New York."

"I trust it wasn't bad news. I came out of my room and saw you sitting there with your head down. And now that you look up I see tears." The words were kind, but his voice held a certain thin edge. "I understand that someone has been calling most of the day, trying to reach you. A man."

Amy had a flashing hope that this was a show of jealousy. It would serve him right! But perhaps he simply didn't want any interference with his plans.

Slowly she got to her feet, placing the chair back beside the table. "Yes," she said coolly, "a man. Someone I knew in New York. It was a—" she couldn't resist it "—a little unfinished business."

"I see." Abruptly the faint air of tension slackened and he pulled her toward him. "As long as you make very certain it is finished now, *cara*."

He gazed down at her, holding her with his eyes. "I've been wanting to do this all day, but not in the midst of a thousand people."

The firm warm lips closed over hers, capturing, probing deeply. His hands slipped down to cup her hips, drawing her against him. Then his mouth moved to breathe against her ear, "All unfinished business finished, do you hear, except with me. Only with me."

Any fought to calm her wild response to his touch. She could not forget Elisa. "Nando, please, not here...someone...the servants...."

He loosened his hold slightly, but his hands still slid over her hips in an intimate caress. There was smoldering fire in the gray eyes, a hard-to-resist invitation, a promise. "Very well, then, come to my room with me. Now."

Any drew back, trying to disentangle herself from those disturbing hands. "No, Nando, please. I'd really like to go to my room now. Alone. I'd like to shower and change my clothes. It will be dinnertime shortly." The problems that existed between them, the troubling questions, could not all be solved in bed, she thought.

He looked down at her. If there had been emotion

in his face it was gone now, replaced with an expression of cynical amusement. "Excuses, always excuses. Is that how people behave in America? Do they plan their lovemaking in such a cool and businesslike manner? Ah, perhaps they do, but not in Italy, *cara*. Here, one makes love when the blood runs hot. You must be taught not to always temper the flame. I can feel the beat of your heart."

He put one hand just below her left breast. "It is racing, it is saying yes to me."

Her treacherous body was yearning achingly to say yes, but once again it was Elisa who stood in the way, Elisa and Nando together this afternoon, walking away from the crowd.

She forced a light laugh. "You do not understand, Nando, that my heart is speaking English, not Italian. And it is saying no."

As Amy started toward her room, Nando fell into step beside her. "You have some important things to learn, Amy, and one of them is that it is well not to throw water on the fire too often, or there may be nothing left but ashes. Let us be certain that doesn't happen, shall we?"

Amy gave him a wry lift of her brows. "I don't think I will try to answer that question. I feel there's really no safe way to do so." Then with a quick diffident smile, she opened her door and slipped into her room, leaving him to walk on down the hall alone.

AMY WAS ALREADY IN BED late that evening when she heard a faint tap at her door, then saw the doorknob turn. She lay quietly, not daring to move until the footsteps finally went away. She had somehow expected Nando might come to her room tonight, and for the first time she had turned the key in the lock.

For a long time she lay there, thinking. There were questions in her mind that had to be answered, troubling questions.

She did not want her body to answer them for her.

CHAPTER THIRTEEN

DURING THE NEXT TWO WEEKS, Amy found to her pleasure that she was being moved from department to department in the winery, learning as she went. But there came a day when she had reason to climb up the spiral iron staircase to the catwalk running around the steel fermenting tanks, and at that she hesitated. She could feel the nerves at the back of her neck becoming tense as wires.

Might as well get it over with, she thought. Going over to the first step, she took a deep breath and started up, her hands gripping the railing tightly, her feet moving cautiously from one step to the next. Her palms were perspiring and her knees felt strangely awkward, as if they didn't quite belong to her. But she continued on.

Halfway up, she turned to stare down at the workers moving about far below. The faint but unpleasant memory of Elisa's trickery with the tank door came flashing back to chill her. She certainly didn't want any more of Elisa's "amusing" little tricks; the climb was frightening enough as it was.

But no one appeared to be following her, or for that matter paying any attention to her ascent, except Signore Calabro, who stood by the bottom of the steps watching her progress. He had shown reluctance about this stage of her indoctrination, shaking his head doubtfully. But he had been handicapped in dissuading her by their lack of a common language.

When Amy realized that this was a normal part of the training, she had stubbornly nodded her head, pointing up at the catwalk and gesturing. It had ended with Signore Calabro giving a grudging shrug of his shoulders and reluctantly walking with her to the stairs.

Perhaps she was being obstinate and foolish, she told herself as she turned back to her climbing. The catwalk was probably token learning where she was concerned. She'd more than likely never be called upon, even in an emergency, to go up to check on or repair tanks. But if others had done this before her, she was going to do it, too. Deep inside she wanted to show Nando Bonavia that no exception had to be made for her because she was a woman.

Amy wondered where Nando was. She had hardly seen him at the winery all week. And even at the villa he was strangely preoccupied. There had been a few fleeting kisses, those also strangely preoccupied and controlled. He had made no more attempts to visit her room after hours.

When the subject of marriage came up, Nando had informed her casually that all arrangements had been made.

Amy had started to voice her doubts, but the eyes he'd turned on her were suddenly cryptic. "Please, Amy, don't tell me we are about to indulge in the vacillating game all over again. Our wedding will be held at the same time as Anna Maria's and Filippo's. Since you seem so unwilling to make plans, I have done so."

Franco had given her a sharp look later. "I must say, you are less the blushing bride-to-be than any woman I've ever seen," he told her. "Anna Maria is all bubbling enthusiasm, but you, you are muted, quiet." He put his hand over hers, covering for a moment the ruby ring. "Are you absolutely sure about this?"

In a way it was what Bert had asked, too. She gave Franco a serene candid gaze. "Yes, Franco. Yes, now I am."

Perhaps it was the conversation with Bert that had really made her decision clear. He had offered her a choice. For several days afterward she had brooded about it, until she realized that deep within her the answer had been there all the time. She had only to accept it. Marriage with Nando, life with Nando, was a little like walking blindfolded into a strange unpredictable world. But a future without him would be forever meaningless. She would rather accept that uncertainty with the volatile Nando than all the security Bert could offer.

As she neared the top of the iron stairs, Amy gave a wry smile. Marriage to Nando was going to be a bit like traversing the catwalk—scary, yes, but nevertheless something she wanted to do.

And this walk *was* scary! Her heart bumped up into her throat as she reached the top and looked down through the grillwork to the floor below. Quickly she raised her eyes again to gaze straight ahead.

Amy started out cautiously. The metal grating beneath her feet felt slippery and somehow insubstantial. But step by step she went toward one of the tanks that was open at the top, peering down into it, then moved on warily.

As Amy rounded one tank at the far end of the building, she stopped short. A man was ahead of her on the catwalk, making some repairs to one of the huge steel containers. He glanced up, obviously startled at the sight of a slender young woman edging along on the grillwork. As she approached he murmured something she couldn't understand, drawing himself close to one side so she could squeeze past. Not knowing what he said, she nodded in what she hoped was some kind of answer.

When she had nearly completed the catwalk circuit, she began to feel nervous relief. For the first time she realized there was a chill of perspiration down her spine. But there was an inner thrill of triumph, too. It had been frightening, it was certainly not much fun, but she had done it! And if ever it should be necessary, she knew she could climb up there again.

Step by step she descended the stairs, still extremely cautious, until she arrived at the bottom. She found Franco there waiting for her.

"Amy!" He was shaking his head in disapproval. "Why did you attempt that? You didn't have to, you know."

Now that she'd completed her walk she felt suddenly exhilarated. "I know, I know! I admit it was a little frightening, but I wanted to. It's part of the training. Someday I might be called on to go up there to check on some problem, and I wanted to be certain I could." She gave a quick happy smile that sparkled in her green eyes. "And I can!"

Signore Calabro walked past, giving her a reluctant nod of approval.

As Franco strolled along beside Amy, he asked, "Was that Nando's idea?" He nodded up toward the catwalk.

"No, he doesn't know. Besides, Signore Calabro is the one who decides things. I'm afraid I bullied him a little, but I don't want to skip anything that anyone else is required to do."

Franco glanced down at his watch. "If you're free for the next few minutes, we'll just have time to complete something before it's time to go home. Nando asked me to run down here and give you a couple of details about the bottling of wines, because that's the next department you'll be going into. This will really only take a moment or two, but it is something you should know about before you start."

Amy gazed at him curiously. "That's fine with me, but I'm surprised Signore Calabro won't be teaching me." She gave him a quick apologetic smile. "Not to insult you, of course, but why you?"

Actually she was a little surprised, for she seldom saw Franco in the wine-making part of the castle. His marketing work seemed to more or less confine him to the office upstairs or to visits to other towns.

"Nando is involved in something else right at the minute, and though the explanation is brief, Signore Calabro can't handle the language problem. But when you start work in there, he can easily demonstrate the process of bottling. This is only to explain to you what kind of bottles and corks we use, and why."

He pulled open a heavy iron-studded wooden door and they entered a long hall. "Say, what's with Nando these days?" Franco asked curiously. "He's seldom in the office." He paused, then said, "Are you two planning a trip to Rome?"

"Rome? No. Why?"

Franco hesitated so long before replying that Amy glanced up at him, saying, "What makes you ask that? Is he going?"

Franco grimaced uncomfortably, a flush of red creeping up his neck into his face. "Maybe I've spilled the milk. He probably means it to be a surprise. I heard him make flight reservations for two, so I naturally assumed.... Oh, Amy, I feel like a blundering fool! I shouldn't have said anything. When he brings it up, for heaven's sake, please act surprised!"

It could be that Nando was planning Rome for their honeymoon, Amy reflected. He was making all the other arrangements. The very thought of the wedding gave her a giddy feeling. But it was still two weeks away. "Did he say when he was going?"

Franco sighed. "Tomorrow. Look, my dear, I'm horribly sorry I spoiled what was no doubt planned as a surprise."

Tomorrow? If she were going with him he surely would have told her by now. No doubt it was a business trip.

The subject was dropped as they entered the bottling room. It was a brightly lighted area, clean to the point of shininess. The workers were all dressed in hygienic white to prevent any possible contamination, Franco explained as he led Amy into a storage room in one corner.

Lifting a pale green bottle from a box, he flourished it. "This, my dear madam, begins our two-minute lecture. Item number one. This bottle is made in this particular shape so that it can be easily stacked on its side. In that way the corks will be kept moist. If they dry out the quality of the wine will be affected. Now notice, if you will, the narrow straight neck, planned to fit snugly around the compressed cork."

Amy was amused by his mock professorial air. She took the bottle, turning it about in her hands. "I know this sounds silly, but are all wine bottles green? I have to admit I've never paid any attention."

"No. Countries and wineries differ, but mostly there's a common standard. Vino d'Oro is put in these light green bottles, as most white wines are. Though some wineries favor clear glass. Red wines usually go into dark green, to keep them from fading. Sherries into amber, vermouths into green and, of course, sparkling wines into heavy champagne bottles."

Franco took the bottle and put it in its box. "One more thing." He reached over into a case and brought out a cork. "You'd think a cork was a cork, but there's a lot of difference between them. A cheap cork can be a faulty one and ruin the wine. All vintners will tell you that a wine is only as good as its cork. They should be at least two inches long to prevent air from entering. Nando will have nothing but the best, and these you see here are expensive.''

"Where does he get them?" she asked, looking at the cork and deciding that if it was expensive, it didn't show it. To her it was simply a cork. One more thing to learn.

"Mostly Spain and Portugal. These are from Spain." He took the cork back and smiled down at her. "There, relatively painless, right? Signore Calabro will show you how the bottles are prepared and filled, and how the corks are treated and inserted. But this takes care of my part."

Before leaving, Amy turned to watch the bottling machines, on which, one by one, scores of the glass containers were being filled and corked.

"There's so much to find out about, Franco, yet everything interests me. Wine making is my life now," Amy said contentedly.

They walked up the hill to the villa together. Franco was silent most of the way, then just before they reached the gate, he said, "Amy, it hurts to lose a battle. It hurts even more to lose someone like you. This marriage of yours neatly prevents Filippo and me from gaining control. . . with your help. It's clear now that we weren't fooling Nando, however. I don't mean necessarily that he's marrying you to prevent it, but it does in fact do so. So he gets not only your share, but he gets you, and that hurts even more."

"Nando won't automatically be getting my share through marriage, Franco. I plan to keep it myself."

He shot her a sudden shrewd look. "Don't bet on

it. You don't know Nando. I told you that once before, and I'm repeating it now. Whatever you think, whatever you plan, Nando intends to have your share of the business, and you can count on that."

And so she found out that evening when she went down to the salon before dinner. Only Nando and Aunt Lucia were there; the others hadn't come down yet.

Nando turned around suddenly as Amy walked into the room. Her heart leaped instinctively at the sight of this coolly aloof man, whom she knew to be so excitingly sensuous under that controlled exterior.

He strode toward her, dark brows scowling. "What's this I hear about you? Do I understand correctly that you actually went up on the catwalk today?"

Amy nodded complacently. "I did."

"Will you tell me why you did such a foolhardy thing? It can be dangerous, and your doing so was entirely unnecessary. Signore Calabro should never have allowed it."

"Don't blame him," Amy said airily. "He objected, to tell you the truth. But I insisted. I'm going to do everything required of any other trainee."

"But you are not any other trainee. You are shortly to be my wife! And if you don't mind, I'd like you to remain in one piece!" The gray eyes sparked with irritation. "I don't have any desire to see you come down the aisle in a wheelchair, or on a litter, either."

"He's really quite right, Amy," Aunt Lucia observed in her firm voice. "I wouldn't think of going up there myself. It is true that I have no head for heights, but even if I had, I should never think of attempting it. The steps are slippery, and the slightest misstep could be dangerous, even though we practice every safety precaution. We have had accidents in the past. No, I really wouldn't try it again, my dear, if I were you.''

"I don't expect I'll ever be called on to go up there, since there are so many other qualified workers. But I felt I had to do it, Aunt Lucia.''

The other woman nodded her white head slowly. "Yes, I believe I understand. Perhaps we—Nando and I—created a climate when you first arrived, one that made you feel you had to prove yourself in spite of us and our opposition.''

This grim-visaged woman was really two people, even as Nando was, Amy thought as she sat down. Aunt Lucia was undeniably arrogant and haughty, but under that frigid surface Amy felt that she could detect a strong current of compassion.

Nando stepped to the table, poured a glass of wine from a carafe and brought it over to Amy. "I'm happy to be able to report to you that all our planning is complete. There will be a brief civil ceremony, followed by a simple wedding in the church of San Zeno in Verona. Then you and I shall depart for Venice, Anna Maria and Filippo to Capri. A double wedding is acceptable, a double honeymoon is not.''

Then he went on in a casual voice, "I say that all is now complete, but one detail needs to be concluded—the matter of your share of the winery. I'm going to Rome tomorrow for several days, and before I leave I'd like to wrap up that last item. So I'd appreciate it if you will bring me your certificate after dinner this evening."

Amy looked up at him over the rim of her glass, instantly cautious. "Do you mean you need it temporarily, for some particular purpose on your trip, or are you asking that I surrender my share to you . . . permanently?"

He laughed; a bit too easily, she thought. "I don't imagine there will be any problem on that subject now. We're going to be married shortly. As your husband, naturally I—"

"*Patria potestas!*" Amy broke in, her voice dismayed.

He nodded. "But of course. In our family, yes indeed." He stood looking down at her, the picture of dominant masculinity. "You certainly shouldn't be too surprised by that."

"I won't give it to you," she said simply.

There was a stiff silence. Though Amy lowered her eyes to her glass, she could still look up through her lashes at the tall figure before her. He had not liked her reply and had shown it with a tightening of his dark brows.

But Aunt Lucia was suddenly lifting her thin regal hand. "No, indeed, Nando, Amy shall keep her share if she wishes."

Nando turned abruptly and said something in Italian to his mother.

She shook her head. "Nonsense! There is absolutely no need for her to surrender her share to you. She has every right to hold on to it exactly as I do mine. Your father didn't demand that I turn my own share over to him, even though it was quite within his right in those days. We worked together.''

The woman went on more slowly. "Yes, my son, I admit that I, too, wanted Amy to surrender her share to you, to us, when she first arrived. Now it is different. She is one of us." The shrewd gray eyes turned toward Amy. "I have a feeling that someday Amy will take my place in the company. She is learning all she can about wine production. She is strong, she is intelligent, she is not afraid. Her share will add to the strength of the company, but it should remain her personal property."

Nando didn't react for several seconds, then he nodded toward his mother. "It seems I'm outvoted," he said. "Very well, then, it appears that *patria potestas* has lost both support and power in the Bonavia family. Thousands of Italian men will turn in their graves." He made an effort to speak lightly, but Amy could tell he wasn't exactly pleased.

If there had been any tension in the room it was quickly dispelled by the entrance of Franco, then Anna Maria and Filippo. The young woman was holding on to her fiancé's arm, chatting excitedly about the coming wedding in a turbulent mixture of Italian and English.

To Amy's intense relief the evening passed pleasantly, without a hint of further talk about shares of the winery. Even Nando no longer showed any sign of his recent reluctance as his eyes caught and held hers from time to time over the dinner table.

After she had gone to her room that evening there

was a knock at her door. She opened it to find Nando standing there, his hands behind him.

"I'm leaving for Rome tomorrow, Amy, but I have a little gift I'd like you to have before I go," he said.

At her initial hesitation he smiled. "We both are completely clothed, so you shouldn't feel particularly threatened about inviting me in. This is a social call."

Though she eyed him suspiciously, she did step back and allow him to enter. Bringing one hand from behind his back he handed her a package several inches square and wrapped in silver paper.

"My mother has already bestowed on you the family ring. Now I wish to give you something I consider particularly appropriate, both as a gift from the groom and as a premature graduation present."

Amy untied the ribbon, took off the paper and opened the box. She lifted out a beautiful silver cup, barely an inch deep and not quite three inches in diameter. The handle was a slender twining silver grapevine, and topping the handle was a thumb rest.

He smiled at her delight. "It's a *tastevin*, a wine-tasting cup. It's made of silver so the shiny surface will reflect light through the wine. You hook your finger through the handle and put your thumb on the silver rest so you can hold the cup steady. You will find that every wine expert has his own. Yours...."

Nando turned it over and she saw Amy Bonavia etched in the silver surface.

She lifted her eyes, her breath catching in her throat. "Nando, it's beautiful, it really is. I love it!"

She fondled it in her hands, gazing at the graceful curving lines.

"Those markings make the light reflect in different ways," he said. "That's so you can gauge the true clarity of the wine from various angles. And now...." He brought his other hand from behind him. It held an open bottle of Vino d'Oro.

"I brought this along to christen it." He poured a little into the *tastevin*.

Any turned the cup about, watching with delight as the silver reflected the light up through the wine. She tasted it, then offered it to Nando. He covered her hand with his as she held the cup, and drank the rest, never taking his eyes from her face.

Gently removing the cup, he set it on a nearby table, then put his arms around Amy. "For an engaged couple we have had precious little time lately to explore love," he said softly.

If she had been going to protest—and she wasn't at all certain she was—there would have been no chance before his lips commanded hers. But he didn't linger. Instead he lifted her in his arms, carrying her over to the bed.

"Nando—" she began, but he gave her no chance to finish.

"Amy, my love, don't send me away tonight." Instantly he was beside her, his hands finding the buttons on her dress, his fingers gently cupping her breasts as his mouth moved hungrily on hers, completely erasing all resistance.

This time he made love to her not wildly, not feverishly passionate, but in a manner that was achingly tender. His hands touched her lightly, his lips moving from hers down to the pulse that was pounding at the base of her neck. He drew her close until she could feel the urgency of his need.

Deny him? How could she, when her love for him filled her with a sweet poignant yearning that flooded through her as she pressed against him, returning his kisses with all her heart? He undressed her slowly, his hands caressing, softly arousing, as he removed each bit of clothing.

Standing up for a moment, he quickly removed his own clothes. His hands, she could see, were trembling. Then he was back beside her again, his body instantly melding with hers. His hands slid down to grip her hips, pulling her close until she could feel the strength of his aroused maleness pressing hard against her thighs. Slowly, deliberately, he rolled her over onto her back so that she lay flat upon the bed. Seductively he let his fingers trail along the curve of her cheek and down her throat to her breasts, cradling them as he bent over above her, his mouth closing over a taut nipple.

He began guiding her gently into new delights of love. Patiently, invitingly, his fingertips and his lips touched, tempted, invaded—until he had unfolded an aching need in her that couldn't be contained, and she was gripping hard at his back as he bent above her.

"Amy, love, look at me."

She gazed up at him, seeing the naked desire burning in the gray depths. "Don't shut your eyes, now, my darling. Don't look away," he whispered huskily.

Her eyes remained locked on his as his warm

throbbing body covered her, his hand guiding, finding, until he had gently entered. For a second he was motionless, then he began a tantalizing, a teasing, a sensual invitation with his body that led her unresisting into a dizzying ecstasy. His eyes, never leaving hers, held them together as the room dissolved around them and they were the only two people left in the world. Somewhere in the midst of passion he gasped, "Oh, Amy, *cara*!" and he gripped her as they went spinning together into an explosive consummation that left them lying breathless and limp in each other's arms.

For countless moments there was silence, broken only by the sound of their uneven breathing. At last, raising his head, Nando looked down at Amy. Her hair was a wanton golden tangle, her skin alive with an almost luminous glow. He bent to kiss her shoulder, her chin, her eyelids, then he drew back. "Amy? Are these tears? Your eyes are wet."

She gazed up at him, trembling. "Not sad tears, Nando. It was so...so lovely. So indescribable," she said softly, feeling the intensity of her love for this complex man.

"Ah, but *cara*, this is only the beginning," he replied huskily. "Marriage will offer us unlimited opportunities for love. I warn you, I will take advantage of them all!"

Before Nando left her, much later that night, he bent to kiss her lips gently as she lay in bed. "I am going to Rome for two days, perhaps three. Then I shall be back here with you, *cara*."

As the door closed behind him, Amy's eyes dreamily roamed about the room, stopping for a long moment on the silver *tastevin* sitting on the table. Amy Bonavia.

"Nando," she whispered softly to herself. "Nando, my love." Love? He had not said he loved her, not even this evening. But it did not matter. He had said it with his body, his kisses, the sweet and tender way he had possessed her. Words hadn't been needed.

Her eyelashes fluttered several times, then, without even turning out the bedside light she drifted off to sleep, a sleep where Nando wandered in and out of her dreams.

THE SUN WAS CREEPING across the floor when she awakened next morning. Amy sat up abruptly, her eyes hurriedly seeking the clock. If she didn't move right along she was going to be late for work.

Yet for a second she hesitated, her eyes soft with the memory of last night. She had read stories of love, had dreamed of finding a passionate lover, but nothing had prepared her for the deep poignant way she felt about Nando. She hugged herself in sheer happiness, every dark cloud of doubt forgotten.

Then, climbing quickly out of bed, she showered and dressed, leaving herself just enough time to step out on the balcony with her cup of coffee and feel the warm sunshine.

As she stood there she noticed a fan of dust on the road as a car circled the castle and came up the hill toward the villa. As it approached she recognized the driver behind the wheel. It was Elisa Antolini.

Amy's brows dipped in an irritated frown. If Elisa thought she was going to waylay her on the way to the winery and deliver another of her gratuitous little warnings, or perhaps even try to talk her out of marrying Nando, then she was going to be met with a blunt refusal. She was too late; permanently too late!

Amy was about to turn away and go back into her room when she heard the front door close and footsteps cross the terrace. She paused, cup in hand, to see Nando hurrying down to the gate. He opened it, put the suitcase he was carrying in the back of the car, then climbed in beside Elisa. They drove off together.

Amy felt frozen. Then sun was no longer warm on her shoulders, for her whole world had shattered into bits. For several moments she couldn't think, could scarcely feel. Then, slowly, she walked back into her room, set the cup on the table, picked up her lunch and left.

Down the stairs and out the front door she went, blindly following her daily routine. Open the gate and go down the road to work.

How could he? After last night, how could he, a voice inside her screamed.

Two reservations for Rome, wasn't that what Franco had said? Maybe, just maybe there was some logical explanation.

Like what?

This was a warning look into the future. A future in which Nando would leave the warmth of Elisa's bed to come home to his wife—his wife who owned a precious share of the winery.

It didn't matter. It didn't matter at all, not anymore. Amy knew now she could never trust him again, could never surrender herself to him as she had last night. That was what hurt the most, that this should happen after the ecstasy they had shared....

Still, she should have known. There had been signs all along the way. Right from the first, when he had tried to take her in his arms with the scent of Elisa's perfume still on him. And at the wine festival they had slipped away...just long enough to lie together in some secret place.

There was no way the trip today was innocent. There was no way to make any of it innocent. Elisa had told her confidently that Nando was hers. Not entirely, Amy reflected bitterly; they were sharing him.

Signore Calabro was waiting for her when she reached the castle. Together they went along to the bottling room. Amy was aware that he glanced at her several times, frowning.

Like an automaton she went through the learning steps of the bottling process, guided by the stocky man, whose dark eyes kept flicking toward her in concern. Once he put a thick heavy-veined hand on her arm. *"Signorina?"*

She shook her head and forced a thin smile.

Somehow Amy managed to get through the morning. At noon she took her lunch, found a deserted part of the courtyard and sat down. She didn't open the box. Instead she set it beside her and leaned back against the hard stone of the castle, her eyes gazing blindly ahead of her.

She didn't need to make a decision, it was already made. This morning had firmly closed one phase of her life. She was going home; it was over. She could not bear to know that whenever she looked at Nando, the face of Elisa would be smiling over his shoulder. His mistress! Probably she had been all the time,

"Amy!" Franco was standing beside her. "I had quite a time finding you. What's wrong?"

She didn't look up at him. "Why do you ask?" For the moment it was all she could trust herself to say.

"Signore Calabro came up to the office a few minutes ago. He's worried, Amy. He says... well, that there's something wrong. He can't ask you himself, but he was concerned enough to come up to speak to Nando. But Nando has gone to Rome, so he talked to me. What is it, Amy?"

She shook her head, her eyes stinging with unshed tears. "Nothing."

"That's not true." He waited for a minute, and when she said nothing, he went on. "I wish I knew. This isn't like you. Did you and Nando have words?"

She shook her head. Words? No, all the words in the world wouldn't help. It was over.

Apparently Franco realized that she wanted to be alone. "I'll see you later, Amy, okay?" he said. "I don't know what it is, but, please, don't worry."

She didn't reply. She didn't even lift her head as he walked away.

That afternoon as she was leaving work, she

walked over to Signore Calabro. Holding out her
hand, she said, "*Grazie,* Signore Calabro."

He had looked at her, obviously puzzled. Concern
and frustration at his lack of communication showed
on his face.

Franco was waiting by the courtyard gate. "Now,
Amy, this can't go on. You must tell me what's
wrong. You aren't sick, or you wouldn't be working.
But you do look rather pale. You look, I don't know,
desperate, I guess. What's happened?"

The words burst out of her. "I'm leaving, Franco." She hadn't meant to say them, but suddenly her
damned-up emotions broke through.

"Leaving?" he echoed in astonishment. "You
mean going back to America?"

She nodded.

"Why, Amy, why?"

She shook her head fiercely. "Don't ask me,
please. I don't want to answer any questions. And
don't tell anyone else."

"Does Nando know?"

"No! I don't want him to know." When he returned from Rome she would be gone. Only the silver
tastevin with the wrong name on it would be left
behind in her room.

"This isn't like you. Something pretty drastic
must have happened. Are you going. . . permanently?"

"Yes." Her voice was low, barely audible.

"But you can't just rush off. If you and Nando
have had a quarrel, don't take it so seriously. People
do, you know; engaged couples frequently. You

ought to at least wait for Nando to return. Don't react on impulse like this.''

Amy took a long steadying breath, managing to exert some control over her voice. "Franco, I'm leaving. At once. Why isn't important. I have my reasons, believe me! But I don't want to talk about it. I should never have told you I'm going, not until I walk out the door. Please don't say anything to Anna Maria or Aunt Lucia—they'd question me, too. I'll just say goodbye and go quickly. It may not be courteous, but I must.''

For several minutes Franco didn't speak. Finally he turned and gave her a thoughtful look. "Very well, if that's what you want," he said. "Now, how are you going? By air? If so, you'll have to get to the airport. You'll need reservations. Would you like me to take care of them?''

She looked at him gratefully. "Oh, Franco, you don't know how I'd appreciate it.''

He stopped her in the middle of the road, lifting her chin with two fingers. "Little one, you're hurting. I don't know why. Can't I help?''

Amy turned her face away. "Yes, by helping me with the reservations. My Italian isn't good enough. And by keeping this from Anna Maria and Aunt Lucia until I'm ready to go.''

He shook his head. "I don't like it, not a bit of it, but I'll do as you say. I'll call the airport as soon as we get to the villa, and I'll let you know what I come up with.''

"Thank you, Franco. And one more thing—I simply can't face dinner tonight. Would you have something sent up? And tell...tell Aunt Lucia I'm resting.''

''Very well. Is there anything else?''

''No, thank you. Though I'd appreciate it if you'd let me know as soon as you can when I can get a flight. I'm going to pack right away so I can be ready at any time.''

But when he came to her room later it was with an apologetic shrug. ''Sorry, Amy, the best I was able to do for you was a late-afternoon plane tomorrow. Will that do?''

It would have to do. She would rather have gone now, within hours, or even tomorrow morning, but as it was she would still be able to avoid Nando's return. Two days, maybe three, he'd said. She harshly shut her mind to other thoughts that came crowding in.

Amy kept to her room next day, sending word by Franco that she'd rather not be disturbed. If Aunt Lucia or Anna Maria thought it strange, she didn't know. Nevertheless they observed her wish.

Her packed suitcases she had shoved under the big bed. She had cleared out everything that was hers. The *tastevin* in its white box was sitting on the dresser. Beside it lay the ruby ring.

The shutters at the window leading to the balcony were closed. Amy hadn't wanted to look down at the castle, at the end of her dreams....

Yes, every bit of it must be ended. She pulled one of her suitcases out from under the bed, opened it and drew out a parchment sheet with a bunch of purple grapes hand-painted on it. This certificate had

marked the beginning of the whole bitter fiasco, of
her disillusionment. She didn't want it any longer.

She walked over to the dresser and set the paper
down beside the ring and the silver cup. If Nando
wanted to send her money in payment for her share,
that was all right. He probably would; it would fit in
with his warped sense of honesty. From now on this
whole episode was going to be wiped from her mind.
She didn't want ever again to think of the winery, or
the family, or Nando. Not even of Italy.

Her departure time was fast approaching. Franco
was going to come up to her room for her suitcases.
She would go downstairs to say a quick goodbye to
Aunt Lucia and Anna Maria, then would hurry off to
the airport.

His knock came. Amy shoved her suitcases over to
the door and opened it.

It wasn't Franco.

Nando stood there, his face stormy. He pushed the
door wide, forcing her back several steps, then
slammed it behind him and locked it. The air between
them sizzled, but he said nothing for several seconds,
his gaze taking in the suitcases ready for departure.

Then both hands shot out to grip her shoulders.
Amy thought he was going to shake her, but he
didn't. Instead his eyes probed hers.

"All right, now what's going on here? Franco
phoned me in Rome and told me to get home fast if I
didn't want to find you gone!"

"He shouldn't have! He didn't have any right to!"
Amy burst out angrily. She tried to jerk away, but
Nando's hands held her immobile.

"Will you please tell me what the hell's going on here? He said you were planning to leave. Obviously you are. I think I have every right to know why."

"I'm going home because...because I don't want to stay here any longer," Amy said unsteadily.

"*Why? Why?*" Now he did shake her, not hard, but as if to force an answer.

"Take your hands off me you...you Casanova!" she flared furiously.

There was an electric silence. Nando's eyes narrowed and for a long minute he stared at her thoughtfully. Then the atmosphere changed. "Did you by any chance see me leave the house yesterday morning? Could that be it?"

She didn't answer, didn't even look at him.

"Hmm." His voice was much less angry as he said, "I suppose it didn't occur to you to interpret that any other way than the way you...obviously have?"

"How else?" Amy's own voice was bitter, accusing. "Not that it matters. But I saw you at the wine festival, too. Maybe I don't understand how you Italian men operate, but it's not my way. Just how would you have interpreted it if I had slipped off to Rome for several days with another man? Especially with one I had...had been...."

"Oh, Amy, Amy!" he sighed, relaxing his fierce grip. "I guess it's my fault. Maybe I should have told you, but it was a delicate situation. I didn't tell Franco, either; only mother knew, as head of the firm. I didn't dare say too much until it was an accomplished fact. You see, we've bought out the Antolini winery. And what you saw at the wine festival was Elisa asking me to come to their wine stall to talk to her father. He'd finally decided to sell, and wanted to begin bargaining."

Amy was stunned. Underneath the hurt, small tender threads of hope were beginning to stir. "Then yesterday . . . ?" she asked.

"Elisa offered to drive her father and me to the plane. At the last minute he had to go to his winery to pick up some papers, so she came by to get me first. Then we collected him and headed for the airport." Abruptly he laughed, pulling her close to him. "Oh, Amy, Amy, I'm sorry, but the whole thing is ridiculous in a way."

She struggled in his embrace, the pain inside too recent, too sensitive for her to be quite trusting. "But—"

"Let me explain, *cara*. It had to be kept quiet, otherwise it might not have worked out. Other wineries would have entered the bidding. Antolini's is not a bad company, even though it's without a good vintner at the moment. We can improve it. When Signore Antolini—and his daughter—found there was no hope of joining us, they decided to cash out."

When Elisa knew Nando was being married, ending her chance to have him, and her father's chance to join the winery? Perhaps, but would she ever know for sure, Amy wondered. Best to let it go at that.

But Nando was continuing, "I'm planning to bring in an expert vintner from Udine, a fellow I know there. And I've been giving some thought to having Franco and Filippo manage the Antolini winery as a branch of Vino d'Oro." He smiled down at her. "That should keep them so busy they won't have time to think of ways to gain more power here."

For the first time in the past day and a half Amy began to sense life pulsing through her veins once again.

"I think, too, that I should ask Franco to be my best man at the wedding," Nando said seriously. "I realize he had his own hopes regarding you. But he was concerned enough to phone me about you, saying he couldn't bear to see you so desperately unhappy. Guessing that something had come up between us, he told me in no uncertain terms that I'd damned well better come back and settle it."

"Then he never did make any reservations for me?" she asked in surprise.

Nando shook his head. "He checked to see when I could make it back here, then arranged to keep you here past that time."

"Did you get all your business taken care of in Rome or did you have to...to come back early?" Amy asked in a small voice.

"It's done, but barely; finished this morning. I hope the entire crisis is over, too. The Antolini winery is ours and—" his eyes met hers "—the Antolini family is moving to Rome. Signore Antolini is retiring, and I think Elisa is anticipating a more exciting social life there. And just in case you have any remaining doubts, Amy, I did tell you the truth about Elisa and me. There was a...a flirtation of sorts in the past. But nothing more than that. It's you I love. Believe me, now and forever."

"You've never said that to me before, Nando, that you loved me," she said wonderingly.

"Nor you to me, my darling one." There was a gentle teasing note in his deep voice.

"Oh, but I did. I'm certain I did. That is, I think...." Amy frowned as she searched back through her memory. "Well, perhaps I didn't, not in so many words. But you should have known, from the way I couldn't help responding to your kisses, the way you kept shaking me up emotionally."

"Indeed? And you think I wasn't 'shaken up' emotionally?" His tone was dry. "You surely can't be so naive, Amy. And that unfortunate day at the lake! I should have recognized right then that it was a whole lot more than a physical response that I was feeling toward you. But at that point I was too immersed in self-disgust over what I was doing to drive you away."

Nando bent and kissed her gently on her forehead, her eyelids. "I think it really hit me when I saw you limping up the hill from the winery after your first day of work. Your face was so pale and you looked so terribly vulnerable. It was at that moment that everything began to change. I fought falling in love; God knows I fought it! It was ruining all the plans I'd set up so carefully."

"How could I have known how you felt, especially when it was your mother who brought up the idea of marriage?" Amy asked.

"How I felt? If you could only have seen *your* face! When I asked you what you thought about it you almost snapped my head off. I'll admit, certainly, that at first her idea of marriage was...precipitous. But you'll notice I came around to it.''

Amy lifted one hand and laid it softly against his cheek. "I did notice," she whispered huskily. "Two nights ago." Her voice was low, but her eyes met his boldly. For the briefest of seconds she thought again of something that had passed fleetingly through her mind that day back in Baltimore, the day she had gone through her mother's possessions. How was it she had phrased it? Oh, yes, that Nando was so thoroughly the Renaissance man, so strongly masculine. His cool manner was just a thin shell underneath which fires smoldered.

How right she had been.

THEIR HOTEL ROOM IN VENICE overlooked the Grand Canal. Amy stood bemused out on the balcony, watching the light of a thin silver moon shatter across the dark water. A gondola carrying a pair of young lovers was passing below, the gondolier singing to them softly as he poled his boat along. In the distance a church bell chimed slowly.

The day had flown by like a dream. First a short civil ceremony in which she had stood beside Nando, their hands clasped. Then the church, an ancient vaulted building where candles flickered before gaunt medieval statues and casual passersby came wandering in to watch the two couples exchanging their vows. The reception, too, she remembered in a daze—people gathering around to express good wishes in an excited babble of Italian, a few in halting English. Amy had floated through it on a cloud of happiness.

Anna Maria and Filippo must now be nearing Capri, she thought as she stood watching the passing boats, the bobbing lights. Waves lapped softly against the steps of the clustered buildings.

A soft night breeze stirred her hair, fluttering the thin white negligee she was wearing, and she went back into the room. Nando was coming toward her, wearing a dark paisley dressing gown.

He stood for a moment gazing down at her, desire beginning to blaze hotly in his eyes. "Amy...?" he spoke softly.

She held up her arms to him. *"Prego!"* she said.

Now's your chance to discover the earlier books in this exciting series.

Choose from this list of great

SUPERROMANCES!

SUPERROMANCE

Complete and mail this coupon today!

Worldwide Reader Service

In the U.S.A.   In Canada
1440 South Priest Drive   649 Ontario Street
Tempe, AZ 85281   Stratford, Ontario N5A 6W2

Please send me the following SUPERROMANCES. I am enclosing my check or money order for $2.50 for each copy ordered, plus 75¢ to cover postage and handling.

☐ # 8	☐ # 14	☐ # 20
☐ # 9	☐ # 15	☐ # 21
☐ # 10	☐ # 16	☐ # 22
☐ # 11	☐ # 17	☐ # 23
☐ # 12	☐ # 18	☐ # 24
☐ # 13	☐ # 19	☐ # 25

Number of copies checked @ $2.50 each = $_____

N.Y. and Ariz. residents add appropriate sales tax $_____

Postage and handling $____.75

TOTAL $_____

I enclose_____

Please send check or money order. We cannot be responsible for cash sent through the mail.)

Prices subject to change without notice.

NAME_____
(Please Print)

ADDRESS_____APT. NO._____

CITY_____

STATE/PROV._____

ZIP/POSTAL CODE_____

Offer expires February 28, 1983   20856000000

Yours FREE, with a home subscription to SUPERROMANCE™

Now you never have to miss reading the newest SUPERROMANCES... because they'll be delivered right to your door.

Start with your **FREE** LOVE BEYOND DESIRE. You'll be enthralled by this powerful love story...from the moment Robin meets the dark, handsome Carlos and finds herself involved in the jealousies, bitterness and secret passions of the Lopez family. Where her own forbidden love threatens to shatter her life.

Your **FREE** LOVE BEYOND DESIRE is only the beginning. A subscription to SUPERROMANCE lets you look forward to a long love affair. Month after month, you'll receive four love stories of heroic dimension. Novels that will involve you in spellbinding intrigue, forbidden love and fiery passions.

You'll begin this series of sensuous, exciting contemporary novels...written by some of the top romance novelists of the day...with four every month.

And this big value...each novel, almost 400 pages of compelling reading...is yours for only $2.50 a book. Hours of entertainment every month for so little. Far less than a first-run movie or pay-TV. Newly published novels, with beautifully illustrated covers, filled with page after page of delicious escape into a world of romantic love...delivered right to your home.